Queenie Hetherton

Mary Jane Holmes

Queenie Hetherton

Copyright © 2025 Bibliotech Press
All rights reserved

ISBN: 979-8-88830-934-6

TO

MRS. JULIE P. SMITH,
OF HARTFORD, CONN.,
I DEDICATE THIS STORY OF QUEENIE,
IN MEMORY OF
THE DEAR LITTLE GIRL WHO SLEEPS AMONG
THE NEW ENGLAND HILLS.

Brockport, June, 1883

CONTENTS

CHAPTER I

INTRODUCING SOME OF THE CHARACTERS

The morning mail for Merrivale had just arrived, and the postmaster was distributing the letters. Col. Rossiter, who lived in the large stone house on the Knoll, had two; one from his wife, who, with his two daughters, was spending the summer at Martha's Vineyard, and one from his son Philip, a young graduate from Harvard, who had been off on a yachting excursion, and was coming home for a few days before joining his mother and sisters at the sea-side. There was also one for Mrs. Lydia Ann Ferguson, who lived on Cottage Row, and was the fashionable dressmaker of the town. Mr. Arthur Beresford, the only practicing lawyer in Merrivale, had six, five of which he read hastily, as he stood in the post-office door, and then for a moment studied the superscription of the other, which was soiled and travel-worn, and bore a foreign postmark.

"From Mr. Hetherton," he said, to himself. "What can he want, I wonder?" and opening the letter, he read as follows:

"Hotel Meurice, Paris, June 10th, 18—.
"Mr. Beresford:

"Dear Sir:—You will undoubtedly be surprised to hear that I am coming home. Once I expected to live and die abroad, but recently, with my failing health, there has come over me an intense longing to see America once more.

"After an absence of nearly twenty-three years, it will seem almost as strange to me as to my daughter Reinette, who has never been in an English-speaking country. She is as anxious to come as I am, and we have engaged passage on the Russia, which sails from Liverpool the 25th. I have no idea whether the old house is habitable or not. All important changes and repairs I prefer to make myself, after Reinette has decided what she wants; but, if possible, I wish you to have a few rooms made comfortable for us. The large chamber which looks toward the town and the river I design for Reinette, and will you see that it is made pretty and attractive. If I remember rightly, there used to be in it a mahogany bedstead older than I am. Remove it, and substitute something light and airy in its place. Reinette does not like mahogany. Put simple muslin curtains at the windows, and have nothing but matting on the floors; Reinette detests carpets. And if you know of a pair of fine carriage horses and a lady's saddle pony, have them ready for inspection, and if they suit Reinette I will take them. If you chance to hear of a trusty, middle-aged woman suitable for a housekeeper at Hetherton Place, retain her until Reinette can see her; and please have the conservatory and garden full of flowers. Reinette is passionately fond of flowers—fond, in fact, of everything bright and pretty. She has just come in, and says tell you to be sure and get her some cats and dogs, so I suppose you must do it; but, for

Heaven's sake, don't fill the house with them—two or three will answer. I can't abide them myself. Reinette is waiting for me to go to dinner, and I must close. Shall telegraph to you from New York as soon as the vessel arrives, and shall follow on first train.

"Truly, Frederick Hetherton.

"Spare no money to make the place comfortable."

Arthur Beresford's face was a puzzle as he read this letter from one whose business agent and lawyer he merely was, and whom he scarcely remembered at all except as a dashing, handsome young man, whom everybody called fast, and whom some called a scamp.

"Cool, upon my word!" he thought, as he folded the letter and returned it to his pocket. "A nice little job he has given me to do. Clean the house; air Miss Reinette's bed-chamber; move the old worm-eaten furniture, and substitute something light and cheerful which Reinette will like; put muslin curtains to her windows; get up a lot of horses for her inspection; fill the garden with flowers, where there's nothing but nettles and weeds growing now; and, to crown all, hunt up a menagerie of dogs and cats, when, if there is one animal more than another of which I have a mortal terror, it is a cat. And this Reinette is passionately fond of them. Who is she, any way? I never heard before that Mr. Hetherton had a daughter; neither, I am sure, did the Rossiters or Fergusons. Mrs. Peggy would be ready enough to talk of her Paris granddaughter if she had one. But we shall see. Mr. Hetherton's letter has been delayed. He sails the 25th. That is day after to-morrow, so I have no time to lose, if I get everything done, cats and all. I wish he had given the job to somebody else. Phil Rossiter, now, is just the chap to see it through. He'd know exactly how to loop the curtains back, while as for cats I have actually seen the fellow fondling one in his arms. Ugh!" and the young lawyer made an impatient gesture with his hands, as if shaking off an imaginary cat.

Just at this point in his soliloquy, Colonel Rossiter, who had been leisurely reading his two letters inside the office, came out, and remembering that he was a connection by marriage with the Hethertons, Mr. Beresford detained him for a moment by laying a hand on his arm, and thus making him stand still while he read the letter to him, and asked what he thought of it.

"Think?" returned the colonel, trying to get away from his companion, "I don't think anything; I'm in too great a hurry to think—a very great hurry, Mr. Beresford, and you must excuse me from taking an active part in anything. I really have not the time. Fred. Hetherton has a right to come home if he wants to—a perfect right. I never liked him much—a stuck-up chap, who thought the Lord made the world for the special use of the Hethertons, and not a Rossiter in it. No, no; I'm in too great a hurry to think whether I ever heard of a daughter or not—impression that I didn't; but he might have forty, you know. Go to the Fergusons; they are sure to be posted, and so is Phil, my son. By the way, he's coming home on next train. Consult him; he's just the one, he's nothing else to do, more's the pity. And, now, really, Mr. Beresford, you must let me go. I've spent a most uncommon length of time talking with you and I bid you good-morning."

And so saying, the colonel, who among his many peculiarities numbered that of being always in a hurry, though he really had nothing to do, started toward home at a rapid pace, as if resolved to make up for the time he had lost in unnecessary talk.

Mr. Beresford looked after him a moment, and then, remembering what he had said of Philip, decided to defer his visit to Hetherton Place until he had seen the young man.

Two hours later, the Boston train stopped at the station, and Phil Rossiter came up the long hill at his usual rapid, swinging gait, attracting a good deal of attention in his handsome yachting-dress, which became him so well. The first person to accost him was his aunt, Mrs. Ferguson, who insisted upon his stopping for a moment, as she had a favor to ask of him. Phil was the best natured fellow in the world, and accustomed to have favors asked of him, but he was tired, and hot, and in a hurry to reach the quiet and coolness of his own home, which was far pleasanter, and more suited to his taste than the close, stuffy apartment into which Mrs. Ferguson led him, and where his cousin sat working on a customer's dress.

Anna Ferguson, who had been called for her mother, but had long ago discarded Lydia as too old-fashioned, and adopted the name of Anna, was eighteen, and a blue-eyed, yellow-haired blonde, who would have been very pretty but for the constant smirk about her mouth, and the affected air she always assumed in the presence of her superiors. Even with Phil she was never quite at her ease, and she began at once to apologize for her hair, which was in crimping-pins, and for her appearance generally.

"Ma never ought to have asked you into the work-room, and me in such a plight," she said. But Phil assured her that he did not mind the work-room, and did not care for crimping-pins—he'd seen bushels of them, he presumed. But what did his aunt want? he was in something of a hurry to get home, as his father was expecting him, and would wonder at his delay.

Phil knew he was stretching the truth a little, for it was not at all likely his father would give him a thought until he saw him, but any excuse would answer to get away from the Fergusons, with whom at heart he had little sympathy.

What Mrs. Ferguson wanted was to know if he had ever heard his mother or sisters speak of a dressmaker at Martha's Vineyard, a Miss Margery La Rue, who was a Frenchwoman, and who had written to Mrs. Ferguson, asking if she wished to sell out her business, and if it would pay for a first-class dressmaker to come to Merrivale.

"Here's her letter, read it for yourself if you can," Mrs. Ferguson said. "Anny and me found it hard work to make it out, the writing is so finefied."

Philip took the letter, which was written in that fine, peculiar hand common to the French, and which was a little difficult at first to decipher. But the language was in good English and well expressed, and the writer, Miss Margery La Rue, late from Paris, wished to know if there was an opening for a dressmaker in Merrivale, and if Mrs. Ferguson wished to sell out, as Miss La Rue had been told she did.

"I wish to mercy ma would get out of the hateful business and take that horrid sign out of her window. I'd split it up quick for kindlings. I'm always ashamed when I see it," Miss Anna said, petulantly, for she was foolish enough and weak enough to ascribe all her fancied slights to the fact that her mother was a dressmaker and had a sign in her window.

Mrs. Ferguson, however, did not share in this feeling, and reprimanded her ambitious daughter sharply, while Philip, who knew how sore she was upon the point, asked her if she really thought she would be any better with the obnoxious sign gone and her mother out of business.

"Of course I wouldn't be any better. I'm just as good as anybody now," Miss Anna retorted, with a toss of her head. "But you know as well as I, that folks don't think so, and ma and I are not invited a quarter of the time just because we work for a living. Even your sisters Ethel and Grace would not notice me if I wasn't their cousin. As it is, they feel obliged to pay me some attention. I hate the whole thing, and I hope I shall live to see the day when I can go to the sea-side, and wear handsome dresses and diamonds, and have a girl to wash the dishes and wait on me. There's the bell, now: somebody to get some work done, of course," and Anna flounced out of the room to wait upon a customer, while her mother asked Philip again if he had ever heard his sisters speak of Miss La Rue.

Philip never had, but promised to inquire when he went to the Vineyard, as he intended doing in a few days. Then, not caring for a second encounter with his cousin, he went out of the side door and escaped into the street, breathing freer in the open air and wondering why Anna need always to bother him about being slighted because she was poor, as if that made any difference.

Mr. Beresford was the next to accost Phil, and as the Hetherton business was uppermost in his mind, he walked home with the young man and opened the subject at once by telling him of the letter and asking if he had ever heard of Reinette Hetherton.

"Reinette Hetherton—Reinette," Philip repeated. "No, never; but that's a pretty name, and means 'little queen.' I wonder what kind of a craft she is? Frenchy, of course, and I hate the French. She must be my cousin, too, as I have never heard that Mr. Hetherton married a second time. When will she be here?"

Phil was interested in the girl at once, but Mr. Beresford, who was several years older, was more interested in the numerous arrangements he was to make for her reception. They had reached the Knoll by this time, and were met in the hall by the colonel, who did not manifest the least annoyance because of Mr. Beresford's presence, but on the contrary seemed glad to have him there, as it relieved him from any prolonged stay with his son.

"Eh, Phil, glad to see you," he said. "Hope you had a pleasant time;" then, in an absent kind of way, with a wave of his hand, "make yourself at home. You are quite welcome, I am sure; both of you," bowing to Mr. Beresford.

"And now, if you'll excuse me, I will leave you. Shall see you at lunch time, good-morning, gentlemen;" and with another very courtly bow, he walked rapidly away to the greenhouse, where he was watching the development of a new kind of bean found in Florida the previous winter.

Left to themselves the two young men resumed their conversation concerning Reinette Hetherton, and Mr. Beresford showed Phil her father's letter.

"Upon my word," said Phil, "one would suppose this Reinette to be a very queen, the way her father defers to her. Everything must bend to her wishes; bedstead, matting, flowers, housekeeper, horses, and cats and dogs; that's rich; but I'll take the last job off your hands. I know of a whole litter of young puppies which I'll have in readiness for her, besides half a dozen or more cats."

"Yes, thank you. I am sure I shall be glad to be rid of the cat business," said Mr. Beresford, "but tell me, please, about Mrs. Hetherton, Reinette's mother, I was too much of a boy when she went away, and you, of course, were a mere child, but you must have heard of her from your mother. They were sisters, I think."

"Half sisters," Philip replied. "My grandfather Ferguson was twice married, and mother was the child of his first wife. Grandma Ferguson, as most everybody calls her, is only my step-grandmother, and Mrs. Hetherton was her daughter Margaret, and, as I've heard, the most beautiful girl in Merrivale. It was her beauty which attracted Mr. Hetherton, and I imagine it was a love match, for he was proud as Lucifer and very rich, while she was poor and—and—well, she was a Ferguson," and Philip changed color a little as he said this: then, as Mr. Beresford looked curiously at him he added, laughingly, "Not that I am in the least ashamed of my relatives. They do not affect me one whit. I am just what I am, and a cart load of Fergusons can't hurt me, though I'll confess that grandma and aunt Lydia do try me at times, but wait and see what Miss Reinette thinks of them. When are you going over to investigate the place, and would you like me to go with you?"

Nothing could suit Mr. Beresford better, for though he was several years older than Phil, the two were fast friends, and later in the day, when it was beginning to grow cool, they rode together toward "Hetherton Place," which had been tenantless since the death of General Hetherton, ten or twelve years before.

CHAPTER II

INTRODUCING MORE OF THE CHARACTERS

Hetherton Place was nearly a mile distant from the village, and on the side of a hill, the ascent of which was so gradual that on reaching the top one was always surprised to find himself so far above the surrounding country, of which there were most delightful views. Turn which way you would the eye was met with lovely landscape pictures of grassy meadows and plains, of wooded hill-sides, sloping down to the river's brink and stretching away to the sandy shores of the ponds or little lakes, which, when the morning sun was shining on them, sparkled like so many diamonds, in the sunny valley of Merrivale, where our story opens.

Merrivale was not a very large or very stirring town, for its sons and daughters had a habit of turning their backs upon the old home and seeking their fortunes in the larger cities or in the West, where nature seems to be kinder and more considerate to her children, in that her harvests there yield richer stores with less of that toil of the hands and sweat of the brow so necessary among the rocky hills of New England. There were no factories in Merrivale, for the waters of the lazily-flowing Chicopee were insufficient for that, but there were shoe-shops there, and the men who worked in them lived mostly in small, neat houses on Cottage Row, or on the new streets which were gradually creeping down the hill to the river and the railroad track, over which almost every hour of the day heavily-laden trains went rolling on to the westward.

Years and years ago, when the Indians still lurked in the woods around Merrivale, and bears were hunted on Wachuset Mt., and the howl of the wolf was sometimes heard in the marshy swamp around old Cranberry Pond, the entire town, it is said, was owned by the Hethertons, who traced their ancestry in a direct line back as far as the Norman conquest. Theirs of course was the bluest blood in Merrivale, and theirs the heaviest purse, but purses will grow light in time, and blood grow weak as well, and the Hetherton race had died out one by one, until, so far as anybody knew, there was but a single member remaining, and he as good as dead, for any good he did to the people of Merrivale. For nearly twenty-three years Frederick Hetherton had lived abroad, and during that time, with one exception, he had never communicated with a single individual except his lawyers, the Beresfords— first Henry, the elder, who had been his friend and colleague, and, after his death, with Arthur, who succeeded to his brother's business.

When Frederick first came home from college he was a dashing, handsome young man, with something very fascinating in his voice and manner; but to the young girls of Merrivale he was like the moon to the humble brook on which it shines, but always looks down. They could watch, and admire, and look up to him from a distance, but never hope for anything like an intimate recognition, for the Hethertons held themselves so high that very few were admitted to the charmed circle of their acquaintance.

Mrs. Hetherton, Frederick's mother, had come from the vicinity of Tallahassee, and with the best blood of Florida in her veins, was, if possible, more exclusive than her husband, and labored assiduously to instill her notions into the mind of her son.

After her death, however, whether it was that he found life at Hetherton Place too lonely, or that he missed her counsels and instructions, he was oftener with the young people of Merrivale; and rumors were at last afloat of frequent meetings between the heir of Hetherton and Margaret Ferguson, whose father was a stone mason, but a perfectly honest, upright, and respectable man, and whose mother was then familiarly known in the community as the Aunt Peggy who sold root beer and gingerbread in the summer time, and Boston brown bread and baked beans in the winter.

During Mrs. Hetherton's life-time her carriage had occasionally stopped before the shop door while she bartered with Peggy for buns and cakes, but anything like social intercourse with the Fergusons the lady would have spurned with contempt.

Great, therefore, was her astonishment when Col. Paul Rossiter, who had been educated at West Point, and whom, in a way, she acknowledged as her equal, fell in love with and married Mary Ferguson, who was the child of her father's first marriage, and in no way related to Peggy, and who was quite as well educated as most of the girls in town, and far prettier than any of them. The Fergusons were all good-looking, and Mary's dazzling complexion and soft blue eyes caught the fancy of Col. Rossiter the first time he reined his horse in front of the shop where root beer and gingerbread were sold.

Col. Rossiter at the time was thirty-five or more, and had never evinced the slightest interest in any one of the opposite sex. Indeed, he rather shunned the society of ladies and was looked upon, by them as a very peculiar and misanthropical person. He belonged to a good family, was an orphan and rich, and had no one's wishes to consult but his own; and so, after that first call at Peggy's establishment, when Mary entertained and waited upon him, it was remarked that he seemed very fond of root beer, and that it took him some time to drink it, for his chestnut mare was often tied before the shop door for half an hour or more, while he sat in the little room where Mary was busy with the shoes she stitched, or closed, as they called it, for the large shop near by. At last the gossip reached Mrs. Hetherton, whose guest the colonel was, and who felt it her duty to remonstrate seriously with the gentleman. The colonel listened to her in a dazed kind of way, until she said, although no harm would come to him, he certainly could not wish to damage the girl's good name by attentions which were not honorable.

Then he roused up, and without a word of reply, started for town, and entering Peggy's shop, strode on to the back room, where Mary sat with her gingham apron on and her hands besmeared with the shoemaker's wax she was obliged to use in her work. They were, nevertheless, very pretty hands, small, and white, and dimpled, and the colonel took them both between his own, and before the astonished girl knew what he was about, he asked her to be his wife, and told her how happy he would make her, provided she would forsake all her family connections and cleave only unto him.

"I do not mean that you are never to see them," he said, "but anything like intimacy would be very undesirable, for there would be a great difference between your position as my wife and theirs, and——"

He did not finish the sentence, for Mary had disengaged her hands from his by this time, and he always insisted that she struck at him, as she rose from her seat and, with flashing eyes, looked him straight in the face, while she said:

"Thank you, Col. Rossiter. You have said enough for me to understand you fully. You may be proud, but I am prouder still, and I decline your offer, which, the way you made it, was more an insult than an honor. I know I am poor, and that father is only a day laborer, but a better, truer, worthier man never lived, and I hate you for thinking to make me ashamed of him; while his wife, though not my mother, has always been kind to me, and I will never turn my back upon her, never! The man who marries me will marry my family too, or at least, will recognize them. I wish you good-morning, sir," and she walked from the room with all the hauteur of an offended duchess, leaving the crest-fallen colonel alone, and very much bewildered and uncertain as to what had happened.

It came to him at last that he was refused by Mary Ferguson, the girl who stitched shoes for a living, and whose stepmother made and sold root beer.

"Is the girl crazy?" he asked himself, as he precipitately left the house. "Does she know what she is doing to refuse me, who would have made her lady! and she says she hates me, because I will not marry her family. Well, well, it's my first experience at love-making, and I think it will be my last."

But it was not, for Mary Ferguson's blue eyes had played the very mischief with the colonel's heart-strings, and he could not give her up, and the next day he told her so in a letter of three pages, which she promptly returned to him, with the words:

"The man who marries me must recognize my family."

A week went by, and then the colonel sent his love a letter of six pages, in which he capitulated generally. Not only would he recognize the family, but in proof thereof, he would buy the large stone house called the Knoll, which was at present unoccupied, and he had heard was for sale. Here they would live, in the summer at least, and during the winter she might like Boston for a change, but he would not insist upon anything which did not meet her approval. All he wanted was herself, and that he must have.

This was a concession, and Mary, who, while standing by her family, had not been insensible to the good fortune offered her, surrendered, and in less than a month was Mrs. Colonel Rossiter, and mistress of the handsome stone house, where her father was always made welcome, and her stepmother treated with kindness and consideration.

We have dwelt thus long upon the wooing and wedding of the colonel, because the Rossiters and Fergusons have as much to do with this story as the

Hethertons, and because the marriage of Mary Ferguson was the means of bringing about another marriage, without which Reinette, our dainty little queen, could never have been the heroine of this romance. Mary would hardly have been human if her sudden elevation to riches and rank had not affected her somewhat. It did affect her to a certain extent, though the villagers, who watched her curiously, agreed that it did not turn her head, and that she fitted wonderfully well in her new place.

"Acts for all the world as if she was born to that grandness, and ain't an atom ashamed of me nuther," Mrs. Peggy said, never once suspecting that Mrs. Rossiter, as she mingled more and more in her husband's world, did sometimes shiver, and grow cold and faint at her old-fashioned ways and modes of speech.

As for the father he enjoyed to the full seeing his daughter a lady, but laughed at her endeavors to change and polish him.

"'Tain't no use, Mollie," he would say. "You can't make a whistle of a pig's tail, and you can't make a gentleman of me. My hard old hands have worked too long in stone and mortar to be cramped up in gloves or to handle them wide forks of yourn. I shall allus eat with my knife; it comes nateral-like and easy, and shall drink my tea in my sasser. But I like to see you go through with the jimcracks, and think you orter, if the colonel wants you to. You allus had the makin' of a lady, even when your hands, where the diamonds is now, was cut and soiled with hard waxed ends, and nobody'll think the wus of you, unless it's some low-minded, jealous person who, when they see you in your best silk gownd may say how you was once poor as you could be, and closed nigger shoes for a livin'. That's human nater, and don't amount to nothin'. But, Mollie, though you can't lift Peggy nor me, there's your sister Margaret growin' up as pretty and smart a gal as there is in Merrivale. You can give her a hist if you will, and mebby she'll make as good a match as you. She's the prettiest creetur I ever see."

And in this John Ferguson was right, for Margaret was even more beautiful than her sister Mary. To the same dazzling purity of complexion, and large, lustrous blue eyes, she added a sweetness of expression and a softness of manner and speech unusual in one who had seen so little of the world. Mrs. Rossiter, who was allowed to do whatever she pleased, acted upon her father's suggestion and had her sister often with her, and took her to Boston for a winter, and to Saratoga for a season, and it was in the Rossiter carriage that Frederick Hetherton first remarked the fresh, lovely young face which was to be his destiny. He might, and probably had, seen it before in church, or in the shop where he occasionally went for beer, but it had never struck him just as it did, when, framed in the pretty bonnet, with the blue ribbons vieing with the deeper, clearer blue of the large bright eyes which flashed a smile on him as he involuntarily lifted his hat.

Fred Hetherton was very fond of pretty faces, and it was whispered that he did not always follow them for good, and there were rumors afloat of large sums of money paid by his father for some of his love affairs, but, however that might be, his intentions were always strictly honorable with regard to

Margaret Ferguson. At first his pride rebelled a little, for he was quite as proud as any of the Hethertons, and he shrank from Aunt Peggy more than Mr. Rossiter had done. But Margaret's beauty overcame every scruple at last, and when his father, who had heard something of it in town, asked him if it were true that he was running after old Ferguson's daughter, he answered boldly, "Yes, and I intend to make her my wife."

A terrible scene ensued, and words were spoken which should never have passed between father and son, and the next day Fred Hetherton was missing from his home and Margaret Ferguson was missing from hers, and two days later Aunt Peggy went over to Hetherton Place and claimed relationship with its owner by virtue of a letter just received from her daughter who said she was married the previous day, and signed herself "Margaret Hetherton." Then the father swore his biggest oaths, said his son was his no longer, that he was glad his wife had died before she knew of the disgrace, and ended by turning Peggy from his door and bidding her never dare claim acquaintance with him, much less relationship. What he wrote to his son in reply to a letter received from him announcing his marriage no one ever knew, but the result of it was that Frederick determined to go abroad at once, and wrote his father to that effect, adding that with the fortune left him by his mother he could live in luxury in Europe, and asked no odds of any one. This was true, and Mr. Hetherton had no redress, but walked the floors of his great lonely rooms foaming with rage and gnashing his teeth, while the Fergusons were crying over the letter sent to them by Margaret, who was then in New York, and who wrote of their intended departure for Europe.

She was very happy, she said, though she should like to come home for a few days and bid them good-by, but Frederick would not allow it. She would write them often, and never, never forget them. Then came a few lines written on shipboard, and a few more from Paris, telling of homesickness, of Frederick's kindness, and the pearls and blue silk dress he had bought her. Then followed an interval of silence, and when Margaret wrote again a change seemed to have come over her, and her letters were stilted and constrained like those of a person writing under restraint, but showed signs of culture and improvement. She was still in Paris, and had masters in French and music and dancing, but of her husband she said very little, except that he was well, and once that he had gone to Switzerland with a party of French and English, leaving her alone with a waiting-maid whom she described as a paragon of goodness.

To this letter Mrs. Rossiter replied, asking her sister if she were really content and happy, but there came no response, and nothing more was heard from Margaret until she wrote of failing health and that she was going to Italy to see what a milder climate would do for her. Weeks and weeks went by, and then Mr. Hetherton himself wrote to Mr. Ferguson as follows:

"Geneva, Switzerland, May 15th, 18—.

"Mr. Ferguson.—Your daughter Margaret died suddenly of consumption in Rome, the 20th of last month, and was buried in the Protestant burying ground.

"Yours,
"F. Hetherton"

Nothing could be colder or more unsatisfactory than were these brief lines to the sorrowing parents, to whom it would have been some comfort to know how their daughter died, and who was with her at the last, and if she had a thought or word for the friends across the water, who would never see her again. But this solace was denied them, for though Mrs. Rossiter wrote twice to the old address of Mr. Hetherton in Paris, she never received a reply, and the years passed on, and the history of poor Margaret's short married life and death was still shrouded in mystery and gloom, when General Hetherton died without a will; and, as a matter-of-course, his property went to his only child, who, so far as the people knew, had never sent him a line since he went abroad.

Upon the elder Mr. Beresford, who had been the general's legal adviser, devolved the duty of hunting up the heir, who was found living in Paris and who wrote to Mr. Beresford, asking him to take charge of the estate and remit to him semi-annually whatever income there might be accruing from it. The house itself was to be shut up, as Frederick wrote that he cared little if the old rookery rotted to the ground. He never should go back to live in it: never return to America at all, but he would neither have it sold or rented, he said. And so it stood empty year after year, and the damp and mold gathered upon the roof, and the boys made the windows a target for stones and brick-bats, and the swallows built their nests in the wide-mouthed chimneys, and, with the bats and owls flew unmolested through the rooms, where once the aristocratic Mrs. Hetherton trailed her velvet gowns; and the superstitious ones of Merrivale said the place was haunted and avoided it after nightfall, and over the whole place there brooded an air of desolation and decay.

Then the elder Beresford died, and Arthur, who was many years younger, succeeded him in business and took charge of the Hetherton estate, and twice each year wrote formal letters to Mr. Hetherton, who sent back letters just as formal and brief, and never vouchsafed a word of information concerning himself or anything pertaining to his life in France, notwithstanding that Mrs. Rossiter once sent a note in Mr. Beresford's letter, asking about her sister's death, but to this there was no reply, except the message that she died in Rome as he had informed her family at the time.

Thus it is not strange that the letter to Mr. Beresford announcing his return to America, and speaking of his daughter, was both a surprise and revelation, for no one had ever dreamed there was a child born to poor Margaret before her death. In fact, the Fergusons themselves had almost forgotten the existence of Mr. Hetherton, and had ceased to speak of him, though John, who had now been dead four years or more had talked much in his last sickness of Margaret, and had said to his wife:

"Something tells me you will yet be brought very near to her. I don't know exactly how, but in some way she'll come back to you; not Maggie herself perhaps, but something; it is not clear quite."

And now at last she was coming back in the person of a daughter, but grandma Ferguson did not know it yet. Only Mr. Beresford and Philip held the secret, for Col. Rossiter counted for nothing, and these two were driving toward Hetherton Place on the warm June afternoon of the day when our story opens.

CHAPTER III

MR. BERESFORD AND PHIL

Scarcely any two men could be more unlike each other than the two who walked slowly through the Hetherton grounds, commenting on the neglected, ruinous condition everywhere apparent, and the vast amount of labor necessary to restore the park and garden to anything like beauty or order.

Mr. Beresford, as the elder, will naturally sit first for his photograph. In age he was probably not more than thirty-five, though he looked and appeared somewhat older than that. He had received a first-class education at Yale, and when he entered the law he devoted himself to it with an energy and assiduity which, had he lived in a larger town than Merrivale, would have placed him at the head of his profession. There was no half way work with him. Whatever he did, he did with all his might, and his services were much sought after by people in the towns around Merrivale, so that he was always occupied and busy.

In stature he was medium size for a man, but finely formed, with a head set erect and square upon his shoulders, and crowned with a profusion of dark brown hair, which curled slightly around his forehead. His complexion was dark, and his eyes those round, bright, restless eyes which make you uncomfortable when fixed upon you, because they seem to be reading your inmost secrets and weighing all your thoughts and motives.

Belonging to one of the oldest and best families in the country, he was proud of his blood and proud of his name—foolishly proud, too, in many things, for had he been Anna Ferguson, that sign in her mother's window would have annoyed him even more then it did the young lady herself, while the memory of the beer and the gingerbread once sold by her grandmother, and the cellar walls and chimneys built by her grandfather, would have driven him nearly frantic. Indeed, it was a wonder to him how Phil Rossiter could endure the Fergusons, whom he considered wholly vulgar and second-class. And yet, Arthur Beresford was a man of sterling qualities, and one whom everybody respected and liked, though not as they liked Phil Rossiter—good-natured, easy-going, indolent Phil, who, though always ready to help whenever his services were needed, had never been known to apply himself for any length of time to a single useful thing.

Business he had none; employment none; but for this useless life his mother was, perhaps, more in fault than he, for she was virtually the moving power of the family, or, as the villagers termed it, "the man of the house."

Always peculiar, Col. Rossiter had grown more and more peculiar and absent-minded with every year of his married life, and as a natural consequence his wife, whose character was stronger than his, had developed into a self-reliant, independent woman, who managed her husband and his affairs admirably, and for the most part let her children manage themselves. Especially was this the case with Phil, who was her idol, and whom she rather encouraged in his idleness. There was money enough, she reasoned, for the colonel was one of those fortunate men in whose hands everything turns to gold, and there was no need for Phil to apply himself to business for several years at least. By and by when he came to marry, it might be well enough to have some profession, but at present she liked him near her ready to do her bidding, and no queen ever received more homage, or a mother more love, than did Mrs. Rossiter from her son. For her sake he would do anything, dare anything, or endure anything, even to the Fergusons, and that was saying a great deal, for they were not a family whose society he could enjoy. But his mother was a Ferguson, and he was bound to stand by them, and if the vulgarity of Mrs. Lydia, his Uncle Tom's wife, or the silly affectation of his cousin Anna, ever made him shudder, he never gave a sign, but bore up bravely and proudly, secure in his own position as a Rossiter and a gentleman.

To his grandmother he was always attentive and kind. She was not his own blood relation, he reasoned, and she was old, and so he allowed her to pet and fondle him to such an extent as sometimes to fill him with disgust. Only once had he rebelled, and that when a boy of ten. "Granny's baby," she sometimes called him, and this sobriquet had been adopted by his schoolfellows, who made his life so great a burden that at last on one occasion, when she said to him as she patted his young, fresh face, "Yes, he is granny's baby," he revolted openly, and turning fiercely upon her, exclaimed:

"You just hush up, old woman, I've had enough of that. I ain't your baby. I'm ten years old, and wear roundabouts, and I'll be darned if I'll be called baby any longer."

She never called him so again, or kissed him either, until the night three years later when he was going away to school next day. And then she did not offer it herself. She said good-by to him at his father's house, and went back to her own home, where she had lived alone since her husband's death, and which seemed lonelier to her than ever, because on the morrow Phil would be gone. Phil was her idol, her pride, and his daily visits had made much of the sunshine of her life, and as she undressed herself for bed, and then went to wind the tall clock in the kitchen corner, the tears rolled down her face and dropped upon the floor. She was a little deaf, and standing with her back to the street door she neither saw nor heard anything until she felt a pair of arms close tightly around her neck, and Phil's lips were pressed against hers.

"For the dear Lord's sake how you scart me. What on airth brought you here!" she exclaimed, turning toward him with her nightcap border flying back, and her tallow candle in her hand.

Phil was half crying, too, as he replied:

"I could not go away without kissing you once more, and having you kiss me. You haven't done so since that time I got so plaguy mad and called you names. I've cried about it fifty times, I'll bet. I want you to forgive it, and kiss me, too. I'm awful sorry granny."

The pet name for her in his babyhood, and which he had long since discarded, dropped from his lips naturally now, and putting down her candle the old lady took him in her arms and nearly strangled him as she sobbed:

"Forgive you, Phil? Of course I will, with all my heart, and kiss you, too. Any woman, young or old, would like to kiss a mouth like yours."

We do not believe our readers will like Philip Rossiter the less for this little incident, or because even in his young manhood he had a mouth which any woman, young or old, might like to kiss. A handsome mouth it was, with full red lips which always seemed just ready to break into a merry, saucy laugh, but which you felt intuitively had never been polluted by an oath, or vulgar word, or low insinuation against any one. In thought, and word, and deed, he was as pure as any girl, and held all women in the utmost respect, because his mother was a woman.

At the time our story opens Phil was twenty-five years old, though from the delicacy of his complexion he looked younger, and might easily have passed for twenty-one. Tall, willowy, and graceful in figure, he was, like all the Ferguson race, blue-eyed and fair, with a profusion of soft brown hair, which curled just enough to save it from stiffness. People called him handsome, with his frank, open, boyish face and winning smile but he hated himself for it, as a handsome man was an abomination, he thought, and he had times of hating himself generally, because of that natural distaste to application of any kind, which kept him from being what he felt sure he was capable of being if he could but rouse himself to action. Had he been a woman, he would have made a capital dressmaker, for he knew all the details of a lady's dress, from the arrangement of her hair to the fit of her boot, and could detect at a glance any incongruity in color, and style, and make-up. To his sisters he was invaluable as a critic, and no article which he condemned was ever worn again. It was strange, considering how unlike to each other they were, that Phil and Mr. Beresford should be such friends, but each understood perfectly the peculiarities of the other, and each sought the other's society continually. With Mr. Beresford the fact that Phil was a Rossiter covered a multitude of sins, while more democratic Phil cared but little who Mr. Beresford's family were, but liked the lawyer for himself, and spent a great deal of time in his office, where he once actually begun the study of law, but gave it up as soon as a party of his college friends asked him to join an excursion to the Adirondacks, and he never resumed it again.

CHAPTER IV

THE INVESTIGATION

"Well, this is a jolly place for the kind of girl I fancy Miss Reinette to be," Phil said, as he strolled through the grounds, putting aside with his cane the weeds, and shrubs, and creeping vines, which choked not only the flower-beds, but even the walks themselves.

Everywhere were marks of ruin and decay, and the house seemed worse than all the rest, it was so damp and gloomy, with doors off their hinges, floors half rotted away, and the glass gone from most of the lower windows.

"Seems like some old haunted castle, and I actually feel my flesh creep, don't you?" Phil said to his companion, as they went through room after room below, and then ascended the broad staircase to the floor above.

"Suppose we first take the room intended for Miss Reinette?" Mr. Beresford suggested, and they bent their steps at once toward the large chamber with the bay-window overlooking the town and the country for miles and miles away.

As they stepped across the threshold both men involuntarily took off the hats they had worn during their investigation below. Perhaps neither of them was conscious of the act, or that it was a tribute of respect to the unknown Reinette, who was in the thoughts of both as they stood in the great silent, gloomy room, from which the light was excluded by the heavy shutters which had withstood the ravages of time. This had evidently been the guest chamber during the life of Mrs. Hetherton, and the furniture was of solid mahogany and of the most massive kind, while the faded hangings around the high-post bed were of the heaviest silken damask. But the atmosphere was close and stifling, and Mr. Beresford drew back a step or two while Phil pressed on until he ran against the sharp corner of the bureau and uttered a little cry of pain.

"For Heaven's sake come out of this," Mr. Beresford exclaimed. "Let's give the whole thing up, and let Mr. Hetherton fix his own old rookery. We can never make it decent."

"Just hold on a minute," said Phil, making his way to a window, "wait till I let in a little air and light. There," he continued, as he opened window after window and pushed back the heavy shutters, one of which dropped from the hinges to the ground. "There, that is better, and does not smell so like an old cheese cupboard, and look, Beresford, just see what a magnificent view. Ten villages, as I live, and almost as many ponds, and the river, and the hills, with old Wachusett in the distance."

It was indeed a lovely landscape spread out before them, and Phil, who had an artist's eye for the beautiful, enjoyed it to the full, and declared it as fine as anything he had seen in Switzerland, where he went once with his father just before he entered college. Mr. Beresford was, however, too much absorbed in the duties devolving upon him to care for views, and Phil himself soon came back to the room and examined it minutely, from the carpet, molding on the floor, to the rotten hangings on the bed, which he began at last to pull down, thereby raising a cloud of dust, from which Mr. Beresford beat a hasty retreat.

"I tell you what," he said, "it's of no kind of use. I shall wash my hands of the entire job, and let Miss Reinette arrange her own room."

"Nonsense! you won't do any such thing," said Phil. "It's not so very terrible, though I must confess it's a sweet-looking boudoir for a French lady to come to, but it can be fixed easy enough. I'll help. I can see the end from the beginning. First, we'll have two or three strong women. I know where they are. I'll get 'em. Then we'll pitch every identical old dud out of the window and make a good bonfire—that falls naturally to the boys. Then we, or rather, the women, will go at the room, hammer and tongs, with soap, and sand, and water, and burnt feathers, if necessary. Then we'll get a glazier and have new window-lights put in, and a painter with paint-pot and brush, and a paperer to cover the walls with—let me see, what shade will suit her complexion, I wonder. Is she skim-milky, with tow hair, like the Fergusons generally, or is she dark, like the Hethertons, do you suppose?"

"I'm sure I don't know or care whether she is like a Dutch doll or black as a nigger. I only wish she would stay in France, where she belongs," growled Mr. Beresford, very hot and very sweaty, and a good deal soiled with the dust from the bed-curtains which Phil had shaken so vigorously.

"Take it cool, old fellow," returned Phil. "You'll be head and ears in love, and go down on your knees to her in less than a month."

"She'll be the first woman I ever went on my knees to," said Mr. Beresford, while Phil continued:

"Reinette is light, of course; there never was a Ferguson yet who had not a complexion like a cheese, so we will have the paper a soft, creamy tint, of some intricate pattern, which she can study at her leisure, mornings when she is awake and does not wish to get up. That settles the paper, and now for the furniture—something light—oak, of course, and real oak, no sham for the queen. Mosquito net—coarse, white lace, trimmed with blue, for blondes and blue always go together. So, we'll loop the muslin window curtains back with blue, and have some blue and white what do you call 'em, Beresford—those square things the girls are always making for backs of chairs, and bureaus, and cushions; you know what I mean?"

"No I don't. I'm not a fool to know all the paraphernalia of a girl's bed-chamber," said Mr. Beresford, while Phil replied, with imperturbable good nature:

"Neither am I a fool because I can no more enter a room without knowing every article and color in it, and whether they harmonize or not, than you can help hearing of a projected law-suit without wondering if you shall have a hand in it; chacun à son goût, my good fellow. You see I am beginning to air my French, as I dare say this little French queen speaks atrocious English. Do you understand French, Beresford?"

"Scarcely a word, and I am glad I do not. English is good enough for me," said Mr. Beresford, thinking to himself, however, that he would privately get out his grammar and French reader, and brush up his knowledge of the language, for if the foreigner, in whom he was beginning to feel a great deal of interest, really could not speak English readily, it would never do to give so much advantage to handsome, winning Phil, who startled him with the exclamation:

"I've got it! Tidies!—that's what I mean. Blue and white tidies on the bureau, with little fancy scent-bottles standing round—new-mown hay jockey-club, eau-decologne, the very best that Mrs. Maria Ferina Regina can make; and soap! By Jove! she shall have the very last cake of the box I got in Vienna nine years ago; I keep it in the drawer with my shirts, and collars, and things, for perfumery; but I've got to give it up now. Not but Miss Reinette will bring out a cart load, but I wish her to know that we Americans have foreign soap sometimes, as well as she. Then, there's powder; I must get sister Ethel to give me some of Pinaud's."

"Powder! What do you mean?" Mr. Beresford asked, in unfeigned surprise; and Philip replied:

"Now, Beresford, are you putting on, or what? Is it possible you have lived to be forty years old——"

"Only thirty-five," interrupted Mr. Beresford, and Phil continued:

"Well, thirty-five, then. Have you lived to be thirty-five, and don't know that every grand lady has a little powder-pot and puff-ball on her dressing bureau, just to touch her skin and make it feel better when she's moist. Some of it costs as high as three dollars a package—that's the kind Reinette must have. You ought to have some, too. It would improve that spot where the dust of the Hethertons has settled under your nose. There—don't rub it with your hands; you make it worse than ever. We must hunt round for some water to wash your face before we go back to town. But let's furnish this room with matting, which we quite forgot, and a willow chair in the bay-window, and a work-table, and another chair close by, with the cat and kittens. That will make the picture complete, and if she is not satisfied, why, then she's hard to suit. I'll make this room my special charge; you needn't bother about it at all. I was going right down to the Vineyard, but shall wait to greet my cousin. And now, come on, and let's investigate the rest of the old hut, while there is daylight to do it in."

Mr. Beresford was not at all loth to leave the close room which smelled so musty and damp, but which really seemed in a better state of preservation than other parts of the house. Everything had gone to decay, and but for Phil he would have been utterly discouraged, and abandoned all attempts to restore the place to anything like a habitable condition. Phil was all enthusiasm, and knew exactly what ought to be done, and in his zeal offered to see to nearly everything, provided his friend did not limit him as to means. This Mr. Beresford promised not to do. Money should be forthcoming even if a hundred workmen were employed, as Phil seemed to think there must be, the time was so short, and they would like to have things decent at least for Miss Reinette, of whom they talked and speculated as they rode back to town.

Was she pretty, they wondered, and the decision was, that as all young girls have a certain amount of prettiness, she probably was not an exception; yes, she was pretty, unquestionably, and Frenchy, and spoiled, and a blonde, Phil said, for no one with a drop of Ferguson blood in his veins was ever anything but that, and the young man spoke impatiently, for he was thinking of his own lilies and roses, and fair hair which he affected to hate.

"Of course she is petite," Mr. Beresford said, but Phil did not agree with him.

He was himself six feet; his mother was tall, his cousin Anna was tall. All the Fergusons were tall, and the young men bet a soft hat on the subject of Reinette's height. They were getting very much interested in the young lady, nor was their interest at all diminished when, as they reached the village, they called at the post-office and found a letter from her, which, though sent by the same steamer with her father's had not reached Merrivale until that evening. The handwriting was very small, but very plain and pretty; the letter was very short and ran as follows:

"Hotel Meurice, Paris, June ——.

"Mr. Arthur Beresford.—Dear Sir: I have just discovered that papa has told you among other things to have a little saddle pony in readiness for me. Now I will not have a pony. I detest a little horse as much as I do a little woman, and I must have a great tall horse, who will carry me grandly and high. The biggest and grandest you can find.

"Truly, Reinette Hetherton."

It almost seemed to the young men that they held the unknown Reinette by the hand, so near did this letter bring her to them, and such insight into her character did it give them.

"She has a mind of her own and means to exercise it," said Mr. Beresford, while Phil, intent upon the soft hat, said:

"You will lose your bet, old fellow. Nobody but an Amazon would insist upon a great tall horse. It is just as I told you. She is five feet eleven at least. I want a nice hat, and if you don't object, I'll pick it out myself, and send you the bill."

"I was just thinking of doing the same by you, for only a wee little creature would want a tall horse to carry her grandly and high," said Mr. Beresford, still studying the gilt-edged sheet of note paper, where there lingered a faint delicate perfume which miles of travel by land and sea had not quite destroyed.

"Ah bien, nous verrons," said Phil: then, bidding good-night to his friend, he walked away humming softly an old French song, of which Mr. Beresford caught the words, "Ma petite reine."

"Confound the boy," he said to himself. "He's better up in French than I am, and that will never do."

Arrived at his rooms, Arthur Beresford's first act after putting Reinette's letter carefully away, was to hunt up his long-neglected Ollendorf, over which he pondered for two hours or more, with only this result, that his head was full of all sorts of useless and nonsensical phrases, and that even in his dreams he kept repeating over and over again, "Avez vous mon chapeau? Oui, monsieur, je l'ai."

CHAPTER V

PHIL INTERVIEWS HIS GRANDMOTHER

After leaving Mr. Beresford Phil concluded, before going home, to call on his grandmother and ask if she had ever heard of a granddaughter in France. The house of grandma Ferguson, as she was now universally called, was the same low, old-fashioned brown building under the poplar trees where she had sold gingerbread and beer in the days when Paul Rossiter and Fred Hetherton came wooing her two daughters, Mary and Margaret. In her youth grandma Ferguson had been a tall, slender, well-formed girl, with a face which always won a second glance from every one who saw it. In fact, it was her pretty face which attracted honest John Ferguson when he was looking for some one to be a mother to his little girl. Margaret Martin was her real name, but everybody called her Peggy, and everybody liked her, she was so thoroughly kind-hearted and good-natured, and ready to sacrifice herself in every and any cause. But her family was against her. Her father was coarse and low, and a drunkard, and her brothers were coarser and lower still, and the most notorious fighters in town, while her mother was a shiftless, gossipy, jealous woman, who would rather receive charity at any time than work, and who always grumbled at the charity when given. But against Peggy's reputation not a whisper had ever been breathed. She was loud-talking, boisterous, and ignorant, and a Martin but perfectly honest, straightforward, and trusty, and from the day John Ferguson, the thrifty stonemason took her to his home to look after his house and child her fortune was made, for in less than six months she became his wife. As Mrs. John Ferguson she was somewhat different from Peggy Martin, and tried, not without success, to lower her voice and soften her manners; but her frightful grammar remained unchanged, and her slang was noted for its originality and force. But she was a good mother, and wife, and neighbor, and after her father and mother died, and her fighting brothers emigrated to California, she shook the Martin dust from her skirts and mounted several rounds higher on the ladder of respectability. But she did not get into society until some years after the Rossiters were established in the great house on the Knoll. Her faithful John was under the sod, and the beer sign gone from the window of the low brown house where she lived in comfort and ease, with a colored servant Axie, who was very serviceable to her indulgent mistress, making her bread, and pies, and caps, and frequently correcting her grammar, for Axie knew more of books than Mrs. Peggy.

To Mrs. Rossiter Grandma Ferguson was a care and sometimes a trouble: to the young ladies, Ethel and Grace, she was an annoyance and a mortification, both from her manners and her showy style of dress, while to Phil, who did not care in the least how she talked or how she dressed, she was a source of amusement, and he frequently spent hours in her neat, quiet sitting-room, or out on the shaded back porch where he found her on the evening of his return from Hetherton Place. With increasing years Grandma Ferguson had lost the slight, willowy figure of her girlhood, and had reached a size when she refused to be weighed. So saucy Phil set her down at two hundred and fifty, and laughed at her form, which he said he could not encircle with both his long arms. All delicacy of feature and complexion had departed, and with her round red face and three chins she might well have passed for some fat old English or German dowager, especially when attired in her royal purple moire antique, which she always called her morey with a long heavy gold chain around her neck, and her best lace cap with mountains of pink bows upon it. Mrs. Ferguson was fond of dress, and as purple and pink were her favorite colors, she sometimes presented a rather grotesque appearance. But on the night when Phil sought her, she had laid aside all superfluities and her silvery hair shone smooth and glossy in the soft moonlight, while her plain calico wrapper looked cool and comfortable and partially concealed her rotund form.

"For the massy's sake," she said, as Phil's tall figure bent under the doorway and came swiftly to her side, "what brung you here so late, and why hain't you come afore? I was round to your Aunt Lyddy Ann's this afternoon, and she told me you was to home, so I made a strawb'ry short-cake for tea, hopin' you'd happen in. There's a piece cold in the buttry now if you want it."

Phil declined the short-cake, and sitting down by his grandmother told her of Mr. Hetherton's letter, and asked if she had ever heard of a daughter.

Mrs. Ferguson was a good deal startled and surprised, or, as she expressed it afterward to Reinette herself, "she was that beat that a feller might have knocked her down with a straw." That there was somewhere in the world a child of her beautiful young daughter who died so far away, was a great shock to her, and, for an instant, she stared blankly at Phil, as if not quite comprehending him. Then she began:

"Fred Hetherton coming back after so many years, and bringin' a darter with him! My Maggie's girl! That's very strange, and makes me think of what your gran'ther said afore he died. Seems as if he had second sight or somethin', which ain't to be wondered at when you remember that he was born with a vail over his face, and could allus tell things. He said that, in some way, Maggie would come back to me, and she is comin': but it's queer I never hearn of a baby when Maggie died. Still, it's like that sneak of a Fred Hetherton to keep it from us. We wasn't good enough to know there was a child. But, thank the Lord, there's as much Ferguson in her as Hetherton, and he can't help that. I never could abide him, even when he came skulkin' after

Maggie, and whistlin' for her to come out. At fust I was afraid he didn't mean fair with her, and I told him if he harmed a hair of her head I'd shoot him as I would a dog. There's fight, you know, in the Martins!"

And the old lady's eyes blazed with all the fire of her two scape-grace brothers, once the prize-fighters of the country.

"What were the particulars of the marriage and her death? I've heard, of course, but did not pay much attention, as I knew nothing of Reinette," said Phil; and Mrs. Ferguson replied:

"'Twas a runaway match, for old Mr. Hetherton rode such a high hoss that Fred was most afraid of his life, and so they run away—the more fools they—and he took her to Europe, and that's the last I ever seen of her, or hearn of her either, as you may say. It's true she writ sometimes, but her letters was short, and not satisfyin' at all—seemed as if she was afraid to tell us she was lonesome for us at home, or wanted to see us. She had a new blue silk gown, and cassimere shawl, and string of pearls, and a waitin'-maid, and she said a good deal about them, but nothin' of Fred, after a spell, whether he was kind or not. He never writ, nor took no more notice of us than if we was dogs, till there came a letter from him sayin' she had died suddenly at Rome and was buried in the Protestant grave-yard. He was in Switzerland then, I believe, skylarkin' round, for he was always a great rambler, and we didn't know jestly where to direct letters; but your mother writ and writ to the old place in Paris, and never got no answer, and at last she gin it up. When old man Hetherton died, Fred had to write about business, but never a word to us."

"It's very singular he did not tell you about the little girl," suggested Phil; and Mrs. Ferguson replied:

"No 'tain't. He wouldn't of let us know if there had been a hundred babies. He'd be more likely to keep whist, for fear we'd lay some claim to her, and we as good as he any day, if he wasn't quite so rich. Why, there never was a likelier gal than your mother, even when she closed boots for a livin'; and there ain't a grander lady now in the land than she is."

"I don't know about the grand," said Phil, "but I know there is not a better woman in the world than my mother, or a handsomer either, when she's dressed in her velvet, and laces, and diamonds. I wish you could see her once."

"I wish to gracious I could," returned Mrs. Ferguson. "Why don't she never put on her best clothes here and let us see 'em once, and not allus wear them plain black silks, and browns, and grays?"

"Merrivale is hardly the place for velvets and diamonds," said Phil. "There is seldom any occasion for them, and mother does not think it good taste to make a display."

"No, I s'pose not," grandma replied; "but mabby Rennet will take me with her to Washington, or Saratoga, or the sea-side, and then I can see it all. And they needn't be ashamed of me nuther. There's my purple morey, and upon a pinch I can have another new silk. Rennet will find her granny has clothes!"

Phil did not usually wince at anything his grandmother said, but now a cold sweat broke out a over him as he thought of her at the sea-side arrayed in her purple morey, which made her look fatter and coarser than ever, with the bright pink ribbons or blue feather in her cap. What would Reinette say to such a figure, and what would Reinette think of her any way? He was accustomed to her; he knew all the good there was in her; but Reinette, with her French ideas, was different, and he found himself seeing with Reinette's eyes and hearing with Reinette's ears, and blushing with shame for the good old lady, who went on talking about her new granddaughter, whom she sometimes called Rennet, and sometimes Runnet, but never by her right name.

At last Phil could bear it no longer, and said:

"Grandma, isn't it just as easy to say Reinette as Rennet? Do you know what a rennet is?"

"No, what is it?" she asked, and he replied:

"It is what farmers put in milk to make cheese curd."

"Bless the boy!" and Mrs. Ferguson laughed till the tears rolled down her fat cheeks. "Bless the boy, that's runnet; as if I didn't know runnet—I, that lived with a farmer three summers, and made cheese every day."

"No matter; it is spelled rennet, and I do not believe my cousin would care to be called that. We want to please her, you know," said Phil, and his grandmother replied:

"To be sure we do, and we must make quite a time when she fust lands here. Your mother and the gals will come home, of course."

"Perhaps so. I shall write them about it," said Phil, and his grandmother continued: "We must get up a percession to meet her, in your father's carriage, and a hired hack, and our best clothes. I'll see Lyddy Ann to-morrow about fixin' me somethin' to wear. Now I think on't, Lyddy Ann talks of sellin' out her business—so she told me this afternoon. Did you know it?"

"I knew some one had written her on the subject, but not that she had decided to sell," was Phil's reply, and his grandmother said:

"She hain't, exactly; but Anny's puttin' her up to it, thinkin' she'll be thought more on if her mother is not a dressmaker, and that sign is out of the winder. Silly critter! She gets that from the Rices, and they was nothin' extra—I know 'em root and branch. I tell you I'm as much thought on as if I hadn't sold gingerbread and beer; but Anny says I'm only noticed on account of the Rossiters—that folks dassent slight Miss Rossiter's mother, and mabby that's so."

How dreadful her conversation was to Phil, who wondered if she had always talked in this way, and if nothing could be done to tone her down a little before Reinette came. Nothing, he finally decided, and then proceeded to tell her what changes Mr. Beresford contemplated making at Hetherton Place, and what Mr. Hetherton had written of his daughter's tastes with reference to cats, and asked if she could help him there.

"That's the Martin blood in her," said Mrs. Ferguson. "We are desput fond of cats, but I can't let her have old Blue, who has lived with me this ten years, but there's Speckle, with three as lovely Malta kittens as you ever see.

They torment me most to death killin' chickens and tearing up the flower-beds. Rennet can have them and welcome."

It was Rennet again, and Phil let it pass, feeling that to change an old lady like his grandmother was as impossible as to change the order of the seasons, and hoping his cousin would have sense enough to overlook the grammar, and the slang, and prize her for the genuine good there was in her. As it was now getting very late Phil at last said good-night and walked toward home thinking constantly of Reinette, wondering how he should like her, and wondering more how she would like him.

CHAPTER VI

GETTING READY FOR REINETTE

Within two days it was known all over Merrivale that Frederick Hetherton was coming home and was to bring with him a daughter of whose existence no one in town had ever heard, and within three days thirty workmen were busy at Hetherton Place trying to restore the house and grounds to something like their former appearance. Nominally Mr. Beresford was the superintendent, but Phil was really the head, the one who thought of everything and saw to everything, and to whom every one finally went for advice. He had written to his mother and sisters telling them of the expected arrival, and asking if they would not come home for a few days to receive Reinette, who would naturally feel more at her ease with them than with the Fergusons.

To this letter his sister Ethel replied, expressing her astonishment that there should be a cousin of whom she had never heard, and saying they should be very glad to be in Merrivale to receive her, but that her mother was suffering from a sudden and acute attack of muscular rheumatism, and required the constant care both of herself and her sister Grace, so it would be impossible for them to leave her.

"Mother is very anxious to have father here; because she thinks he can lift her better than any one else," Ethel wrote in conclusion, "but she says perhaps he ought to stay and welcome Miss Hetherton; he must do as he thinks best."

This letter Phil showed to his father, of course, and as Col. Rossiter was not particularly interested, either in Frederick Hetherton or his daughter, and as it was very obnoxious to have Grandma Ferguson coming to him every day as she did to discuss the percession which ought to go up to meet the strangers, he started at once for the sea-side, and as Mr. Beresford was confined to the house with a severe influenza and sore throat Phil was left to stem the tide alone. But he was equal the emergency and enjoyed it immensely. Every day was spent at Hetherton Place, except on the occasions when he made journeys to Springfield or Worcester in quest of articles which could not be found in Merrivale. It was astonishing to Mr. Beresford, to whom daily reports were made, how much Phil knew about the furnishing of a house. Nothing was forgotten from a box of starch and pepper up to blankets, and spreads, and easy-chairs. Phil seemed to be everywhere at the same time, and by his own enthusiasm spurred on the men to do double the work they would otherwise have done. He superintended everything in the grounds, in the garden, and in the house, where he frequently worked with his own hands. He cut the paper and the border for Reinette's bed-chamber, put down the matting himself, looped the muslin curtains with knots of blue ribbon, and from his own room at the Knoll brought a few choice pictures to hang upon the walls. He asked no advice of any one, and was deaf to all the hints his cousin Anna gave him with regard to what she thought was proper in the furnishing of a house. But when toward the last she insisted upon going to Hetherton Place, he consented and took her himself in his light open buggy.

Anna was never happier than when seen by the villagers in company with Phil, or with any of the Rossiters of whose relationship to herself she was very proud, parading it always before strangers when she thought there was any likelihood of its working good for herself. Like her grandmother she thought a great deal of dress, and on this occasion she was very dashingly arrayed with streamers on her hat nearly a yard long, her dress tied back so tight that she could scarcely walk, her fan swinging from her side, a black lace scarf which came almost to her feet, and a white silk parasol which her mother had bought in Boston at an enormous price. Anna was very much in love with her parasol, and very angry with Phil for telling her it was more suitable for the city than for the country. She liked city things, she said, and if the Merrivale people were so far behind the times as not to tolerate a white silk parasol she meant to educate them. So she flaunted her parasol on all occasions and held it airily over her head as she rode to Hetherton Place with Phil, and was very soft, and gentle and talkative, and told him of a schoolmate of hers who had just been married, and made a splendid match, only some might object to it, as the parties were own cousins, not half, but own? For her part she saw nothing out of the way if they were suited. Did Phil think it wrong for cousins to marry each other?

Yes, Phil thought it decidedly wicked, and he urged his pony into a pace which drowned the rest of Miss Anna's remarks on the subject of cousins marrying.

Arrived at Hetherton Place, the young lady criticised things generally with an unsparing tongue. Every thing was so simple and plain, especially in Reinette's room. Of course it was pleasant, and neat, and cool, and airy, but why did Phil get matting for the floor, and that light, cheap-looking furniture. There was a lovely pattern of Brussels carpeting at Enfair's for a dollar fifty a yard and a high black walnut bedstead and dressing bureau at Trumbull's; and why didn't he get a wardrobe with a looking-glass door, so Reinette could see the bottom of her dresses. Then she inspected the pictures, and asked where he found those dark-looking photographs, and that woman in the clouds with her eyes rolled up, and so many children around her. Why didn't he get those lovely pictures, "Wide Awake" and "Fast Asleep?" They would brighten up the room so much!

Phil bit his lips, but maintained a very grave face while he explained to the young lady that what she called photographs were fine steel engravings, which he found in Frankfort, one a landscape after Claude Lorraine, and the other a moonlight scene on the Rhine, near Bingen, with the Mouse Tower and Ehrenfels in sight, while the woman with her eyes rolled up was an oil copy of Murillo's great picture, the gem of the Louvre.

Anna Ferguson had been to boarding-school two or three quarters, and had botanies, and physiologies, and algebras laid away on the book-shelf at home; but for all that she was a very ignorant young lady, and guiltless of any knowledge of the Louvre or Murillo and Claude Lorraine. But she liked to appear learned, and had a way of pretending to know many things which she did not know; and now she hastened to cover her mistake by pretending to examine the pictures more closely, and saying, "Oh, yes, I see; lovely, aren't they? and so well done! Why, Mr. Beresford, you here!" and she turned suddenly toward the door, which Arthur Beresford was just entering.

He was much better, and had ridden over to Hetherton Place with a friend who was going a few miles farther, and, hearing voices up stairs, had come at once to Reinette's room, where he found Phil and Anna.

Just then a workman called Phil away, and Mr. Beresford was left alone with Anna, who was even better pleased to be with him than with her cousin, and who assumed her prettiest, most coquettish manners in order to attract the grave lawyer, whose cue she at once followed, praising the arrangement of the room generally, and finally calling his attention to the pictures, one of which, she said, was drawn by Mr. Lorraine, and the other by—she could not quite remember whom, but—the oil painting was the portrait of Murillo, whose hands and hair she thought so lovely. That came from Loo, in France, but the engravings were from somewhere in Kentucky—Frankfort, she believed.

Mr. Beresford was disgusted, as he always was with Anna, but did not try to enlighten her, and, as Phil soon joined them, they went over the rest of the house together. Only the upper and lower halls, the dining-room, the library, Mr. Hetherton's and Reinette's bedchambers, the kitchen and servants' rooms had been renovated, and these were all in comfortable living order, with new matting on the floors, fresh paint and whitewash everywhere, and furniture enough to make it seem homelike and cozy. But it was in the grounds that the most wonderful change had been wrought, and Mr. Beresford could scarcely credit the evidence of his eyes when he saw what had been done. Weeds and obnoxious plants dug up by the roots; gravel walks cleaned and raked; quantities of fresh green sod where the grass had been almost dead; masses of potted flowers here and there upon the lawn and in the flower-garden; while the conservatory, which opened from the dining-room, was partly filled with rare exotics which Phil had ordered from Springfield.

In its palmy days Hetherton had been one of the finest places in the country, and, with some of its beauty restored, it looked very pleasant and inviting that summer afternoon; and Anna felt a pang of envy of her more fortunate cousin, for whom all these preparations were made, and of whom Phil talked so much. Anna was beginning to be jealous of Reinette, and, as she rode home with Phil, she asked him if he supposed he would make as much fuss for her if she were coming to Merrivale.

"Why, yes," he answered her, "under the same circumstances I should, of course."

"Yes, that's just the point," she retorted. "Under the same circumstances, which means if I were rich like her, and belonged to the Hethertons. I tell you what, Phil, 'Money makes the mare go,' and though this girl is not one whit better than I am, whose mother is a dressmaker and whose father keeps a one-horse grocery, you and that stuck-up Beresford, whom I hate because he is stuck-up, would run your legs off for her, when you, or at least he, would hardly notice me. You have to, because you are my cousin, but if you were not you would be just as bad as Beresford. Wouldn't you now?"

Phil did not care to argue with his cousin, whose jealous nature he understood perfectly, so he merely laughed at her fancies and tried to divert her mind by asking her where she thought he could find a blue silk spread to lay on the foot of the bed in Reinette's chamber.

Anna did not know, but promised to make it her business to inquire, and also to see that some pots of ivies were sent to Hetherton Place before the guests arrived.

The ruse had succeeded, and Miss Anna, who felt that she was deferred to, was in a much better frame of mind when she was at last set down at her mother's door. She found her grandmother in the sitting-room, and at once recounted to her all she had seen at Hetherton Place, and how she was to send over some ivies and hunt up a blue silk quilt for Reinette's bed.

"A blue silk bed-quilt this swelterin' weather? What under the sun does she want of that?" grandma asked, and Anna explained that Cousin Ethel had a pink silk quilt because her room was pink, and Cousin Grace had blue because her room was blue. It was a fashion, that was all.

"Fiddlesticks on the fashion!" her grandmother replied. "Better save the money for something else. If Rennet must have an extra comforter, there's that patch-work quilt, herrin'-bone pattern, which her mother pieced when she was ten years old. It took the prize at the cattle show, and I've kep' it ever sense as a sort of memoir. If Rennet is any kind of a girl she'll think a sight on 't because it was her mother's work. I shall send it over with the cat and kittens."

"Cat and kittens! What do you mean?" Anna asked, in unfeigned surprise, and her grandmother explained that Rennet's father had written she was very fond of cats, and Phil wanted some for her, and she was going to give her Speckle and the Maltas.

Anna, who was above such weaknesses as a love for cats, sniffed contemptuously, and thought her cousin must be a very silly, childish person; "but then grandma," she added, "you may as well call her by her right name, which isn't Rennet, but Reinette, with the accent on the last syllable."

"Oh, yes, I forgot," said grandma. "Phil told me not to call her Rennet, but what's the difference? I mean to do my duty by her, and show Fred Hetherton that I know what is what. We must all go up in percession to meet 'em, and, then, go with 'em to the house, and your mother is goin' to fix me a new cap in case we stay to tea, and if it ain't too hot I shall wear my morey, and if it is, I guess I'll wear that pinkish sprigged muslin with my lammy shawl, and you, Anny, must wear your best clothes, for we don't want 'em to think we are back-woodsy."

There was no danger of Anna's wearing anything but her best clothes, and for the next three days she busied herself with thinking what was most becoming to her, deciding at last upon white muslin and a blue sash, with her long lace scarf fastened with a blush-rose, her white chip hat faced with blue and turned up on one side, with a cream-colored feather drooping down the back. This she thought would be altogether au fait, and sure to impress Reinette with the fact that she was somebody.

Anna was getting quite interested in her new cousin, with whom she meant to stand well; and though she said the contrary, she was really glad that Ethel and Grace Rossiter were both absent, thus leaving her to represent alone the young-ladyhood of the family.

Such was the state of affairs on the morning when the paper announced that the Russia had reached New York the previous afternoon—a piece of news which, though expected, threw Mr. Beresford, and Phil, and the Fergusons into a state of great excitement.

Fortunately, however, everything at Hetherton Place was in readiness for the strangers. The rooms were all in perfect order; a responsible and respectable woman in the person of a Mrs. Jerry, had been found for housekeeper, and with her daughter Sarah installed in the kitchen. Two beautiful horses, with a carriage to match, were standing in the stable, awaiting the approval of Miss Reinette; while in another stall a milk-white steed, tall and large, was pawing and champing, as if impatient for the coming of the mistress he was to carry so grandly and high. Chained in his kennel to keep him from running away to the home he had not yet forgotten, was a noble Newfoundland dog, which Phil had bought at a great price in West Merrivale, and whose name was King. Could Phil have had his way, he would have bought a litter of puppies, too, for the young lady; but Mr. Beresford interfered, insisting that one dog like King was enough to satisfy any reasonable woman. If Miss Hetherton wanted puppies, let her get them herself. So Phil gave them up, but brought over Speckle and the three Maltas, and these were tolerably well domesticated, and had taken very kindly to the stuffed easy-chair which stood in Reinette's window. The blue silk quilt had been found in Worcester, and Grandma Ferguson had sent over the "herrin'-bone" which Margaret pieced when ten years old, and which had taken the prize at the "Cattle show." This Mrs. Jerry had promised faithfully to put on Rennet's bed, and to call the young lady's attention to it as her mother's handiwork.

And so all things were ready, and Grandma Ferguson's sprigged muslin, and lammy shawl, and new lace cap were laid out upon the bed when Phil came with the news that the ship had arrived, and that in all probability, they should soon get a telegram from Mr. Hetherton himself.

This was early in the morning, and as the hours crept on, Mr. Beresford and Phil hovered about the telegraph office, until at last the message came flashing along the wires, and the operator wrote it down, and, with a white, scared face, handed it to Mr. Beresford, who, with a whiter face and a look of horror in his eyes, read the following:

"New York, July ——, 18—.

"To Mr. Arthur Beresford:

"Papa is dead. He died just before the ship touched the shore, and I am all alone with Pierre. But every body is so kind, and everything has been done, and we take the ten o'clock train for Merrivale, Pierre and I and poor dead papa. Please meet us at the station, and don't take papa to his old home. I could not bear to have him there dead. I should see him always and hate the place forever; so bury him at once. Pierre says that will be better. I trust everything to you.

"Reinette Hetherton."

CHAPTER VII

ON THE SEA

The Russia was steaming slowly up the harbor to her moorings on the Jersey side of the Hudson, and her upper deck was crowded with passengers, some straining their eyes to catch the first sight of familiar forms among the crowd waiting for them on shore, and others to whom every thing was strange, looking eagerly from side to side at the world so new to them. Standing apart from the rest, with her hands locked tightly together, her head thrown back, and a long blue vail twisted around her sailor hat, was a young girl with a figure so slight that at first you might have mistaken her for a child of fourteen, but when she turned more fully toward you, you would have seen that she was a girl of twenty summers or more, whose face you would look at once, and twice, and then comeback to study it again and wonder what there was in it to fascinate and charm you so. Beautiful in the strict sense of the word it was not, for if you dissected the features one by one there was much to find fault with. The forehead was low, the nose was short and inclined to an upward turn, as was the upper lip, and the complexion was dark, while the cheeks had lost something of their roundness during the passage, which, though made in summer, had not been altogether smooth and free from storm.

During the first three days Reinette had been very sick, and Pierre, her father's attendant, had carried her on deck, and wrapped her in blankets and furs, and watched over and cared for her as if she had been a queen. Then, when the rain came dashing down and the great green waves broke over the lower deck, and she refused to return to the close cabin and said she liked to watch the ocean in a fury, because it made her think of herself in some of her moods, he staid by her and covered her with his own rubber cloak and held an umbrella over her head until the wind took it from him and turning it wrong side out, carried it far out to sea, where it rode like a feather on the waves, while Reinette laughed merrily to see it dance up and down until it was lost to sight. Others than Pierre were interested in and kind to the little French girl, whose father had kept his berth from the time he came on board at Liverpool.

It was whispered about that he was a millionaire, and that Reinette was his only child, and heiress of his vast fortune; and as such things go for a great deal on shipboard as well as elsewhere, this of itself was sufficient to interest the passengers in Reinette, who, as soon as she was able, danced about the ship like the merry, lighthearted creature she was, now jabbering with Pierre in his native tongue, and sometimes holding fierce altercations with him, now watching the sailors at their work, and not unfrequently joining her own clear, bird-like voice in the songs they sung, and again amusing some fretful, restless child, whose tired mother blessed her for the respite, and thought her the sweetest type of girlhood she had ever seen. Everybody liked her, and, after a little, everybody called her beautiful, she was so bright and sparkling, with the rich, warm color in her cheeks, her pretty little mouth always breaking out in exclamations of surprise or bursts of laughter, her long eyelashes and heavy brows, her black, wavy hair, which in some lights had in it a tinge of golden brown, as if it had been often kissed by the warm suns of Southern France, and, more than all, her large, dark, brilliant eyes which flashed upon you so suddenly and so swiftly as almost to blind and bewilder you with their brightness. Taken as a whole, Reinette Hetherton was a girl, who, once seen, could never be forgotten; she was so sunny, and sweet, and willful, and piquant, and charming every way; and the passengers on the Russia, who were mostly middle-aged people, petted, and admired, and sympathized with her, too, when, with the trace of tears in her beautiful eyes, she came from her father's bedside and reported him no better.

For months his health had been failing, and he had hoped the sea voyage would restore him somewhat; but he was growing steadily worse, though as yet there was no shadow of fear in Reinette's heart; she was only sad and sorry for him, and staid with him whenever he would let her. Generally, however, he would send her away after a few passionate hugs and kisses, and inquiries as to how he was feeling. She must get all the sea air she could, he said, for he wanted her to be bright and fresh when he presented her to his friends in America.

"Not that I have many friends there," he said, smiling a little bitterly. "It has been so many years, and so much has happened, since I left home, that I doubt if any remember or care for me; but they will forgive me, perhaps, for the sake of you, my daughter," and he stroked fondly the long silken curls which Reinette wore bound at the back of her head, and looked lovingly into the eyes meeting his so tenderly.

Then he sent her away, and turning in his narrow berth, thought again, as he had thought many times, of all the sin and evil doing he had heaped up against himself and others since the day he last saw his native land. Many and terribly bitter were the thoughts crowding his brain and filling him with remorse, as he lay there day after day, and knew that with each turn of the noisy screw he was nearing the home where there was not a friend to welcome him.

"But once there," he said to himself, "once back in the old place, I'll begin life anew. I'll make friends even of my enemies for the sake of my darling; oh, Queenie, my child, there is so much I would undo for you—for you—to whom the greatest wrong of all has been done, and you so unconscious of it. Would you kiss me as you do? Would you love me as you do, if you knew all the dark past as I know it? Oh, my child! my child!" and, covering his face with his hands, the sick man sobbed aloud.

"If I live to get there," was now the burden of his thoughts; but could he live he asked himself, as, day by day, he felt he was growing weaker, and counted the rapid heart-beats and saw the streaks of blood upon the napkin his faithful Pierre held to his lips after a paroxysm of coughing.

The desire for life was stronger within him now than it had been in years; but the candle was burned out; there was only the snuff remaining, and when at last the scent of the land breeze was borne through his open window, and Reinette came rushing in to tell him they were entering the harbor, and she had seen America, he knew the hand of death was on him, and that the only shore he should ever reach would be the boundless shore of eternity, which was looming up so black before him. But he would let Reinette be happy as long as possible, and so he sent her from him, and then with a low moan, he cried:

"Pity me, oh, God! I have so much need to be forgiven."

In his gayest, most reckless moods, with his skeptical companions round him jeering at all that was sacred and holy, he had said there was no God, that the Bible was only an old woman's fable, but he had never quite believed it, and now, with death measuring his life by heart-beats, he knew there was a God and a hereafter by the stings of his own conscience, and the first prayer uttered in years fell from his white lips. Oh, how many and how great were the sins which came back to him as he thought of his wasted life, remembering his mother dead so long ago; his father, too, whose last words to him had been a curse; and the beautiful Margaret, whom for a short period he had loved with a love so impetuous that in a few short months it had burned itself out and left only poisonous ashes where the fierce passion had been. How gentle, and patient, and forgiving she was, and how basely he had requited her faithfulness and love.

"Oh, Margaret," he whispered, "I am so sorry, and if I could undo the past I would."

Then, as another phantom, darker, more terrible than all the others flitted before his mind, he shivered as with a chill, while the great drops of sweat came out upon his forehead, and the palms of his hands which he clasped so tightly together, were dripping with perspiration. And while he lay there alone suffering the torments of remorse he could hear the rapid movements of the sailors and the excited crowd on deck watching for the shore. And Reinette, he knew, was with them, looking eagerly upon the new world which recently he had tried to teach her to love as her future home.

"Home—America," he murmured; "I must see it again!" and, regardless of consequences, he got out of his berth, and, tottering to his window, looked out upon the beautiful bay, and saw in the distance the city, which had grown so much since he last looked upon it.

But the exertion was too great for him, and, dizzy and faint, he crept back to his bed, where he lay unconscious for a moment; then rousing himself, and alarmed by the terrible feeling stealing over him so fast, he called aloud for Reinette.

The call was heard by Pierre, who was never far away, and who came at once, greatly alarmed by the pallor in his master's face and the flecks of blood upon the lips and chin.

To go for Reinette was the work of an instant, and like a frightened deer, she bounded down the stairway to her father's side, and in her impetuosity almost threw herself upon him. But he motioned her back, and whispered.

"Not so close; you take my breath away. Pierre," he added faintly as his valet started for the physician, "don't go for him; it's too late now. I am dying; nothing can help me, and I must not be disturbed. I must be alone with Queenie. Stand outside till I call."

The frightened Pierre obeyed, and then Reinette was alone with her dying father. She knew he was dying, but the awful suddenness stunned her so completely that she could only gaze at him in a stupefied kind of way, as his eyes were fixed so earnestly upon her.

"Little Queenie," he said, using the pet name he always gave her, "kneel down beside me and hold my hands in yours while I tell you something I ought to have told you long ago."

She obeyed, and, covering his cold hands with kisses, whispered:

"Yes, father, I am waiting."

But if he heard, he did not answer at once; and when at last he spoke, it was with difficulty, and like one who labors for breath. His mind, too, seemed wandering, and he said:

"I can't tell, but if it ever comes to you, promise you will forgive me. I have loved you so much, my darling oh, my darling, promise while I can hear you!"

"Yes, father, I promise," Reinette replied, knowing nothing to what she pledged herself, thinking nothing except of the white face on the pillow, where the sign of death was written.

"Queenie, are you here?" the voice said again, and she replied, "Yes, father," while he continued: "I meant to have told you when we reached New York, but cannot now, I am too weak. It is too late, forever too late. Oh Queenie—oh, Margaret, forgive!"

"Is it of mother you wish to tell me?" Reinette asked bending forward eagerly, and fixing her great dark eyes upon him.

"Your mother, child—your mother. Yes—no—don't speak that name aloud. We've left her way over there, or I thought we had. That's why I was going home—to get away from it, and—if——Queenie, where are you? I can't see you, child. You are surely here? You are listening?"

"Yes, yes, father, I am here. I am listening," and the girl's rigid face and fixed, wide-open eyes showed how intently she was listening.

"Yes, child, that's right; listen so close that nobody else can hear. We are all alone?"

"Yes, father, all alone; only Pierre is outside, and he understands English so little. What is it, father? What are you going to tell me?"

There was silence for a moment, while Mr. Hetherton regarded his daughter fixedly, and with an expression in his eyes which made her uneasy and half afraid of him.

"What is it?" he said, at last. "I don't know; it comes and goes, as she did. Ah! now I have it: Queenie, remember how much I love you, and if you ever meet your mother, remember it was my fault, and do not blame her too much."

"Oh, poor father! his mind is wandering," Reinette thought; but she said to him, soothingly: "Mother is dead; she died in Rome when I was born."

Again the eyes regarded her wistfully as the dying man replied:

"Yes, I know; but she's here, or she was over there in the corner just now, laughing at my pain. Oh, Queenie! do the torments of the lost begin before they die? I'm sorry—oh, I am so sorry! It's too late now—too late. I can't think how it was, or tell you if I could."

He was quiet a moment, and seemed to be himself again, as his hands caressed the shining hair of the head bowed down so near to him.

"Too late, Queenie. I ought to have told you before, but it's my nature to put off; and now when they claim you in Merrivale, accept it; try to like everybody and be pleased with everything. America is very different from France. Trust Mr. Beresford; he is my friend. He comes of a good race. Tell him everything. Go to him for everything necessary, but don't trouble any one when you can help yourself. Don't cry before people; it bothers and distresses them. Be a woman; learn to care for yourself. Govern your temper; nobody will bear with it as I have. Be patient with Pierre—and—and—Queenie, child, where are you? It's getting so dark. I can't see you anywhere, nor feel you either. Have you left me, too? and Margaret is gone now."

"No, no; I'm here!" Reinette cried, in an agony of fear; and her father continued:

"Remember, when it comes to you, as it may, that you promised to forgive."

"Yes, father. I don't know what you mean, but if I ever do, I'll forgive everything—everything, and love you just the same, forever and ever," Reinette said to him; and the cold, clammy hands upon her head pressed harder in token that he had heard. But that was the only response for a moment, when he said again, and this time in a whisper, with heavy, labored breath:

"One thing more comes to my mind. There will be letters for me—some on business, and possibly some others, and you must let no one see them if there is any thing in them the world ought not to know. Promise Queenie."

"I promise," Reinette said, frightened at the strange look in his face and his evident eagerness for her reply.

"God bless you, darling! Keep your promise and never try to find—"

He did not say what or whom, but lay perfectly quiet while overhead on deck the trampling of feet was more hurried and noisy, and the ship gave a little lurch as if hitting against something which resisted its force and set it to rocking again. The motion threw Reinette backward and when she gathered herself up and turned toward the white face upon the pillow, she uttered a wild cry in French:

"Oh Pierre, Pierre, come quickly, father is dead!" and tottering toward the door she fell heavily against the tall custom-house officer just entering the state-room.

He had come on board to do his duty; had seen the bustling little Frenchman speak hurriedly to the young girl on deck; had seen her dart away, and fancied she cast a frightened look at him. When others came to declare the contents of their trunks she had not been with them.

"Secreting her goods and chattels, no doubt," he thought, and made his way to the state-room, where he stood appalled in the awful presence of death.

Reinette might have had the wealth of all Paris in her trunks and carried it safely off, for her boxes were not molested, and both passengers, ship's crew, and officers vied with each other in their care for and attention to this young girl, whose father lay dead in his berth, and who was all alone in a foreign country. Understanding but little of the language, and terrified half out of his wits at the sight of death, Pierre was almost worse than useless, and could do nothing but crouch at his mistress' feet, and holding her hands in his, gaze into her face in dumb despair, as if asking what they were to do next.

"Children, both of them. We must take it in hand ourselves," the captain said to his mate, and he did take it in hand, and saw that Reinette was made comfortable at the Astor, and that the body was made ready for burial.

When asked if she had friends or relatives expecting her, Reinette replied:

"No, papa was all I had. There's only Pierre now, and Mr. Beresford, papa's agent. I am to trust him with everything."

Later, when something was said to her of telegraphing to Mr. Beresford to come for her, she answered, promptly:

"No, that would make unnecessary trouble, and father said I was not to do that. Pierre and I can go alone. I have traveled a great deal, and when papa was sick in Germany and Pierre could not understand, I talked to the guards and the porters. I know what to do."

And on the pale face there was a resolute, self-reliant look, which was in part born of this terrible shock and partly the habit of Reinette's life.

"To-morrow morning I will telegraph," she added. "You see us to the right train, and I can do the rest, I can find the way. I have been studying it up."

And she showed him Appleton's Railway Guide, to which she had fled as to a friend.

Since leaving the ship she had not shed a tear in the presence of any one, but the anguish in her dry bright eyes, and the drawn, set look about her mouth told how hard it was for her to force back the wild cry which was constantly forcing itself to her lips. Her father, to whom in life her slightest wish had been a law had said to her, "Don't trouble people, nor cry if you can help it. Be a woman;" and now his wish was a law to her, which she would obey if she broke her heart in doing it. She did not seem at all like the airy, merry-hearted, laughing girl she had been on shipboard, but like a woman with a woman's will and a woman's capacity to act. That she could go to Merrivale alone she was perfectly sure, and she convinced the captain of it, and then with a voice which shook a little, she said:

"Mr. Beresford will meet me, of course, at the station, and some others, perhaps. I don't quite know the ways of this country. Will they bury him at once do you think, or take him somewhere first?"

The captain understood her meaning and replied by asking if she had friends—relatives—in Merrivale.

"None," she said. "Nobody but Mr. Beresford, father's friend and lawyer."

"But you have a house—a home—to which you are going?"

"Yes, the home where father lived when a boy, and which he was so anxious to see once more," Reinette said, and the captain replied:

"Naturally, then, they will take your father there for a day or two, and then give him a grand funeral, with——"

"They won't; they sha'n't," interrupted Reinette, her eyes blazing with determination. "I won't have a grand funeral, with all the peasantry and their carts joining in it. Neither will I have him carried to the old home. I could not bear to see him there dead. I should hate the place always, and see him everywhere. He is my own darling father to do with as I like. Pierre says I'm my own mistress, and I shall telegraph Mr. Beresford to-morrow that father must be buried from the station, and I shall make him do it."

She was very decided and imperious, and the captain let her have her way, and sent off for her next morning the long telegram which she had written, regardless of expense, and which so startled the people in Merrivale and changed their plans so summarily.

CHAPTER VIII

REINETTE ARRIVES

Mr. Beresford, to whom the telegram was addressed, read it first, feeling as if the ground was moving from under his feet, and leaving a chasm he did not know how to span.

"What is it?" Phil asked, as he saw how white Mr. Beresford grew, and how the hand which held the telegram shook.

"Read for yourself," Mr. Beresford said, passing the paper to Phil, to whose eyes the hot tears sprang quickly, and whose heart went out to the desolate young girl, alone in a strange land, with her dead father beside her.

"If I had known it last night I would have gone to her," he said, "but it's too late now for that. All we can do is to make it as easy for her as possible. Beresford, you see to the grave in the Hetherton lot, and that the hearse is at the station to meet the body, and I'll notify them at the house not to go on with the big dinner they are getting up, and I'll tell grandmother that her flounced muslin and pink ribbons will not be needed to-day."

Shocked and horrified as he was, Phil could not refrain from a little pleasantry at the expense of the dress and cap which grandma Ferguson was intending to wear "to the doin's," as she termed it. That she should accompany her son-in-law and granddaughter home to dinner she did not for a moment doubt, and her dress and cap and "lammy" shawl were ready when Phil came with the news, which so shocked her that for a moment she did not speak, and when at last she found her voice her first remark was wholly characteristic and like her.

"Fred Hetherton dead! Sarves him right, the stuck-up critter! But I am sorry for the girl, and we'll give him a big funeral jest on her account."

But Phil explained that Mr. Hetherton was to be buried from the station, as Reinette would not have the body taken to Hetherton Place.

"'Fraid of sperrits, most likely," said Mrs. Ferguson, thinking to herself that now she should spend a great deal of time with her granddaughter who would be lonely in her great house.

Then, as her eye fell upon her muslin dress and lace cap, her thoughts took another channel. Out of respect to Reinette, who would of course be clad in the deepest mourning she could find in New York, she and her daughter-in-law, Mrs. Tom, and Anna, must at least wear black when they first met her. "Not that she cared for Fred Hetherton," she said, "who had thought no more of her than he did of a squaw. But Margaret's girl was different," and in spite of Phil's protest against the absurdity of the thing, the old lady bustled off in the hot sun to consult with Mrs. Lydia. The news of Mr. Hetherton's death had preceded her, and she had only to plunge into business at once, and insist that a bombazine which she had never worn since she left off her widow's weeds, and which was now much too small for her, should be let out and made longer, and fixed generally, and she talked so fast and so decidedly that Mrs. Tom, who never had any positive opinions of her own, and who liked to please her mother-in-law because of the money she was supposed to hold in store for Anna, was compelled to take her apprentice from a piece of work promised for the next day, and put her upon the bombazine which grandma had brought with her. Against mourning for herself, however, Miss Anna stoutly rebelled. She had tried the effect of the Swiss muslin the lovely lace scarf, the blush-rose and white parasol, and was not to be persuaded to abandon it, she said, for "forty dead Hethertons." So the young lady was suffered to do as she liked, but the entire village was ransacked after shawls, and vails, and bonnets, for the two Mrs. Fergusons, who were to go up in the Rossiter carriage and appear as sorry and miserable as the deepest black could make them. Mr. Tom Ferguson, of whom scarcely anything has been said, and who was a plain, quiet, second-class grocer, and as obstinate in some matters as a mule, refused to have any thing to do with the affair.

"Fred Hetherton had never spoken to or looked at him when a boy, and he shouldn't go after him now," he said. "He should stay at home and mind his own business, and let Phil and the women folks run the funeral."

This resolution Anna in her secret heart thought a very sensible one. If possible she was more ashamed of her father than of the sign in her mother's window; and she would far rather that handsome stylish Phil should ride with her then her old-fashioned father, whom Reinette was sure to take for a peasant. But when the carriage came round for the mourning party Phil was not in it; nor did the coachman know where his young master was; his orders were to drive the ladies to the station, and that was all he knew, and Anna, always suspicious, felt like striking him because of the insolent look in his face when she bade him dismount from his box and open the carriage door for them.

"He would not dare treat her Aunt Rossiter and cousins like that; neither would Phil have left them to go up alone," she thought, as she took her seat poutingly, wondering where Phil was, and if he would keep aloof from them at the station, just to show Reinette that he recognized the difference between himself and his relatives.

And while she thought thus jealously of Phil, he, with the perspiration standing in great drops upon his face, and with his cuffs pulled up from his white wrists, was working like a beaver in the "Hetherton lot," which Mr. Beresford, on his return from selecting the site for the grave, had reported "a perfect swamp of briers and weeds." It would never answer, Phil said, to let Reinette tear her dress on briers, and get her feet entangled in weeds. Something must be done, although there was but little time in which to do it, and he began to hunt about for some man to help him: but no one was to be found, while even the sexton was busy with the grave of a town pauper who was to be buried that afternoon.

Phil was very tired, for he had been busy since the arrival of Reinette's telegram at his grandmother's, his Aunt Lydia's, his own home, and at Hetherton Place, where he filled the rooms with flowers brought from the Knoll gardens and conservatory and with the beautiful pond lilies which he went himself upon the river to procure. The most of these he arranged in Reinette's chamber, for there was a great pity in Phil's heart for the young girl whose home-coming would be so sad. Of himself, or how he would impress Reinette, he never but once thought, and that when, chancing to pass the mirror, he caught sight of his hat, which was rather the worse for wear.

"I certainly must honor my cousin with a new hat, for this is unpardonably shabby," he thought, and remembering his bet with Arthur Beresford, and how sure he was to win, he went into a hatter's on his return to town, and selecting a soft felt, which was very becoming, and added to his jaunty appearance, he had it charged to his friend, and then went in quest of some laborer to take with him to the grave-yard.

But there was none to be found, and so he set off alone with hoe and rake, and sickle, and waged so vigorous a warfare upon the weeds, and grass, and briers, that the lot, though far from being presentable, was soon greatly changed in its appearance. But Phil had miscalculated the time, and while pruning the willows which drooped over Mrs. Hetherton's grave, he suddenly heard in the distance the whistle of the train not over a mile away.

To drop his knife, don his coat, and wipe the blood from a bramble scratch on his hand, was the work of an instant, and then Phil went flying across the fields the shortest way to the station, racing with the locomotive speeding so swiftly across the meadows by the river-side until it reached the station, where a crowd of people was collected, and where grandma and Mrs. Lydia waited in their black, and Anna in her white, while Mr. Beresford, who had come up in his own carriage, stood apart from them, nervous and expectant, and wondering where Phil could be—poor Phil! tumbling over stone walls, bounding over fences, and leaping over bogs in his great haste to be there, and only stopping to breathe when he rolled suddenly down a bank and was obliged to pick himself and his hat up, and wipe the dirt from his pants and rub his grazed ankle. Then he went on, but the train had deposited its freight, living and dead, and shot away under the bridge, leaving upon the platform a young girl with a white, scared face, and great bright black eyes, which flashed upon the staring crowd glances of wonder and inquiry.

It was an exquisite little figure, with grace in every movement; but the crape which Grandma Ferguson had expected to see upon it was not there. Indeed, it had never occurred to Reinette that mourning was needed to tell of the bitter pain at her heart; and she wore the same gray camel's hair which had done duty on shipboard, and which, though very plain, fitted her so admirably, and was so unmistakably stylish and Parisian, that Anna began at once to think how she would copy it. Reinette's sailor hat was the color of her dress, and twisted around it and then tied under her chin was a long blue veil, while her gloves were of embroidered Lisle thread, and came far up under the deep white cuff, which was worn outside her closely fitting sleeve.

All this Anna noted at a single glance, as she did the dainty little boot, which the short dress made so visible.

"She isn't in black; you might have saved yourself all that bother," Anna said, under her breath, while her grandmother was thinking the same thing and sighing regretfully for the cool muslin lying at home, while she was sweating at every pore in her heavy bombazine.

But she meant well, and secure in this consciousness, she pressed forward to welcome and embrace her grandchild, just as Mr. Beresford stepped up to the young lady.

The crowd of people had confused and bewildered Reinette, and, for an instant she had thought of nothing but the box which was being lifted from the car, and which Pierre, half crazed himself, was superintending, while he jabbered first his unintelligible French, and then his scarcely more intelligible English. But when the box was carefully put down and the train had started, she threw rapid glances around her in quest of the only one on whom she felt she had any claim, Mr. Beresford, her father's friend and agent who was looking at her, curiously, and thinking at first that though very stylish she certainly was not handsome. But when, in their rapid sweep, the dark eyes fell upon him and seemed to rest there inquiringly he began to change his mind; and as the Ferguson party were evidently waiting for him to make the first advance, and Phil was not there, he walked up to her, and offering her his hand, said, in his well-bred, gentlemanly way.

"Miss Hetherton, I believe?"

In Reinette's mind Mr. Beresford had always seemed a gray-haired, middle-aged man, as old or older than her father, and she had no idea that this young, good-looking stranger, with the handsome teeth and pleasant smile and voice, was he; so she withheld her hand from his offered one, and stepping back a little, said in perfect English, but with a very pretty foreign accent:

"I am looking for Mr. Beresford, please; do you know him?—is he here?"

It was such a sweet, musical voice, and had in it something so timid and appealing that Mr. Beresford felt his pulses quicken as they had never done before.

"I am Mr. Beresford," he replied, and the lightning glance which the bright eyes flashed into his face almost blinded him, for Reinette's eyes were wonderful for their brilliancy and continually varying expression, and few men ever stood unmoved before them.

"Mr. Arthur Beresford? Are you Mr. Arthur, father's friend?" she asked:

"Yes, Mr. Arthur, your father's friend," and again his hand was extended toward her.

Reinette had kept up her composure ever since the moment when she knew her father was dead, and had even tried to seem cheerful on the train and had talked of the places they were passing to some people who had been on the Russia with her, and were on their way to their home in Boston, but at sight of Mr. Beresford, her father's friend, whom she was to trust with everything, her forced calmness gave way, and she broke down entirely. Taking both his hands in hers, she bent her face over them and sobbed like a little child.

It was a very novel position in which the grave bachelor Beresford found himself—a girl crying on his hands, with all those people looking on; and still he rather liked it, for there was something very touching in the way those fingers clung to his, and in his confusion he was not quite sure that he did not press them a little, but before he could think what to say or do Grandma Ferguson stood close to him, and as Reinette lifted her head a pair of arms was thrown around her neck, and a voice which her patrician ears detected at once as untrained and uneducated, exclaimed:

"My dear Rennet, I am so glad to see my daughter's girl."

With a motion as swift and graceful as the motions of a kitten, Reinette freed herself from the smothering embrace, and the eyes, in which the tears were still shining, blazed with astonishment and indignation at the liberty taken by this strange woman, whose tout ensemble she took in at a glance, and who said again, "My dear child, I am so sorry for you."

"Madam, I don't understand you," Reinette replied, drawing nearer to Mr. Beresford, and holding faster to his hand, as if for protection and safety.

Neither did grandma understand, but Mr. Beresford did, and knew that the existence of the Fergusons was wholly unknown to Reinette, who, as if to breathe more freely, untied the blue veil, and taking it from her neck and hat, stood like a hunted creature at bay; while Mrs. Ferguson, nothing abashed, and simply thinking the girl might be a little deaf, raised her voice and said:

"I am your grandmarm—your mother's mother; and this," turning to her daughter-in-law, "is your A'nt Lyddy Ann—your Uncle Tom's wife; and this one," nodding to Anna, who understood the state of things better than her grandmother, and was hot with resentment and anger, "this is your Cousin Anny."

Releasing her hand from Mr. Beresford's, Reinette, with dexterous rapidity, wrenched off her gloves, as if they, like the veil, were burdensome; and Anna, who hated her own long, slim fingers, with the needle-pricks upon them, saw, with a pang of envy, how soft and small, and white were her cousin's hands, with the dimples at the joints, and the costly jewels shining on them.

Mrs. Lydia, who felt quite overawed in the presence of this foreign girl, did not speak, but courtesied straight up and down; while Anna put on a show of cordiality, and, offering her hand, made a most profound bow, as she said:

"I am glad, Cousin Reinette, to make your acquaintance, and you are very welcome to America."

"Thanks," murmured Reinette in her soft, foreign accent, just as Grandma Ferguson spoke again:

"And this is another cousin, Philip Rossiter—your A'nt Mary's boy."

Phil had come at last, and stood looking over his grandmother's shoulder at the new arrival. His face was very red with his recent exercise, and a little soiled by the hands which had come in contact with fences and walls, and bogs, and then wiped the perspiration from it, so that he was not quite as jaunty and handsome as usual. At a glance he had seen how matters stood. Miss Reinette did not take kindly to her new relatives, if indeed she believed they were her relatives at all. Miss Reinette was neither an Amazon nor a blonde; she was petite and a brunette. He had lost his bet; the new hat he wore so airily was not his, but Mr. Beresford's, and quick as thought he snatched it from his head and exchanged with his friend, just as he was presented to Reinette as another cousin.

Instantly the large, bright black eyes darted toward him a perplexed, wondering look, but aside from that there was no response to the lifting of Phil's old hat. Another cousin was the straw too many, and Reinette fairly gasped as she involuntarily said to herself in French, "I believe I shall die;" then, taking the sailor hat from her head, she fanned herself furiously, while the look of a hunted, worried creature deepened on her dark, flushed face and shone in her flashing eyes.

Just then Pierre came to the rescue, and said something to her in his own language, whereupon she turned swiftly to Mr. Beresford and said:

"You received my telegram? You will bury him straight from here?"

"Yes," he answered, "and I believe every thing is ready. Shall I take you to your carriage?"

"Yes, yes! Oh, do!" she replied, and placing her hat on her head again, she took his arm, and Anna always insisted that she held her skirts back as with the air of a grand duchess, she walked past them to the carriage, the door of which the coachman held open with as much respect as if she had been a queen.

Reinette must have guessed the intention of her new relatives to ride with her, for she said, rapidly and low, to Mr. Beresford:

"You go with me, of course, and Pierre; he loved father; he is nearer to me now than any one in the wide world."

"Why, yes; only I think your relatives—your grandmother will naturally expect to accompany you," Mr. Beresford answered, and Reinette said quickly:

"My relatives! my grandmother! Mr. Beresford, father said I was to ask you everything. Are they my grandmother? Tell me true."

Mr. Beresford could not repress a smile at the way she put the question, in her vehemence, but he answered her very low and cautiously, as the Ferguson party was close behind:

"I think they are."

Then, as a sudden idea flashed upon him, he continued:

"Was your father twice married?"

"No, never, never!"

"Tell me, then, please, your mother's name?"

"Margaret Ferguson, and she died in Rome, when I was born."

He had her in the carriage by this time, and her eyes were looking straight into his as he began:

"If your mother was Margaret Ferguson, and died in Rome, I am afraid-"

He did not go on, for something in the black eyes stopped him suddenly, and warned him that if these people were indeed her relatives she would suffer no insinuations against them. She was like Phil in that respect; what was hers she would defend, and, when Mrs. Ferguson's red face appeared at the door, Reinette moved to the other side of the seat, and said:

"Here, grandmother, sit by me, please."

She had acknowledged her by name, at least, and Reinette felt better, and only clenched her hands hard as Mrs. Lydia and Anna disposed of themselves on the soft cushions opposite, the young lady stepping on and tearing her long lace scarf.

"You didn't orter wear it. Such jimcracks ain't for funerals. Rennet hain't got on none," grandma said, while Anna frowned insolently, and Reinette looked on and shivered, and held her hands tighter together, and thought how dreadful it all was, and how it could be that these people belonged to her, who at heart was the veriest aristocrat ever born.

Phil did not come near her, but kept close to Mr. Beresford's carriage, and to Pierre, to whom he spoke in French, thereby so delighting the old man that he began to jabber so rapidly and gesticulate so vehemently that Phil lost the thread entirely, and shook his head in token that he did not understand. Without exactly knowing why, Phil felt uncomfortable and ashamed, and the Ferguson blood had never seemed so distasteful to him as now. Reinette had seen them first, and so ignored him, and he did not like it at all. Had there been no step-grandmother, nor aunt, nor Cousin Anna, he could have come up by himself, he thought, in his father's handsome carriage, with the high-stepping bays, and the coachman, who, without the aid of livery, looked so respectable and dignified upon the box, and it would all have been so different. But now he felt slighted and overlooked, and shabby, and there was a soiled spot on the knee of his pants, and his hands were cut with briers and dirty, too, and there was nothing airy or exquisite about him as he entered Mr. Beresford's barouche with that gentleman and Pierre, and followed the other carriage where Reinette sat, silent and motionless, with her blue veil tied closely over her face as if to hide it from the eyes opposite scanning her so curiously.

Never once did she look from the carriage window, or evince the slightest interest in any thing around her, and when, as they reached the village and turned into the main street, Mrs. Ferguson motioned with her hand to the right, and said:

"There, Rennet—way down there under them popple trees is the house where I live, and where your mother was born," she never turned her head, or gave a sign that she heard; only the hands locked so tightly together, worked a little more nervously, and there was an involuntary shrug of her shoulders, which Anna resented hotly.

At last, as the silence became unbearable to grandma, she said to Reinette:

"I s'pose you don't remember your mother."

Reinette shook her head, and grandma continued:

"How old was you when she died?"

"I don't know."

"Don't know how old you was when your mother died? That's curis. Didn't your father never tell you?"

"No, madam."

"Wall, now. Don't you think that's singular?" and grandma looked at her daughter-in-law and Anna, the latter of whom seized the opportunity to spit out her venom, and said:

"Not singular at all, and if I's you, grandma, I wouldn't bother Reinette with troublesome questions, for I've no idea that she ever heard of us until to-day, let alone her knowing how old she was when her mother died."

Anna spoke spitefully, and had the satisfaction of seeing the black eyes under the thin veil unclose and flash at her just once, while grandma replied:

"Never heard of us till to-day! Never heard she had a grandmother! Be you crazy, Anny? Do you s'pose her father never told her of her mother's folks? Rennet, do you hear that? I hope you can contradict it."

Thus appealed to Reinette roused herself, and in a voice choking with sobs, said:

"Oh, please—don't worry me now; by and by I can talk with you, but now—oh, father, father, why did you die and leave me here alone."

The sob was a wailing, heart-broken cry, and the little hands were upraised and beat the air in a paroxysm of nervous pain for an instant, then dropped helplessly, and Reinette never moved again until they turned into the cemetery and stopped before the Hetherton lot. Then she started, and throwing back her veil, said, hurriedly:

"What is it? Are we there?"

Grandma Ferguson, who, since Reinette's pitiful outburst, had been crying softly to herself, wiped her eyes and said:

"Yes, darling, this is the Hetherton lot. It has been left to run down this many a year, but will look better by and by. Hadn't you better stay in the carriage? You can if you want to."

"No, no, oh, no. I must be with father," Reinette replied, and opening the door herself, she sprang to the ground, and was first at the open grave, where she stood immovable until they began to lower the body. Then she exclaimed:

"Oh, are there no flowers for him? Did no one bring a flower, when he loved them so much?" and her eyes flashed rebukingly upon those who had brought no flowers for the dead man.

Then she was quiet again until there was a creaking sound in the ropes and the coffin slipped a little, when, with a cry of alarm, she sprang forward and bent over the grave as if to see that no harm was coming to her father. There was danger in her position, and Phil went quickly to her side, and laying his hand on her shoulder, said to her, very gently:

"Please stand farther back. There is quicksand here, and the earth might crumble."

She never looked at him, but she stepped backward a few paces and did not move again until the grave was filled, and her father—he who had so longed to come home that he might begin anew and make amends in part for his past life—was hidden forever from sight with all the dark catalogue of his sins unconfessed save as he had whispered them into the ear of the Most High when death sat on his pillow and counted his heart-beats.

Meanwhile Phil, with his usual forethought, had interviewed his grandmother in an aside and suggested to her that as Reinette would undoubtedly prefer going alone with Mr. Beresford to her new home, the ladies should return to town in the carriage of the latter and call on his cousin the following day.

Grandma, whose heart was set upon going to Hetherton Place, where she had not been since she was turned from its door by its enraged master, would have demurred at this arrangement were it not that her heavy crape was weighing her down, and making her long for the coolness of her own house and her thin "muslin." As it was, she made no objection, and when it was time to go, she went to Reinette and said:

"Phil thinks you'd ruther be alone the fust night home, and I guess he's right, so if you'll excuse your A'nt Liddy, and me and Anny, we'll come early to-morrow and see you, and have a long talk about your mother. Good-by, and Heaven bless you, child."

While she was speaking Reinette looked steadily in her face, and something in its expression attracted more than it repelled her. It was a good, kind, honest face, and had seen her mother, and Reinette's lip quivered as she held out her hand and said:

"Thank you, it will be better so; good-by."

There was another up and down courtesy from Mrs. Lydia, another cold, stately bow from Miss Anna, whose turned-up hat, cream feather, blue sash, and long lace scarf, Reinette noted a second time, and then the ladies walked to the Beresford carriage, where Phil was waiting for them.

"Well, we've seen the great sight. Pray, what do you think of her?" Anna asked him when they left the cemetery and turned into the highway.

Phil did not like the tone of her voice, and was on his guard at once.

"I've not seen enough of her yet to have an opinion," he said; "nor can she appear herself. She is in great trouble, and all alone in a strange country. We must make every allowance for her."

"Yes, of course; I knew you'd stand up for her, just because she's a Hetherton and rich," Anna replied. "For my part, I hate her!"

This was Anna's favorite expression if she did not like a person, and she went on:

"If we had been the lowest people living she could not have shown more contempt for us. I know she had never heard of a soul of us till to-day, and I just wish you could have seen her when grandma claimed her as a grandchild. Where were you, Phil? What was keeping you?"

He explained where he was, and she continued:

"You might have spared yourself the trouble. I don't believe she'll thank you. She just threw her head back and stared at grandma in such an impertinent way that I wanted to box her ears, especially when she said so haughtily, 'Madam, I don't understand you.' She might have added, 'and I don't believe you either; my mother never came from such stock.' That's what she meant, and what her eyes and voice expressed. I don't believe she looked at ma or me, though she did just touch the tips of my fingers. She had taken off her veil at grandma, and torn off her gloves for us—cotton, they were, too; and when you came, and grandma said, 'Here's another cousin,' she snatched off her sailor hat and fanned herself rapidly, as if you were the straw too many. Yes, I hate her, and I think her just as homely as she can be, with her turn-up nose and lip. She's as black, too, as the ace of spades, and those great, big, staring eyes are as insolent and proud as they can be, but I dare say you and Mr. Beresford are both in love with her."

Phil did not care to discuss the matter with his unreasonable cousin, who rattled on until the carriage stopped at Mrs. Ferguson's door. Glad of the chance to escape from Anna's tirade, Phil said he would walk home, and so the carriage drove on, leaving him standing by the gate with his grandmother, who said:

"Such a tongue as Anny's got!—hung in the middle, I do believe. She must git it from the Rices, for the Fergusons ain't an atom backbity. Of course Rennet ain't exactly what I thought Margaret's girl would be, but—then—everything is strange and new to her. She's all Hetherton, and the very image of the old lady, Fred's mother. But you and I'll stand by her Phil. Poor little lonesome critter! how I pity her, alone in that great house, with her father dead in the grave-yard, and her mother dead over the seas!"

There were tears in grandma's eyes, and Phil felt a lump in his own throat as he walked rapidly away, repeating her words to himself.

"Poor little girl! Alone in that great house, with her father dead in the grave-yard, and her mother dead over the sea."

Phil was still a little sore and disappointed. He had made no impression upon Reinette, except it were one of disgust. And everything had turned out so differently from what he had hoped. Even Reinette was wholly different from his idea of her. The tall Amazon, with pink and white complexion and yellow hair, had proved to be a wee little creature, with dark eyes, and hair, and face, but still with something indescribably bewitching and graceful, in every turn of her head and motion of her body, while the clear, bell-like tones of her voice, with its pretty accent, rang continually in his ears, and he began to envy Mr. Beresford the pleasure of having her all to himself for an indefinite length of time.

What would she say to him? Would she talk like any girl, and ask him "who the Fergusons were," and who "the long-legged spooney with the dirty face and hands and the grass stains on his pants?" Phil had reached home by this time, and had seen in the glass that his personal appearance was not as prepossessing as it might be.

"Upon my word," he said, as he contemplated himself in the mirror, "I am a beauty. Look at that streak of dirt upon my forehead, and that spot on my nose, and that blood stain under my eye, and, to crown all, Beresford's old hat. I look for all the world like a prizefighter, I who fancied there was something so distingue and high-toney about me that Reinette would see it at once, and she never even bowed to me, but said she felt like dying."

Here the ludicrousness of the whole affair came over Phil so forcibly that he burst into a loud, merry laugh, which was like thunder on a sultry day. It cleared the atmosphere, and Phil was himself again, or would be after the long ride on horseback which he determined to take into the country.

Calling John the stable-boy he bade him saddle Pluto, his riding horse, and was soon galloping off at a furious rate, going eastward first until he came to a fork in the road, where he turned and rode in the direction of Hetherton Place. He had no intention of stopping there—no expectation of seeing Reinette, unless Providence should interfere. But Providence did not interfere, and he saw no sign of human life about the house.

The windows of Reinette's chamber were open and in one of them sat Mrs. Speckle, the cat, evidently absorbed in something going on inside—the gambols of her three kittens, perhaps.

The Rossiter carriage was not in the yard, and by that token Phil knew that Mr. Beresford must have returned to town, and that he had missed meeting him by having made the circuit of what was called the Flatiron.

Phil did not quite understand why he felt glad to know that his friend had not made a long stay with Reinette, but he was glad, and rode on quite cheerfully for three or four miles, when he turned and came back more slowly, reaching Hetherton just as the sun was setting.

As before, everything was quiet, and no one was to be seen until he came opposite a great ledge of rocks on the hill-side higher up than the house itself and commanding a still better view of the surrounding country. This ledge, which covered quite a space of ground and was in some places as level as the floor, presented in other sections a broken, uneven appearance, like a succession of little rooms, and one niche in particular was called the "Lady's Chair" from its peculiar formation of seat, sides and back. Here with the fading sunlight falling upon it, sat a little figure in gray with the blue veil twisted round the hat, and the hands folded together and lying upon the lap, reminding Phil of that picture of Evangeline sitting by the river and watching the distant boat. Pierre was kneeling upon the rock beside his mistress, and stretched at her feet was the watch-dog, King, with whom she had already made friends. The three made a very pretty picture far up the hill-side with the western sky behind them, and Phil, without knowing whether he was seen or not, involuntarily raised his hat. But the courtesy was not acknowledged, and he bit his lip with vexation as he galloped rapidly on thinking to himself:

"Hang the girl, I believe Anna is half right. She is proud as Lucifer, and means to cut us all. Well, let her. Maybe she'll find some day that a Rossiter is quite as good as a Hetherton!"

In Phil's estimation Reinette was not altogether a success, but then he did not know her.

CHAPTER IX

REINETTE AT HOME

When Phil envied Mr. Beresford his opportunity for being alone with Reinette and listening to her conversation, he made a mistake, for during the first of the drive from the cemetery to Hetherton Place, she scarcely spoke to him, but sat with closed eyes and locked hands, leaning back in a corner of the carriage, as motionless as if she had been asleep. Once, however, when they were crossing the river, she looked out and asked:

"Isn't this the Chicopee?" and on being told it was, she said to Pierre, in French:

"This is the river, Pierre, where papa used to gather the pond lilies when he was a boy. It empties into the Connecticut as the Seine does into the sea. You know you looked it out on the map for me."

Pierre nodded, and Reinette, although she now kept her eyes open, did not speak again until they reached the long hill which wound up to the house Then, as she saw to her left a lovely little sheet of water sparkling in the sunlight, she started up, exclaiming:

"That must be Lake Petit, where father used to keep his boat, the Waif."

"Yes," said Mr. Beresford, surprised at her knowledge of the neighborhood. "Your grandmother, Mrs. Hetherton, called it Lake Petit, I believe, but to most of the people here it is the Mill Pond."

Reinette shrugged her shoulders, and asked:

"Isn't it on papa's land?"

"Yes, it belongs to the Hetherton estate," was the reply, and she continued, in a decisive tone:

"Then it is never any more to be Mill Pond. It is Lake Petit forever."

They were half way up the hill by this time, and as one after another views of the surrounding country greeted Reinette's wondering gaze, her delight knew no bounds, and, forgetting for a moment the load of pain at her heart, she gave vent to her delight in true girlish fashion, uttering little screams of surprise and gladness, and occasionally seizing Pierre by the shoulder and shaking him to make him see what she was seeing, and appreciate it, too.

"It's better than Switzerland, better than France—better than anything! I like America," she cried, but Pierre shook his head, and gave a sigh for "La Belle France," the best country in the world, where he wished he had staid, he said, adhering to his opinion in spite of all his mistress could say.

Mr. Beresford could not understand them, but he knew that some altercation was going on between them, and was astonished to see the different expressions which passed in an instant over Reinette's face, and how beautiful she grew as the bright color came and went, and she sparkled, and flashed, and laughed, and frowned, and shook up the stupid Pierre all in the same breath. They were driving up to the house by this time, and the moment the carriage stopped she sprang to the ground and began to look about her, gesticulating rapidly, and talking now in French and now in English, now to Mr. Beresford and now to Pierre, who was almost as excited as she was. The chateau, as she called it, was so much larger than she supposed, and the grounds more pretentious, and "Oh, the flowers!" she cried, darting in among them like a little humming-bird, and filling her hands with the sweet summer pinks, which she pressed to her lips and kissed as if they had been living things and sharers of her joy.

"The flowers are the same everywhere, and I love them so much, and the world is so bright just like a picture, up here where it is so high; so near Heaven, and I am so happy," she exclaimed, as she hopped about; then suddenly as a cloud passes over the sun on an April day, a shadow came over her face and great tears rolled down her cheeks as, turning to Mr. Beresford, she said, "What must you think of me to be so gay, and he dead over in the grave-yard? But it is one part of me; there are two natures in me you see, and I can't help it, though all the time I'm missing him so much, and there's a pain in my heart and a lump in my throat till it feels as if it would burst. And still I must love the brightness even though it's all dark where he lies alone. Oh, father, if you, too were here!"

She was sobbing bitterly, and Pierre was crying too, even while he tried to comfort her. Suddenly at something he said her sobbing ceased, and dashing the tears from her eyes she smiled brightly at Mr. Beresford and said:

"Forgive me, do, for troubling you with an exhibition of my grief. I forgot myself. Father told me not to cry before people, and I will not again. Come, let us go into the chateau; it looks so cool and inviting with the doors and windows open and the muslin curtains blowing in and out, and the scent of clover and new hay everywhere. The world is very beautiful, and I mean to be happy."

During this scene in the grounds Mrs. Jerry, the housekeeper, had been inspecting the little lady from behind the kitchen blinds, and now, as the party entered the wide hall, she came forward to meet her in her neat calico dress and clean linen collar, with her hair combed smoothly back from her frank, open brow. She knew she was there on trial, subject to Miss Reinette's fancy, and as she liked the place, and was desirous of keeping it, she naturally felt some anxiety with regard to the impression she should make upon the girl. She was not long kept in suspense, for something in her face attracted Reinette at once, and without the least hauteur in her manner she went forward with outstretched hands, and said:

"Mrs. Jerry, I am so glad you are here, I know I shall like you, and you must like me in all my moods, for I am not always alike. There are two of me, one good and one bad—though I mean to shut the bad one out of doors in this my new home. And now, please, take these flowers and put them in water for me. I don't wish any one to show me over the house."

Turning now to Mr. Beresford she said,

"I'd rather find my way alone and guess which is my room and which was meant for him,"—here her lip began to quiver, but she kept up bravely and went on: "You will come and see me to-morrow, and I shall ask you so many things. Father said I was to trust you and go to you for everything. By and by, though, I shall take care of myself. And now, good-by till to-morrow afternoon."

She gave him her hand, and he had no alternative but to go, although he would so gladly have lingered longer, so deeply interested was he already in this strange girl with the two natures, one proud, cold, scornful, and passionate; the other gentle, and soft, and sweet as the flowers she loved so dearly. He might have been more interested still had he seen her standing in the door with the great tears drooping from her long eyelashes as she watched him going down the hill and felt that now, indeed, she was alone in her desolation with her new life all before her.

"I like him because he was father's friend, and because he seems a gentleman," she thought; and then as she remembered those other people who had claimed her for their own, and who were not like Mr. Beresford, she shuddered and felt her other self mastering her again.

Just then Mrs. Jerry appeared, asking if she could do anything for her, and if she would not like to go to her room.

"No, no—go away!" Reinette answered, almost angrily; "I want nothing but to be let alone. I can find my way. I must work it out myself."

So Mrs. Jerry went back to the kitchen, and Pierre, who knew the first approaches of his mistress' moods, sat down upon the grass quietly waiting the progress of events.

Reinette's face was very white, and as was usual when she was trying to repress her feelings, her hands were locked together as she stood looking about her at the trees under which her father had played when a boy, and the honeysuckle which grew over the trellis-work and which must have blossomed for him, and more than all at his initials cut by himself on the door-post. Then with a little smothered cry she turned suddenly, and ran up stairs to the room which she had heard described so often, and which at a glance she knew was hers.

CHAPTER X

THE TWO REINETTES

"Oh, how lovely it is!" she cried, as she entered the room and took it all in as rapidly as Phil himself could have done. "What perfect taste Mr. Beresford must have!" she continued. "It is just as I would have it, except the blue ribbons, which do not suit my black face. But I can soon change them, and then everything will be faultless; and—oh—oh—the cats!" she screamed, as she caught sight of Mrs. Speckle, who, with her three children, was purring contentedly in the cushioned arm-chair by the window. "Cats! and I love them so much; he has remembered everything!" and bounding across the floor, Reinette knelt by the chair and buried her face in the soft fur of the kittens, who, true to their feline instincts, recognized in her a friend, and began at once to pat her neck and ears with their velvety paws, while Mrs. Speckle, feeling a little crowded, vacated the chair and seated herself upon the window-stool, where Phil saw her when he rode by.

The sight of the cats carried Reinette back to the day when her father had written his directions to Mr. Beresford and she had made suggestions. How careful he had been to remember all her likes and dislikes, and how pale and tired he had looked after the letter was finished, and how unjust and thoughtless she had been to feel aggrieved because he said he was not able to drive with her in the Bois de Boulogne after dinner was over. And now he was dead, and she was alone in a strange new world, with only Mr. Beresford for a friend, unless it were those people who claimed her for a relative—those people of whom she had never heard, and against whom she rebelled with all the strong force of her imperious nature. She had not had time to consider the matter seriously; but now, alone in her own room, with the doors shut between her and the outside world, it rose before her in all its magnitude, and for a time drove every other feeling from her. The proud aristocratic part of her nature was in the ascendant, and battled fiercely against her better self.

Was it possible, she thought, that the loud-voiced old lady, who used such dreadful grammar and called her Rennet, and the Aunt Lyddy Ann, who looked like a bar-maid, and the tall, showily-dressed Anna, with the yellow plume, the cheap lace scarf, and the loud hat, such as only the common girls of Paris wore—were really the relatives of her beautiful mother, who she had always supposed was an Englishwoman, and whom she had cherished in her heart as everything that was pure, and lovely, and refined! Her father had said of her once:

"I never knew my wife to be guilty of a single unlady-like act, and I should be glad, my daughter, if you were half as gentle and gracious of manner as she was."

It is true she had never been able to learn anything definite of her mother's family, for her father, when questioned, had either answered evasively, or not at all. Once he had said to her, decidedly:

"There are reasons why I do not care to talk of your mother's family and it is quite as well that you remain in ignorance. Mrs. Hetherton was everything that a perfect lady should be. You must be satisfied with that, and never trouble me again about your mother's antecedents."

He had seemed very much excited, and there was a strange look on his face, as he walked the salon, which frightened Reinette a little; and still she persisted so far as to say:

"I am sure mother was an Englishwoman, by her picture."

"Be satisfied then that you know so much, and don't seek for more knowledge. Whatever her friends were, they are nothing to me; they can be nothing to you. So never mention them again."

And she never did; but she almost worshiped the beautiful face, which had been painted on ivory in Paris when her mother was a bride and had rooms at the Hotel Meurice. It was a fair, lovely face, with hair of golden brown, and great tender eyes of lustrous blue, with a tinge of sadness in them, as there was also in the expression around the sweet mouth just breaking into a smile. The dress was of heavy creamy satin, with pearls upon the neck and arms, and on the wavy hair. A refined aristocratic face, Reinette thought it, and in spite of her father's evident dislike of her mother's friends, she never for an instant had thought of them as other than fully her equals in position and social standing. Probably there had been some quarrel which had resulted in lasting enmity, or her mother might have been the daughter of some nobleman, and eloped with the young American, thus incurring the life-long displeasure of her family. This last was Reinette's pet theory, and she had more than once resolved that when she was her own mistress she would seek her mother's friends, never doubting that she should find them fully equal to the Hethertons, who, her father said, had in their veins the best blood of the land.

Everything pertaining to her mother was guarded by Reinette with great fidelity, and in the box where her favorite treasures were hidden away was a long, bright tress of hair and a few faded flowers, tied together with a bit of blue ribbon, to which was attached a piece of paper, with the words, "My mother's hair, cut from her head after she was dead, and some of the flowers she held in her hands when she lay in her coffin."

Among Reinette's books there was also an old copy of "The Lady of the Lake," on the fly-leaf of which was written in a very pretty hand. "Margaret, From her sister Mary. Christmas, —." This was the only link between herself and her mother's family which Reinette possessed, and she built upon it a multitude of theories with regard to the Aunt Mary whom she meant some time to find, and whom she always saw clad in velvet, jewels, and old laces, with possibly a coronet on her brow.

Such were Reinette's ideas of her mother's friends, which her father had suffered her to cherish, only smiling faintly at some of her extravagant speculations, but never contradicting them. And now, in place of lords, and ladies, and English nobility, to have these people thrust upon her, this grandmother, and aunt, and cousin, with unmistakable marks of vulgarity stamped upon them, was too much, and for a time the proud, sensitive girl rebelled against it with all the fierceness of her nature, while, mingled with her bitter humiliation was a better and deeper feeling, which hurt her far more than the mortification of knowing that she was not what she had believed herself to be. Her father, whom she had so loved, and honored, and believed in, had not dealt fairly with her.

Why had he not told her the truth, especially after he knew they were coming to America, and that she must certainly know it some time?

"If he had told me, if he had said a kind word of them, I should have been prepared for it, and loved them, just because they were mother's people. Oh, father, whatever your motive may have been, you did me a grievous wrong," she said, and into her eyes there crept a look of resentment toward the father who had kept this secret from her.

Then, as her thoughts went backward to the state-room where he died, and the words he said to her, she cried out:

"I understand now what he meant, and what I was to forgive. He meant to have told me before, he said; he was sorry he had not. Yes, father, I see. While we were in France there was no need for me to know, and when we started for America it was hard to confess it to me, and destroy my beautiful air castles filled with a line of ancestry nobler, better, even, than the Hethertons, and so you put it off, as you did everything unpleasant, as long as possible. You were going to tell me when you reached New York, but before we were there you were dead, and I was left to meet it alone. Oh, father, I promised to forgive and love you just the same, and I will, I do—but it's very, very hard on me, and I must fight it out and cast the demon from me before I meet one of them again."

And in truth Reinette did seem to be fighting with some foe as she stood in the center of the room, her face as white as ashes, her tearless eyes flashing fire, and her hands beating the air more rapidly and fiercely than they had done when in the carriage her grandmother questioned her of her knowledge of her mother. That was a feeble effort compared to what she was doing now as she flew about the room striking out here and there as if at some tangible object, and sometimes clutching at the long curls floating over her shoulders. It was a singular sight and not strange at all that Mrs. Speckle, from her seat in the window, looked curiously at the young girl acting more like a mad than a sane woman, and at the three kittens upon the floor, who, fancying all these gyrations were for their benefit, jumped and scampered, and spit, and pulled at Reinette's feet and dress in true feline delight.

Suddenly the door opened cautiously and Pierre looked in, saying, softly:

"Please, Miss Reinette, wouldn't you come out of it quicker if you was to shake me a bit. I shouldn't mind it if you didn't use your nails, and would let my hair alone. There isn't much of it left, you know!"

Pierre had not lived in his master's family fourteen years without understanding his mistress thoroughly, and that in his heart he worshipped her was proof that he had found far more good in her than bad. He knew just how kind, and loving, and self-sacrificing she was, and how she had cared for him when he had the fever in Rome, and her father was away in Palestine. In spite of the remonstrances of friends she had stood by him night and day, for weeks because he missed her when she was absent and called for her in his delirium. It did not matter that the gayeties of the carnival were in progress and that rare facilities were offered her for seeing them. She turned her back on them all and staid by the sick man who needed her, and who, the physicians said, owed his life to her nursing and constant care. Pierre had never forgotten it any more than he had forgotten the time when, in a fit of anger she had pounced upon his back like a cat and scratched, and bit, and pulled his hair until he shook her off and held her till her passion had subsided. Her father had punished her severely, and she had never behaved so badly since, though she sometimes shook Pierre furiously, for by contact with some living thing which resisted her she could conquer herself more readily, she said; and when there was no one near whom she dared touch she occasionally gave vent to her excitement by whirling round in circles and beating the air with her hands. Pierre knew this peculiarity, and when he came to the door and heard the tempest within, he offered himself at once as a kind of breaker for the storm to beat against. But Reinette did not need him. The battle was nearly over, for at its height, when it seemed to her that she could not lose one grain of respect for her father for having thus deceived her—could not exchange the ideal friends of her mother for these people so different from herself, there came suddenly before her mind a fair, handsome face, with eyes as tender and pitiful as those of a woman, and yet with something strong and masterful in their expression as they smiled a welcome upon her.

It was when she was most bewildered and confounded by the unknown relations claiming her that somebody had said, "This is another cousin;" but in her excitement she had scarcely heeded it, and made no response when the young man's hat was lifted politely by way of a greeting.

It was the same young man, she was sure, who had held her back from the open grave, and spoken to her in a voice which she recognized at once as belonging to her class. Reinette laid great stress upon the human voice, insisting that by it she could tell how much of real culture or natural, inborn refinement its owner possessed. The sharp, loud voices of the Fergusons, with their peculiar intonation, had grated upon her nerves, but the well-modulated, well-trained tones of the young man had fallen on her ear like a strain of music among jarring discords.

Who was he? Not the brother, surely, of that tall blonde with the yellow plume and long lace scarf. That was impossible; and yet some one had said, "Here is another cousin," and he had acknowledged it with a smile, which came to her now like sunshine breaking through a rift of clouds and clearing up the sky.

"Oh! if he only were my cousin, I could bear it so much better," she thought, just as Pierre came in, offering himself as a victim, provided she spared his hair, of which he had so little.

The whole thing was so unexpected and droll that it quieted Reinette at once, and, sitting down in a chair, she laughed and cried alternately for a moment; then dashing her tears away and taking the kittens upon her lap, she bade the old man sit down beside her, as there was something she wished to ask him.

"Pierre," she began, "it was right nice in you to offer yourself a victim to my fury; and, had you come sooner, I might have shaken you a little, for when I'm fighting with my other self I always like to feel something in my power—something which stands for that other girl I'm trying to conquer, and I was half tempted to take one of these little kittens and wreak my temper on that, but I didn't, and I am glad, and I am going to govern myself hereafter, for I must be a woman now and not a child."

"Yes, miss, that's very good," Pierre said, wondering how he should like his little mistress if she were always as mild and gentle as she seemed now, without any fire or spirit at all.

"Pierre," Reinette continued, "how long have you lived with us?"

"Fourteen years come Christmas."

"I thought so; and did you know papa before you came to us?" she asked, and he replied:

"No, miss: only as I had heard of him as the rich American, who lived so extravagantly at the Hotel Meurice, and had such a handsome chateau in the country."

"Yes, Chateau des Fleurs. It was lovely, and I was so happy there. Then, of course, you never saw my mother."

"Never," said Pierre, and Reinette continued:

"And did you never hear anything of her from strangers? Did you never hear where she came from, where papa found her?"

"I heard from you that she was very beautiful and good, and died at Rome when you were born, and I think you told me she was English. Surely you would know about your own mother;" and Pierre looked curiously at his young mistress, who colored painfully and beat the matting with her boot.

Reinette was hesitating as to how much she would tell Pierre, for it hurt her to confess to any one how little she really knew of her mother's antecedents, so wholly silent and non-committal had her father been on the subject. At last, deciding that she must be frank with Pierre if she wished him to be so with her, she said:

"Pierre, you are all I have left of the life in France, and I must tell you everything. There was always a mystery about mamma which I could not solve, and all I know of her was her name, Margaret Ferguson, and that papa loved her so much that he could not bear to talk of her, and all I know besides the name I guessed, and now I am afraid I did not guess right. I have never met anybody who had seen her but papa, except the nurse Christine Bodine, who was with her when she died, and who brought me to Paris. She, too, left me when I was a year or so old, and I have not seen her since, and it made father very angry if I ever spoke of her. She was not a nice woman, he said, and he did not wish me to mention her name. Do you know anything of her?"

"What was the name, please?" Pierre asked, and Reinette replied:

"Christine Bodine, and if living now she must be forty or more. Mother would be forty-three."

"I don't know where she is, and I never saw her," said Pierre, "but the name brings something to my mind. Years ago, a dozen or more, when we were staying at Chateau des Fleurs, I went with monsieur to Paris—to the office of Monsieur Polignie, a kind of broker or money agent in town, and your father gave him a note or check of francs to be sent to Mademoiselle Christine Bodine. I remember the name perfectly, Christine Bodine, because it rhymed, and I said it to myself two or three times, but who she was or where she lived I didn't know; only master's face was very dark, and he was silent and gloomy all day, and I thought maybe Mademoiselle Bodine was some woman to whom he had to pay money, whether he liked it or not. You know many fine gentlemen in Paris do that."

He saw that she did not understand him, and though he might have told her that her father had not always been the spotless man which she believed him to be, he would not do it, preferring that she should be happy in her ignorance.

"I remember that day so well," he continued, "your father bought you a big wax doll in the Palais Royal, and although you were in bed when we returned to the chateau, he had you up to give it to you, and fondled and caressed you more than usual, as if making up for something."

Reinette's eyes were full of tears at these reminiscences of Pierre's, but she forced them back, and said:

"You have no idea where Christine is now?"

"None whatever, but I think monsieur heard from her or of her when we were in Liverpool waiting to sail. You remember that several letters were forwarded to him, and one excited him very much. I was in the room when he read it, and heard him say something in English which I think was a swear, and I know he said something angry about Christine, for I understood that plain. He was very white and weak all day, and that night asked you if you would feel very badly to turn back to Paris and not go to America after all. You remember it, don't you?"

Reinette did remember it, though at the time she had laid little or no stress upon it, thinking it a mere idle remark, as her father was naturally changeable. Now she could recall how sick and sad he had looked, and how much he had talked of France and she could see, or thought she could, that had she been willing, he would have gone back so gladly.

Surely there could have been nothing in a letter from Christine, which should make him angry or wish to go back. Pierre did not understand English well; it was easy for him to blunder, though he had not done so in the name "Christine Bodine" to whom her father had sent money. Why had he done so, and where was Christine now?

Turning to Pierre, she said:

"This money agent, Polignie, is still in Paris?"

"Yes, miss, I think so."

"And you know his address?"

"I know where we went that day your father paid the money, but he may have moved since many times."

"No matter. He must be well known: a letter will find him, and I shall write and ask for Christine Bodine, for I mean to find her if I cross the ocean to do it. She knew mother, and I must know something of her too, for—oh, Pierre, my brain is all in a whirl with what has happened to-day; but I can't tell you in here, I feel so smothered when I think of it. Let's go to that ledge of rocks yonder on the hill-side. We must see the sun set from there, and maybe we can see poor papa's grave."

She put on her hat and preceded Pierre down the stairs and through the dining-room, where she found Mrs. Jerry arranging a very dainty-looking tea-table.

"Supper will be ready very soon," Mrs. Jerry said, suggesting that her young mistress wait till it was served, as the muffins would all be cold. But Reinette was not hungry, she said, and Mrs. Jerry must eat the muffins herself. By and by she would perhaps have some toast and tea in her room; she would tell Mrs. Jerry when she wanted it, and she flashed upon the woman a smile so sweet and winning that it disarmed her at once of the resentment she might otherwise have felt because her nice supper was slighted and she must keep up the kitchen fire in order to have toast and tea whenever it should suit the young lady's fancy.

Meanwhile Reinette went on her way, through the back yard toward the ledge of rocks, when suddenly she heard a pitiful whine, and, turning, saw the dog tugging at his chain to get away. In an instant she was at his side, with her arms round his neck, while she cried:

"Look, Pierre, what a noble fellow he is! Why do they keep him tied up? I mean to set him free."

And she was about to do so, when the coachman, who was watching her at a little distance, called out:

"Miss Hetherton, you must not do that. He is strange here, and will run home. He has done so twice already."

"Who are you?" Reinette asked, rather haughtily, and he replied:

"I am Stevens, and take care of the horses. Maybe you would like to see them; they are real beauties."

"Yes, when I unchain the dog," Reinette replied. "He'll not run from me; I can tame him. What's his name?"

"King," said Stevens; and taking the dog's face between her hands, and looking straight, into his eyes, Reinette said:

"Mr. Doggie, you are my king, and I am your queen. You must not run away from me. I'll take such good care of you, and love you so much; and in proof thereof I give you your liberty."

She slipped the chain from his neck, and, with a joyful bark, King sprang upon her, licking her face and hands in token of his grateful allegiance. Every brute recognized a friend in Reinette, and King was not an exception, and kept close to her side as she went toward the stables to see the horses, which Stevens led out for her inspection.

First, the splendid bays, Jupiter and Juno, with which she could find no fault, unless it were that Juno carried her head a trifle higher than Jupiter, and might be freer in the harness. She could not quite decide until she saw them on the road, she said; and then she turned to the milk-white steed, her saddle pony, with which she was perfectly delighted; she was so white and clean, and tall and gentle, and ate grass from her hand, and followed her about as readily as King himself.

"What's her name?" she asked.

And on Stevens replying that he did not know, she said:

"Then she shall be Margery, after the dearest friend I ever had except

55

papa. She was so fair, and beautiful, and tall, and I loved her so much. Oh, Margery!" she continued, laying her hand upon the neck of her steed; "where are you now, and do you know how sad and lonely your little Queenie is?"

There was a shadow on Reinette's bright face, but it quickly passed away; and sending the horses back to their stalls, she went, with Pierre and King, toward the ledge of rocks on the grassy hill-side.

CHAPTER XI

ON THE ROCKS

It was very pleasant on the ledge of rocks, with the soft, rose-tinted glow of the summer sunset in the western sky, and the long line of wooded hills and grassy meadows stretching away to north, and south, and east, as far as the eye could reach. Through a deep cut to the westward a train of cars was coming swiftly into view, while over the tops of the pine trees, to the east, wreaths of smoke were curling, heralding the approach of another train, for Merrivale was on the great thoroughfare between Boston and Albany. At the foot of the hill the waters of Lake Petit lay like a bit of silvery moonlight amid the green fields around it, while further to the left another lake or pond was seen, with the Chicopee winding its slow course through strips of meadow land and green pastures, where the cows fed through the day and from which there now came a faint tinkle of bells as they were driven slowly home. Everything was quiet, and calm, and peaceful, and Reinette felt quiet and peaceful, too, as she seated herself in the "Lady's Chair" and scanned the lovely landscape spread out below her.

"America is beautiful," she said to Pierre, who stood at her side; "and I should be so happy in papa's old home, if only he were here. And I mean to be happy, as it is, for I know he would wish it to be so, and I understand now what he meant when he said such strange things to me just before he died. He was preparing me for a surprise—a—a—Pierre—" and forcing down a great sob, Reinette began rapidly, "Pierre, did you notice those people—those ladies, I mean, who came to meet me at the station?"

"Yes," said Pierre; "they rode with you to the grave. I thought, maybe, they were the servants of the house: who were they, mademoiselle?"

"Servants," and the dark eyes flashed angrily, for if they were hers—her flesh and blood—nobody must speak against them. "Servants! Pierre, you are an idiot!"

"Yes, mademoiselle," the old man answered, humbly, and Reinette continued:

"You don't yet understand how different everything is in America. There is no nobility here—no aristocracy like what we have in Europe. Your son, if you had one born here, might be the President, for all of his birth. It's worth and education which make nobility here, with, perhaps, a little bit of money, and, Pierre, those ladies—mind you, ladies—whom you thought servants, were my own grandmother, and aunt, and cousin, my mother's relatives."

"Mon Dieu!" dropped involuntarily from the old man's lips, as he looked searchingly at his mistress for an instant, and then dropped his eyes meekly as he met her threatening gaze.

"Yes I do not quite know how it is, or why papa never told me of them; some family quarrel most likely," Reinette continued. "He tried to tell me when he was dying. He said there was something he must explain; something he ought to have told me, and this was it. My mother was American and not English, as I supposed, and these are her relatives and mine, and it's nice to find friends where one did not expect them."

"Yes, mademoiselle, very nice," Pierre said with a nod of assent, though, knowing the proud little lady as he did, he knew perfectly well how hotly she was rebelling against these new friends, and how it was her great pride which prompted her to exalt them in his estimation if possible.

But it was not for him to express any opinion, so he remained silent, while Reinette went on:

"Mother's own blood relations, who can tell me all about her, though I mean to find Christine Bodine just the same, and hear what she has to say of mamma. Pierre, there was another cousin at the station—a young man, with such a fair, winning face and perfect manners. He was at the grave, too. You must have seen him. He was a gentleman, I am sure."

"Yes, mademoiselle," and Pierre brightened at once. "He is quite the gentleman, the nobility, the aristocracy, like Monsieur Hetherton. He rode with Monsieur Beresford and myself, and spoke to me in my own tongue; not as you talk it, but fair, very fair, though he did not understand me so well."

Pierre was growing eloquent on the subject of Phil, and Reinette was greatly interested, and asked numberless questions concerning him.

"What was his name? What did Mr. Beresford call him, and what did he say?"

"He asked much of you," Pierre replied, "and once there was something like tears in his eyes when I told him how sad you were, but seems like he was ashamed to have the other one see him, for he pulled his hat down over his eyes, and said something about it in English which made them both laugh, he and the other gentleman who called him Pill."

"Pill!" Reinette repeated. "What a name. You could not have understood."

But Pierre insisted that he did; it was Pill, and nothing else; and as at that moment Phil himself rode by, the old man pointed him out to Reinette just after the bow, which she did not see, and consequently could not return; but she watched him as far as she could see him, admiring his figure, admiring his horse, and wondering how it could be that he was so different from those other people, as she mentally designated the Fergusons, whom, try as she would, she could not accept willingly as her mother's friends. If she could find Christine Bodine, she could solve all doubts on the subject; and she meant to find her, if that were possible, and set herself about it at once—to-morrow, perhaps, for there was no time to be lost. If Christine had, as Pierre believed, been a pensioner of her father's, and if he had heard from her at Liverpool, then of course she was living, and through the Messrs. Polignie she could trace her, and perhaps bring her to America to live with her, as something to keep fresh in mind her past life, now so completely gone from her.

Thus thinking, she walked back to the house just as it was growing dark, and Mrs. Jerry was beginning to feel some anxiety with regard to the tea and toast, and the time they would be called for.

Reinette's long fast, and the fatigue and excitement of the day were beginning to tell upon her, and after forcing herself to swallow a few mouthfuls of the food which the good woman pressed upon her, she announced her intention of retiring to her room.

Mrs. Jerry carried up the wax candles, which she lighted herself, and after setting them upon the table and seeing that everything was in order, she stood a moment, smoothing the hem of her white apron, as if there was something she had to say. She had promised Grandma Ferguson to call Reinette's attention to the patch-work spread, quilted "herrin'-bone" and which, as the work of a young girl, had taken the prize at the Southbridge Fair, but she did not quite know how to do it. "Herrin'-bone" quilts did not seem to be in perfect accord with this little foreign girl, who, though so plainly dressed, and so friendly and gracious of manner, bore unmistakable marks of the highest grade of aristocracy. Like the most of her class, Mrs. Jerry held such people in great esteem, and as something quite different from herself, whose father had worked side by side, many a day, in plaster and mortar, with honest John Ferguson, and she could not understand how one like Reinette Hetherton could care for a patch-work quilt, even if her mother had pieced it in years gone by. But she had promised, and must keep her word, and laying her hands upon it, and pulling it more distinctly into view, she began:

"I promised your grandmother to tell you about this bed-quilt, which 'pears kind of out of place in here, but she sent it over—the old lady did—thinkin' you'd be pleased to know that your mother did it when she was a little girl, and that many of them is pieces of her own gowns she used to wear. I remember her myself with this one on; it was her Sunday frock, and she looked so pretty in it;" and Mrs. Jerry touched a square of the blue and white checked calico which had once formed a part of Margaret Ferguson's best dress.

"I don't think I quite understand you," said Reinette, who was wholly ignorant of that strange fashion of cutting cloth in bits for the sake of sewing them up again.

But one idea was perfectly clear to her. Mrs. Jerry had seen her mother, and her great dark eyes were full of eager inquiry as she continued:

"You have seen mother; you knew her when she was a little girl; knew her for certain and true?"

There was still a doubt—a rebelling in Reinette's mind against the new relatives, but Mrs. Jerry knew nothing of it, nor guessed that Reinette was not fully acquainted with all the particulars of her mother's early life and marriage.

"Yes," she answered, "Margaret Ferguson and I was about the same age; mabby I am two years or so the oldest; but we went to school together and was in the same class, only she was always at the head and I mostly at the foot, and we picked huckleberries together many a time out in old General Hetherton's lot, never dreaming that she would one day marry Mr. Fred. I beg your pardon, your father I meant," she added hastily, as she met the proud flash of Reinette's eyes, and understood that to speak of her father as Fred was an indignity not to be tolerated.

But for this slip of the tongue Reinette might have questioned her further of her mother, but she could not do it now, though she returned to the bed-quilt and managed to get a tolerably clear comprehension with regard to it. "Made every stitch of it and I warrant she pricked herself over it many a time," Mrs. Jerry said, and being fairly launched on her subject she was going on rapidly when Reinette suddenly interrupted her with:

"Yes, yes, I know: I see; mother did it. Mother's hands have touched it; and now go away, please, quick, and leave me alone."

She pointed to the door, and Mrs. Jerry went swiftly out, half frightened at the look in the young girl's eyes as she bade her leave the room.

"It must be true; everybody and everything confirms it, and I have lost my ideal mother," Reinette whispered to herself as she closed the door after Mrs. Jerry.

Yes, she had lost her ideal mother, but the loss had not been without its gain, and Reinette felt that this was so as she knelt in her anguish by the bedside and laid her hot, tear-stained cheek against the coarse fabric which had been her mother's work.

"Mother's dear hands have touched it," she said, "and that brings her so near to me that I almost feel as if she were here herself. Oh, mother, did your hands ever touch your baby, or did you die before you saw me? Nobody ever told me. Why was father so silent, so proud? I would have loved these people for her sake, and I will love them now in time. But it is all so strange, and mother's girlhood was so different from what I have fancied it to be."

Then, remembering what Mrs. Jerry had said of the bits of calico, she brought the candle close to the bed and examined the pieces carefully, especially the blue and white one in which Mrs. Jerry had said her mother had looked so prettily. It was delicate in color and in pattern, but to Reinette, who had never in her life worn anything coarser than the fine French cambrics, it seemed too common a fabric for the picture she held in her heart of her mother. It did not at all match the lovely pearls she kept so sacredly among her treasures. Her trunks and boxes had been brought from the station, and in one of them were the pearls.

Unlocking the box, Reinette took out the exquisite necklace, bracelets, and ear-rings which her father told her her mother had worn to a ball, where she had been noted as the most beautiful woman present.

Taking them now to the bedside, she laid them upon the squares of blue and tried to picture to herself the beautiful woman in creamy white satin who had worn them and the girl who had picked berries with Mrs. Jerry, and worn the dress of blue.

"Pearls and calico! There is a great gulf between them," she thought, "but no greater than the distance between my old life and the new, which I must live bravely and well."

Then, returning the pearls to their casket, with a feeling that now she should never wear them, she undressed herself rapidly, for her head was beginning to ache, and throwing herself upon the bed drew the patch-work quilt over her, caressing it as if it had been a living thing, and whispering, softly:

"Dear mother, I do not love you one whit the less because you once picked berries in father's fields and wore the cotton gown, and you seem near to me to-night, as if your arms were round me, and you were pitying your desolate little girl, who has nobody to pity her, nobody to love her, nobody to pray for her now, and she so wretched and bad."

Poor little Reinette was mistaken when she thought there was no one to pity or pray for her now, for across the river, over the hill, and under the poplar trees, a light was still burning in the chamber where Grandma Ferguson knelt, in her short night-gown and wide frilled cap, and prayed for Margaret's child, that God would comfort her and have her in his keeping, while at the Knoll, Phil was thinking of the great sad eyes which, though they had flashed only one look at him, haunted him persistently, they were so full of pathos and pain.

"Poor little girl," he said, "alone in a new country, with such a lot of us whom she never heard of thrust upon her. I pity her by Jove!"

CHAPTER XII

REINETTE AND MR. BERESFORD

Reinette slept heavily that first night in her new home—so heavily, that the robins had sung their first song, and the July sun had dried the dew-drops on the greensward and flowers before she awoke, with a very vague perception as to where she was, or what had happened to her. Through the window which she had left open came the warm summer air, sweet with the scent of clover and the newly-mown hay, which a farmer's boy was turning briskly, not far from the house. And Reinette, who was keenly alive to everything fresh and beautiful, inhaled the delicious perfume and felt instinctively how much of freshness and beauty she was losing. But when she rose and, going to the window, threw back the shutters and looked for an instant at the lovely picture of the Merrivale hills and valleys spread out before her, a sharp cutting pain across her forehead and in her eyes warned her that her old enemy, the nervous headache, was upon her in full force, and there was nothing for her that day but pain and suffering in the solitude of her room. Then, as she remembered what Mrs. Ferguson had said of an early visit, for the sake of "talking over things," she shuddered, and grew cold and faint, and thought, with that strange feeling of incredulity to which she clung:

"If I were only positive and sure, beyond a doubt that mother did once pick huckleberries with Mrs. Jerry, and wear the cotton gown, I could bear everything so much better. Mr. Beresford knows all about it; he will tell me, and I must see him first, for those people will not be long in coming to pay their respects. I'll send Pierre immediately with a note asking him to come to me as soon as possible."

What Reinette willed to do she did at once, and in spite of the blinding pain in her head, she opened her desk and wrote as follows;

"Mr. Beresford:—I must see you. Come without delay.

Miss Hetherton."

This done, she attempted to dress, but finding an elaborate toilet too much for her, she contented herself with a cool, white cambric wrapper, with rows of lace and embroidery down the front, and bows of delicate pink ribbon on the pockets and sleeves. Over this she threw a dainty Parisian jacket or sacque of the same hue, letting her dark wavy hair fall loosely down her back. She always wore it so when she had a headache, and she made a most beautiful and striking picture for Mrs. Jerry to contemplate when, in answer to her ring, that lady presented herself at the door to know what her mistress would have. Like most women, Mrs. Jerry had a hundred remedies for the headache, but Reinette wished for none of them. Nothing was of any avail until the pain ran its course, which it usually did in twenty-four hours, and all she asked was to be left in quiet in the library below, where she proposed going to wait for Mr. Beresford, whom Pierre found in his office and with him Phil Rossiter, the two talking together of the young lady at Hetherton Place and comparing their impressions of her.

"Not so very pretty, but bright and agreeable, with a will of her own," Mr. Beresford said, guardedly, remembering what Phil had predicted with regard to the immediate surrender of his heart to the foreigner.

"Yes, and proud as Lucifer, too, or I'm mistaken," answered Phil. "Why, I really believe she means to ride over us all. Odd, though, that she'd never heard of a soul of us. That snob of a Hetherton must have been a queer chap."

At this moment Pierre appeared in the door, bowing and gesticulating, and jabbering unintelligibly as he handed the note to Mr. Beresford, who read it aloud, while Phil said laughingly, though in reality he secretly felt aggrieved;

"You see, it is you for whom she has sent. She does not care for me."

Strangely enough, notwithstanding his imperfect knowledge of English, Pierre understood the last part of Phil's speech, and his gestures were more vehement than ever as he assured Phil that he was mistaken. Miss Reinette cared for him very much indeed, and had asked much about him, and noticed him at the grave, and when he went by on horseback. It was business alone which had prompted her to send for monsieur; later she would be most happy to see young monsieur, her cousin.

Phil could not follow the old man readily, but he thought he made out that Reinette had sent this message to him, or something like it, and he changed his mind about starting for Martha's Vineyard that afternoon, as he had half resolved to do. He would see Reinette first, and hear her speak to him face to face.

"Tell her I shall be there some time to-day," he said to his more fortunate friend, the lawyer, who, nothing loth to meet the glance of Reinette's bright eyes once more, was soon riding rapidly toward Hetherton Place.

Reinette's head was worse than it had been earlier in the morning, but she insisted upon seeing Mr. Beresford, who was admitted at once to the room, which Mrs. Jerry had made as dark as possible, but which was still light enough for him to distinguish distinctly the little figure in pink and white, reclining in the easy-chair, with masses of long dark hair rippling down its back, and a wet napkin upon the forehead, partially concealing the eyes, which nevertheless, flashed a welcome upon him as he came in, feeling a little abashed in the presence of this foreign girl in her pretty dishabille, with her loose wide sleeves showing her round, white arms to her elbows, and her little high-heeled pink-rosetted slippers resting on the footstool. She, on the contrary, was as composed and unconscious as if he had been a block of wood, instead of a man, with all a man's impulse to worship and admire.

"Oh, Mr. Beresford," she began, offering him one wet hand, while with the other she took the napkin from her head, and, dipping it in the bowl of water on the stand beside her, wrung it lightly and replaced it on her forehead, letting a little of the fringe hang over her eyes while drops of water ran down her face and fell from the end of her nose. "Oh, Mr. Beresford, it was so kind in you to come so soon when you must have so much to do, but you see I could not wait, even though I have this headache. Mrs. Jerry said it was hardly the thing to receive you in this way, but a girl with the headache cannot be expected to dress as for a dinner, and I can't bear my hair bound up, though I might fix it a little," and with a dexterous, quick movement, Reinette took the whole mass of wavy hair in her hand, and giving it a twist and a sweep backward, wet the napkin again, and spatting it down on her forehead, went on:

"I must see you this morning, because father said I was to ask you every thing—trust you with everything—and I want to know—I want you to tell me—those peo—those ladies—my grandmother said she was coming to-day to talk over matters, and how can I talk if I don't know what to say?"

Mr. Beresford was sure he didn't know, and she continued:

"It may seem strange to you, who did not know father intimately, to knew how little he talked of his affairs to any one. Even with regard to mother, he was very reticent, and never told me anything, except that she died in Rome, when I was born, and that her name was Margaret Ferguson. I always thought she was English, and built many castles about her and her relatives, and so, you see, I was a little surprised yesterday when they claimed me—such a number of them, it seemed. Were there many?"

"Only three," Mr. Beresford replied, knowing that she had no reference to Phil when she talked of "those people."

"Yes, three," she continued, "and I fear I was not as gracious as I might have been, for I was so astonished to be claimed when I did not know for sure that I had a relative in the world. Mr. Beresford, would you mind telling me all you know about my mother? Did she ever live in Merrivale? Did father find her here? Did she pick huckleberries with Mrs. Jerry, and cut up bits of calico for the sake of sewing them together again?"

The napkin went into the water with a great splash, and then back to her forehead as she said this, but her eyes were fixed on Mr. Beresford, who, not knowing what she meant by the bits of calico, said he did not, but continued, laughingly:

"I dare say she did pick berries; for almost every girl born in Merrivale does so at some period of her life."

"Then she was born here, and you have seen her, and there is no mistake, and these people, they are—they are my grandmother?"

This was the second time Reinette had put her questions in this form, and this time Mr. Beresford laughed heartily, as he replied:

"Yes, they are your grandmother decidedly; but," he added, more quietly, "it is strange your father never told you."

"Not strange at all if you knew him," Reinette said, resolved that no blame should attach to her father. "But tell me," she went on, "tell me all about it—the marriage, I mean, and who are the Fergusons—nice people, of course, or my mother would not have been one. Who are they, Mr. Beresford?"

The lawyer could not look that proud, high-bred girl in the face and tell her of Peggy Ferguson's beer shop under the elms, of the Martins, or of the wonder and surprise when Fred Hetherton made Margaret Ferguson his wife. But he dwelt upon the honesty and respectability of John Ferguson, and the great beauty of his daughter Margaret, whose loveliness had attracted the heir of the Hethertons.

Reinette saw he was evading her questions, and with an impatient stamp of her little slipper, she said:

"Mr. Beresford, you are keeping things from me, and I will not bear it. If there is anything wrong about the Fergusons I wish to know it. Not that I shall turn against them," she said, with a flash in her eyes which made her visitor wince. "They are mother's people, and if they are thieves and robbers I am a thief and robber, too. I see by your face that there is something—that you don't fancy these people of mine, but I tell you I do. If they are mine they are mine, and I won't hear a word against them!"

What a strange contradictory creature she was, one moment insisting that he must tell her something, if there was any thing to tell, and the next warning him that she would not listen to a word. What could he do but stare wonderingly at her, as, dropping the napkin into the bowl of water, she leaned back in her chair and holding him with her bright eyes, said, imperiously:

"I am waiting, go on; father made a mesalliance, I suppose."

"Yes, that's about the fact of the case," Mr. Beresford replied, feeling compelled to speak out. "Your mother's family did not stand as high socially as your father's. They were poor, while Mr. Hetherton, your grandfather, was rich, and that makes a difference, you know."

"No, I didn't," she replied. "I thought nothing made a difference in America, if you behaved yourself. But go on. How poor were they? Did they beg? What did they do?"

The look in her eyes brought the answer promptly:

"Your grandfather built chimneys and laid cellar walls."

"Well, that's dirty, sticky, nasty work, but no disgrace—people must have chimneys and cellar walls, and I've no doubt he built them well. What did she do—grandmother, I mean? Was she a bar-maid?"

She had almost hit it, but not quite, and Mr. Beresford replied:

"She sold gingerbread and beer; kept a kind of baker's shop."

Reinette drew a quick, gasping breath, put the wet napkin again on her head without wringing it at all, and said:

"Yes, I see—I understand. They were unfortunate enough to be born poor; they did what they could to get their living; but that is nothing against them; that is no reason why you should despise them. They are mine, and I won't have it, I say."

"My dear Miss Hetherton," Mr. Beresford began, puzzled to know how to treat this capricious creature, "what can you mean? I do not despise them."

"Yes, you do," she answered; "I see it in your face. I saw it there yesterday when they claimed me. But I won't have it; they are mine. Who was that young man with them? Why don't you tell me about him, and not of them all the time? He is not a Ferguson, sure?"

No, Phil was not a Ferguson, and Mr. Beresford launched at once into praise of Phil, and the Rossiters generally, dwelling at length upon their handsome house at the Knoll, the high position they held in both town and country, the accomplishments of the young ladies, Ethel and Grace, the sweetness and dignity of Mrs. Rossiter, and, lastly, Phil himself, the best-hearted, most popular fellow in the world, with the most exquisite taste in everything, as was shown in what he had done to make Hetherton Place attractive.

It was strange how Reinette's whole attitude and expression changed as she listened. The Rossiters were more to her liking than the Fergusons, and she became as soft and gentle as a purring kitten, forgetting in her interest to wipe the drops of water from her face, as the napkin made frequent journeys to the bowl and back.

Mr. Beresford felt that he deserved a great deal of credit for thus extolling Phil, feeling, as he did, a horrible pang of jealousy when he saw the bright, eager face flush, and the dark eyes light up with pleasure and expectancy.

"And cousin Philip will call on me soon—to-day, I hope. I am so anxious to see him. It is so nice to have a real flesh and blood cousin, to whom I can talk more freely even than to you. Tell him, please, how I want to see him," she said; and again a pang, like the cut of a knife, thrilled Mr. Beresford's nerves, as he felt that his kingdom was slipping away.

Reinette was growing tired, and as there was no necessity to prolong the interview longer, she gave a little wave of her hand toward the door, and said:

"Thank you, Mr. Beresford; that is all I care to ask you now. You will, of course, continue to look after me as you did after papa until I am of age, and then I shall look after myself. Until then I wish you to see to everything, only stipulating that you let me have all the money I want, and I give you warning that I shall ask for a great deal. I mean to make this place the loveliest spot in the world. You accept, of course? You will be my agent, or guardian, or whatever you choose to call it but you must let me do exactly as I please, or you will find me troublesome."

She smiled up at him very brightly, while he bowed his acceptance, thinking to himself that he might sometimes find it hard to deal with this spoilt girl who warned him so prettily, and yet so determinedly, that she must have her way.

"I will serve you to the best of my ability," he said, "and if I am to look after your interests it is necessary that I fully understand how much your father died possessed of, and where it is invested. I know, of course, about affairs in this country, but he must have had money, and perhaps lands, abroad. Do you know? Did he have any box where he kept his papers; and will you let me have that box as soon as possible; not to-day, of course, but soon?"

For an instant Reinette looked at him fixedly, while the remembrance of what her father had said to her with regard to letters which might come to him flashed upon her, and with the instincts of a woman who scents danger there came to her mind the thought that if there were letters no one must read, there might be papers which no eye but hers must see. She would look them over first before intrusting them to the care of any one, and if there were a secret in her father's past life, only she would know it.

"Yes," she said at last, "there are papers—many of them—in a tin box, and when you come again I will give them to you. Father had houses in Paris, and Avignon, too, I think. Pierre knows more of that than I do. Ask him anything you please. But hush! Isn't that a carriage driving up to the door? It may be cousin Philip. I hope so. I am quite sure of it; and now go, please, and send Mrs. Jerry or Susan to me. I must do something with all this hair, or he'll think me a guy;" and gathering her long, heavy hair in a mass she twisted it into a large flat coil, which she fastened at the back of her head with a gold arrow taken from her morning jacket.

It was not very complimentary to Mr. Beresford to know that while she was willing to receive him en dishabille, as if he had been a block, the moment Phil came she was at once alive to all the proprieties of her personal appearance. Nor was it very gratifying to be thus summarily dismissed to make way for another, and that other the fascinating, good-for-nothing Phil, whom every woman worshipped; but there was no help for it, and bidding good-morning to the little lady who was standing before the mirror with her back to him, fixing her hair, he went out in the hall to meet—not Phil, but Grandma Ferguson and Anna. They had entered without ringing, and as Mr. Beresford opened the door of the library grandma caught sight of Reinette, and went unannounced, into her presence.

CHAPTER XIII

THOSE PEOPLE

With a little start of surprise and disappointment, Reinette recognized her visitors, and for an instant her annoyance showed itself upon her face, and then she recovered herself, and went forward to meet them with far more cordiality in her manner than she had evinced toward them the previous day.

"Good-morning, Rennet," grandma began. "I meant to have come earlier, so as to have a good long visit before noon, for I sha'n't stay to dinner to-day. We are going to have green peas from my own garden, and they'd spile if kept till to-morrow. Oh, my sakes, how hot I am!" and settling herself in the chair Reinette had vacated, the good lady untied her bonnet-strings, took off her purple gloves, and fanned herself rapidly with the huge palm-leaf she carried. "Please open one of them blinds," she continued; "it's darker than a pocket here, and I want to see Margaret's girl by daylight."

Reinette complied with her request, and then for the first time Mrs. Ferguson noticed the bowl of water, and the dark rings about Reinette's eyes.

"Why, what's the matter?" she asked. "Got the headache? Oh, I'm so sorry. You take it from your mother. She never could go nowhere, without comin' home with sick headache. 'Twas her bile that was out of kilter, and you look bilious. Better take some blue mass, or else sulphur and molasses, and drink horehound tea. That'll cleanse your blood."

As she listened Reinette began to grow rebellious again, and she could have screamed with disgust at what she knew was well meant, but what seemed to her the height of vulgarity. Sinking into a chair, with her back to the window, and her visitors in front where she could see them distinctly, she scanned them closely; but said very little to them.

"She evidently cares nothing for us," Anna thought, and she was beginning to feel angry and resentful, when Mrs. Jerry looked in, and seeing Mrs. Ferguson exclaimed:

"Just the one I wanted. I'm making some currant jam, and wish you'd come to the kitchen a minute."

Mrs. Ferguson went out at once, and, left to themselves, the two girls began to talk, Reinette asking numberless questions by the way of drawing her cousin out and judging what she was. It did not take long for her to learn that Anna had been for three quarters to a young ladies' seminary in Worcester, that she had studied algebra, geometry, astronomy, chemistry, physiology, botany, rhetoric, zoology, English literature, German and French; she had dabbled a little in water-colors, had taken lessons on the piano, and sometimes played the melodeon in Sunday school.

"Dear me," said Reinette, drawing a long breath, "how learned you must be. I have never studied half those things. I hate mathematics, and rhetoric, and geology, and literature, and you are posted in them all. But tell me, now you are through school, what do you do? Merrivale is a small place; there cannot be much to occupy one outside. What do you do all day, when it rains, for instance, and you can't go out? and when you first came from school; time must have hung heavily then."

Reinette had no particular object in asking so many questions; she only wished to make talk, and she had no suspicion of the effect her words had upon Anna, who turned scarlet, and hesitated a moment; then, thinking to herself, "It don't matter; I may as well spit it out," she said:

"Reinette, you will know some time how I live, and so I'll tell you myself, and let you judge whether my life is a happy one. You know of course that we are poor. I don't mean that we have not enough to eat and wear, but we work for a living, and that in America makes quite as much difference as it does in Europe. Father keeps a small grocery and mother is a dressmaker and, talk as you please of the nobility of labor, and that 'a man's a man for a' that,' the man must have money and the woman, too; and there are lots of girls in town no better than I am, with not half as good an education, who look down upon me because my mother makes their dresses, and I help her sometimes. You ask what I did when I first came from school. I'll tell you. Mother was very busy, for there was a grand wedding in progress to which I was not bidden, but I had to work on the dresses, and take some of them home, and when I rang the front door-bell at Sue Granger's, I was told by an impudent house-maid to step round to the side door as her lady had visitors in the parlor, and it was no place to receive parcels. I tell you I was mad, and I've never carried a budget since, and never will; and I shall be so glad if we ever get out of the business, for I hate it, and I am just as good as Sue Granger, whose mother they say once worked in a cotton mill. Thank goodness, I am not as low as that. There's good blood in my veins, too, if I am poor. The Rices (mother was a Rice) are highly connected with some of the best families in the State. Governor Rice is a distant relative of mine, and the Fergusons are well enough."

Here Anna paused to take breath, and Reinette, who had listened to her wonderingly, said:

"And do your cousins, Ethel and Grace, share your opinions?"

"Of course not. Why should they? Aren't they big bugs, Colonel Rossiter's daughters? Don't they go to Saratoga, and Newport, and Florida, and the sea-side, and have a maid, and drive their carriage, and live in a big house? Such people can never understand why girls like me feel as I do. Ethel and Grace laugh at me, and say I am just as good as they are; and so I am, though the world don't think so. Their mother used to stitch shoes for the shop when a girl, and sell gingerbread across the counter sometimes, just as your mother did. You know, perhaps, that Grandma Ferguson kept a kind of baker's shop."

Reinette flushed to the roots of her hair as she replied;

"Yes, I know, but I supposed one's respectability depended upon himself—his conduct, I mean, rather than what he does for a living—if the business is honest and justifiable."

"There's where you are grandly mistaken," said Anna. "One's position depends upon how much money he has, or how many influential friends. Is my Aunt Mary any better than when she stitched shoes and sold gingerbread? Of course not. She's John Ferguson's daughter just the same; but she's rich now. She is Mrs. Colonel Rossiter, and looked up to, and admired, and run after by the whole town, while ma and I are just tolerated because of our relationship to her. 'Who is that stylish-looking girl?' I once heard a stranger say to Sue Granger, who replied: 'That's Anna Ferguson; her mother is a dressmaker,' and that settled it. The stranger—a stuck-up piece from Boston—cared nothing for a girl whose mother made dresses for a living. Sometimes I get so mad I hate everything and everybody."

Here Anna stopped a moment, and Reinette scanned her very closely from her head to her feet, deciding, mentally that she was good-looking, and had about her a certain style which strangers would naturally remark, even though it was rather fast than refined. But she was not a lady, either by nature or education, and Reinette, who, in some things was far-seeing for her years, saw readily the difficulty under which her cousin labored. She was not naturally refined, but on the contrary, vulgar and suspicious, and jealous of those who occupied a position above her; and while she took pains with her person, and affected a certain haughtiness of manner, her language was decidedly second-class and frequently interlarded with slang and harsh denunciations of the very people whose favor she wished to gain.

While Reinette was thinking all this, Anna began again:

"I wish mother would sell out and take that odious sign from our front window; we can live without dressmaking, but I've given it up. She had a chance a few weeks ago. A Frenchwoman from Martha's Vineyard wrote, asking her terms, which she put so high that Miss La Rue declined, and so that fell through."

"What did you call the woman?" Reinette asked, rousing up suddenly from her reclining posture and looking earnestly at Anna, who replied:

"Miss Margery La Rue, from Martha's Vineyard. She has done some work, I believe for my cousins, who think highly of her, and suggested her buying out ma's business. Why, how excited you seem! Do you know her?" she asked, as Reinette sprang up quickly, her cheeks flushing, her eyes sparkling, and her whole appearance indicative of pleasurable surprise.

"Margery La Rue," she repeated. "The name is the same, and she is French, too, you say, but it cannot be my Margery, for the last I heard from her she was in Nice, and talked of going to Rome, but it is singular that there should be two dressmakers of the same name. What do you know of her? Is she old or young?"

"I know nothing except the name," Anna said, astonished at her cousin's interest in and evident liking for a mere dressmaker. "Is your Miss La Rue young, and was she your friend?" she asked, and Reinette replied:

"Yes, she was my friend—the dearest I ever had, and the only one, I may say, except papa, and she is beautiful, too; she has the loveliest face I ever saw—sweet and spirituelle as one of Murillo's Madonnas, with soft blue eyes, and sunny hair."

"But how came you so intimate with her, and she only a dressmaker?" Anna asked.

"It is too long a story to tell you now," Reinette replied. "I have known her since I was a child. I never thought anything about her being a dressmaker. She is educated, and refined, and good, and true, with not a single low instinct in her nature, and that, I think, is what constitutes a lady rather than money or what one does for a living."

Anna shrugged her shoulders incredulously. In her own estimation she was refined and educated, and yet she was not recognized as a lady by those to whose notice she aspired; but she made no reply, and Reinette continued:

"I shall take steps at once to ascertain if this Miss La Rue you speak of is my Margery, and if she is, and it is merely a matter of money which keeps her from accepting your mother's offer, I think I can make two people happy; you first, if taking that sign from your window will do it, and myself, by bringing her here where I can see her every day, if I wish to."

Before Anna could reply, Grandma Ferguson came in, puffing with exercise, and apologizing for her long absence.

"I didn't mean to be gone more'n a minit," she said, "but Mrs. Jerry offered to show me all over the house, and I kinder wanted to see it, as it's my fust chance. The last, and I may say the only time I was ever here, I was turned out o' door afore I could look about me."

"Turned out of doors! For what, and by whom?" Reinette asked, in astonishment, and grandma replied:

"Turned out by your Granther Hetherton, because I came over to tell him his son Fred had run off with your mother. Why, Rennet, child, what's the matter! you are white as a sheet," she continued, as with a long gasp for breath Reinette clasped both hands to her forehead and leaned helplessly back in her chair.

"It's nothing," she said faintly, "only the pain in my head has come back again. What you told me was so dreadful—my mother ran off with my father! What for? Why, were they not married at home? Was there any reason?"

"Reason? No," grandma returned. "There was a nice big room back of the shop, and if it was good enough for Paul Rossiter to be married in, and for your father to spark your mother in, as he did many a time, it was good enough for him to be married in. But no; he was afeard, mabby, that he should have to notice some of us, who he thought no more on than so much dirt, and so he ran off with her to New York and got married, and then started for Europe, and I've never seen her sence. But surely, Rennet you must have known something about it, though Anny here, and Phil too—that's Miss Rossiter's son—will have it that you never heard of us till yesterday, and so never knew who your mother was. Is that so?"

It was a direct question and hurt Reinette cruelly suffering as she was both mentally and physically. The wet napkin was again applied to her throbbing temples, and then, in a voice full of anguish, and yet with something defiant in its tone, she said rapidly, like one who wishes to have a disagreeable task ended:

"No, I did not know who my mother was; father never told me."

"That's smart, but just like him," grandma interposed; but Reinette stopped her short, and said:

"Hush, grandma! I will not hear my father blamed for anything. He may have acted hastily and foolishly when he was young, but he was the dearest and best of fathers to me. He did not talk much, ever, and never of his private affairs, and since I know—that—that—he ran away with my mother, I am not surprised that he did not tell me who she was or anything of her early life. He knew it would pain me, and so he let me think her an English woman, as I always did——"

"Yes, but when you started for America a body would s'pose he would have told. He knew you'd have to see us then and know," grandma said, and Reinette replied:

"Yes, and he meant to tell me when we reached New York. He had a habit of putting off things, and he put that off, and when he was dying on the ship he tried to tell me so hard. I know now what he meant when he said: 'When it comes to you forgive me and love me just the same;' and I do—I will—and I'll stand by father through everything;" and Reinette's eyes, where the great tears were standing, fairly blazed, as she defended her dead father; and her grandma cried, too, a little, but her animosity toward the Hethertons was so great and this silence of her son-in law seemed so like a fresh insult, that she was ready to fire up in an instant, and when Reinette said to her, "It is very painful for me to hear it, and still I wish you to tell me all I ought to know of mother and father both. Why did you say they ran away?" she began as far back as the first time her daughter Margaret handed Fred Hetherton a glass of beer across the counter, and in her own peculiar way, told the story of the courtship and marriage, ending with a graphic description of her call on Gen. Hetherton, who turned her from his house, and bade her never enter it again.

"And I never have till to-day," she said, "when I wouldn't wonder if he'd stir in his coffin if he knew I was here, seein' he felt so much above me. If I'd been a man, I b'lieve I'd a horse-whipped him, for there's fight in my make-up. My two brothers, Jim and Will Martin, were the prize-fighters of the town, and could lick any two men single-handed. They are dead now, both on 'em—died in the war, fightin' for their country, and I s'pose it's better so than if they'd lived to do wus."

"Yes, oh, yes," Reinette said, faintly, neither knowing what she said or what she meant, knowing only that every nerve was quivering with excitement and pain, and that she felt half crazed and stunned with all she had heard of the father and mother she had held so high.

Nothing had been omitted, and she knew all about the beer and the gingerbread her grandmother sold,—the shoes her mother closed,—the berries she had picked to buy the blue chintz gown—the pride of the Hethertons and the inexcusable silence of her father with regard to her mother's death and her own existence. There was nothing more to tell, and Reinette could not have heard it, if there had been. Proud and high-spirited as she was, she felt completely crushed and humiliated, and as if she could never face the world again. And yet in what she had heard there was nothing derogatory to her mother's character, or her father's either for that matter. Only it was so different from what she had believed. By and by, when she could reason more calmly, she would feel differently and see it from a different standpoint, but now she felt as if she should scream outright if her visitors staid another minute, and she was glad when, reminded by the twelve o'clock whistle of her green peas cooking at home, grandma arose to go. She had had no intentions of wounding Reinette, but she had no sensitiveness herself, no delicacy of feeling, no refinement, and could not understand how crushed, degraded, and heart-broken Reinette felt as she fled up the stairs to her own room, and throwing herself upon the bed sobbed and moaned in a paroxysm of grief and despair.

"And these people are mine," she said; "they belong to me, who was once so proud of my blood. Prizefighters, and brewers, and bakers, and mercy knows what, in place of the dukes and duchesses I had pictured to myself! Why did father bring me here, when he had kept the knowledge of them from me so long, or at least why did he not tell me of them? It is dreadful, and I hope I may never see one of them again."

Just then her ear caught the sound of horse's feet galloping into the yard, and starting up from her crouching position among the pillows and pushing back her heavy hair from her forehead, Reinette listened intently, feeling intuitively that she knew who the rider was, and experiencing a thrill of joy when, a few moments later, Pierre brought her a card with the name of "Phil Rossiter" engraved upon it. Taking the bit of pasteboard in her hand she examined it critically, and pronouncing it au fait in every respect, announced her intention of going down to meet her cousin.

"But, mademoiselle, your dress, your hair; monsieur is a gentleman," Pierre said; but Reinette cared nothing for her dress then—nothing for her hair, which had again fallen over her shoulders.

Gathering it up in masses at the back of her head, and letting a few tresses fall upon her neck, she wrapped her pink sacque a little more closely around her, and went hurriedly down to the library where Phil was waiting for her.

CHAPTER XIV

REINETTE AND PHIL

He was gotten up after the most approved manner of a young man of leisure and taste. From his short, cut-away coat to the tip of his boots everything was faultless, and his fair, handsome face impressed you with the idea that he was fresh from a perfumed bath, as, with his soft hat under his arm, he stood leaning on the mantel and looking curiously about the room. She, in pink and white dishabille, a good deal tumbled and mussed, her hair just ready to fall down her back, her cheeks flushed and her eyelids swollen and red, showed plainly the wear and tear of the last few days. And still there was a great eagerness in her face, and her eyes were very bright as she stood an instant on the threshold looking intently at Phil, as if deciding what manner of man he was. Something in the expression of his face which won all hearts to trust him, won her as well, and when he stepped forward to meet her, she went swiftly to him, and laying her head upon his bosom as naturally as if he had been her brother, sobbed like a child.

"Oh, Philip, oh, cousin, I am so glad you have come at last," she said. "Why didn't you come sooner, come first of all, before—those—before my— Oh, I am so glad to see you and find you just like my father!"

Phil did not quite know whether he felt complimented or not to be likened to her father, but to say that he was astonished faintly portrays his state of mind at the novel position in which he found himself. Although warm-hearted and affectionate he was not naturally very demonstrative, or if he were, that part of his nature had never been called into action, except by his grandmother. His sisters were very fond and proud of him, but they never caressed or petted him as some only brothers are petted, and only kissed him when parting with him, or after a long absence. As to the other girls of his acquaintance, his lips had never touched theirs since the days of his boyhood when he played the old-time games in the school-house on the common, nor had he held a girl's hand in his except in the dance, and when assisting her to the carriage or her horse; and here was this stranger, whom till yesterday he had never seen, sobbing in his arms, with his hands clasped in hers and her face bent over them so that he could feel the touch of her burning cheek, and the great tears as they wet his imprisoned fingers. And with that queer perversity of man's nature Phil liked it, and drew her closer to him, and felt his own eyes moisten, and his voice tremble as he said gently and pityingly, as women are wont to speak:

"Poor little Reinette, I am so sorry for you, for I know how you have suffered: and you have the headache, too, grandmother told me. She was here this morning. I hope you liked her. She is the kindest-hearted woman in the world."

"Yes," came faintly from the neighborhood of his hands, where Reinette's face was hidden for an instant longer; then, freeing herself from him and stepping backward, she looked at him fixedly, until all the tears left her eyes, which twinkled mischievously as she burst into a merry laugh, and said: "No, I will be honest with you, Philip, and let you know just how bad I am. I didn't like her! Oh, I know you are horrified and hate me, and think me awful," she continued, as she sank into an easy-chair, and plunging the napkin into the bowl of water still standing there, spread it upon her head. "But you can't understand how sudden it all is to me, who never knew I had a relative in America, unless it were some distant one on father's side, and who, had I been told that I was first cousin to Queen Victoria, would not have been surprised, but rather have thought her majesty honored by the connection, so proud was I of my fancied blood. And to be told all these—"

"What have you been told?" Phil asked, and she replied:

"Everything, I am sure, or if there is anything more I never wish to hear it. I know about the chimneys and the cellar walls, the gingerbread and the beer, and closing shoes, though what that is, I can't even guess, and the runaway match, worse than all the rest unless it be those dreadful men who fought each other like beasts. What were their names? I cannot remember."

"You mean Uncle Tim and Uncle Will Martin," Phil said, calling the men uncle for the first time in his life, although there was not a drop of their blood in his veins.

But he would not hint that he was not as much a Martin as herself.

"You mean Uncle Tim and Uncle Will, grandmother's brothers; they were only great uncles, and had the good taste to get killed in the war. They can't hurt you."

"I know that, but something hurts me cruelly," Reinette replied, clenching her hands together. "And you don't know how much I hate it all—hate everybody—and want to fight and tear somebody's hair; that would relieve me, but it would not rid me of these dreadful people."

She looked like a little fury as she beat her hands in the air, and forgetting that they were strangers, Phil said to her:

"You surprise me, Reinette, by taking so strange a view of the matter. Can you not understand that in America, where we boast of our democracy, there is no such commodity as blood, or if there is, it is so diluted and mixed that the original element is hard to find. It does not matter so much who you are, or who your parents were, as it does what you are yourself.

"'Honor and shame from no condition rise,
    Act well your part, there all the honor lies.'

"That used to be written for me in my copy-book at school, and I puzzled my brain over it to know what it meant, understanding at last that it was another version of that part of the church catechism which tells us to do our duty in that state of life to which God has called us."

"I'm sure I don't know what you mean by talking poetry and catechism to me," Reinette said, tartly, and Phil replied:

"I mean that you should look on the brighter side and not hate us all because we chance to be your relatives and not rebel so hotly and want to fight and tear somebody's hair because, instead of being the granddaughter of a duchess, you prove to be the granddaughter of—of a Ferguson."

"Who calls me Rennet, and talks such dreadful grammar, and wears purple gloves," interrupted Reinette, with a half-laugh in her eyes, where the great tears were shining.

Phil smiled a little, for the purple gloves, into which Grandma Ferguson persisted in squeezing her coarse red hands, shocked his fastidious taste sorely, but he was bent upon defending her, and he replied:

"Yes, I know all that; grandma is peculiar and old-fashioned, but she does not harm you, as Reinette Hetherton, one whit. She never had a chance to learn; circumstances have been against her. She had to work all her early life, and she did it well, and is one of the kindest old ladies in the world, and some day you will appreciate her and think yourself fortunate to have so good a grandmother, and you'll get used to us all."

"I never shall," Reinette replied, "never can get used to these people. You know I don't mean you, for you are not like them, though I do think it very mean in you to stand there lecturing me so, when I wanted you to come to me so badly, and thought you would comfort me and smooth the trouble away, and instead of that you have done nothing but scold me ever since you've been here, and nobody ever dared to do that before but father, and you know how awfully my head is aching, and you've made it ten times worse. I am disappointed in you, Philip Rossiter; and I meant to like you so much. But you don't like me, I see it in your face, and you are a Ferguson, too, and I hate you—there!"

As she talked Reinette half rose from her chair, and in her excitement upset the bowl of water, which went plashing over the floor. Then, sinking back into her seat, she began to cry piteously as Phil had never heard a girl cry before. Crossing swiftly to her side he knelt down before her, and taking her flushed, tear-stained face between both his hands, kissed her upon her forehead and lips, while he tried to comfort her, assuring her that he was not scolding her, he was only defending his friends, that he was sorry for her, and did like her very much.

"Please forgive me, Reinette," he said, "and let us be friends, for I assure you I like you."

"Then don't call me Reinette," she said. "Father always called me Queenie, and so did Margery, and they are the only people I ever loved, or who ever loved me. Call me Queenie, if you love me, Philip."

"Queenie, then, it is—for by Jove, I do love you; and you must call me Phil, if you love me, and so we seal the compact," the young man said, touching again the sweet, girlish lips, which this time kissed him back without the least hesitancy or token of consciousness.

And so they made it up, these cousins who had quarreled on the occasion of their first interview; and Phil picked up the bits of broken china and the napkin, and wiped up the water with his handkerchief, and told her he could cure her headache by rubbing, just as he often cured his mother's. And

Queenie, as he ever after called her, grew as soft and gentle as a kitten, and, leaning her head upon the back of her chair, submitted to the rubbing and manipulations of her forehead until the pain actually ceased, for there was a wonderful mesmeric power in Phil's hands, and he threw his whole soul into the task, and worked like a professional, talking learnedly of negative and positive conditions, and feeling sorry when his cousin declared the pain gone, and asked him to throw open the blinds and let in the light, and then sit down where she could look at him.

There was perfect harmony between them now, and for an hour or more they talked together, and Reinette told Phil everything she could think of with regard to her past life, and asked him numberless questions concerning his own family and the Fergusons generally.

"I am ashamed of myself," she said, "and I am going to reform—going to cultivate the Fergusons, though I don't believe I can ever do much with Anna. What ails her, Phil, to be so bitter against everybody? Are they so very poor?"

"Not at all," said Phil. "Uncle Tom—that's her father—is a good, honest, hard-working man, odd as Dick's hat-band, and something of a codger, who wears leather strings in his shoes, and never says his soul is his own in the presence of his wife and daughter; but he is perfectly respectable, though he doesn't go to church much on Sundays, and always calls my mother 'Miss Rossiter,' though she's his half-sister."

"What?" and Reinette looked up quickly. "Aren't we own cousins, and isn't your mother my own aunt?"

"No," Phil answered reluctantly; then, thinking she would rather hear the truth from him than from any one else, he told her of his grandfather's two wives, one of whom was his grandmother and one hers.

"And so the Martins and the prize-fighters are not one bit yours; they are all mine," Reinette said, the tears rushing to her eyes again.

"Nonsense, Queenie; that doesn't matter a bit. Remember what I told you; blood does not count in this country. Nobody will think less of you because of those fighters, or fancy you want to knock him down."

"But I feel sometimes as if I could; that must be the Martin in me," Reinette said, laughingly; and then she spoke again of Anna, who Phil said was too sensitive, and jealous, and ready to suspect a slight where none was intended.

"But once give her a chance," he added, "and she would ride over everybody's head, and snub working people worse than she thinks she is snubbed because her mother makes dresses."

This allusion to dressmaking reminded Reinette of what Anna had said with regard to Miss La Rue who had proposed buying her mother's business, and she questioned Phil of her, but he knew nothing, and Reinette continued:

"Oh, if it only were my Margery, I should be so happy. You don't know how I love her; she is so sweet, and good, and beautiful. I've known her since we were little girls at school together. It was a private English school in Paris, where I was a boarder, and she a day scholar at half rate, because they were poor. I never saw Mrs. La Rue but once or twice, and she is not at all like Margery. She had been a hair-dresser at one time, I think. Oh, if this Miss La

Rue should prove to be my friend! When will you see her? When are you going to the Vineyard?"

Phil could not tell. He had intended going at once, but since coming to Hetherton Place he had changed his mind, for there was something in this willful, capricious sparkling girl which attracted him more than all the gaieties of the Sea View House, and he said it was uncertain when he should go to the Vineyard—probably not for two weeks or more.

"Oh, I am so sorry," Reinette said frankly, "for I do want to know about Margery; but then," she added, with equal frankness, "it is real nice to have you here, where I can see you every day. We must be great friends, Phil, and you must like me in all my moods; like me when I want to tear your eyes out just the same as when I would tear mine out to serve you. Will you promise, Phil?"

"Yes," was his reply, as he took in his the hand she offered him, feeling strongly tempted to touch again the girlish lips which pouted so prettily as she looked up at him.

One taste of those lips had intoxicated him as wine intoxicates the drunkard; but there was a womanly dignity now in Reinette's manner which kept him at a distance, while she went on to tell him of her good intentions. She was going to cultivate the Fergusons, especially her grandmother, and she should commence by calling there that very afternoon, and Phil must go with her. She would order an early dinner, at half-past four, to which Phil should stay, and then they would take a gallop together into town.

"You have nothing to do but to stay with me. Your business will not suffer?" she asked; and coloring at this allusion to his business, Phil replied that it would not suffer very much from an absence of half a day or so, and that he was at her disposal.

"Then I'll interview Mrs. Jerry, and have dinner on the big piazza which overlooks the river, and the meadows. That will make it seem some like Chateau des Fleurs, where we ate out doors half the time," she said, as she disappeared from the room in quest of Mrs. Jerry who heard with astonishment that dinner was to be served upon the north piazza instead of in the dining-room.

But a few hours' experience had taught her that Miss Hetherton's ways were not at all the ways to which she had been accustomed, and so she assented without a word, while Reinette went next to her room and transformed herself from an invalid in a wrapper into a most stylish and elegant young lady.

How lovely she was, in her dress of dark-blue silk with a Valenciennes sleeveless jacket, such as was then fashionable, her hair arranged in heavy curls, which were fastened at the back of her head with a scarlet ribbon, while a knot of the same ribbon was worn at her throat.

Phil had thought her bewitching in her wrapper, with the wet napkin on her head, but when she tripped into the room in her new attire he started with surprise at the transformation. There was a bright flush on her cheeks, and her eyes shone like stars as they flashed smile after smile upon him, until he became so dazed and bewildered that he scarcely knew what he was doing.

She had her sun-hat in her hand, and led him out into the grounds, where she told him of the improvements she meant to make, and asked what he thought of them.

She should not change the general appearance of the house, she said. She should only add one or two bay-windows and balconies, and enlarge the north piazza, as she wished the rooms to remain as they were when her father lived there, but the park was to undergo a great change, and be modeled, as far as possible, after the park at Chateau des Fleurs. There were to be winding walks, and terraces, and plateaus of flowers, and fountains, and statuary gleaming among the evergreens, and clumps of cedar trimmed and arranged into a labyrinth of little rooms, with seats and tables in them, and lamps suspended from the branches. But the crowning glory of the whole was to be a rustic summer-house, large enough to accommodate three or four sets of dancers, when she gave an outdoor fete, and to seat at least forty people at a breakfast or dinner. Her ideas were on a most magnificent scale, and Phil listened to her breathlessly till she had finished, and then asked if she had any idea how much this would cost.

"A heap of money, of course," she said, arching her eyebrows and nose a little, as she scented disapprobation; "but what of that? Father had a great deal of money, I know, and never denied me anything. What is money for, except to spend and let other people have a good time? I mean to fill the house with company, summer and winter, and make life one grand holiday for them, and you must stay here most of the time and help me see to things, or would that interfere too much with your business—your profession?"

This was the second time she had alluded to his business, and Phil's cheeks were scarlet, and he was conscious of a feeling of shame in the presence of this active, energetic girl, who took it for granted that he must have some business—some profession. He could not tell her that he had none, and had she pressed the point, would have fallen back upon that two months' trial in Mr. Beresford's law office, when he started to have a profession; but fortunately for him the dinner was announced, and they went together to the north piazza, where Reinette presided at one end of the table, and he at the other.

"It was quite like housekeeping," Reinette said, and she made Phil promise to dine with her every day when he was in town.

"Not always here," she said, "but around in different places—under the trees, and in my new summer-house, which must be built directly, and every where."

She was the fiercest kind of a radical, always seeking something new, and Phil felt intuitively that to follow her would be to lead a busy, fatiguing life, but he was ready for it; ready for anything; ready to jump into Lake Petit, if she said so, he thought, a little later, when he saw her in her riding habit, mounted upon the snow-white Margery, who held her neck so high, and stepped along so proudly, as if conscious of the graceful burden she bore. Reinette was a fine horsewoman, and sat the saddle and handled the reins perfectly, and she and Phil made quite a sensation as they galloped into town, with King in close attendance, for Reinette had insisted that he should accompany them as a kind of body-guard.

Their first call was upon Mr. Beresford, who came out and stood by Reinette's horse as he talked to her, marveling at the change in this sparkling, brilliant creature, so different from the tear-stained swollen-eyed girl he had seen in the morning. She told him of her plans for improvements, which she meant to begin immediately, and which Phil had said would cost at least two thousand dollars, but that did not matter. When she wanted a thing, she wanted it, and would Mr. Beresford give her the money at once, as she had only two or three hundred dollars in her purse at home. She talked as if gold grew on bushes, and Mr. Beresford listened to her aghast, for unless he advanced it himself, there were not two thousand dollars for her in his possession. The repairs at Hetherton Place had already cost enormously, and there were still debts waiting to be paid. Mr. Hetherton's death would of course retard matters a little, but it was impossible to refuse the eager, winsome girl, whose eyes looked so straight into his own, and he promised to give her what she asked for, and said he had already written to Paris to Messrs. Polignie & Co., who he believed had charge of her father's foreign business, adding that he should like the papers as soon as possible.

Reinette said he should have them the next day, and added:

"I, too, am going to write to Messrs. Polignie, to inquire for my old nurse, Christine Bodine. She knew mother, and I mean to find her if she is alive.

"Not that it matters much, as there is no doubt that my mother was Margaret Ferguson," she said to Phil, as they rode off, "and I am getting quite reconciled to it now that I know you. Would you mind," and she dropped her voice a little, "would you mind showing me the chimneys and cellar walls our grandfather built? and the beer shop where mother sewed the pieces of cloth together, and those shoes and things?"

Phil could not show her the chimneys John Ferguson had built, for though there were those in the town who often pointed them out when Mrs. Rossiter, his daughter drove by in her handsome carriage, he didn't know where they were, but he could show her the beer shop, as she termed it, though it bore no traces now of what it used to be. It was long and low, like many of the old New England houses, but it looked deliciously cool and pleasant under the tall elms, with its plats of grass and its sweet, old-fashioned flowers in full bloom. Grandma Ferguson, too, in her clean calico dress and white apron, with her hair combed smoothly back, made a different picture from what she did in the morning, with her wide ribbons and purple gloves. She was delighted to see them, and took Reinette all over the house, from the parlor where she said Paul Rossiter and Fred Hetherton had courted their wives, to the room where Reinette's mother used to sleep when she was a girl, and where the high-post bed she occupied, and the chair she used to sit in, were still standing.

"Mary—that's Miss Rossiter—wanted me to git some new furniture," she said, as they stood in the quiet room, "and I could afford it as well as not, for your gran'ther left me pretty well off, with what Mary does for me; but somehow it makes Margaret seem nigher to me to have the things she used to handle, and so I keep 'em, and sometimes when I'm lonesome for the days that are gone, and for my girl that is dead, I come up here and sit awhile and think I can see her just as she used to look when I waked her in the mornin', and she lay there on that piller smilin' at me like a fresh young rose, with her hair fallin' over her pretty eyes; and then I cry and wish I had her back, though I know she's so happy now, and some day I shall see her again, if I'm good, and I do try to do the best that I know how. Poor Maggie, dear little Maggie, dead way over the seas."

Grandma was talking more to herself than to Reinette, and the great tears were dropping from her dim old eyes, and her rough, red hands were tenderly patting the pillows, where she had so often seen the dear head of the child "dead way over the seas." But to Reinette there was now no redness, or roughness about the hands, no coarseness about the woman, for all such minor things were forgotten in that moment of perfect accord and sympathy, and Reinette's tears fell like rain as she bent over the hands which had touched her mother.

"Blessed child," grandma said, "I thank my God for sending you to me, and that you are good and true, like Margaret."

This was too much for the conscious-smitten Reinette, who burst out impulsively:

"I'm not good; I'm not true; I'm bad and wicked as I can be, and I am going to confess it all here in mother's room, hoping she can hear me, and know how sorry I am. I was proud and hot, and felt like fighting yesterday when I met you all, because it was so sudden, so different; and this morning I rebelled again, and wanted to scream, but I'll never do so again, and I am going to make you so happy; and now, please, go away and leave me for a little while."

Grandma Ferguson understood her in part, and went out, leaving the girl alone in the low, humble room, which had been Margaret's. Kneeling by the bed, and burying her face in the pillows, Reinette sobbed like a child as she asked forgiveness for all her proud rebellion against the grandmother whom in her heart she knew to be kind and loving. The prayer did her good, and as hers was an April nature, she was as bright and playful as a kitten when she went down the steep, narrow stairs, and bidding her grandmother good-night, mounted her horse and started with Phil for Mrs. Lydia Ferguson's. They found that lady very hot and nervous over a dress which must be finished that night, and on which Anna was working very unwillingly. Through an open door Reinette caught a glimpse of a disorderly supper-table, at which a man was sitting in his shirt sleeves, regaling himself with fried cakes and raw onions.

"Come, father," Mrs. Lydia called, in a loud, shrill voice, "here's Reinette, your niece. Reinette, this is your Uncle Tom, who is said to look enough like your mother to have been her twin."

His face was pleasant, and his manner was kindly, as he shook hands with Reinette, and said he was glad to see her, and told her that she favored the Hethertons more than the Fergusons, but Reinette saw that he belonged to an entirely different world from her own, and when they were going over the house at the Knoll, she said to Phil that she felt as if she were backsliding awfully.

"Isn't there a couplet," she asked, "which runs thus:

"'The de'il when sick a saint would be,
But when he got well, the de'il a saint was he.'

"Now I am just like that. Over at grandmother's I felt as if I never could be bad again; and I never will to grandmother. I shall make her caps and fix her dresses, and coax her not to wear purple gloves, or call me Rennet. But O, Phil, shall I be so wicked that I can never go to Heaven if I don't rave over those other people? They are so different from anything I ever saw before. Now, this suits me; this is more like Chateau des Fleurs," she said, as she followed Phil through the house until they came to his room, where, on the table, he found a telegram from his father, which was as follows:

"Come to us at once as I must go to Boston on business, and your mother needs you.

"Paul Rossiter."

He read it aloud to Reinette, who exclaimed:

"I am so sorry, for now I shall be alone, and I meant to have you with me every day."

Phil was sorry, too, for the dark-eyed French girl had made sad havoc with his heart during the few hours he had known her. But there was no help for it; he must go to his mother, and the next morning, when the Springfield train, bound for Boston, left Merrivale, Phil was in it on his way to Martha's Vineyard.

CHAPTER XV

DOWN BY THE SEA

Mrs. Rossiter occupied the handsomest rooms at the Sea View House, and on the morning of Phil's arrival she lay on her couch by the open window, occasionally looking out upon the water, but mostly with her eyes fixed fondly upon her handsome boy, who sat by her side, fanning himself with his soft hat, and answering the numerous questions of his sisters, concerning Reinette, their new cousin, whose existence had taken them so by surprise. How did she look? What was she like? What did she wear? What did she say, and who was to live with her in that great lonely house?

"Don't hurry a chap so!" said Phil. "There's a lot to tell, and I'd better begin at the beginning."

So he described first the arrival at the station, where grandma and Aunt Lydia were waiting in their weeds, and Anna was gorgeous in her white muslin and long lace scarf, while he flourished with a dirty face and torn, soiled pants.

"Oh, if you could have seen her face when we were presented to her as her 'cousins, and her uncles, and her aunts!' I tell you it was rich. I never saw such eyes in a human being's head as those which flashed first upon one and then upon another of her new relations."

"Do you really mean she had never heard of us at all?" both Ethel and Grace asked in the same breath, and Phil replied by telling them everything which had transpired since Reinette's arrival up to the time he had left her at her own door, dwelling at length upon her sparkling beauty, which he said might not perhaps be called beauty in the strict sense of the word. Some might think her too small and too dark, while others would object to her forehead as too low, and her nose as a little too retrousse, but to Phil, who had seen the rich warm color come and go on her clear olive cheeks, who had seen her dark eyes flash, and sparkle, and dance until her whole person seemed to shine and glow like some rare diamond, she was supremely beautiful, and he dwelt upon her loveliness and piquancy, and freshness, while his mother and sisters listened breathlessly, but not so breathlessly as the girl in the adjoining room, who sat making some changes in a dress Miss Ethel was to wear that night to a hop in the hotel.

The door between the two rooms was only slightly ajar, and Margery La Rue had not heard a word of the conversation between the brother and sisters until her ear caught the name of Reinette, followed soon by Hetherton and Paris. Then the work dropped from her hands, and a sudden pallor crept into her cheeks, which ordinarily were like the sweet roses of June.

"Reinette; Reinette Hetherton," she whispered. "Is there another name like that in all the world? Is it my Reinette, my Queenie, the dearest, best friend I ever had? Impossible, for what can she be doing here in America, in Merrivale, where I have thought to go!"

There was a death-like faintness in the heart of this girl, whose whispered words were in French, and were scarcely words so softly were they spoken.

"Reinette, Reinette!" she repeated, as with clasped hands, and head bent forward in the attitude of intense listening, she heard the whole story Phil told, and laughed a little to herself at the ludicrous description of the Fergusons, and the impression they made upon the stranger. "I can imagine just how cold and haughty, and proud she grew, and how those great eyes blazed with scorn and incredulity, if it is my Reinette he means," she thought; "but it cannot be. There is some mistake." Then as the name Queenie was spoken she half rose to her feet and laid both hands upon her mouth to force back the glad cry which sprang to her lips. There could be no longer a doubt. This foreigner, this girl from France, this cousin of the Rossiters, this near relation of the Fergusons, whoever they might be, was her Queenie, her darling, whom she loved with such devotion as few women have ever inspired in another. How she longed to rush into the next room and pour out question

after question concerning her friend; but this she could not do; she was only a
seamstress and must remain quiet, for the present at least, for she did not
know how the Rossiters would like her to claim acquaintance and friendship
with their kinswoman. So she resumed her work while the talk in the next
room flowed on, always of Queenie, as they called her because Phil did, and in
whom the mother and sisters were so greatly interested. They had intended
stopping at the sea-side for the summer, but now they spoke of an earlier
return to Merrivale on Queenie's account, a plan of which Phil highly
approved, for he would far rather be at home than there, especially as his
mother was improving daily.

"And Anna? How is she?" Ethel asked. "Does she take kindly to our
cousin, or is she jealous of her, as of us?"

This mention of Anna reminded Phil of the Miss La Rue, who had
written to his aunt, and in whose identity with her friend, Queenie had been
so much interested.

"By the way," he said, "there's a dressmaker here somewhere, a Margery
La Rue, from Paris, whom Queenie thinks she knows, and over whom she
goes into rhapsodies. Do you know her, and is she the person who wrote to
Aunt Lydia with regard to her business?"

A warning "sh-sh" came from both the young ladies, with a nod toward
the slightly open door, indicating that the person inquired for was there. Then
the voices were lowered and the door was shut, and the wonder and interest
increased as Ethel and Grace heard all which Reinette had said of their
dressmaker, whose taste and skill they esteemed so highly that they had
suggested her going to Merrivale, but did not then know that she had written
to their aunt, for the girl was very reticent concerning herself and her
business, and only spoke when she was spoken to.

"It is very strange that she should know our cousin so well," Ethel said. "I
mean to sound her on the subject, and hear what she has to say," and as it
was time for Mrs. Rossiter to take her airing in her invalid chair the
conference broke up, and on pretext of seeing to her dress Ethel went into the
room where Margery now sat sewing as quietly and composedly as if she had
never heard of Queenie Hetherton.

CHAPTER XVI

MARGERY LA RUE

She was a tall, beautiful blonde, with reddish golden hair, and lustrous
blue eyes shaded with long curling eyelashes and heavy eyebrows, which
made them seem darker than they really were. The features were finely cut

and perfectly regular, and the whole face and figure were of that refined, delicate, type supposed to belong mostly to the upper classes in whose veins the purest of patrician blood is flowing. She said she was twenty-one, but she seemed older on account of that air of independence and self-reliance habitual to persons accustomed to care and think for themselves. She had come to America the April previous and stopped at Martha's Vineyard with her mother, who was short, and stout, and dark, but rather prepossessing in her manner, with more signs of culture and education than is usual with the ordinary type of French woman. In her girlhood she must have been very pretty and attractive, with her bright complexion and large black eyes, which had not yet lost their brilliancy, though there was in them a sad thoughtful expression, as if she were continually haunted with some bitter memory.

Margery had been introduced to the Misses Rossiter by a friend from Boston who had employed her in Paris, but occupied as they were with their mother and the gay world around them, they had hardly thought whether she were unusually pretty or not, until Phil electrified them with the news that she was the friend of their cousin, who said she was beautiful.

"I will look at her now for myself," Ethel thought, as she entered the room where Margery sat sewing, with a deep flush on her cheek and a bright, eager look in the blue eyes lifted respectfully but inquiringly to the face of her employer.

During the last ten minutes Margery's thoughts had been traveling back over the past to the early days of her childhood, when her home was on the upper floor of a high dwelling in the Rue St. Honore, where her days were passed in loneliness, except for the companionship of a cat and her playthings, of which she had a great abundance. Her parents were poor, and her mother was busy all day at a hair-dresser's, going out early and coming home late, while her father worked she did not know where, and sometimes it entered her little active brain that perhaps he did not work at all, for on the days when she went to walk, as she occasionally did, with the woman who had the floor below, and who looked after and was kind to the lonely little girl in the attic, she often saw him lounging and drinking at a third-class cafe which they passed when her friend, Lisette Vertueil, had clothes to carry to her patrons, for Lisette was a laundress, and washed for many of the upper class. Sometimes, too, Margery heard her mother reproach her father for his indolence and thriftlessness, and then there was always a quarrel, into which her name was dragged, though in what way she could not tell. She only knew that after these quarrels her mother was, if possible, kinder to her than before—and said her prayers oftener in a little closet off from the living room. Her father, too, was kind to her in his rough, off-hand way, but she did not love him as she did her pretty mother, and when at last he died, her grief for him though violent at first was very short-lived and soon forgotten, as the griefs of children are.

Among the patrons of Lisette Vertueil was Mr. Hetherton, the reputed millionaire, whose elegant carriage and horses sometimes stood on the St. Honore while his housekeeper talked to Lisette of the garments she had brought to be washed for her little mistress, Miss Reinette—garments dainty enough for a princess to wear, and which Lisette took great pride in showing to her neighbors, as a kind of advertisement for herself.

One morning when Margery was spending an hour or two with the laundress, helping to fold the clothes preparatory to being sent home, Lisette had shown her the lovely embroidered dresses, and told her of the little black-eyed girl who occasionally came there with her maid, and seemed so much like a playful kitten, in her quick, varying moods.

"Oh, how I wish I was rich like her, and had such lovely dresses, and how I'd like to see her! Do you think she'd come up to our room, if you asked her?" Margery said, and Lisette replied that she did not know but would try what she could do.

Accordingly, the next time Reinette came to the laundry, in her scarlet hood and cloak, trimmed with white ermine and lined with quilted satin, Lisette told her of the little girl who lived on the floor above, and who was alone all day, with only her doll and cat to talk to, and who would like to see her.

The cat and doll attracted Reinette quite as much as the little girl, and with the permission of her maid, she was soon climbing the steep, narrow, but perfectly clean stairway which lead to Numero . Mr. La Rue had been home to lunch that day, and Margery, though scarcely nine years old, was clearing away the remnants of their plain repast, and brushing up the hearth, when the door was pushed softly open, and a pair of bright, laughing eyes looking at her from under the scarlet and ermine, and a sweet bird-like voice said:

"Please, Margie, may I come in? I am Reinette Hetherton—Queenie, papa calls me, and I like that best. Lisette said you lived up here all alone with only the cat. Where is she? I don't see her."

Margery was standing before the fire, broom in hand, with a long-sleeved apron on, which came to her feet and concealed her dress entirely, while her hair was hidden in a cap she always wore at her work. At the sound of Reinette's voice she started suddenly, and dropping her broom, gazed open-mouthed at the vision of loveliness addressing her so familiarly. The mention of the cat struck a chord of sympathy, and she replied at once:

"She isn't she; she's he, and his name is Jacques. There he is, under father's chair," and the two girls bumped their heads together as they both stooped at the same moment to capture the cat, who was soon purring in Reinette's lap, as she sat before the fire, with Margery on the floor beside her, admiring her bright face and beautiful dress.

"I've nothing half so pretty as this," Margery said, despondingly, as she touched the scarlet cloak. "My best coat is plaid, and I only wear it on Sundays."

"Oh my!" Reinette replied, with a great air of self-importance, "I have three more. One is velvet, lined with rose color, which I wear to church, and when I drive with papa in the Bois. Do you ever go there, or on the Champs d'Elysees?"

"I walk there sometimes on Sundays with mother, but I was never in a real carriage in my life," was Margery's reply, and Reinette rejoined:

"Then you shall be. I'll make Celine—that's my maid—take us this very afternoon. There'll be a crowd, and it will be such fun! But why do you wear that big apron and cap?—they disfigure you so."

Margery blushed and explained that she wore them to keep her clothes clean; then, divesting herself of the obnoxious garments, she shook down her rippling hair, and stood before Reinette, who exclaimed:

"How sweet you are, with that bright sunny hair and those lovely blue eyes! I wish mine were blue. I hate 'em—the nasty old things, so black and so vixenish, Celine says, when I am mad, as I am more than half the time. But tell me, do you really live here all alone with the cat?"

"Oh no." And in a few words Margery explained her mode of life, which to the pampered child of luxury seemed desolate in the extreme.

"Oh, that's dreadful!" she said; "and I am so sorry for you! You ought to see our apartments at the Hotel Meurice. They are just lovely! and Chateau des Fleurs our country home, is prettier than the Tuilleries—the grounds are, I mean—and most as pretty as Versailles."

Margery listened with rapt attention to Reinette's description of her beautiful home, and then, as she said her father was an American, she suddenly interrupted her with:

"Can you speak English?"

"Of course I can," said Reinette. "I always speak it with papa, who wishes me to know it as well as French. Mamma was English, and died at Rome when I was born, and I go to an English school, and when papa is away, as he is a great deal, I board at the school, and have such fun, because they don't dare touch me, papa is so rich."

"Oh, if I could only speak English! Mother wishes me to learn it, and says I shall by and by, when she can afford it. She speaks it a little," Margery said; and, after a moment, Reinette replied:

"I'll tell you what I'm going to do. Papa has more money than he knows what to do with, and I mean to tease him till he gives me some for you, and you shall go to that school with me."

"Oh, I shall be so glad, and I'll tell mother to-night!" Margery exclaimed, feeling unbounded faith in Reinette's ability to accomplish anything.

Nor was her faith at all shaken when, a few minutes later Reinette's smart maid Celine came up the stairs after her little mistress, who horrified her with the announcement that she meant to take her new friend for a drive in the Champs d'Elysees.

"I shall; I will," she said, as Celine protested against it. "I like her, and she's never been in a carriage in her life, and she stays here all day with the cat, and washes the dishes, and she's going to ride with me, and I'll spit and bite, if you don't let her."

Celine knew better than to oppose the imperious child when in this mood, and besides, there was something very winning and attractive in the bright-haired, blue-eyed little girl, whose dress, though plain, was becoming and faultlessly clean. She certainly was no ordinary child, and that beautiful face would not disgrace the carriage. So Celine consented, and with joy beaming in every feature Margery brought out her plaid cloak and hood, which presented so striking a contrast to the rich scarlet one of Reinette that she drew back at once, and with quivering lip said to Celine:

"I must not go. I am so shabby beside her. She would be ashamed, and that I could not bear. Oh I wish I was she and she me, just for once—wish I could wear a scarlet cloak and see how it seemed."

"You shall!" Reinette cried, with great tears in her eyes. "You shall know how it seems. We'll make believe you are papa's little girl, and I am Margery," and before Celine could divine her intention, she was removing her dainty scarlet cloak and hood, and putting them on Margery, who was too much astonished to resist, but stood perfectly still, while Reinette wrapped the ermine, and satin, and merino around her, and put the plaid cloak and hood upon herself. "Oh, how lovely you are," she said, gazing admiringly at Margery, "and how ugly I am in this plaid. Nobody will know but what you are really Queenie Hetherton, and I am Margery," and she dragged the child down the stairs, and out into the street, where at a corner the Hetherton carriage was waiting.

Reinette gave Margery the seat of honor, and then sat down beside her, looking somewhat like a dowdy bit of humanity in the plain plaid cloak, with the large hood hiding her face. But she enjoyed it immensely, playing that she was Margery, and bade the coachman drive straight to the Champs d'Elysees.

It was a lovely winter afternoon, and all the Americans and English, with many of the Parisians, were out, making the Champs d'Elysees and the Bois beyond seem like a brilliant procession of gayly-dressed people and splendid equipages. And among the latter none was handsomer or more noticeable than the fine bays and elegant carriage of Mr. Hetherton, in which Margery sat making believe that she was Queenie, and enjoying it as much as if she had really been the daughter of the millionaire, instead of humble Margery La Rue, whose mother was a hair-dresser, and whose father was a nothing.

How happy she was, and how in after years that winter when she rode in the Champs d'Elysees in borrowed plumes, stood out before her as the bright spot in her life from which dated all the sunshine and all the sorrow, too, which ever came to her. Nor was it hard for her to go back to the humble lodgings—to give up the scarlet cloak and be Margery again, for she had so much now to think of; so much to tell her mother, whom she found waiting at the head of the narrow stairs, with a white, scared look on her face, and an eager, wistful expression in her eyes which seemed to look past Margery, down the dark stairway, as if in quest of some one else.

"Oh mother," Margery cried, "you are home early to-night, and I am so happy. Heaven can never be any brighter than this afternoon has been to me, playing that I was Mr. Hetherton's little girl, and wearing her scarlet cloak."

She was in the room by this time, taking off her own plaid coat, which she had put on in the court below, and talking so fast that she did not see the pallor on her mother's face, or how tightly her hands clinched on the back of a chair as she stood looking at her.

Mrs. La Rue had been dismissed by her employer earlier than usual, and finding Margery gone, had been to Lisette's room to make inquiries for her.

"Are you sick?" Lisette asked, as Mrs. La Rue dropped suddenly into a chair when she heard where Margery had gone and with whom. "You look as if you had seen a ghost."

Making an excuse that she was tired, and not feeling quite as well as usual, Mrs. La Rue soon went back to her own apartment, and kneeling down by the wooden chair before the fire, cried bitterly, as people only cry when some great wrong done in the past, or some terrible memory which they had thought dead and buried forever, rises suddenly from the grave and confronts them with all the olden horror.

"Reinette and Margery together, side by side!" she said. "Oh, if I could see it—see her; but no, I have promised, and I must keep my vow. I dare not break it."

For a long time she lay with her head upon the chair, and then remembering that Margery would soon be coming home and must not find her thus, she arose, and wiping the tear stains from her face, busied herself with preparations for the evening meal until she heard upon the stairs the bounding step which always sent a thrill of joy to her heart, and in a moment Margery came in with her blue eyes shining like stars and her cheeks glowing with excitement, as she talked of the wonderful things she had seen, and of Queenie, "who," she said, "acted as if I was just as good as she, and her father so rich, too, with such a lovely chateau, and she was like a picture, as she sat talking to me on this hard old chair," and she indicated the one by which her mother had knelt, and on which the tears were scarcely yet dried.

"This one? Did she sit on this one?" Mrs. La Rue asked, eagerly, laying her hand caressingly on the chair where Queenie Hetherton had sat and talked to Margery.

"And what is the very best of all," Margery continued, "she goes to an English school, and when I told her how much I wanted to learn English, she said she'd tease her father for the money to pay for me, too; and she knew she'd get it, for he gives her every thing she wants. Oh, I do hope he will. I mean to ask God to-night to make him. Lisette says I must ask for what I want, and Jesus will hear and answer. Do you think he will? Does He answer you?"

"Oh, Margery, Margery, I never pray. I am too wicked, too bad. God would not hear me, but he will you: so pray, child, pray," Mrs. La Rue replied, and seizing the little girl she hugged her passionately, and raining kisses upon her forehead and lips, released her as suddenly, and turned quickly away to hide her anguish from her.

CHAPTER XVII

QUEENIE AND MARGERY

That evening Mr. Hetherton sat in his handsome salon at the Hotel Meurice, smoking his after-dinner cigar, and occasionally reading a page or two in the book on the table beside him. He was a very handsome man in his middle age—handsomer even than he had been in his youth, for there was about him now a style and elegance of manner which attracted attention from every one. And yet he was not popular, and had no intimate friends. He was too reserved and uncommunicative for that, and people called him proud, and haughty, and misanthropical. That he was not happy was evident from the shadow always on his face—the shadow it would seem of remorse, as if some haunting memory were ever present with him, marring every joy. Even Reinette, whom he idolized, had no power to chase away that brooding shadow; on the contrary, a close observer would have said that it was darkest when she caressed him most, and when her manner was most bewitching. Sometimes when she climbed into his lap, and, winding her arms around his neck, laid her soft, warm cheek against his, and told him he was the best and dearest father in the world, and asked him of her mother who died, he would spring up suddenly, and pushing her from him, exclaim, as he walked rapidly up and down the room:

"Child, you don't know what you are saying. I am not good. I am very far from being good, but she was—my Margaret. Oh, Queenie, be like her if you can!"

On these occasions Queenie would go away into a corner, and with her bright, curious eyes watch him till the mood was over, and then stealing up to him again would nestle closer to him and half-timidly stroke his forehead and hair with her little hand and tell him no matter how bad he was she loved him just the same and should forever and ever. Queenie was his idol, the sun of his existence, and he lavished upon her all the love of which a strong nature is capable. She could do anything with him, and take any liberty, and as he sat alone in his room he was not greatly surprised when the door opened softly and a pair of roguish black eyes looked in upon him for an instant—then a little white-robed figure in its night toilet crossed the floor swiftly, and springing into his lap began to pat his face, and kiss his lips, and write words upon his forehead for him to guess. This was one of the child's favorite pastimes since she had learned to write, and she had great fun with her father making him guess the words she traced upon his brow. But he could not do it now until she helped him to the first three letters, when he made out the name of Margery, and felt himself grow suddenly faint and cold, for that was the pet name he had sometimes given his wife in the early days of their acquaintance and married life. But how did Queenie know it? How came she by that name which burned into his forehead like letters of fire and carried him back to the meadows, and hills, and shadowy woods of Merrivale, where a blue-eyed, golden-haired girl had walked with him hand in hand, and whom he had called Margery?

"Guess now what is her name and who she is?" Queenie said, holding his face between her hands, and looking straight into his eyes.

"Margery is the name," he said, and his voice trembled a little. "But who is she?"

And then the story came out of the little girl who lived all day with the cat on the top floor of a tenement house, in Rue St. Honore, and who wanted so badly to go to school, but could not because her mother was poor and had no money to send her.

"But you have," Queenie continued; "you have more than you know what to do with, people say, and I want you to give me some for her, because I like her—I don't know why exactly, only I do, and did the first minute I saw her. I felt as if I wanted to hug her hard—as if she belonged to me; and you'll do it, papa, I know you will! You'll send little Margery La Rue to the same school with me."

Mr. Hetherton did not reply to this, but asked numerous questions concerning his daughter's acquaintance with Margery La Rue, whose mother was a hair-dresser, and expressed his displeasure with Celine for having taken her to such places.

"You are never to go there again, under any circumstances," he said, and Reinette replied, promptly:

"Yes, I shall. I'll run away every day and go there, and to worse places, too. I will go the Jardin, if you don't give me the money for Margery, but if you do I will promise never to go there again—only Celine shall go for her to ride with me. I am bound to do that!"

And so she gained her point, and the next day Celine was sent to Lisette to make inquiries concerning Mrs. La Rue. As these proved satisfactory, arrangements were made with the principal of the English school to receive little Margery as a day pupil at half pay, in consideration of her performing some menial service in the school-room by way of dusting the desks and putting the books in order after school was over.

Queenie was delighted, and from the day when Margery became a pupil in the English school, she was her avowed champion, and stood by her always, and fought for her sometimes when a few of the French girls sneered at her position as duster of their books.

Naturally quick to learn, and easier to retain than Queenie, as Margery always called her, she soon outstripped her in all their studies, and was of great service in helping her to master her lessons, and acquit herself with a tolerable degree of credit.

But for Margery, who would go patiently over the lesson time after time with her indolent friend, Queenie would often have been in disgrace, for she was not particularly fond of books, and lacked the application necessary to a thorough scholar. Once, when she had committed a grave misdemeanor which had been strictly forbidden on pain of heavy punishment, Margery was suspected and found guilty, and though she knew Queenie to be the culprit, she did not speak, but stood up bravely to receive the chastisement which was to be administered in the presence of the whole school, and was to be unusually severe as a warning to others. Margery was very pale as she took her place upon the platform, and held out her beautiful white arm and hand to the master, and her blue eyes glanced just once wistfully and pleadingly toward the corner where Queenie sat, her own eyes shut, and her fists clenched tightly together until the first blow fell upon the innocent Margery. Then swift as lightning she went to the rescue, and before the astounded master knew what she was doing she had wrested the ruler from him, and hurling it across the room sprang into a chair, and had him by the collar, and even by the hair, while she cried out:

"You vile, nasty man, don't you touch Margery again. If you do I will pull every hair out of your head. You might have known she didn't do it. It was I, and I am nastier and viler than you, for I kept still just because I was afraid to be hurt, and let her bear it for me. I am the guilty one. I did it, and she knew it and never told. Beat me to a pumice if you want to. I deserve it:" and jumping from the chair and crossing the floor, Queenie picked up the ruler, and giving it to the master, held out her little fat hand for the punishment she merited. But by this time the entire school had become demoralized, as it were, and the pupils thronged around their bewildered teacher, begging him to spare Queenie, who became almost as much a heroine as Margery, because that, notwithstanding her cowardice at the first, she had at the last shown so much genuine moral courage and nobleness.

Queenie wrote the whole transaction to her father, who was in Norway, and asked that as a recompense to Margery she be invited to spend the summer vacation at Chateau des Fleurs, where Queenie was going with Celine. To this Mr. Hetherton consented, and all the long, bright days of summer Margery was at Chateau des Fleurs, which seemed to her like Paradise. Nothing could exceed Queenie's devotion to her from that time onward, and when at eighteen she left school, Queenie stood by her still, and found her a situation as governess in an English family who lived in Geneva, and when, after a few months, Margery said she did not like the life of a governess, as it deprived her of all her independence of action, and made her a mere block, subjecting her to insults from the sons of the house and guests of the family, Reinette, who knew her perfect taste in everything pertaining to a lady's toilet, and the skill with which she fitted her own dresses, suggested that she should try dressmaking as an experiment, without the formality of regularly learning the trade, which would take so much valuable time. So Margery set up as an amateur in the pleasant apartments in Rue de la Paix, where Mrs. La Rue had lived since the death of her husband, which occurred during Margery's second year in school.

It would seem that Mr. La Rue, with his indolent habits, had been a great draft upon his wife's earnings, for, after he died, there was a perceptible change in her manner of living. Money was more plenty, and everything was on a larger, freer scale, so that Margery's home was a very comfortable one, especially after her wonderful skill in fitting, and perfect taste in trimming, and, more than all, the patronage of Miss Hetherton, began to attract people to her rooms. Now, as in her school days, Queenie was her good angel, and brought her more work, and paid her more money than any four of her other customers.

Once, and only once, did Reinette meet Mrs. La Rue, who seemed rather to avoid than to seek her, and that was on an occasion when she came in from the country unexpectedly, and found Margery busy with a lady in the fitting-room.

"Tell her I am Miss Hetherton, and that I will wait," Reinette said to the small, dark woman whom she found in the reception-room, and whom she mistook for an upper servant or housekeeper.

"Miss Hetherton! Margery's Reinette!" the woman exclaimed, turning quickly and coming close to the young lady, whose pride rebelled at once at this familiarity, and who assumed her haughtiest, most freezing manner, as she replied:

"Yes, I am Miss Hetherton. Tell your mistress I am here, at once."

All the blood rushed to Mrs. La Rue's face, and her voice shook as she said:

"She is my daughter, and I am Mrs. La Rue. I beg your pardon if I seemed rude, but you have been so kind to Margery, and I have so wished to see you."

"Deliver my message first," Reinette, said, with the air of a princess, for the woman's manner displeased her and she could see no reason why she should stand there staring so fixedly at her with that strange look in her glittering eyes as of one insane.

At this command Mrs. La Rue turned to leave the room, but ere she went she laid her hand on Reinette's tenderly, caressingly, as we touch the hands of those we love, and said:

"Excuse me, but I must touch you once, must thank you." So saying she left the room and did not return, nor did Reinette ever see her again, except on one occasion when she was driving with Margery in the Bois de Boulogne, and passed her, sitting upon a bench beneath a shade tree. The recognition was mutual, but Reinette did not return her slight nod, or pretend to see her at all.

This was in October, and not long afterwards Margery startled Reinette by telling her that she was going for a winter to Nice, and possibly to Rome.

"Mother has not seemed herself for several weeks," she said, "and I think she needs a change of air; besides, I am most anxious to see Italy."

And so, two weeks later, the friends bade each other good-by, and after one or two letters had passed between them, the correspondence suddenly closed on Margery's side, and the two friends knew nothing more of each other's whereabouts, until each was startled to hear that the other was in America.

Such was in part the history of Margery up to the day when Miss Ethel Rossiter entered the room where she was sewing, and after moving about a little and inspecting the trimming of her dress, began hesitatingly:

"By the way, Miss La Rue, my brother has been telling us about our cousin, Miss Reinette Hetherton, who has just come from Europe, and who says she knew a Margery La Rue in Paris. Is it possible she means you?"

"Yes, oh, yes!" and Margery's face was all aglow with excitement as she looked quickly up. "Yes, Miss Rossiter; you must excuse me, but the door was open, and I could not help hearing some things your brother said—he talked so loud; and I know it is my Queenie. I always called her that because she bade me do so. She is the dearest friend I ever had, and I have loved her since that wintry afternoon when she brought so much sunshine into my life—when she came into our humble home, in her scarlet and rich ermine, and sat down on the hard old chair, and acted as if I were her equal. And she has been my good angel ever since. She persuaded her father to send me to the English school where she was a pupil. She got me a situation as governess, and when I rebelled against the confinement and the degradation—she persuaded me to take up dressmaking, for which I had a talent, and encouraged and stood by me, and brought me more work than any ten of my other customers. Oh, I would die for Queenie Hetherton!"

Margery had talked rapidly, and her blue eyes were almost black in her eagerness and excitement, while Ethel listened to her intently, and thought how beautiful she was, and wondered, too, when or where she had seen a face like the face of this fair French girl, whose accent was so pretty, and whose manners were so perfect.

"And she is your cousin," Margery said: "that is strange, for I always understood that her mother was an English woman."

Ethel colored a little, and replied:

"Yes, her mother and mine were sisters. Mr. Hetherton's old home was in Merrivale. Did you ever see him?"

"Once, on horseback, in the Bois. I was driving with his daughter, and she made him stop and speak to us. He was very fine-looking and gentlemanly, but I thought him proud and reserved, and I believe he had that name in Paris."

Mrs. Rossiter had returned by this time, and entering the room, joined in the conversation, asking many questions of the Hethertons and their life in Paris and at Chateau des Fleurs, which Margery described as a perfect palace of beauty and art.

"Is Reinette pretty?" Grace asked, and Margery replied:

"You might not think her so when she is quiet and her features in repose, but when she is excited and animated, she sparkles, and glows, and flashes, and shines, as if there were a blaze of light encircling her, and then she is more beautiful than anything I ever looked upon, and she takes your breath away with her brilliancy and brightness."

"You must have heard her speak often of her mother, my sister," Mrs. Rossiter said, and Margery replied.

"Yes, many times; and at Chateau des Fleurs there was a lovely portrait of Mrs. Hetherton, taken in creamy white satin, with pearls on her neck and in her wavy hair. She must have been beautiful. There is a resemblance, I see, between you all and that portrait."

"Do you know where that portrait is now?" Mrs. Rossiter asked; and Margery replied by telling her that, nearly six years before, Chateau des Fleurs was burned, with all there was in it, and she believed there was now no portrait of Mrs. Hetherton in the family.

It seemed so strange to the Rossiters that this foreigner should know so much more than themselves of the Hethertons, and for a long time they continued to ply her with questions concerning the new cousin whom they had never seen.

After a time Phil came sauntering into the room in his usual indolent, easy manner, and was presented to Margery, whose blue eyes scanned him curiously and questioningly. She had heard enough of his conversation to guess that he was already far gone in love with Queenie, and she was anxious to know what manner of man he was. Something in his manner and the expression of his face fascinated her strangely, while he, in turn, was equally drawn toward her; and when at last her work was done and she started for home, he exclaimed, under his breath, as he watched her going down the street:

"By Jove, Ethel, if I had never seen Queenie, I should say this dressmaker of yours was the loveliest woman I ever saw. Look at that figure, and the way she carries her head. I don't wonder Queenie raves over her; such eyes, and hair, and complexion I never saw."

Meanwhile Margery was walking rapidly toward the cottage where she and her mother had rooms.

"Oh, mother," she began, as she took off her hat and scarf and began to arrange her hair before the little mirror, "I have such news to-day! Queenie—Miss Hetherton—is here!"

"Here! Reinette Hetherton here! and her father!" Mrs. La Rue exclaimed, springing to her feet as suddenly as if a bullet had pierced her.

But Margery's back was toward her, and she did not see how agitated she was, or how deathly white she grew at the reply.

"Her father died on shipboard just as they reached New York, and Queenie is all alone in Merrivale."

"Mr. Hetherton dead!" Mrs. La Rue repeated, as she dropped back into her chair, while the hot blood surged for a moment to her face and then left it pallid and gray as the face of a corpse.

Something unnatural in the tone of her voice attracted Margery, who turned to look at her.

"Why, mother, what is it? Are you sick?" she cried, crossing swiftly to her and passing her arm around her as she leaned back heavily in the chair.

"I have been very dizzy-like all the morning. It is nothing: it will soon pass off," Mrs. La Rue replied.

But when Margery insisted that she should lie down and be quiet, she did not refuse, but suffered her daughter to lead her to the lounge and bring her the hartshorn and camphor.

"Cover me up, Margery," she said, as a shiver like an ague chill ran through her veins. "I'm so cold. There, that will do; and now sit down beside me, and let me hold your hand while you tell me of your friend and her father, and how he died, and who told you. It will interest me, may be, and make me forget my bad feelings."

So Margery sat down beside her, and took the hot hand which held hers with a grasp which was sometimes actually painful as the narrative proceeded, and Margery told all she had heard from the Rossiters.

"And to think, her mother was an American, and that the Rossiters are her cousins, and her father's old home is Merrivale, where I thought of going! Oh, if I could only go there now!" Margery said; but her mother did not express surprise at anything.

On the contrary, a more suspicious person than Margery would have said that the story was not new to her, for she occasionally asked some question which showed some knowledge of Queenie's antecedents. But this Margery did not observe. She only thought her mother a little strange and sick, and was glad when her closed eyes and perfectly motionless figure indicated that she was sleeping.

Covering her a little more closely and dropping the shade so that the light should not disturb her, she stole softly out, leaving the wretched woman alone with herself. She was not asleep, and clenching her hands together so that the nails left their impress in her flesh, she whispered:

"Dead! Frederick Hetherton dead! and does that release me from my vow? Do I wish to be released? No, oh, no, a thousand times no! And yet when she was talking to me I felt as if I must scream it out. Oh, Margery; oh, my daughter, my daughter! Dead! And will his face haunt me as hers has—the sweet face of her who trusted me so? There surely is a hell, and I have been in it this many a year! Margery! Margery!"

"Did you call me, mother? I thought I heard my name," Margery said, opening the door and looking into the room.

"No, no; go away. You waken me when I want to sleep," Mrs. La Rue said almost angrily, for the sight of that beautiful young face, and the sound of that voice nearly made her mad; so Margery went away again, and left her mother alone to fight the demon of remorse, which the news of Frederick Hetherton's death had aroused within her.

CHAPTER XVIII

OLD LETTERS

Reinette was up and at her window on the morning when Phil left Merrivale, and had his seat been on the opposite side of the car from what it was, and had his powers of vision been long enough, and strong enough, he might have seen a pair of little white plump hands waving kisses and goodbyes to him as the train shot under the bridge, round the curve, and off into the swamps and plains of East Merrivale.

"I shall miss him so much," Reinette thought. "He is just the nicest kind of a boy cousin a girl ever had. We can go all lengths without the slightest danger of falling in love, for that would be impossible. Falling in love means getting married, and I have been educated too much like a Roman Catholic ever to marry my cousin. I would as soon marry my brother if I had one. I think it wicked, disgusting! So, Mr. Phil, I am going to have just the best time flirting with you that ever a girl had. But what shall I do while you are gone? Mr. Beresford is nice, but I can't flirt with him. He is too old and dignified, and has such a way of looking you down."

This mental allusion to Mr. Beresford reminded Reinette that he was to come that day for any papers of her father's which she had in her possession, and that she must look them over first. Ringing for Pierre, she bade him bring her the small black trunk or box in which her father's private papers were kept. Pierre obeyed, and was about leaving the room when Reinette bade him bring a lighted lamp and set it upon the hearth of the open fire-place.

"I may wish to burn some of them," she said.

The lamp was brought and lighted, and then Queenie began her task, selecting first all the legal-looking documents which she knew must pertain strictly to her father's business. A few of these were in English and related to affairs in America, but the most were in French, and pertained to matters in France and Switzerland, where her father held property. These Queenie knew Mr. Beresford could not decipher without her help, and so she went carefully over each document, finding nothing objectionable—nothing which a stranger might not see—nothing mysterious to her, though one paper might seem so to others. It was dated about twenty years before, and was evidently a copy of what was intended as an order setting apart a certain amount of money, the interest to be paid semi-annually to one Christine Bodine in return for services rendered: the principal was placed in the hands of Messrs. Polignie, with instructions to pay the interest as therein provided to the party named, who, in case of Mr. Hetherton's death, was to receive the whole unless orders to the contrary should be previously given. This paper Reinette read two or three times, wondering what were the services for which her old nurse received this annuity, and thinking, too, that here was a chance to find her. The money must have been paid, if she were living, and through the Messrs. Polignie she could trace her and bring her to America.

"I ought to have some such person living with me, I suppose," she said, "and I hate a maid always in my room and in my way."

The business papers disposed of and laid away for Mr. Beresford's inspection, Queenie turned next to the letters, of which there were not very many. Some from Mr. Beresford on business—one from her father's mother, Mrs. General Hetherton, written to him when he was at Harvard, and showing that the writer was a lady in every thought and feeling, and one from herself, written to her father when he was in Algiers, and she only ten years old. It was a perfect child's letter, full of details of life at the English school, and of Margery, who was with her there.

"Queenie's first letter to me," was written on the label, and the worn paper showed that it had been often read by the fond, proud father.

Over this Reinette's tears fell in torrents, for it told how much she had been loved, by the man whose hand she seemed to touch as she sorted the letters he had held so often.

Putting aside the envelope which bore her childish superscription, she took up next a packet, which, to her aristocratic instincts, seemed out of place with those other papers, in which there lingered still a faint odor of the costly perfume her father always used.

There were three letters inclosed in one large envelope, on which was written "Papers pertaining to the Avignon business." Queenie knew her father had once owned some houses in Avignon, and taking first the largest letter in the package, she studied it carefully, noting that the paper was cheap, the handwriting cramped, and Chateau des Fleurs, to which it was directed, spelled wrong. "This is not business—it is a letter which by mistake papa must have put in the wrong place, for it looks coarse, it feels coarse, and it smells coarse," Queenie said, elevating her little nose as she caught a whiff of something very different from the delicate perfumery pervading the other papers. "Who sent this to papa, and what is it about?" were the questions which passed rapidly through her mind, as she held the worn, soiled missive between her thumb and fingers, and inspected it curiously.

Once something prompted her to put it away from her sight, and never seek to know its contents. But woman's curiosity overcame every scruple, and she at last drew the letter itself from the envelope. It was quite a large sheet, such as Reinette knew ladies seldom used, and the four pages were closely written over, while there seemed to be something inside which added to its bulk.

Turning first to the last page, Queenie glanced at the signature, and saw the two words "From Tina," but saw no more, for the something inside, which, slipping down, dropped upon her hand, around which it coiled like a living thing, with a grasp of recognition. It was a tress of long, blue-black hair, with just a tendency to wave perceptible all through it.

Shaking it off as if it had been a snake, Queenie's cheek paled a moment with a sensation she could not define, and then crimsoned with shame and resentment; resentment for the dead mother, who, she felt, had in some way been wronged, and shame for the dead father to whom some other woman had dared to write, and send a lock of hair.

"Who is this Tina?" she said, with a hot gleam of anger in her black eyes, "and how dare she send this to my father—the bold, bad creature! I hate her, with her vile black hair" and she ground her little high heel upon the unconscious tress of hair, as if it had been Tina herself upon whom she was trampling. "I'll burn it," she said at last, "but I'll never touch it again."

And reaching for the tongs which stood upon the hearth, she took up the offending hair and held it in the lamp, watching it with a grim feeling of satisfaction, and yet with a sense of pain, as it hissed, and reddened, and charred in the flame, and writhed and twisted as if it had been something human from which the life was going out.

Through the open window a breath of the sweet summer air came stealing in, and catching up a bit of the burnt, crisped hair carried it to Queenie's white morning wrapper, where it clung tenaciously until she shook it off as if it had been pollution.

"Tina!" she exclaimed again. "Who I'd like to know is Tina?" Then remembering the surest way to find out who she was, was to read the letter, she took it up again, but hesitated a moment as if held back by some unseen influence; hesitated as we sometimes hesitate when standing on the threshold of some great crisis or danger in our lives. "If it is bad," she said, "I do not wish to think ill of him. Oh, father, it isn't bad: it must not be bad;" and the hot tears came fast, as the daughter who had believed her father so pure and good turned at last to the first page to see what was written there.

It was dated at Marseilles twenty years before, and began:

"Dear Mr. Hetherton, are you wondering why you do not hear from your little Tina?—"

"Miss Hetherton, your grandmother is here asking for you," came from the door outside at which Pierre stood knocking, and starting, as if caught in some guilty act, Reinette put the letter back in its envelope, and went down to meet her grandmother, who had come over for what she called a "real sit down visit," and brought her work with her.

There was nothing now left for Reinette but to leave the letters and devote herself to her guest, who staid to lunch, so that it was not until afternoon that Queenie found an opportunity to resume the work of the morning. Meanwhile her thoughts had been busy, and over and over again she had repeated to herself the words, "Your little Tina," until they had assumed for her a new and entirely different meaning from the one she had given them in the first moment of her discovery. There might be—nay, there was no shame attaching to them—no shame in that blue-black tress of hair which she could feel curling around her fingers still, and see as it hissed and writhed in the flame. The letter was written after her mother's death. Her father was human—was like other men—and his fancy had been caught by some dark-haired girl of the lower class who called herself his "Little Tina;" she had undoubtedly bewitched him for a time, so that he might have thought to make her his wife. His first marriage was what they called a mesalliance; and here Queenie felt her cheeks flush hotly as if a wrong was done to her mother, but she meant none; she was trying to defend her father; to save his memory from any evil doing. If he stooped once, he might again, and the last time Tina was the object. He had meant honorably by her always, and tiring of her after a little had broken with her, as was often done by the best of men. Of all this Queenie thought as she talked with her grandmother, answering her numberless questions of her life in France, and her plans for the future; and by the time the good lady was gone and she free to go back to her work, she had changed her mind with regard to Tina's letters, and a strange feeling of pity for the unknown girl had taken possession of her, making her shrink from reading her words of love, if they were innocent and pure, as she fain would believe them to be for the sake of her dead father; and if they were not innocent and pure, "I do not wish to know it. I should hate him—hate him always in his grave!" she said, as she picked up the letter and resolutely put it back in the envelope with the other two.

Once she thought to burn them, as she had the hair and thus put temptation away forever; but as often as she held them toward the lamp she had lighted again, as often something checked her, until a kind of superstitious conviction took possession of her that she must not burn those letters written by "Little Tina."

"But I will never, never read them," she said; and dropping on her knees, with the package held tightly in her hand, she registered a vow, that so long as she lived she would not seek to know what the letters contained unless circumstances should arise which would make the reading of them a necessity.

This last condition came to her mind she hardly knew how or why, for she had no idea that any circumstances could arise which would make the reading of the letters necessary.

Searching through her trunks and drawers, she found four paper boxes of different sizes, and putting the envelope in the smallest of them, placed that in the next larger size, and so on, writing upon the cover of the last one. "To be burned without opening in case of my death." Then tying the lid securely with a strong cord, she mounted upon a chair, and placed the package upon the highest shelf of the closet, where neither she nor any one could see it.

"There, little black-haired Tina," she said, as she came down from the chair and out into her chamber, "your secret, if you had one with my father, is safe—not for your sake, though, you blue-black-haired jade!" and Queenie set her foot down viciously: "not for your sake, but for father's, who might have been silly enough to be caught by your pretty face, and to be flattered by you, for, of course, you ran after him, and widowers are fools, I've heard say."

Having thus settled the unknown Tina, and dismissed her from her mind for the time being at least, Queenie went back to the remaining package in the box—the one tied with a blue ribbon, and labeled "Margaret's letters."

"Mother's," she said, softly, with a quick, gasping breath; "and now I shall know something of her at last;" and she kissed tenderly the time-worn envelope which held her mother's letters.

There were not many of them, and they had been written at long intervals, and only in answer to the husband's, it would seem, for she complained in one that he waited so long before replying to her. Queenie felt no compunctions in reading these; they were something which belonged to her and she went through them rapidly, with burning cheeks, and eyes so full of tears at times that she could scarcely see the delicate handwriting, so different from that other, the blue-black haired Tina's as she mentally designated her. And as Queenie read, there came over her a feeling of resentment and anger toward the dead father, who, she felt sure, had often grieved and neglected the young wife, who, though she made no complaint, wrote so sadly and dejectedly, and begged him to come home, and not stay so long in those far-off lands, with people whom Margaret evidently did not like.

"Dear Frederick," she wrote from Rome, "please come to me; I am so lonely without you, and the days are so long, with only Christine for company, for I seldom go out except to drive on the Pincian or Campagna, and so see scarcely see any one. Christine is a great comfort to me, and anticipates my wishes almost before I know that I have them myself. She is as faithful and tender as if she were my mother, instead of maid, and if I should die you must always be kind to her for what she has been to me. But oh, I do so long for you, and I think I could make you very happy. You used to love me in dear old Merrivale. How often I dream of home and the shadowy woods by the pond where we used to walk together, and the moonlight sails on the river when we rowed in among the white lilies, and you said I was lovelier and sweeter than they. You loved me then; do you love me now as well? I have sometimes feared you did not; feared something had come between us which was weaning you from me. Don't let it, Frederick; put it away from you, whatever it may be, and let me be your Queen, your Daisy, your Margery again; for I do love you, my husband, more than you can guess, and I want your love now when I am so sick, and tired, and lonely. Christine is waiting to post this for me, and so I must close with a kiss right there where I make the star (*.) Put your lips there, Frederick, where mine have been and then we shall have kissed each other. Truly, lovingly, and longingly, your tired, sick Margery."

"Margery? That was, then her pet name, the name I like the best in all the world, because of my Margery," Queenie cried, as her tears fell fast upon the letter, which seemed to her like a voice from the dead. "Poor mother, you were not so very happy, were you? Why did you die? If I only had you now, how I would love and pet you," she said, as she passionately kissed the place which her mother's lips had touched, and her father's, too, she hoped, for how could he resist that touching appeal? He must have loved the writer of that letter, and yet there was a cloud between the husband and wife which cast its shadow over their child and made her weep bitterly as she wondered what it was which had crept in between her father and his tired, sick Margery.

"Was it the blue-black haired Tina;" she said, as she clenched her fists together, and then beat the air with them, as she would have beaten the blue-black-haired Tina had she been there with her. "Poor mother," she said again, "so tired and sick, with no one to care for her but Christine, who was so good to her. I know now why father settled that money on her; it was because she was so kind and faithful to mother, who knows now, perhaps, that father did love her more than she thought; for he did, I am sure he did; and he loved me, too, and I believed him so noble and true. Oh, father, father, forgive me, but I have lost something. I cannot put it in words—I don't know what I mean," and stooping over the package which held her mother's letters, Reinette cried out loud, with a bitter sense of something lost from her father's memory which had been very sweet to her. "Oh, how much has happened since I came to America, and how long it seems, and how old I feel, and there is no one to tell it to—no one to talk with about it."

Just then there was a second knock at the door, and Pierre announced Mr. Beresford waiting in the library. He was a prompt, business man, and had come for the papers, Reinette knew, and, bathing her flushed cheeks, and crumpling her wavy hair more than it was already crumpled, she went down to meet him, taking the papers with her, and trying to seem natural and gay, as if no tress of blue-black hair had been burned in her room, no letters from Tina were hidden away in her closet, and no sting when she thought of her father was hurting her cruelly.

Queenie was a perfect little actress, and her face was bright with smiles as she entered the room and greeted Mr. Beresford, who, being a close observer, saw that something had been agitating her, and guessed that it was the examining of her father's papers, which naturally would bring back her sorrow so freshly. There was a great pity in his heart for this lonely girl, and his manner was very sympathetic and gentle as he took the box from her and said:

"I am afraid this has been too much for you."

Instantly the great tears gathered in her eyes, but did not fall, and only made her all the sweeter and prettier, as she sat down beside him and said:

"I must read some of them over for you, for I don't believe you understand French very well, do you?"

"Not at all," he replied, glad to be thought ignorant of even the monosyllable oui, if by this means he could sit close to her and watch her dimpled hands sorting out the papers, and hear her silvery, bird-like voice, with its soft accent, translating what was written in them into English.

Especial pains did she take to make him understand about the money paid to Christine Bodine, and why it was paid.

"She was so kind to mother, who requested him to care for her. I've been reading all about it in mother's letters to him," she said, without lifting her eyes to his face, for in spite of herself and her avowed confidence in her father's honor, there was in her heart a feeling of degradation when she remembered Tina, as if the shame, if shame there were, was in some way attaching to her, and robbing her of some of her self-respect.

But Mr. Beresford had no suspicion of Tina, and only thought how lovely Queenie was and what a remarkable talent for understanding business she developed, as they went over the papers together and formed a pretty fair estimate of the value of the Hetherton estate.

"Why there is over half a million, if all this is good," she said, looking up at him with pleased surprise. "And I am so glad, for I like a great deal of money. I have always had it, and should not know what to do without it. I want a great deal for myself, and more for other people. I am going to give grandma some, because—well," and Queenie hesitated a little, "because I was mean to her at the station when she claimed me; and I'm going to give some to Aunt Lydia, so she can afford to sell out her business which is so obnoxious to Anna, and if that girl down at the Vineyard proves to be my Margery, I shall give her money to buy Aunt Lydia out, and then I shall have her all to myself, and you'll be falling in love with her—remember that! You'll be in love with Margery La Rue the second time you see her!"

"Margery La Rue! Who is she?" Mr. Beresford asked; and then came the story of Margery, mixed with so extravagant praises of the young lady that Mr. Beresford began to feel an interest in her, although the idea of falling in love with her was simply preposterous.

Sensible as he was, Mr. Beresford had a great deal of foolish pride, and would have scouted the thought of a dressmaker ever becoming Mrs. Arthur Beresford. That lady was to be more like this dark-eyed fairy beside him, who chattered on, telling him what she meant to do with her half million, which it seemed was literally burning her fingers. She would give some to everybody who was poor and needed it, some to all the missionaries and churches, and even some to him, if he was ever straitened and wanted it.

Mr. Beresford smiled, and thanked her, and said he would remember her offer; and then she added:

"I will give some to Phil now, if he wants it, to carry on his business. Does it take much money, Mr. Beresford? What is his business—his profession? I do not think I know."

"I don't think he has any," Mr. Beresford replied; and Reinette exclaimed:

"No business! no profession! That's bad! Every young man ought to do something, father used to say. Pray, what does Phil do! How does he pass his time?"

"By making himself generally useful and agreeable," Mr. Beresford said, and in his voice there was a tinge of irony, which Queenie detected at once, and instantly flamed up in defense of her cousin.

"Of course he makes himself useful and agreeable—more agreeable than any person I ever saw. I have only known him a day or two, and yet I like him better than anybody in the world except Margery."

"Phil ought to feel complimented with your opinion which, I assure you, is well merited," Mr. Beresford said, while a horrid feeling of jealousy took possession of him.

Why would girls always prefer an indolent, easy-going, good-for-nothing chap like Phil Rossiter, to an active, energetic, throughgoing man like himself? Not that he had heretofore been troubled by what the girls preferred, for he cared nothing for them in the abstract; but this restless, sparkling French girl was different, and he felt every nerve in his body thrill with a strange feeling of ecstasy when at parting she laid her, soft warm hand on his, and looking up at him with her bright, earnest eyes, said to him:

"Now you will write at once to Messrs. Polignie and inquire about Christine; and I shall write, too; for I must find her and bring her here to live with me. Grandma says I ought to have somebody—some middle-aged, respectable woman, as a kind of guardian—but, ugh! I hate guardians!"

"Oh, I hope not!" Mr. Beresford said, laughingly, managing to retain the hand laid in his so naturally. "In one sense I am your guardian, and I hope you don't hate me."

"Certainly not," Reinette said. "I think you are very nice. You are father's friend, and he said I must like you, and tell you everything, and I do like you ever so much, though not the way I do Phil. I like him because he's so good and funny, and my cousin, and—well, because he is Phil."

"Happy Phil! I wish I was good and funny, and your cousin!" Mr. Beresford said, as he bade her good-afternoon and rode away.

"I hope he is not falling in love with me, for that would be dreadful. I wouldn't marry him any sooner than I would Phil. He is too old, and dignified, and poky," Reinette thought, as she watched him going down the hill, while he was mentally registering a vow to enter the lists and compete with the young man who was so much liked because he was Phil.

CHAPTER XIX

THE LITTLE LADY OF HETHERTON

Within a week after Phil's departure the whole town was full of her, and rumor said she was running a wild career with no one to advise or check her except Mr. Beresford, who seemed as crazy as herself. Everybody thought her wonderfully bright, and fresh, and pretty, but her ways astonished the sober people of Merrivale, who, nevertheless, were greatly interested and amused with watching her as she developed phase after phase of her variable nature— visiting Mr. Beresford at his office two or three times a day, ostensibly to translate foreign letters and papers for him, but really, it was said by the gossips, to see the man himself; galloping off miles and miles into the country on her spirited horse, with the little old Frenchman in attendance; worrying Mrs. Jerry by having chocolate in her room in the morning, breakfasting at twelve, dining at six, with as much ceremony as if a dozen people were seated at the table instead of one lone girl, who sometimes never touched the dishes prepared with so much care—dining, too, in all sorts of places as the fancy took her; on the north piazza, and on the south piazza; giving her money away by the hundreds to the Fergusons, and by the tens, and fives, and ones to anybody asking for it; sinking a little fortune on the grounds at Hetherton Place, which she was entirely metamorphosing, with fifteen or twenty men at work there all the time, while she superintended them, and gave them lemonade or root beer two or three times a day, as an incentive to swifter labor.

Such was the state of affairs when Phil, improving the very first opportunity for leave of absence, came back to Merrivale. It was A.M. when he reached the station, and exactly half-past ten to a minute when he found himself at Hetherton Place, his hand locked in that of Queenie, who in her big garden hat, with trowel, and pruning-knife, led him all over the grounds, where the fifteen men were at work, pointing out her improvements, and asking what he thought of them. And Phil, who had promised his mother to check his cousin if he found her going on recklessly, as they had heard from Anna, proved a very flunky, and instead of checking her, entered heart and soul into her plans, and even made suggestions as to how they could be improved. So useful, in fact, did he make himself, and so much skill and taste did he display, that Queenie forgot entirely to chide him for his lack of a profession. Indeed, she was rather glad than otherwise that he had no profession, as it left him free to be with her all the time and to become at last the superintendent of the whole, with this difference, however, that while he directed the men, Queenie directed him and made him her very slave.

Queenie never shrank from anything, but plunged her white hands into the dirt up to her wrists, while Phil took off his coat and worked patiently at her side, transplanting a rose-bush or geranium to one place in the morning, and in the evening to another, if so the fancy took his mistress. She could not always tell where she wanted a thing until she studied the effect of certain positions, and then, if she did not like it, if it did not harmonize with the picture she was forming, it must be moved, she said. And so the moving and changing went on, and people marveled to see how rapidly what had first seemed chaos and confusion began to assume proportions until the grounds bade fair to become more beautiful and artistic than any place which had ever been seen in the county. What had been done before Queenie's arrival was for the most part unchanged, but the remainder of the grounds were entirely overturned. The plateau and summer-house, on which Queenie had set her heart, were made, and the terraces, and the new walks, and the pasture land, west of the house, was robbed of its greensward for turf to cover the terraces and plateau, which were watered twice each day until the well and cisterns gave out, and then the heavens, as if in sympathy with the work, poured out plentiful showers, and so, not withstanding that it was summer, the turf, and the shrubs, and the vines, and flowers were kept green and fresh, and scarcely stopped their growing. Everything went beautifully Queenie said, as she issued her orders, and, busy as a bee, worked from morning till night, with Phil always in attendance, while even Mr. Beresford at last caught the fever, and went himself into the business of planting and transplanting, and working in the dirt. The Hetherton gardeners the people called the two young men, Phil being the head and Mr. Beresford the sub; but little did they care for the merry-making, so long as that bright, sparkling girl worked with them, and then at night rewarded them with a bouquet, which she fastened to their button-holes, standing up on tiptoe to do it, and looking up at them with eyes which nearly drove them crazy.

Nor was Hetherton Place the only spot where Queenie was busy. A few days after Phil went to the sea-shore there had come to her a letter from Margery, who wrote:

"My Darling Queenie.—You do not know how surprised and delighted I was to hear that you were in America, or how sorry I was to hear of your loss.

You must be so lonely and sad, alone in a strange country. What is Merrivale like? and do you think it would be a good place for me? Is it not funny that I had thought to go there, and have actually written to a Mrs. Ferguson, who turns out to be your aunt? But she asks more for her business than I feel able to pay, and so the plan has been abandoned for the present. But I must see you, and, remembering all your kindness in the years past, you will not think me intrusive when I tell you, that before the summer is gone I am coming to Merrivale, just to look into your dear eyes again, and see if you are changed. I like your aunt and cousins; they are genuine ladies, and I am glad they belong to you."

The first thing Queenie did after reading this letter, was to mount her horse and gallop in hot haste to the village, where she astonished Mrs. Lydia Ferguson by offering her more for her business than she had demanded of Miss La Rue.

"It is my Margery—my friend, and I am going to have her here, if I turn my own house into a dressmaker's shop," she said, and she talked so fast, and gesticulated so rapidly, that Mrs. Lydia grew quite bewildered, but managed to comprehend that a price was offered her which would be well for her to accept, as it might never be offered her again.

Anna, too, was all eagerness to "get out of the vile thing and be somebody," as she expressed it, and so the bargain was closed, and Mrs. Lydia was to retire at once into the privacy and respectability of private life; the obnoxious sign was to be taken from the front window, and Miss Anna was to be merely the daughter of a grocer which she considered quite an ascent in the social scale.

Mrs. Lydia did not wish to sell her house, nor Queenie to buy it.

She had heard there was a charming little cottage on Maple Avenue, for sale, and she swooped down upon the owner like a hurricane, asking him what his terms were, and if he would vacate at once.

"You see I wish to get him out immediately, for I mean to make it just like a palace for Margery," she said to her grandmother, who tried to restrain the reckless girl, telling her she was going on at a ruinous rate, and that, of herself she could not transact business, until she was of age.

"But Mr. Beresford can transact it for me, and I shall have it," she said; and she took Mr. Beresford by storm and compelled him to make an arrangement whereby the cottage and her aunt's business came into her possession. Then she wrote to her friend:

"You Dear Old Darling Margery:—I do know just how surprised and glad you were to hear that I was in America, for wasn't I just as glad to know that you were near me when I thought you in Nice or Italy. Why didn't you answer my letter, you naughty girl? I wrote you six and only had two in return. It is just like a story, isn't it—our being together in America? And, Margie, my grandmother is not that English duchess I used to talk so much about, but a real, live Yankee woman, of the very Yankee-est kind, red, and fat, and good, and calls me Rennet, and wears purple gloves—or she did till I coaxed her into some black ones, which she thinks are not very dressy. And you will like her ever so much, and you are coming to Merrivale to live at once, now, right away. So, pack up your things as soon as you read this. I have bought that business for you of Mrs. Ferguson, who is my aunt, or rather the wife of my mother's brother; and she has a daughter Anna, who is my cousin, and very stunning and swell. That last is slang, which I have learned in America of Phil, who is another cousin, and a Ferguson, too: or rather his mother was, which is the same thing. There are a great many Fergusons, you see; but then there are Fergusons and Fergusons. But you will learn all this when you come. I have a pretty little cottage engaged, with a bit of fresh greensward in front, and the loveliest old-fashioned garden at the side, with June pinks, and roses, and tiger-lilies, and a nice bed of tansy, I like tansy, don't you? There was a patch of it at dear old Chateau des Fleurs. Then there are two front rooms for the work, and a sitting and dining-room back, with the kitchen, and three chambers communicating with each other. One of these I shall fit up with blue for you; it will just suit your lovely complexion and eyes; the other is scarlet, for your mother, who is dark; and the third—well, that is to be mine when I stay with you nights, as I intend doing often. But I can't have the same color as your mother, so I shall take pink, which will make me look just like a—a—nigger. That's another word I caught from Phil. I wish he would come back. Tell him so, please.

"And now, Margery, come as soon as you can. And don't be silly about my buying the cottage and business for you. It is only a little bit of payment on the big sum I owe you for that sacrifice you were ready to make for me. How well I remember that day, and how plainly I can see you now, as you went up to the master, with your face as white as paper, and your eyes so pitiful and appealing as they looked at me, and yet so full of love. And I, the coward, shut my eyes, and clenched my fists, and said to myself just as fast as I could, 'Nasty beast! nasty beast!' till the first blow fell, which hurt me more than it did you, for it cut right into my conscience, and there has been a little smart there ever since, while your dear hand is just as white and fair as if that vile old man's ferrule had never reddened and wounded it. Splendid old Margery! I want to hug you this minute!

"And—oh, Margie, don't think I have forgotten papa, because I have not said more of him; for I haven't, and there is a thought of him and a little moan in my heart for him all the time. No matter what I am doing, or how gay I seem, I never forget that he is dead, and that there is nobody to love me now but you, who seem so near to me, because you knew of the old life at home now gone forever. Answer at once, and say when I may expect you."

To this letter Margery replied within a few days, thanking Queenie for her generous interest, but saying she could not accept so much from her; she should come to Merrivale with her mother as soon as they could arrange matters where they were, but she should insist upon paying rent for the cottage, and also upon paying for the business.

"I can do that in a short time," she wrote, "if I have work, and I shall be happier to be independent even of you, my darling. Besides I do not think the

Rossiters and Fergusons would like you to do so much for a stranger. I am nothing to them, you know, except their dressmaker—"

"I think her a very sensible girl. I could not respect her, if she were willing to receive so much from you," Mr. Beresford said when Queenie read him Margery's letter; whereupon Queenie flew into a passion, and said he did not understand—did not appreciate the nature of the friendship between herself and Margery; adding that she should never tell Margery how much she paid her Aunt Lydia, and that she would never take any rent and she should furnish the house herself.

And she did, and, with Phil to help her after he came, she accomplished more at the cottage and at Hetherton Place than any ten ordinary women could have accomplished in the same length of time. Every day she managed to spend two or three hours at the cottage, which, with plenty of money and perfect taste, was soon transformed into a little gem of a house. It is true there was nothing expensive in it in the way of furniture, except the upright Steinway, which Queenie insisted upon; but everything was so well chosen and so artistically arranged, that the whole effect was like a lovely picture, and the villagers went to see it, and wondered what this Margery could be that Miss Hetherton was doing so much for her.

"She is only a dressmaker, after all," Miss Anna said, with a toss of her head, as she sat in what had been her mother's work-room entertaining a visitor and discussing the expected Margery.

Anna had lost no time in removing the sign from the window, and had even carried out her threat of splitting and burning it up, thinking thus to wipe out a past which she foolishly thought had been a disgrace, because of her mother's honest labor. The work-room, too, had been dismantled of everything pertaining to the obnoxious dressmaking, and Mrs. Lydia, deprived of her occupation, found the time hanging heavily upon her hands, for she had no taste for housekeeping, and could not at once interest herself in it. Besides, she missed the excitement of the people coming in and going out, and missed the gossip they brought, and almost every hour of her life repented that to gratify her daughter she had been persuaded to retire from business and set up for a lady.

Anna, on the contrary, enjoyed it immensely, and held her head a good deal higher, and frizzed her hair more than ever, and wore her best dresses every day, and spoke slightingly of Margery La Rue as only a dressmaker, and told half a dozen of the neighbors, confidentially, that she thought her cousin Reinette fast and queer, though she supposed it was the French of her, to go on, as she did, with Phil and Mr. Beresford, both of whom were making fools of themselves. For her part she could see nothing attractive in her whatever, except that she was bright, and witty, and small, and tall men, as a rule, liked little women. To Queenie herself, however, she was sweetness itself, and as the latter never heard of her ill-natured remarks, there was a show of friendship between the two girls, and Anna was frequently at Hetherton Place, where the envy of her nature found ample food to feed upon, as she contrasted Reinette's surroundings with her own.

CHAPTER XX

ARRIVALS IN MERRIVALE

For three or four years Merrivale had boasted of a weekly paper, and in the column of "Personals" the citizens read one Thursday morning that the Rossiters were coming home on Friday, and that Mrs. and Miss La Rue, the French ladies who were to succeed Mrs. Ferguson in her business, were also expected on that day. Everybody was glad the Rossiters were coming, for Merrivale was always gayer when they were home, as they were hospitable people, and entertained a great deal of company. Usually they brought guests with them, but this time no one was coming, Phil said, except a cousin of his father's—an old bachelor, who rejoiced in the highsounding name of Lord Seymour Rossiter, though to do him justice, he usually signed himself Major L. S. Rossiter, as he had once been in the army. He was very rich, Phil said, and rather good-looking, and he laughingly bade Queenie be prepared to surrender at once to his charms. But Queenie cared little for Lord Rossiter or any other lord just then. All her thoughts and interests were centered in the one fact that Margery was coming, and she spent the whole of Friday morning at the cottage, seeing that everything was in readiness, and literally filling it with flowers from her garden and greenhouse.

"I wish her to have a good first impression," she said to Phil, who was with her as she inspected the rooms for the last time before going home to the early dinner she had ordered that day, so as to be at the station in time.

The train was due at six o'clock, and, a few minutes before the hour, the Rossiter carriage with Phil in it, and the Hetherton carriage with Reinette in it, drew up side by side at the rear of the depot.

Reinette was full of excitement and expectation, and made a most lovely picture in her black dress of some soft, gauzy material, with knots of double-faced scarlet and cream ribbons twisted in with the bows and loops of satin— a scarlet tip on her black hat, and a mass of white illusion wound round it, and fastened beneath her chin.

Phil thought her perfectly charming as she walked restlessly up and down the platform, waiting for the first sound which should herald the approaching train. It came at last—a low whistle in the distance, growing gradually louder and shriller, until the train shot under the bridge, and the great engine puffed and groaned a moment before the station, and then went on its way, leaving two distinct groups of people to be stared at by the lookers-on. One, the Rossiters and a middle-aged man, dressed in the extreme of fashion, with eye glasses on his nose and a little slender cane in his hand, which he twisted nervously, while, with the other members of his party, he looked curiously at the second group farther down the platform—the three French ladies, who spoke their native tongue so volubly, and were so demonstrative and expressive in their gestures and tones. Mrs. La Rue was in black, with a strange expression on her face and in her eyes, as she watched the two young girls.

The moment Margery alighted, Reinette had precipitated herself into her arms, exclaiming:

"You dear old Margie! you have come at last;" while kiss after kiss was showered upon the girl, whose golden hair gleamed brightly in the sunlight, and whose blue eyes were full of tears as she returned the greeting.

Suddenly remembering Mrs. La Rue, Queenie turned toward her, and, offering her hand very cordially, utterly ignored the fact that she had ever seen her before by saying:

"I think you are Mrs. La Rue, and I am happy to meet you, because you bring me Margie."

"Thanks. You are very kind," Mrs. La Rue replied, with a tone which a stranger might have thought cold and constrained but for the face, which had something eager and almost hungry in its expression, as the great black eyes were riveted upon Queenie whose hand the woman held in a tight clasp until it was wrenched away, as the girl turned next to the Rossiters.

"Wait, Margie," she said, in passing. "Our carriage is here, and I am going to take you to your new home."

Then hurrying on she went up to her aunt, and cousins, and the major, who had been watching her curiously, and mentally commenting upon her.

"Quite too much sentiment and gush for me. I like more manner; more dignity," he thought, while Mrs. Rossiter saw only her sister's child, and Ethel and Grace felt a little disappointed with regard to the beauty, of which they had heard so much.

But when she came toward them, her head erect, her cheeks flushed, and eyes shining like diamonds and seeming almost to speak as they danced, and laughed, and sparkled, they changed their minds, and when the great tears came with a rush, as she threw herself into Mrs. Rossiter's arms, exclaiming, "Oh auntie, I am going to love you so much, and you must love me with all my faults, for I have neither father nor mother, now," they espoused her cause at once, and never for a moment wavered in their allegiance to her. Giving each of them a hand, and kissing them warmly, she said, laughingly: "You are all alike, aren't you? tall and fair, and blue-eyed—so different from me, who am nothing but a little black midget."

"That's the Ferguson of us," Phil said, with a meaning smile, which brought a flush to his sister's cheeks, and made Queenie laugh, as she retorted:

"I wish I were a Ferguson then, if that would make me white."

"A deuced pretty girl, after all," the Major thought, as she beamed on him her brightest smile when Phil introduced her, and then the parties separated. And returning to Margery, Queenie led her in triumph to the carriage, while Mrs. La Rue followed after them.

Her black gauze vail was drawn closely over her face, but both girls caught a sound like a suppressed sigh, and turning to her, Margery said:

"I believe mother is homesick, and pining for France she seems so low spirited."

"Oh, I hope not. America is a great deal better than France, and Merrivale is best of all," Queenie said, glancing at Mrs. La Rue, and noting for the first time how pale and tired she looked, noticing, too, that she was all in black, though not exactly in mourning.

"She has lost some friend, perhaps," she thought, and then chatted on with Margery, unmindful of the woman who leaned wearily back among the soft cushions of the luxurious carriage.

Of what was she thinking?—the tired, sad woman, as the carriage wound up the hill, across the common, past the church where Margaret Ferguson used to say her prayers, and past the yellowish-brown house which Queenie pointed out as her Aunt Lydia's, and where, on the door-step Anna sat fanning herself, rejoicing that she was now a grocer's daughter. It would be hard to fathom her thoughts, which were straying far back over the broad gulf which lay between the present and the days of her girlhood. And yet nothing escaped her, from Anna Ferguson on the door-step to the handsome house and grounds at the Knoll, which Queenie said was her Aunt Rossiter's house; but when at last the cottage was reached, and she alighted from the carriage, she was so weak and faint that Margery led her into the house, and even Queenie was alarmed at the death-like pallor of her face, and stood by her while Margery hunted through her bags for some restorative.

"You are very tired, aren't you?" Queenie said, kindly, to her, at the same time laying her hand gently upon her head, for her bonnet had been removed.

At the touch of those cool, slender fingers and the sound of the pitying voice Mrs. La Rue gave way entirely, and grasping both Queenie's hands, covered them with tears and kisses; as she said:

"Forgive me, Queenie, and let me call you once by that pet name; let me thank you for all you have done for us—for Margery and me. God bless you, Queenie! God bless you!"

"Mother, mother, you frighten Miss Hetherton!" Margery said, coming quickly forward, and guessing from the expression of Queenie's face, that so much demonstration was distasteful to her. "You are tired and nervous; let me take you up stairs," she continued as she led the unresisting woman to her room, where she made her lie down upon the couch, and then went back to Queenie, who was standing in the door-way and beating her little foot impatiently, as she thought:

"I wonder what makes that woman act so? The first time I ever saw her she stared at me as if she would eat me up; and just now there was positively something frightful in her eyes as they looked up at me; I do not believe I like her."

Just here Margery appeared, apologizing for her mother, who, she said was wholly overcome with all Queenie's kindness to them.

"Yes, I know. I do it for you," Queenie said, a little petulantly, for she did not care at all if Margery knew of her aversion to her mother.

It was time now for her to go if she would see her cousins, and promising Margery to look in upon her in the morning and bring her a pile of dresses which needed repairing, she entered her carriage, and was driven to the Knoll, where the family were just sitting down to supper.

Taking a seat with them, Queenie talked and laughed, and sparkled, and shone, until the room seemed full of her, and the bewildered major could have sworn there were twenty pairs of eyes flashing upon him instead of one, while Ethel and Grace held their breath and watched her as the expression of her bright face changed with every new gesture of her hands and turn of her head.

"She is so bright and beautiful, and different from anything we ever saw," they thought, while Mrs. Rossiter, though no less fascinated than her daughters, was conscious of a feeling of disappointment because she could discover no resemblance to her sister in her sister's child. She was unmistakably a Hetherton, though with another look in her dark face and wonderful eyes which puzzled Mrs. Rossiter as she sat watching her with constantly increasing interest, and listening to her gay bad-Phil and the major, the latter of whom seemed half afraid of her, and was evidently ill at ease when her eyes lighted upon him.

Supper being over Reinette arose to go, saying to her aunt and cousins:

"I shall expect you to dine with me to-morrow at six o'clock. It is to be a family party, but Major Rossiter is included in the invitation. I am going now to ask grandma and Aunt Lydia. Will you go with me, Phil?"

They found Grandma Ferguson weeding her flower borders in front of her house, with her cap and collar off, and her spotted calico dress open at the throat.

"It is too hot to be harnessed up with fixin's," she said, and when Reinette, who did not like the looks of her neck, suggested that a collar or ruffle did not greatly add to one's discomfort in warm weather and gave a finish to one's dress, she replied: "Law, child, it don't matter an atom what I wear. Everybody knows Peggy Ferguson." Reinette gave a little deprecating shrug and then delivered her invitation, which was accepted at once, grandma saying, "She could come early so as to have a good visit before dinner, though she presumed Mary and the gals wouldn't be there till the last minit."

Reinette gave another expressive shrug, and drove next to her Aunt Lydia's, where she found that lady seated in the parlor with a tired look on her face as if doing nothing did not agree with her, while Anna was drumming the old worn-out piano which, having been second-hand when it was bought, was something dreadful to hear.

"Oh, Phil, you here?" she said turning on the musicstool. "I was going by and by to see the girls. I hope they are well. Who was that dandyish-looking old man with them, sitting up as straight as a ramrod, with eyeglasses on his nose? Have they picked up a beau somewhere?"

Phil explained that the dandyish-looking old man was his father's cousin, Major Lord Seymour Rossiter, from New York, where he had for twenty years occupied the same rooms at the same hotel.

"Oh, yes, I've heard of him; rich as a Jew, and an old bach," Anna said. "Yes, I'll come to dinner, Queenie, and mother too, I suppose, but I've no idea you'll get father there—he doesn't like visiting much."

In her heart Reinette cared but little whether her uncle came or not. His presence would add nothing to her dinner; but something in Anna's manner awoke within her a spirit of opposition, and sent her to the grocery where her Uncle Tom sold codfish, and molasses, and eggs, and where she found him in his shirt sleeves, seated upon a barrel outside the door, smoking a tobacco pipe. He did not get up, nor stop his smoking, except as he was obliged to take his pipe from his mouth while he talked to Reinette, who gave him the invitation, and urged his acceptance as warmly as if the success of her dinner depended upon it.

"He was much obliged to her," he said but he didn't think he should go. He wasn't used to the quality, and hadn't eaten a meal of victuals outside his own house in years except at Thanksgivin' time when he had to go to his mother's.

"And that is just the reason you will come to-morrow," Queenie said, coaxingly. "It is my first family party, and you will not be so uncivil as to refuse. I shall expect you without fail," and with a smile and flash of her eyes, which stirred even staid Tom Ferguson a little, Reinette drove away, saying to Phil, who was going to ride home with her and then walk back to the Knoll: "I hope he will come, for I could see that Anna did not wish him to. Such airs as she has taken on since she split up that sign and quit the business, as she terms it! Does she suppose it is what one does which makes a lady? Oh, Phil, why is there such a difference between people of the same blood? There's your mother, as cultivated and refined as if she had been born a princess, and there's Anna and grandma, and Uncle Tom. Is it American democracy? If so, I am afraid I don't like it;" and, leaning back in the carriage, Queenie looked very sober, while Phil said good-humoredly:

"In rebellion against the Fergusons again, I see. It will never do to go against your family; blood is blood, and there's no getting rid of it or of us."

"I have no wish to be rid of you, but I may as well confess it, I do wish mother had been somebody besides a Ferguson," Reinette replied; then added, laughingly: "Don't think me a monster—I can't help the feeling; it was born in me, and father fostered it; but I am trying to overcome it, you see, for haven't I invited them all to dinner? You must come early, Phil—very early, so as to help me through."

Phil promised, and as they had reached Hetherton Place by this time, and it was beginning to grow dark, he bade her good-night, and walked rapidly back to the Knoll.

True to her promise, Reinette drove round to see Margery the next morning, and carried a pile of dresses which scarcely needed a stitch, but which she insisted should be changed, as she knew Margery needed work. She found her friend well and delighted with the cottage, which suited her in every particular. Mrs. La Rue, too, was very calm and quiet, and only spoke to Reinette when spoken to, until the latter, in speaking of Hetherton Place and how lonely she was there at times, especially in the evening, when Phil was not with her, said:

"I am going to hunt up my old nurse, who was with mother when she died. She is alive, I am sure, and somewhere in England or France. I shall have her come to live with me."

Mrs. La Rue was standing with her back to Reinette, picking the dead leaves from a pot of carnations, but she turned suddenly, and facing the girl, said quickly:

"Better leave the nurse where she is; you will be happier without her."

"I don't know why you should say that," Reinette retorted, in a tone which showed her irritation that Mrs. La Rue should presume to dictate; "you certainly can know nothing of Christine Bodine."

"Of course not, but I know that old nurses do not often add to the happiness of young ladies like you, so leave her alone; do not try to find her," Mrs. La Rue replied, and there was a ring in her voice like a note of fear which Reinette would have detected had she been at all suspicious.

But she was only resentful and answered proudly, "I shall certainly find her if I can," then with a few directions to Margery with regard to the dresses, she drove away to order some necessary articles for her dinner, which she meant to make a success. As the new summer-house on the plateau was not yet completed, the table was laid on the broad piazza overlooking the river and town beyond, and everything was in readiness by the time Grandma Ferguson arrived, for true to her promise, she came early, and in her sprigged muslin and lavender ribbons, was fanning herself in the large rocking-chair just as the clock was striking four. She had tried, she said, to bring Lyddy Ann and Anna with her, but Anna had got some highfalutin' notions about not goin' till the last minit; and so she presumed she wouldn't come till the last gun was fired, but if she's Reinette she wouldn't wait for her.

Miss Anna was really putting on a great many airs and talking etiquette to her mother and grandmother until both were nearly crazy. She had been to the Knoll that morning to call upon her cousins, both of whom were struck with the accession of dignity and stiffness in her manner, but never dreamed that the splitting up of the sign had anything to do with it; they attributed it rather to the new and pretty muslin the young lady wore and the presence of

Major Rossiter, who was presented to her, and who, with a freak of fancy most accountable, surrendered to her at once. The major was fifty, and bald and gray, and near-sighted and peculiar, and though he admired pretty women, he had never been known to pay one more attention than was required of him as a gentleman. He had thought his cousins, Ethel and Grace, very attractive and lady-like and sweet, while Reinette had taken his breath away with her flash and sparkle, but neither of the three had ever moved him as he was moved by Anna's stately manner when she gave him the tips of her fingers and bowed so ceremoniously to him. The major liked a woman to be quiet and dignified, and Anna's stiffness suited him, and he walked home with her and sat for half an hour in the parlor and talked with her of Europe, which she hoped one day to see, and sympathized with her when she deplored most eloquently the fate which tied her down to a little country place like Merrivale, when she was by nature fitted to enjoy so much. But poverty was a hard master and ruled its subjects with an iron rod, she said, and there were tears in the blue eyes which looked up at the major, who felt a great pity for and interest in this girl so gifted, so dignified, and so pretty, for he thought her all these, and said to her at parting that he hoped to see her later in the day at Hetherton Place, where he was going with the Rossiters.

After the major left her Anna sat down to think, and the result of the thinking was that though Major Rossiter was old, and tiresome, and fidgety, and not at all like Mr. Beresford or Phil, he was rich and evidently pleased with her, and she resolved that nothing should be lacking on her part to increase his interest in her, and make him believe that whatever her surroundings were, she was superior to them and worthy to stand in the high places of the land. She was ashamed of her father and mother, especially the former, and when at noon he asked what time the dinner was to come off, she felt a fear lest he might be intending to go as he was. Reinette's eyes and manner when she gave the invitation had done their work with him.

"I really b'lieve the girl wants me to come, odd and homespun as I am," he thought, and he made up his mind to do so, and Anna felt a cold sweat oozing out from her finger tips, as she wondered what Major Lord Rossiter would think of him.

"Are you sure you will enjoy it?" she said. "You know how long it is since you have been anywhere, and Reinette is very particular how her guests comport themselves—foolishly so, perhaps. You cannot eat in your shirt sleeves there, no matter how warm you may be."

"Who in thunder said I would eat in my shirt sleeves," Mr. Ferguson said, doggedly, feeling intuitively that his daughter did not wish him to go, and feeling also determined that he would.

And so it happened that simultaneously with the major, in his elegant dinner costume, with his white neck-tie and button-hole bouquet, came honest Tom Ferguson, in the suit he had worn to church for at least six years or more, and which was anything but stylish and fashionable. But Tom was not a fashionable man, and made no pretense of being other than he was, but he did not eat in his shirt sleeves or commit any marked blunders at the dinner table, where six or seven courses were served, with Pierre as chief waiter and engineer. Reinette was an admirable hostess, and so managed to make her incongruous guests feel at home, that the dinner was a great success, and the fastidious major, who was seated far away from both grandma and Tom, did not think the less of Anna because of any shortcomings in her father or mother, though he knew they were not like the people of his world. But the Rossiters were, and they were Anna's relations, and she was refined and cultivated, if her parents were not, he thought, for the glamour of love at first sight was over and round him, and Anna was very pretty in her white muslin dress, and very quiet and lady-like, he thought, and when, after the dinner was over, he walked with her upon one of the finished terraces and saw how well she carried herself and how small and delicately-shaped were her hands and feet—for he was one to notice all these things—he began vaguely to wonder how old she was and what his bachelor friends at the club would say if he should present her to them as his wife. The major was unquestionably attacked with a disease, the slightest symptoms of which he had never before had in his life, and when at last it was time for the guests to leave, and the Hetherton carriage came round to take Grandma Ferguson and Mrs. Lydia and Anna home, he suggested to the latter that she walk with him, as there was a moon and the night was fine.

If there was anything Anna detested it was walking over a dusty dirt road in slippers, and she wore that day a dainty pair with heels so high that her ankles were in danger of turning over with every step. But slippers and dusty highways weighed as nothing against a walk with Major Rossiter down the winding hill, between hedges of sweet-brier and alder, and across the long causeway where the beeches and maples nearly met overhead, and the river wound like a silver thread through the green meadows to the westward. Such a walk would be very romantic, and Anna meant to take it if she spoiled a dozen pairs of slippers. So she acceded to the major's proposition, and the two started together for home, while Phil looked curiously after them and said in an aside to Queenie: "The old chap is hard hit, and if I'm not mistaken, Anna will be my Lady Rossiter, and then won't we second-class mortals catch it."

CHAPTER XXII

MARGERY AND THE PEOPLE

Margery was a success in Merrivale as a dressmaker, at least. Mrs. Lydia had done very well, it is true. Her work was always neatly finished and her prices satisfactory, but she never went farther from home than Springfield or

Worcester, so that there was a sameness and stiffness in her styles wholly unlike the beautiful garments which came from Margery's skillful hands, no two of which were alike, and each one of which seemed prettier and newer than its predecessor, so that in less than two weeks her rooms were full of work, and her three girls busy from morning till night, and she had even proposed to Miss Anna to help her a few hours each day during the busy season. But Anna spurned the proposition with contempt, saying her days of working for people and being snubbed by them on account of it were over.

When Queenie heard of this she laughed merrily, and went herself into Margery's workshop and trimmed Hattie Granger's wedding-dress with her own hands and promised to make every stitch of Anna's should she succeed in capturing the major, as she seemed likely to do; but Anna answered that her wedding-dress, if she ever had one, would not be made in the country, and so that point was settled.

From the first Margery's great beauty attracted unusual attention but upon no one did it produce so great an effect as upon Grandma Ferguson, who first saw the girl the Sunday after her arrival in Merrivale. Reinette had told the sexton to give Miss and Mrs. La Rue a seat with her in the Hetherton pew, describing the two ladies to him so there could be no mistaking them. But Margery came alone, and whether it was that the old sexton's mind was intent upon a short woman in black, or whether something about Margery herself carried him back to the Sundays of long ago, when a girlish figure used to glide up the aisle to John Ferguson's pew, he made a mistake and Grandma Ferguson had just settled herself on her cushion and adjusted her wide skirts about her, when a rustling sound caught her ear, and turning her head she saw a face which made her start suddenly with a great throb of something like fear as a tall young girl, simply but elegantly attired in black silk and white chip bonnet, with a wreath of lilacs around it, took a seat beside her. Mrs. Rossiter had seen something in the French girl's face which puzzled and bewildered her. And grandma saw it, too, and defined it at once, and drew a long breath as she gazed at the face so like the face of her Margaret dead over the sea. Who was she, grandma asked herself and forgot to say her prayers or listen to the sermon, as she wondered and watched. Others had seen only a likeness to Margaret Ferguson, but the mother who could never forget saw more than that; she saw her dead child repeated in this beautiful young girl, who grew restless and nervous under the scrutiny of the eyes she knew were fastened so constantly upon her, and was glad when the sermon was over and she could thus escape them.

Reinette, who occupied the Hetherton pew, had turned once, and seeing where Margery was, had nodded to her, and the moment church was over she came down the aisle, tossing her head airily, and with the strange witchery and magnetism of her smile and wonderful eyes, throwing into the shade the fair blonde whose beauty had been noted by the people as something remarkable. And how unlike they were to each other, golden-haired, blue-eyed, rose-tinted Margery, so tall, and quiet, and self-possessed, and dark-haired, dark-eyed, dark-faced Reinette, petite and playful, and restless as a bird, with a flash in her brilliant eyes, before which even Margery's charms were, for the time, forgotten.

"Who is she, Rennet?" grandma whispered, catching her granddaughter's arm as she came near, and pointing toward Margery. "Who is she, with a face so like your mother's that for a minute I thought it was my Margaret come back again."

"Like my mother? Oh, I am so glad, for now I shall love her more than ever," Reinette replied; then, touching Margery, she presented her to her grandmother, saying, as she did so: "She thinks you look like my mother, and perhaps you do, for I am sure you are more like a Ferguson than I am."

The next day grandma went to the cottage, ostensibly to make some inquiries with regard to a dress, but really to see again the girl who was so like her daughter, and who was very kind and gentle with her, and said to her so sweetly:

"I am glad if I am like Mrs. Hetherton, for she was Reinette's mother, and I am sure you will like me for it. I want people to like me."

And in this wish Margery was gratified, for from the first she became very popular and took her place among the best young ladies in town. For this she was in part indebted to Reinette, who insisted that she should be noticed, and who, if she saw any signs of rebellion or indifference on the part of the people, opened her batteries upon the delinquents, and brought them to terms at once.

When the grounds were completed at Hetherton Place, she gave a garden party to which all the desirable people in Merrivale were bidden. It was in honor of Margery, she said, and she treated the young girl as a subject would treat a queen, and made so much of her, and talked of her so much, that Mr. Beresford said to her as they were standing a little apart from the others, and she was asking if he ever saw any one as beautiful as Margery:

"Yes, she is very pretty and graceful and all that, but she cannot have had the training which you did. Her early associates must have been very different from yours, and I am somewhat surprised at your violent fancy for her."

Then Reinette turned upon him hotly, and he never forgot the look of scorn in her blazing eyes, as she said:

"I know perfectly well what you mean, Mr. Beresford, and I despise you for it. Because Margery works—earns her own living—is a dressmaker—you, and people like you, look down upon her from your lofty platform of position and social standing, and I hate you for it; yes, I do, for how are you better than she, I'd like to know. Aren't you just as anxious for a case to work up as she for a dress to make, and what's the difference, except that you are a man and she a woman, and so the more to be commended, because she is willing to take care of herself instead of folding her hands in idleness. I tell you, Mr. Beresford, you must do better, or I'll never speak to you again. There's Margery now, over there by the summer-house, talking with Major Rossiter, and looking awfully bored. Go and get her away, and dance with her. See, they are just forming a quadrille there in the summer-house;" and she pointed to the large, fanciful structure on the plateau, which, with its manycolored lights, was much like the gay restaurants on the Champs d'Elysees in Paris. Indeed the whole affair bore a strong resemblance to the outdoor fetes in France, and the grounds seemed like fairy-land, with the flowers, and flags, and arches, and colored lights, and groups of gayly-dressed people wandering up and down the broad walks and on the grassy terraces, or dancing in the summer-house, near which the band was stationed.

Mr. Beresford never danced; he was too dignified for that, but he carried Margery away from the major, and walked with her through the grounds, and wondered at her refinement and lady-like manners, which seemed so natural to her. Mr. Beresford was an aristocrat of the deepest dye, and believed implicitly in family and blood, and as Margery had neither, he was puzzled, and bewildered, and greatly interested in her, and thought hers the most beautiful face he had ever seen, excepting Reinette's, which stood out distinct among all the faces in the world.

Reinette was at her best that night, and like some bright bird flitted here and there among her guests, saying the right word to the right person, and doing the right thing in the right place, and so managing, that when at a late hour the festivity was at an end, and her guests came to say good-by, it was no fashionable lie, but the truth they spoke when they assured her that evening had been the most enjoyable of their lives, and one never to be forgotten.

CHAPTER XXIII

PERFECTING THEMSELVES IN FRENCH

That was what Mr. Beresford and Phil were said to be doing during the weeks when they went every day to Hetherton Place, Phil, who had nothing to do, riding over early every morning, and Mr. Beresford, who had a great deal to do, going in the evening, or as early in the afternoon as he could get away from his office. It was not unusual for the two to meet on the causeway, Phil coming from and Mr. Beresford going to the little lady, who bewitched and intoxicated them both, though in a very different way. With Phil, her cousin, she laughed, and played, and flirted, and quarreled—hot, bitter quarrels sometimes—in which she always had the better of Phil, inasmuch as her command of language was greater, and her rapid gestures added point to her sarcasm. But if her anger was the hotter and fiercer, she was always the first to make overtures for a reconciliation; the first to confess herself in error, and she did it so prettily and sweetly, and purred around Phil so like a loving kitten, that he thought the making up worth all the quarreling, and rather provoked the latter than tried to avoid it.

Sometimes, when she was more than usually unreasonable and aggravating, Phil would absent himself from Hetherton Place for two or three days, knowing well that in the end Pierre would come to him with a note from Queenie begging him to return, and chiding him for his foolishness in laying to heart anything she had said.

"You know I do not mean a word of it, and it's just my awful temper which gets the mastery, and I think you hateful to bother me by staying away when you know how poky it is here without you," she would write, and within an hour Phil would be at her side again, basking in the sunlight of her charms, and growing every day more and more infatuated with the girl, whose eyes were just as bright, and whose smile was just as sweet and alluring, when, later on, Mr. Beresford came, more in love, if possible, than Phil, but with a different way of showing it.

Queenie was morally certain that he was either in love with her or would be soon; and she was always a little shy of him, and never allowed the conversation to approach anything like love-making; and if he praised a particular dress and said it was becoming, as he sometimes did, she never wore it again for him, but when she knew he was coming, donned some old-fashioned gown in which she fancied herself hideous.

"If Mr. Beresford would be foolish, it should not be from any fault of hers," she thought, never dreaming that if she arrayed herself in a bag he would still have thought her charming, provided her eyes and mouth were visible.

Ostensibly Mr. Beresford's relations with her were of a purely business nature; for in managing so large an estate there was much to be talked about, and Queenie would know everything, especially with regard to foreign matters.

There were many letters from France, and these she read to Mr. Beresford, who, with Phil's help, might have made them out: but he brought them religiously to Queenie, who had insisted upon it with a persistence which surprised him, and insisted, too, upon receiving them from him with the seals unbroken and reading them first herself. She had not forgotten her father's dying injunction: "If letters come to me from France burn them unread."

No letters had come to him from any source, proving that he had no friends who cared to know of his welfare: but with a woman's subtle intuition, heightened by actual knowledge, Queenie knew there was something somewhere which she was to ward off if possible, and, as it might come in some business letter, she made it a condition that all documents should be brought to her first. As yet, however, everything had been open and clear, and Queenie was beginning to think her fears groundless, when Mr. Beresford brought her one day a letter from Messrs. Polignie & Co., who, among other things, wrote that the money invested with them for the benefit of a certain Christine Bodine had been paid by them to her agent, who had been empowered by her to receive the same. The name of the agent was given, and enclosed was his receipt, and then M. Polignie wrote:

"For reasons which may or may not be just, I would not advise the young lady to continue her search for this woman Bodine, whom we shall make no effort to find nor shall we answer Miss Hetherton's letter with regard to her, unless greatly pressed to do so."

Reinette was white to her lips as she read this, with Mr. Beresford sitting by and watching her, but she uttered no sound She merely took a pencil from the table, and on a slip of paper wrote the name and address of Christine's agent, which she put into her pocket; then, still keeping the letter from Mr. Beresford, she scratched out every word concerning Christine so effectually that it would be impossible for any one to decipher it, much less Mr. Beresford, whose knowledge of the language was so imperfect.

"Miss Hetherton! what are you doing? You may be erasing something very important for me to know. Stop, instantly! You have no business thus to mutilate a letter which does not belong to you," he cried, growing more and more in earnest, and even irritable, as she paid no heed to him, but went coolly on with her erasures.

"It is my business," she answered, at last, and her voice was low and strange. "It is my business, and no one's else. It has nothing to do with you. It only concerned me. You can have your letter now; they have paid my nurse's agent and sent you his receipt."

She handed him the letter, which, as it was written in an unusually hurried manner, he could not read, and so she read it to him, unconsciously laying a good deal of stress upon the fact that Christine had been paid, and that there was an end of that.

"You see they do not tell you where she is," she said, trying to speak naturally, though there was a kind of defiant tone in her voice. "And you need not make any further inquiries. I might not like her, and if I brought her here I should feel obliged to keep her."

She looked straight at Mr. Beresford, who nodded assent to what she said, but was not wholly deceived. That the erasure had something to do with Christine he was certain, and, with his curiosity roused by Reinette's excited manner, he resolved to ascertain for himself who and what the woman was. He, too, had the address of her authorized agent, and the mail for New York which left Merrivale next day carried two letters, one in English and one in French, directed to M. Jean Albrech, Mentone, France, and in the one written in French was a note for Christine Bodine, in whom Reinette had implicit faith as a true, good woman, notwithstanding what the Messrs. Polignie had insinuated against her. They were vile, suspicious people, Reinette said to herself, who, because her father paid money to a poor woman, thought she must be bad. They did not know, as she did, how kind and faithful Christine had been to her mother, who asked that she should be rewarded and cared for, and this was the way her father had done it. Thus Queenie reasoned and tried to reassure herself, but for days there was a shadow on her bright face and a dull pain in her heart as she wondered what the mystery could be concerning the woman Bodine.

But Queenie could not be unhappy long, and in visiting Margery as she did every day, and calling upon her cousins at the Knoll, and watching what had become a decided flirtation or rather genuine love affair between Major

Rossiter and Anna, she recovered her spirits, and resuming her old, fascinating manner with Mr. Beresford and Phil, drove them both to the point of seeking to know their fate, whether for good or evil.

CHAPTER XXIV

"I LOVE YOU, QUEENIE"

Mr. Beresford was the first to say it. As he did not often see Phil and Queenie together, except in company with Grace and Ethel, or Anna, he had no reason to know how much they were to each other, or he might not have been as confident of success as he was when at last he made up his mind to speak and know the worst or best there was to know. It had been his boast that no woman living could affect his happiness one way or the other. As a general thing he did not believe in them; that is, did not believe them real, or worth the love so many strong, sensible men wasted upon them.

But the little, bright-eyed French girl had torn down all his fortifications, and he did believe in her, and wanted her for his own, as he had never wanted anything before in his life. She was so fresh, so original, so piquant, so different from any one he had ever seen. Ethel and Grace Rossiter were sweet and lady-like, but they never affected him, while Margery La Rue was, he acknowledged, the most beautiful girl he had ever seen.

Everybody conceded that, and Mr. Beresford was not an exception to the rule.

Since the night when Reinette berated him so soundly for what she thought his lack of appreciation for Miss La Rue, he had called upon her a few times, and felt a growing interest in her, as he saw how pure and sweet she was, with an inborn delicacy and refinement of manner seldom found in persons of her class, for she never tried to hide the fact that her mother was a hair-dresser in Paris, and her father a nothing.

This, of itself, would have been a terrible obstacle in Mr. Beresford's way had he been greatly interested in Margery. Her family was against her, but with Queenie it was different, and he loved her as men of his mature age usually love when the grand passion seizes them for the first time, and he told her so one night when they sat together upon the ledge of rocks which overlooked the town and the river wandering through it.

Reinette had quarreled with Phil that day—hotly and fiercely quarreled, and had told him to go away and never come near her again, for she did not like him, and thought big cousins bores any way. And Phil had answered back, and said he was quite ready to go, and glad to be rid of such a termagant, and that she need not expect him to put himself in the way of her temper again, even though she wrote him a hundred notes of apology.

Then Phil went away and slammed the door after him, and was soon riding rapidly down the hill, while Queenie from her window watched him, wondering if she had offended him past all reconciliation, and what her life would be without patient, good-for-nothing Phil to come and go at her nod.

And then she wondered if it was true, as he had said, that she was vixenish and catty (those were the terms he had used), and if others thought so too—Mr. Beresford, for instance, who was so different from Phil, and of whom she was a little afraid. She had never treated him with such bursts of temper as she had Phil, but she had been hot and imperious in her manner toward him when he did not please her, and with Phil's words, "You are a vixen and a termagant," ringing in her ears, she resolved to be very gracious to Mr. Beresford when he came that evening, as he was sure to do. Every claw should be sheathed, and if she were a cat, she would be a very gentle, purring one, and she wore the dress she knew Mr. Beresford liked, and put knots of scarlet ribbon here and there, and was altogether lovely when he came, earlier than usual, and this time without any papers or foreign letters for her to read. There was nothing to do but talk, and Queenie was very soft and gentle, and acquiesced readily in his proposition that they walk out to the ledge of rocks, which was her favorite seat.

The early October night was warm and still, and the young moon hung in the western sky giving a pale silvery light to everything, and falling upon the dark hair and bright, glowing face of the young girl who was full of life and animation, and talked, and laughed, and coquetted with her companion until he could restrain himself no longer, and catching her suddenly in his arms, he said to her:

"Queenie, I love you, and want you for my wife; I have loved you, I believe, since the moment I first saw you at the station, and you clung to me as your father's friend, whom you were to trust with everything. So trust yourself to me; let me have a right to call you mine. I have lived many years with no thought or care for womankind, and such men love all the more when at last their heart is touched. Surely, surely, Queenie, you will not tell me no."

This last was said in a tone which had in it something of fear, for Queenie had wrenched herself from him, and standing a little apart was looking fixedly at him with wide-open, wondering eyes as if asking what he meant.

"Say, Queenie," he continued, "you will let me love you. You will be my wife."

"No, never, never! Always your friend but never your wife," she said, and her voice rang out clear and full as if the answer were decisive. "I am sorry," she began very gently as she saw how he staggered back as if smitten with a sudden blow, "I am sorry that you care for me this way; sorry if I have encouraged you. I thought you knew me better than that. I have laughed, and talked, and flirted with you, just as I have with Phil, but with no intention to make you love me. Forgive me, Mr. Beresford, if I have misled you. I cannot be your wife. I have no love for you."

He knew she was in earnest, quite as much by the expression of her face as by her words, and for a moment he felt bewildered and stunned with his sense of loss and pain which was all the greater because he had expected a different answer from her. Not expected her to say yes at once, for that was not her nature. She would tease him, and maybe laugh at him, and call him old, as she had sometimes done, when he was conscious of trying to act young. She would assume all these coquettish manners which he thought so charming, and then in the end she would lay her little hands in his, and answer in her saucy way:

"You can have me if you really want me, but you will get a bad bargain."

This, or something like it, was what he had fondly imagined, and alas, the result was so different. The little hands he had expected to be laid in his were locked firmly together, and the girl stood up erect and dignified before him, with no coquetry in her manner, or even shyness, as she gave him her answer which hurt him so cruelly. He was not one to beg and plead as a younger, more impetuous man might have done, and so the blow hurt him worse and made him shiver with a cold, faint feeling as he looked at her for a moment, while she looked back as curiously at him, seeing something in his face which awoke within her a feeling of great pity for him.

"Oh, Mr. Beresford," she said, coming a little nearer to him. "Don't look at me like that. Don't care for me so much—I am not worth it. I should not make you happy, I am so high-tempered, and passionate, and bad, and say things you never would forget. Nobody could forget them but Phil, and he has sworn never to do it again. Only to-day he called me a vixen and a termagant, and left me in hot anger, and if I can make him feel like that, what could I not do to you, who are so different—so much more matter-of-fact."

The mention of Phil was unfortunate, and awoke in Mr. Beresford a feeling of bitter jealousy which made him say things he would have given worlds to unsay when it was too late to do so.

"Phil!" he repeated, sneeringly. "Yes, I see; I understand; Phil is my rival, and I might have known it. Women always prefer idlers like him, who have—" he stopped suddenly, checked by the expression of the black eyes confronting him so steadily, and growing so fierce and bright, as the girl said:

"Well, go on. You did not finish. You said 'idlers like him, who have—' Have what? I insist upon knowing what you mean. What is it Phil has which you have not?"

Her tone and manner made him angry, and he answered at last:

"He has plenty of time at his disposal to make love to you; he has nothing else to do, and women like men with no aim, no object in life; nothing to do but to play the Sardanapalus."

"Mr. Beresford," and Reinette's eyes blazed with scorn, "I did not dream you were so mean—so dastardly. Idler as you say he is, Phil Rossiter would cut his tongue out sooner than it should say a word against you, his friend, were you a thousand times his rival; and you, in your foolish jealousy, accuse him of wearing women's dresses, and spinning, and—"

"Queenie, I did nothing of the sort," Mr. Beresford said, interrupting her, and she continued:

"Yes, you did. You likened him to Sardanapalus, which is the same thing, and I hate you for it!"

"Not more than I hate myself," Mr. Beresford said, for he was beginning to be very much ashamed of the weakness which prompted him to speak against Phil Rossiter, whom he liked so much. "Forgive me, Queenie; it was unmanly—cowardly in me to attack my rival, and nothing but cruel disappointment and bitter pain could have induced me to do it. Phil is my friend, and the most unselfish, kind-hearted fellow in the whole world. Can you forgive me for saying aught against him?"

Queenie knew he was in earnest, and, as ready to forgive as to take offense, she answered at once:

"Yes, I know you did not mean it; you could not. Phil may be an idler, I rather think he is, but he is so noble, so good, so unselfish, and bears with me as no one else ever could. But, Mr. Beresford, you are mistaken. Phil is not your rival, and it was no thought of him which led me to refuse you. He is my cousin, and if I loved him ever so much, I could no more marry him than I could my brother, if I had one. I am enough of a Roman Catholic to think such a marriage unnatural and wicked. I could not do it, and I have no desire to—no love for him that way. Why, I would sooner marry you than Phil; upon my word, I would."

She had forgiven him, and he knew it, and hope rose suddenly within him, and taking her hands in his, and holding them tightly there, he began again:

"Oh, Queenie, you give me new life, new hope, for if Phil is not my rival, you may come in time to think of me, not now, not for a year, perhaps, or more, but some time, when you have learned how much I love you. Promise me that you will try. Put me on trial for a year, during which time I will not bother you with love-making. I'll be your staid old guardian, nothing more. Will you—will you think of it a year!"

"Of what use would that be," she said, "when at the end of the year I should think just the same?"

"But you might not," he replied. "At least give me that chance; give me one ray of sunlight, for without it the world will be very dreary. I shall put myself on probation whether you will or not."

She did not answer him, but stood looking off across the moon-lit meadows with a troubled look in her dark eyes which he could not fathom. At last releasing her hands from his, she said, with a little shiver:

"It is growing cold. I must go in now, and you must go home, and never speak to me again as you have to-night."

"Not until a year, and then if no other love has come between us, I shall tell you again that I love you," he said, and she replied:

"A year is a long time, and so much may happen to us both."

It did seem long to her, but to him, who was so much older, it seemed as nothing, if at the end he could hope to win the girl who walked so silently by his side until the house was reached, where he said good-night to her and then rode back to town, feeling, in spite of her assertion to the contrary, that there was a grain of hope for him, if he would bide his time patiently, and feeling, too, a great remorse and hatred for himself for what he had said of Phil.

CHAPTER XXV

PHIL'S WOOING

When Phil left Reinette so suddenly he was full of resentment, for she had been unusually unreasonable and exasperating, and he meant what he said when he told her he would not come to her again if she wrote him a hundred notes of apology. She had called him a bore, and a spooney, and a Miss Nancy, and he did not know what else; and his anger continued all through the day and night when he lay awake thinking of her, and how she looked with the great tears standing in her flashing eyes as she bade him leave her and never come again.

"And I won't, by Jove!" he said, as he was dressing himself in the morning; but when breakfast was over, and he had sat for an hour or more with his mother and sisters he began to feel terribly ennuied, and to wonder why Grace and Ethel would be so dull and tame, and take so much interest in their worsteds, as if their lives depended upon having the right shades of wool in their roses.

They were nice girls, of course, he thought, but quite commonplace and old-maidish, and he was puzzled to know how he should dispose of his time, now that he could not go to Reinette. It had been his custom to ride over to Hetherton Place quite early in the day, and stay until late in the afternoon, but that was over now; he was never going there again, and life had rather a dreary lookout for Phil when he at last left the house and sauntered slowly toward Mr. Beresford's office.

The lawyer was busy, but he greeted Phil even more cordially than usual, for there was in his heart a feeling of keen regret for having allowed himself to say aught against the young man whom he really liked so much, and who, it seemed to him, looked rather sober and abstracted, as he seated himself near the window and began idly to turn the leaves of a law book. The mail was just in, and among Mr. Beresford's letters was one from his uncle, in New York, who wrote asking if his nephew, knew of any honest, trusty, winning young man who would like to go out to India for a year or more on business for the firm. Tact, and patience, and suavity of manner were the essential qualifications, he wrote, and to a person possessed of these, the firm would pay a liberal salary. On many accounts he preferred a man from the country, and so had written to his nephew first.

Mr. Beresford read the letter carefully, then glanced at Phil, and asked himself whether it were not a desire to remove a possible rival from his way, which prompted him to think him just the man for the place. Phil was trusty and winning, with any amount of tact and perseverance if once roused to action. The post would suit him exactly; and deciding at last that he was not wholly selfish in the matter, Mr. Beresford handed him the letter, saying:

"Here is something which may interest you, and possibly you may like the situation."

Phil read the letter through, and his first impulse was that he would go. He should enjoy the voyage immensely, for he liked the sea, and he should enjoy the new life, too, only—and Phil gave a little gasping breath, as he thought of going away where he could not even see Reinette. Of course, she would never be to him what she had been, but it would be some pleasure to see her come in and go out of his father's house, and to watch her in the street, and hear occasionally the sound of her voice, and all this would be impossible in India. And still the chance to do something, which he had so longed for at times, was too good to be lightly thrown away, and he said to Mr. Beresford:

"I am half inclined to go; at all events, I will see what father says, and let you know to-night."

"Bon jour, Monsieur Rossiter," fell suddenly on Phil's ear, and turning, he saw Pierre, who handed him a dainty note, and waited while he read it.

It was dated at "Hetherton Place, 9 o'clock A.M., and read as follows:

"Dear Phil:

"What a simpleton you must be to think I was in earnest when I told you to go and never come back again. I know I tried you awfully and so you did me, and you called me such dreadful names—a vixen, a virago, a cat, and a termagant, and the dear knows what, and I called you a bore, and a spooney, and said I hated you, but, Phil, I do not, and I am just as lonesome without you as I can be, and last night, after I went to my room, I cried real hard, and said to myself, 'I am sorry, Phil,' and I am, and want you to forgive me, and come right over here with Pierre and stay to lunch. I have ordered broiled chicken, with pop-overs and maple sirup. You know you can eat a dozen. I shall be out on the rocks, and see you when you come down the hill, and I will tie my pocket-handkerchief to my parasol and wave it for a signal. And now you will come, won't you, and we will make it up, and never, never fight again?

"Your repentant
"Queenie"

Phil Rossiter was not the man to withstand an appeal like this, and, as he read it, India and everything else was forgotten in his intense desire to fly to the girl waiting for him.

Mr. Beresford saw Pierre hand him the note, knew it was from Reinette, and watched him as he read it, while his color came and went like that of some young schoolgirl, and he was not greatly surprised when Phil said to him, as he rose to leave the office:

"By the way, I've been thinking it over, and I don't believe I care to go to India; it is too far away. There is Will Granger—just the fellow they want, and he needs money badly; offer it to him."

Phil was in the street by this time, and ten minutes later he was galloping toward Hetherton Place and the girl whose signal he saw as she waved it aloft to let him know she was there. And Phil rode hard and fast until he was at her side, sitting just where Mr. Beresford had stood the night before and asked her to be his wife.

How sweet and lovely she was with that air of shyness and penitence! for she was very sorry for what had passed, and very glad to have Phil back; and she gave him both her hands, and offered no resistance when he kissed them more than once, and held them while he talked to her, and asked if she did not think him weak and silly to come the minute she sent for him.

"No, I don't," she said; "I knew you would come back, just as I knew I should send for you. It is useless for us to try to live apart, for what would the world be to either of us without the other?"

"Nothing, Queenie, nothing," Phil said, eagerly, as he drew her down beside him and passed his arm around her waist, while the light of a new hope and joy shone all over his face.

Phil had long ago told himself that he loved Queenie with more than a cousin's love, and had only been deterred from telling her so by her fitful moods, sometimes all sunshine, sometimes all storm. But now he surely might speak with the full assurance of a favorable answer, for what but this could her manner mean, and her assertion that they could not live apart. She loved him, he was certain; and with his arm around her, he began rapidly and impetuously to tell her how inexpressibly dear she was to him, and to speak of the future when she would be his wife, as if everything were understood and settled between them.

"We will never quarrel then, will we, darling?" he said. "I should not like to see a frown on my wife's face, and know it was meant for me, and I will be so good and loving that you will not wish to call me a bore, and send me away from you. And we will be married at once. You need a husband to care for you, and there is no reason why we should wait a day. I will tell mother to-night, and she will be so glad, and so will Ethel and Grace, for they all love you dearly. Why don't you speak to me, Queenie?" he said, as she did not answer him, but sat like one dead to all sense of speech or hearing. "Why, Queenie, what is the matter? How white you are," he continued, as he stooped at last to look into the face, which was pale as ashes, with an expression of pain, and even horror, upon it, which he could not understand.

"Oh, Phil, you have killed me," Queenie said, at last, as she released herself from him and moved to another rock, where she sat down and looked at him with eyes from which the hot tears were falling like rain.

"Killed you, Queenie!" Phil cried. "How could I kill you by telling you that I loved you, when you must have known it already? Surely, surely, you have not been deceiving me all this time—not been leading me on to believe you loved me, just as I love you, only to mock me at the last? That would be cruel, indeed."

And this he said because of something in her face and eyes which filled him with dread and fear.

"Oh, Phil," Queenie replied, beating the air with her hands, as she always did when excited, "if my conscience reproved me one whit, and said I had purposely misled you for my own amusement, I would drown myself in Lake Petit, but I have not, I certainly have not. I thought——"

"You thought," Phil interrupted her, as she hesitated a moment—"thought what? That I was a stock—a stone to be unmoved by your beauty and sweetness, and—I will say it—your wiles and witcheries, which, if they meant nothing, were damnable, to say the least, and prove you to be the most heartless coquette that ever breathed. Girls do not usually write notes to men such as you have written me, begging them to come back, and then, when they go, receive them as you have received me, without meaning something, and if you do not mean marriage, may I ask what you do mean?"

He spoke bitterly, but not at all as he had ever spoken to her before when his temper and hers were at their height. It was the outraged, insulted man, not the passionate boy speaking to her now, and Queenie recognized the difference, and shivered from head to foot, as she crouched down on her knees beside him and sobbed:

"Listen to me, Phil, before you judge so harshly, and believe me, as I hope for heaven, I never tried to make you love me this way. You are my cousin—my blood relation; our mothers were sisters, and I have been taught that such unions were wicked, unnatural, such as God disapproves and curses."

"You are not a Roman Catholic?" Phil said, quickly, and she replied:

"No, but I had much of that teaching in my childhood, at home in France, and this is one of the things which took deep root in my mind. I had a governess who married her own cousin in spite of everything, and two of her children were idiots, while the third was deaf and dumb, and when the poor mother knew that, she drowned herself in the Seine. Phil, I would no sooner marry my cousin than I would my brother, if I had one, and I looked upon you as a brother, and loved you as such, and thought you understood. Surely, you cannot think me so brazen-faced and bold as to treat you as I have, with a view to making you want me for your wife. I am sorry, Phil, so sorry, and I wish I had never crossed the sea, for I can never be your wife—never! My whole nature revolts against it, the same as if you were my brother, and I know that all is over between us—that we can never be to each other again what we have been in the past. You will come here no more as you have come, and the days will be so long without you, Phil, and, worse than all, you will perhaps think always that I meant to deceive you; but I didn't. Oh, I didn't, and you must believe it and forgive me! Will you?"

She was still kneeling before him, her white face upturned to his, and every muscle quivering with anguish, as she thus importuned him. He could not resist her, and stooping down he kissed the quivering lips, but did not say he forgave her; he asked, instead: "If I were not your cousin, could you marry me?"

"I don't know, Phil. You see, I never thought about you in that way. I might, perhaps, in time, but I could not now, for you are like a brother, and I must go back to the beginning and build up a new kind of love for you; and then, Phil, I should wish you to be a little different from what you are now. Girls do not generally marry men who have—"

Here Queenie stopped suddenly, appalled at her own temerity, but Phil bade her go on in a tone she must obey, and she went on, and said:

"Who have nothing to do but amuse themselves and others. It is all very nice in cousins and brothers to know how to run our sewing-machines and how our dresses should be trimmed and ought to hang, but we wish our husbands to be different from that; wish them to have some aim in life—some occupation, and you have none. You have never done anything toward earning your own living. Your father is rich, it is true, and able to support you, but it is more manly to support one's self—don't you think so?"

She spoke very gently, but every word was a sting, and hurt Phil, if possible, more than her rejection of him had done.

"Yes, I see," he answered bitterly. "You think me a lazy dog, whom people generally despise, and so I am, but it is very hard to hear it from you, Queenie; hard to know that I have neither your love nor your respect, when, fool that I was, I believed I had both."

"And so you have, Phil; so you have," Reinette said, eagerly, touched by the grieved, hopeless expression of his face, which was not at all like Phil's face, usually so bright and happy. "You have both my love and respect—love as a sister—for neither Ethel nor Grace can love you better than I do, in a certain way, and I respect and esteem you as the kindest, and best, and most unselfish Phil in all the world. Don't, Phil, oh, don't cry!" she continued, in a tone of agonized entreaty, as the great tears, which he could not restrain, rolled down his white face, which was convulsed with pain. "If you cry like that, I shall wish I were dead, and I almost wish so now," she added, frightened by the storm of sobs and tears to which he at last gave vent.

She was still kneeling by him, and she crept down closer to him, and took his hands from his face, where he had put them, and wiped his tears away, while her own fell fast as she tried to comfort him and could not, for in only one way could she do that, and, with her view of the matter that was impossible. On that point she was as firm and conscientious as the most rigid Roman Catholic. To marry her cousin would be wicked, and so there was no hope for him in that way; but may be she could comfort him in another, and she said, at last:

"Phil, I can never marry you; that is just as impossible as for your sister to do it, but I can promise never to marry any one else. That would not be hard, for I do not believe I shall ever see any one for whom I care as I do for you; and, if you wish it, I'll swear to remain single for your sake forever. Shall I?"

"No, Queenie; no. I am not so selfish as that," he said. "You ought to marry; you need a husband here at Hetherton Place—somebody with energy and will, and not an effeminate idler like me."

He was still smarting from the hurt of her last objection to him, and he went on:

"Whether you marry or not cannot affect me, for I am going away—going to do something and be a man, whom you will never taunt again with his laziness and sloth."

"Oh, Phil, you misunderstood me! I did not taunt you. I only told you that girls would rather their lovers had some occupation. It was not a taunt at all. Forgive me, Phil. I am so sorry—oh, so sorry for this morning's work, when I meant to be so happy!"

Phil had risen to his feet, and she had risen, too, and stood looking up at him with an expression which, if it was not born of love, was near of kin to it, and nearly maddened Phil.

"Queenie," he began, laying his hands upon her shoulders and looking fixedly into her eyes, "do you mean to send me away with no word of hope?—mean that you cannot be my wife?"

"Yes, Phil; I mean it. I can never be your wife; because I am your cousin, and because I do not love you in that way," she said.

And Phil knew she meant it, and was conscious of a death-like sickness stealing over and mastering him, and making him sit down again upon the rock, while every thing grew dark around him, and Queenie's voice seemed a long way off, as she spoke to him in affrighted tones, and asked if he were fainting.

He did not faint, though it was some minutes before he was himself again and arose to say good-by. There was no question of lunch, no thought of broiled chicken and pop-overs, for both were past caring for such things now, and only remembered that in some sense, this good-by was forever.

She thought he would, of course, come to Hetherton Place again—to-morrow, perhaps—but not as he had come heretofore; not as in the old happy days; not as the Phil with whom she could play and coquette, but more as a stranger; more like Mr. Beresford before he troubled her with his tale of love.

He knew he should not come again to-morrow, nor for many, many to-morrows—never, perhaps; for there was danger in that far-off eastern land to which he now meant to go. Possibly his grave was there waiting for him, or he might tarry years and years, until the bright, beautiful girl standing before him had grown old and gray with the cares of life. And so, to him, it was good-by forever; but he would not tell her so. He would wait and write his farewell. But he must kiss her once, for the sake of all she had been to him, and that he had hoped she would be. He was a tall young man of six feet and she a wee little girl, whom he could take in his arms as he would a child; and he took her in his arms, and kissed her forehead and lips, and said to her:

"Remember, Queenie, whatever comes, my love for you will remain unchanged; for it was not the love of a day or a year, but love till death, and after, too, if such a thing can be. Good-by! I'm going now."

And he went swiftly from her, while she watched him with a throbbing heart; and neither of them guessed just where or how they would meet again.

CHAPTER XXVI

PHIL GOES AWAY

Mr. Beresford was alone in his office when Phil came in after his return from Hetherton Place, and asked, abruptly:

"Have you seen Will Granger about going to India?"

"Not yet; no, I thought I would wait till to-night," Mr. Beresford replied, and Phil continued:

"Don't see him, then; I will take the place. Write so to your uncle at once, or perhaps I had better write myself."

Something in the tone of his voice made Mr. Beresford turn quickly and look at him.

"Why, Phil," he said, "what ails you? What has happened to make you look so white and strange?"

"Nothing," Phil answered—"that is, nothing of any consequence to any one but myself." Then, moved by a sudden impulse to tell somebody, Phil burst out: "Beresford, I can trust you, I know, for you have always been my friend."

"Yes," faltered Mr. Beresford, thinking remorsefully of what he said to Reinette, and wondering if Phil would think that friendly, if he knew.

"I must tell somebody—talk to somebody, or go crazy," Phil continued. "The fact is, I have made a fool of myself and been rejected, as I deserved."

"You rejected! By whom?" Mr. Beresford asked, although he felt that he knew perfectly well what the answer would be.

"By Reinette, of course. What other woman is there on the face of the earth whose no is worth caring for? I asked her to be my wife, and she refused, and made me know she meant it; and now I am going to India, for I cannot stay here."

"What reason did she give for her refusal?" Mr. Beresford asked, feeling like a guilty hypocrite, and Phil replied:

"She had three reasons, each of them good and sufficient in her own mind. First, she did not love me in that way, as she expressed it; second, I am her cousin, and, with her Roman Catholic notions, it is an unpardonable sin to marry one's cousin; and third, she could not marry a man with no aim, no occupation, no business except to loop up dresses and run a sewing-machine. That's what she said, or something like it, and that hurt me worst of all, for it made me feel so small, so contemptible: and, after she said it, I knew how impossible it was for her even to respect such a dawdling, effeminate Sardanapalus as I must appear to her."

At the mention of Sardanapalus Mr. Beresford started, for that was the name he had used when speaking of Phil to Reinette. Had she told him? It was not likely, else he had never come there with his confidence, which seemed so like a stab to the conscience-stricken man, who at last could bear it no longer, and as Phil went on with his story, showing in all he said how implicitly he trusted him, he burst out:

"Stop, Phil, stop a minute, while I make a confession to you, and then you will not think me so much your friend, though Heaven knows I am, and that there is no man living I like as well. But, Phil, I went back on you once, and in a moment of weakness said things for which I blush. I, too, have offered myself to Reinette Hetherton."

"You! When?" Phil exclaimed, and Mr. Beresford replied:

"Only last night, and when she refused me, and said she did not love me, I accused you of being my rival, and in my mad jealousy said things of you which only a coward could have said of his friend. I sneered at your idle, aimless life, and said that women generally preferred a Sardanapalus to energetic, strong men, or something like that."

"You said this of me to Reinette, and I thought you my friend! I would never have served you so," Phil said, and in his eyes there was an expression which hurt Mr. Beresford cruelly, and made him think of the wounded Cæsar when he cried out, "Et tu, Brute!"

"Yes, I said it, Phil, but I took it all back, and made what amends I could. Queenie will tell you so if you ask her. She flew in my face like a yellow-jacket, and defended you bravely. Forgive me, Phil; I am greatly ashamed of myself."

He offered his hand to the young man, in whose eyes tears were shining, but who did not refuse to take it, though he was still smarting under this new pain.

"I can forgive you," he said, with a faint smile, "because Queenie defended me, but it is very hard to bear. You say she refused you and gave you no hope?" Mr. Beresford thought of the year's probation he had insisted upon, and spoke of it to Phil, but added:

"She told me, however, that it was useless, for at the end of the time her answer would be the same, so you see there is no hope for me either;" and this he said because he saw how utterly crushed and heart-broken Phil was, and he would not add to his pain by confessing that away down in his heart there was a shadowy hope that Queenie might change her mind, especially with Phil away, for he was going. He had made up his mind to that, and before returning home he wrote himself to the firm in New York, accepting the situation, and saying he would be in the city the next evening, as he wished for a few days before sailing in which to post himself with reference to the business.

"But why go to-morrow? There is no such haste necessary," Mr. Beresford said, when he heard the contents of the letter, and Phil replied:

"I must go before I see her again; the sight of her might unman me and make me give it up."

So the letter was sent, and when Phil went home to dinner at night he startled his family by telling them that he was going to India for a year, and possibly longer.

"To India!" both mother and sisters exclaimed, and then Phil explained it to them.

The former opposed the plan with all her strength, for life without Phil would be nothing to the mother who loved him so much. Mr. Rossiter, on the contrary, approved it. It was no way for a young man to hang on to his mother's apron strings all his days, he said; Phil ought to do something for himself. This was only a repetition of the old story of idleness and ease, and confirmed Phil in his purpose. He would make something of himself—would show that he was capable of higher occupation than devising trimming for dresses and running a sewing-machine. He was very sore on the subject of the sewing-machine, and very reticent all through the dinner, and when it was over excused himself to his sisters, saying he had letters to write and some few matters which must be attended to. It was very sudden to them all—his going away—but, as he said, he was his own master and must act for himself, and when his mother tried to persuade him to give it up, he answered:

"No, I have staid with you too long. You are the best and dearest mother in the world, but you have done wrong not to send me away before this, and make me stay away, too. I should have been more of a man among men. I see it now, and must take the first chance offered me. A year is not very long, and I shall write to you every week."

So Mrs. Rossiter gave it up, and busied herself with various preparations for his comfort, and said she should go to New York to see him off, and tried to seem cheerful and happy, and tried, with his sisters, to fathom the cloud which overshadowed his face, and made him so unlike himself. What had happened to him, and was Reinette in any way connected with it? They thought so, and when in the morning he said he was going to bid his grandmother and Anna good-by, and they asked if he were not going to see Reinette, too, and he answered: "I saw her yesterday, but give her this letter when I am gone," they were sure of it, and for the first time since they had known her, they felt a little vexed with the girl, who even then was watching from her window for the rider coming over the river, across the causeway, and up the long hill as he would not come again, for when, later in the day, the express train for New York stopped at West Merrivale, it carried him along toward the new life which was to have an aim and occupation.

CHAPTER XXVII

HOW QUEENIE BORE THE NEWS

She saw the long train as it came across the plains from East Merrivale—saw it shoot under the bridge, past the station, and glide swiftly on by the river-side until it was lost to view in the deep cut by the old gold-mine, and remembered that afterward she heard the whistle as the train stopped at

132

West Merrivale a few minutes and then went speeding on to the West But she never dreamed that it carried with it a young man whose face was pale as ashes as he sat with folded arms, and hat pulled over his eyes, seeing nothing of what was passing around him, and thinking only of her, listening even then for the sound of his horse's feet coming up the hill. For Queenie felt sure he would come back to her, and that in some way they would make it up, and resume their old, delightful relations with each other. And she watched for him all day long, and was beginning to get restless and impatient, when, about sunset, the Rossiter carriage came slowly up the hill and into the yard.

In a trice Queenie was at the door, feeling certain that the recreant Phil had driven over with his sisters, as he sometimes did. But only Ethel and Grace were there, and it struck Queenie that there was something a little strange in their manner, while Grace had evidently been crying.

"I am so glad you have come!" she said, as she led the way into the house. "I have been so lonely to-day, with not a person to see me except the major and Anna, who were here a few moments this morning, and who are so absorbed in each other as to be of no account to any one else. I do believe he is in earnest, and means to marry her; and then won't we have to bow to my Lady Rossiter! Where's Phil, and why has not he been here to-day?"

"Phil has gone; you surely knew that, or, at least, that he was going; he was here yesterday," Ethel said; and in her voice there was a hardness, as if her cousin were trifling with her thus to ask for her brother.

But she knew better when she saw how white Queenie grew, as she repeated after her:

"Gone, and I knew of his going! You are mistaken; I know nothing. Where has he gone?"

"To India!" Ethel said.

And then Reinette grasped the chair near which she was standing with both hands, and leaning heavily upon it, asked, in a half whisper, for something was choking her so that she could not speak aloud:

"To India! For what? And how long will he be gone?"

As rapidly as possible Ethel told all she knew of a matter which had taken them so by surprise, and which had so affected her mother that she was sick in bed.

For a moment Queenie did not speak, but stood staring at Ethel, who, sure that she was in fault, went pitilessly on:

"We thought you had something to do with it; that you sent him away, for it was after he came from here yesterday that he decided to go; he had given it up before."

"I sent him away!—sent him to India to die, as he will! No, no; I did not do that," Queenie cried, piteously. "I said I could not marry him, and he my cousin; and I could not, any more than you could marry him, he being your brother. But I did not think he'd go away. Oh! what shall we do without Phil?"

Reinette was sobbing passionately, and Ethel and Grace were crying with her, for Phil had made the happiness of their lives, and without him they were very desolate.

"Did he speak of me?" Queenie asked, at last. "Did he leave no word? no message? no good-by?"

"He left this for you," Ethel said, passing the letter to Queenie, who clutched it eagerly, but would not read it there with the sisters looking on. That they blamed her, and held her responsible for Phil's India trip, she was certain, and she felt glad when they at last said good-night, and left her to herself and her letter—Phil's letter—which she read in the privacy of her room, and which nearly broke her heart.

"Dear Queenie," he began, "I am going away—for a year certainly, and perhaps, forever, for men of my habits, who have never been accustomed to hardships of any kind, die easily in that hot climate."

"Oh-h!" and Reinette groaned bitterly, as she thought, "Why did Phil say what will make me feel like his murderer, if he should die out there."

Then she read on:

"I am going to India on business for a firm in New York, of which Mr. Beresford's uncle is the head. The salary is good, and the duties such as I can perform, and so I am going. Mr. Beresford made me the offer this morning, and with my usual indolence I declined it, but I did not then know your opinion of me; did not know how you despised me for my effeminacy and laziness. Queenie, I do believe that hurt me more than your refusal of me. I might live without your love, perhaps, but not without your respect, and so I am going to begin life anew, with some aim, some occupation, and you shall never taunt me again with my idleness. But oh, Queenie, how I love you, and how I long to hold you in my arms as my own darling. It is a strange power which you have over us men—a power to hold us at your will by one glance of your eyes, or toss of your head. Other faces may be more beautiful than yours; some would say that Margery La Rue's was one of them, but there is something about you more attractive than mere regularity of feature or purity of complexion, and men go down before it as I have done, body and soul, with no hope or wish for anything else, if you must be denied me. May you never know how my heart is aching as I write this, my farewell to you; and yet to have known and loved you is the dearest thing in life, and the memory of you will help to make me a man. I know you will be sorry when I am gone, and miss me everywhere, but you will get accustomed to it in time. Some one else will take my place; and, just here, although I do not pretend to be so good or unselfish that it does not cost me a pang to do it I would say a word for Mr. Beresford. He knows why I go away, for I told him, and like the splendid fellow he is, he confessed what he said of me to you, and asked my pardon for it, and I forgave him, and you must do so, too, and not be hot, and rash, and bitter against him, as something tells me you may be, when you know I am gone, and that possibly Mr. Beresford suggested to you the words which made me go. He told me of your refusal of himself, but he hopes time may change you; and if it does—oh, my darling, how can I say it, loving you as I do?—if it does, don't worry and tease him, but deal with him honestly and openly, as a true woman should deal with a true, honest man. And now, good-by, and if it is forever—if I never come back again—remember that I love you always, always! and I shall carry your image with me wherever I go, and so, in fancy, I put my arms around you and hold you for a moment as my own, and kiss your dear face, feeling sure that if it were really so, that I was saying good-by to you forever and you knew it, you would kiss me back once at least, in token of all we have been to each other."

"Oh, Phil, Phil, yes, a thousand times would I kiss you, if you were back again! and I am so sorry for the nasty words I said about your idleness," Reinette cried, as, with Phil's letter clutched tightly in her hand, she lay upon her face sobbing bitterly, and wondering what life was worth to her now, that Phil was gone.

"I couldn't marry him, I couldn't, for he is my cousin!" she said; "and I do not love him that way, but he was so much to me, how can I live without him?"

And then there began to creep into her heart hot, resentful feelings toward Mr. Beresford, who had put it into her mind to taunt Phil with his idleness.

"I hate him—I hate him!" she said, stamping her little feet by way of emphasis, but when she remembered that Phil had forgiven him, and still held him as his friend, and wished her to do so, she grew more calm and less resentful toward him, but declined to see him, when, next morning, he rode over to Hetherton Place and asked for her.

"Tell him I am sick," she said to Pierre, "and can see no one, unless it is Margery. Ask him, please, to call at her door, and tell her to come to me, for I am in great trouble."

With a suspicion as to the nature of Queenie's trouble, Mr. Beresford rode back to town and delivered the message to Margery, who went at once to her friend and tried to comfort her. But Queenie refused to be comforted. Phil was gone, and what was there now for her?

"You can bring him back. The ship does not sail for some days you say, and a word from you will change his mind," Margery said, caressing the bowed head resting on her lap.

"Do you think—do you believe he would come back, if I were to write and beg him?" Queenie asked, quickly, lifting up her tear-stained face.

"I've no doubt of it," Margery said; "but, darling, if you do that he will have a right to expect you to marry him. Sending for him to come back would mean nothing else, nor would anything else satisfy him."

"Then he must go," Queenie answered, with a rain of tears. "I cannot marry my cousin; that is a part of my religion. It would be hideous to do it. Phil must go; but my whole life goes with him. Oh, Phil, I am nothing, nothing without you. Why were you so silly as to fall in love and so spoil everything?"

That night, as Margery sat with her mother over their tea talking of Queenie, Mrs. La Rue said to her;

"If Mr. Rossiter were not her cousin, do you think she would marry him?"

"I have no doubt of it," Margery replied. "She fancies she does not love him in that way, as she expresses it, but if the obstacle of cousinship were removed, I believe she would feel differently. Poor little girl, she is so cast down and wretched, thinking she has driven him away to die, as she declares he will."

Mrs. La Rue had listened intently to all Margery told her of Reinette's distress, and there were tears in her eyes as she cleared away the tea things, and busied herself with her household cares.

"Poor little girl," she whispered to herself. "Would her love for him outweigh everything—everything, I wonder? Is it mightier than her pride?"

CHAPTER XXVIII

MRS. LA RUE'S RESOLUTION

There was a worn, tired look on Mrs. La Rue's face next morning, which she accounted for by saying she had not slept well, and that her head was aching. A walk in the crisp autumn air would do her good, she said; and soon after breakfast she left the house, and started toward Hetherton Place. Twice on the causeway she sat down to rest, and once on the bank by the side of the road which led up the long hill. Here she sat for a long time, with her head bowed upon her knees, while she seemed to be absorbed in painful, and even agonized reflection, for she rocked to and fro, and whispered occasionally to herself. In the distance there was the sound of wheels—some one was coming; and not caring to be seen, she arose, and climbing the low stone wall, went up the steep hill-side to the ledge of rocks, where Phil had sat with Queenie and heard his doom. It was the first time Mrs. La Rue had ever been there, and for a moment she stood transfixed with surprise and delight at the lovely view before her. In the clear autumn air objects were visible for miles and miles away, but it was not so much at the distant landscape she gazed as at the scene directly about her—at the broad, rich acres of Hetherton Place, stretching away to the westward, and southward, and eastward, and embracing some of the most valuable land in Merrivale; at the house itself, standing there on the heights so stately and grand, with aristocracy and blood showing themselves from every casement and door-post; and lastly, at the beautiful grounds, so like the parks of some of the old chateaus in France, with their terraces, and winding walks, and pieces of statuary gleaming here and there among the evergreens.

"A goodly heritage truly," the woman said. "And would she give it all for love? God only knows, and I can only know by trying. If she will see me, I must go forward; if she refuses, I shall take it as a sign that I must forevermore keep silent."

Thus deciding, she walked quickly across the fields, and soon stood ringing at the door, which was opened by Pierre himself.

"Miss Hetherton was still in her room," he said, "but he would take any message madame chose to give him;" and his manner showed plainly the great distance he felt there was between his mistress and the woman who, he knew, was born in the same rank of life as himself.

"Tell her Margery's mother is here, and very anxious to see her," Mrs. La Rue said; and with a bow, Pierre departed, leaving her alone in the hall.

He had not asked her to sit down, but she felt too faint and tremulous to stand, and, sinking into a chair, leaned her head against the hat-stand, and shutting her eyes, waited as people wait for some great shock or blow which they know is inevitable. How long Pierre was gone she could not guess, for she was lost to all consciousness of time, and was only roused when he laid his hand upon her shoulder and demanded what was the matter, and if she were sick. Then she looked up, and showed him a face so white, so full of pain, and dread, and horror, that he asked her again what was the matter.

"Nothing, nothing," she answered, sharply. "Tell me what did she say? Will she see me?"

"She bade me tell you she could not see you, but if your errand was very particular or concerned Miss Margery, you were to give it to me," Pierre replied, and in an instant the whole aspect of the woman changed, the deathly pallor left her face, and the look of dread and anguish was succeeded by one of intense relief as she exclaimed:

"Thank God! thank God! for I could not have borne it. I could not have done it at the last, and now I know it is not required of me. I have no errand, no message; good-morning," and she darted from the door, while Pierre looked wonderingly after her, saying to himself, "I believe the woman is crazy."

And in good truth insanity would best describe Mrs. La Rue's condition of mind as she sped down the winding hills and across the causeway, until the bridge was reached, and then she paused, and leaning far over the railing looked wistfully down into the depths below, as if that watery bed would be most grateful to her. Suicide was something of which Mrs. La Rue had thought more than once. It was the phantom which at times haunted her day and night, and now it looked over her shoulder and whispered:

"Why not end it now and forever? Better to die than live to ruin that young life, and know yourself loathed and despised by the creature you love best. Sometime in your fits of conscientiousness you will tell, as you were tempted to do just now, and then——"

Mrs. La Rue gave a long, gasping shudder as she thought, "What then?" and leaned still farther over the parapet beneath which the waters of the Chicopee were flowing so sluggishly.

"Yes, better die before I am left to tell and see the love in Margery's face turn to bitter hatred. Oh, Margery, my child. Mine, by all that is sacred! I cannot die and go away from her forever, for if there be a hereafter, as she believes, we should never meet again. Her destiny would be Heaven, and mine blackness and darkness of despair, where the worm dieth not, and the fire is not quenched! She read me that last night, little dreaming that I carry about with me the worm which dieth not, and have carried it so many years, and oh, how it does gnaw and gnaw at times, until I am tempted to shriek out the dreadful thing. Oh, God, forgive me, and help me to hold my tongue, and keep the love of Margery."

She had drawn back from the railing by this time and, gathering her shawl around her, she started for home, where she found Margery in the reception-room alone, busily engaged on a dark-blue silk, which Anna Ferguson had deigned to give her to make, and for which she was in a hurry. She had been there that morning to see about it, and had found a great deal of fault with some trimming which she had ordered herself, and had insisted that the dress must be finished by twelve o'clock, as she was going with Major Lord Rossiter to West Merrivale to see a base-ball match on the Common.

"The match does not come off until four," Margery said, "and if you can give me till half-past two I shall be so glad."

But Miss Anna was decided; she must have it at twelve, or not at all, and when Margery asked if she would send for it, as the girl who usually took parcels home was sick, she answered promptly;

"No, it is not my business to do that."

And Margery bore the girl's insolence quietly, and promised that the dress should be done, and put aside Mrs. Col. Markham's work to do it, because she knew Mrs. Markham was a lady and would not insult her if she chanced to be disappointed. But she felt the ill-bred girl's impertinence keenly, and her cheeks were unusually red, and her lips very white, when her mother entered the room, and, bending over her, kissed her with a great, glad tenderness as we kiss one restored to us from the gates of death.

"You look tired and worried, ma petite," she said, "and you are working so fast. I thought that dress was not to be finished till to-morrow."

"Nor was it," Margery answered, "but Miss Ferguson has been here and insists upon having it at twelve, and she was so overbearing, and found so much fault, and made me feel so keenly that I was only her dressmaker, that I am a little upset, even though I know she is not worth a moment's disquietude."

"Poor Margery! It is to the caprices of such people as she that you are subjected because you are poor," Mrs. La Rue said, caressing the golden head bent so low over Anna's navy-blue, on the sleeve of which a great tear came near falling. "You ought to be rich, like Miss Hetherton. You would be happier in her place, would you not, my child?"

"No, mother," and Margery's beautiful blue eyes looked frankly up into her mother's face. "I should like money, of course, but I am very happy as I am except when people like Anna insult me and try to make me feel the immeasurable distance there is between themselves and a dressmaker. I like my profession, for it is as much one as that of the artist or musician, and if I were rich as Queenie I do believe I should still make dresses for the love of it. So, mother mine, don't bother about me. I am very happy—happier far, just now, than Queenie, who, though she may have riches in abundance, has no mother to love her, and care for her, and pet her, as I have."

"Oh, Margery, child, you do love me, then you are glad I am your mother, unlike you as I am?" Mrs. La Rue cried in a voice which was like a sob of pain, and made Margery look wonderingly at her, as she said:

"Why, mother, how strangely you act this morning. Of course I am glad you are my mother—the dearest and kindest a girl ever had. I cannot remember the time when you would not and did not sacrifice everything for me, and why should I not love you?"

"You should, you ought," Mrs. La Rue replied, "only you are so different from me that sometimes when I think how refined and lady-like you are, and then remember what I am—an uneducated peasant woman—I feel that I am an obstacle in your way, and that you must feel it, too, and wish you were some one else—somebody like Miss Hetherton—but you don't, Margery, you don't."

"Of course I don't," Margery answered, laughingly, "for if I were Miss Hetherton, don't you see, Anna would be my cousin, and that would be worse than a hundred peasant women; so, little mother, don't distress yourself or bother me any more, for my Lady Anna must have her dress by twelve, and it is nearly eleven now."

Taking the girl's lovely face between her hands Mrs. La Rue kissed it fondly, and then left the room, while Margery wondered what had happened to excite her so. Such moods, or states of mind, in her mother were not unusual, and since coming to Merrivale they had been more frequent than ever, so Margery was accustomed to them, and ascribed them to a naturally morbid temperament, combined with a low, nervous state of health.

"I wonder why she asks me so often if I love her and am happy? Maybe I do not show her my affection enough. I am not demonstrative, like her; there's very little of the French gush in me. I am more like the cold Americans, but I mean to do better and pet her more, poor, dear mother, she is so fond and proud of me," Margery thought, as she kept on with her work, while her mother busied herself in the kitchen, preparing the cup of nice hot tea and slice of cream toast which at twelve she carried to her daughter, who could not stop for a regular meal.

The navy-blue was at a point now where no one could touch it but herself, and she worked steadily on until after one, when Anna again appeared, asking imperiously why the dress was not sent at twelve, as she ordered.

"Because it was not done," Margery replied, adding, "It is a great deal of work to change all that trimming as you desired."

"It ought not to have been made that way in the first place," Anna rejoined, and then continued, "I must have it by two at the latest, and will you bring it yourself, so as to try it on me and see if it hangs right?"

"Yes, I'll bring it," Margery said, and an hour later she was trudging along Cottage Row with a bundle almost as large as herself, for the dress had many plaitings, and puffs, and bows, and must not be crushed by crowding into a small space.

But Margery did not feel one whit degraded or abased, even though she met Mr. Beresford fade to face, and saw his surprise at the size of the bundle.

Mr. Beresford was the only man who had ever interested Margery in the least, and she often wondered why she should feel her blood stir a little more quickly when she saw him. He was so proud, and dignified, and reserved, though always a gentleman and courteous to her, and now he lifted his hat very politely, and, with a pleasant smile, passed on, thinking to himself how beautiful the French girl was, and what a pity, too, that she had not been born in the higher ranks of life, with such people as the Rossiters, and Hethertons, and Beresfords.

Miss Anna was waiting impatiently, and all ready to step into her dress, which fitted her perfectly, and was so becoming, and gave her so much style that she condescended to be very gracious and familiar, and as she looked at herself in the glass, she said:

"Why, La Rue, you are a brick; how lovely it is! I have not a word of fault to find!"

"I am glad if it suits you. Good-afternoon, Miss Ferguson," Margery said, quietly, and then walked away, while Anna thought:

"If she were a grand duchess she could not be more airy. I wonder who she thinks she is, any way? Queenie has just spoiled her with so much attention, and she only a dressmaker!"

CHAPTER XXIX

LETTERS FROM MENTONE

Whether we are sorry or glad, time never stops for us, but the days and nights go on and on, until at last we wonder that so long a period has elapsed since the joy or sorrow came which marked a never-to-be-forgotten point in our lives.

And so it was with Queenie; she could not be as wretched and disconsolate always as she was during the first days of Phil's absence. She was of too light and buoyant a temperament for that, and after a little she woke to the fact that life had still much happiness in store for her, even though Phil could not share it with her. She had received a few words from him written just before the steamer sailed—words which made her cry as if her heart would break, but which were very precious to her because of their assurance that whatever might befall the writer she would always be his queen, his love, whose image was engraven on his heart forever.

And Queenie had answered the note, for it was nothing more, and filled four sheets with her passionate longings for the naughty boy, as she called him, who was not satisfied to be her cousin, but must needs seek to be her lover, and so had made her life miserable.

This letter was sent to Rome, for Phil was to take the overland route to India and visit the Imperial City on the way. He had promised to write from every point where he stopped, and so he did not seem so very far away, and Queenie grew brighter and gayer, and consented to see Mr. Beresford, whom she had persistently ignored, and after rating him soundly for the part he had had in sending Phil away, she became very gracious to him, for Phil had forgiven him, and she must do so, too, and she rode with him one day after his fast horse, and was so bright, and coquettish, and bewitching, that Mr. Beresford forgot himself, and in lifting her from the carriage held her hand tighter in his than was at all necessary. But Queenie withdrew it quickly, and with her usual frankness, said:

"You are not to squeeze my hand that way, Mr. Beresford, or think because I rode with you, that you are on probation, as you call it, for you are not. I am not trying to reconsider, and never shall."

This state of things was not very hopeful for Mr. Beresford, who, nevertheless, drove away more in love than ever with the little lady of Hetherton, who, after he was gone, went to her room, where she found on her dressing-table a letter which Pierre had brought from the office during her absence. It was a foreign letter, postmarked at Mentone, France. Reinette's first exclamation was:

"From the agent. Now I shall hear from Christine."

This was the thing of all others which she had greatly desired, but now that it seemed to be within her grasp, she waited and loitered a little, and took off her hat, and shawl, and gloves, and laid them carefully away, and picked a few dead leaves from a pot of geraniums in the window, before breaking the seal. And even then she hesitated with a strangely nervous feeling, as if from fear that the letter might contain something she would be happier not to know—something her father would have withheld from her, had he been there with her.

"But no," she said at last, "how foolish I am. Christine was faithful to my mother, and father pensioned her for it, as he ought to do, and those vile, evil-minded Polignies thought there was harm in it. They did not know my father, or what stuff the Hethertons are made of. So saying, she opened the letter and read:

"Mentone, France, Oct. 18, 18—.

"To Miss Hetherton, of Merrivale,

Worcester Co., Mass., U. S. A.

"My employer, M. Albrech, is gone away for a few days, and told me to open his letters, and, if necessary, answer them for him. So when yours and Monsieur's came, I opened and read; that is, read yours, but Monsieur's was in English, and it took a long time for me to make out that it meant the same as yours, and asked information of one Christine Bodine, pensioner of M. Hetherton, deceased."

"That was Mr. Beresford who sent him an English letter. What business

141

has he to pry into my affairs?" Reinette exclaimed, and her cheeks were scarlet, and her breath came hurriedly, and then seemed to cease altogether, as she read on:

"I could not remember any one by that name, but there is a certain Madame Henri La Rue, to whom, by reference to M. Albrech's books, I find that moneys were paid regularly by Messrs. Polignie & Co., Paris, for a M. Hetherton, until last summer, when the entire principal was sent to Madame La Rue, at 'Oak Bluffs, Martha's Vineyard, Mass, U. S. A.,' where it seems she is living, though whether she is the person you are wishing to find I do not know. Your billet to Christine Bodine I will keep until M. Albrech returns, and if he knows the woman he will forward it.

"Hoping my letter is satisfactory, I am

"Your obedient servant,
"Louis Arnaud."

"Madame Henri La Rue, Oak Bluffs, Martha's Vineyard, Mass. U. S. A.," Reinette kept repeating to herself, while a feeling of terror took possession of her, and made her for a moment powerless to move or reason clearly. "Who is this Madame La Rue, and where have I seen her?" she asked herself in a bewildered kind of way, and then at last it came to her who Mrs. La Rue was, and where she had seen her.

"Margery's mother! Christine Bodine! impossible!" she cried, reading Louis Arnaud's letter again and again, while her thoughts went backward, and with lightning rapidity gathered up every incident connected with Mrs. La Rue which had seemed strange to her, and made her dislike the woman for her unwarrantable familiarity.

As distinctly as if it were but yesterday she recalled their first meeting in Paris in Margery's receiving-room, when Mrs. La Rue had stared at her so, and seemed so strange and queer; and since then she had so often offended with what appeared like over-gratitude for kindness shown to Margery.

"And all the time when I was talking of my nurse and my desire to find her, she knew she was Christine and made no sign," Queenie said; "and once she bade me stop searching for her, as finding her might bring more pain than pleasure. What does she mean, and why does she not wish me to know who she is? Was there anything wrong about her—No, no, no!" and Reinette almost shrieked as she said the emphatic "no's." "Mother trusted her; mother loved her. I have it in her own words written to papa. 'Christine is faithful and tender as if she were my mother, instead of my maid; and if I should die, you must always be kind to her for what she has been to me,' she wrote, and that's why he sent her the money. But why has she never told me? What has she done? What is she? Yes, she was right. It is more pain than pleasure to find her; but if she had only told me who she was, it would have been such joy to know she was Margery's mother—my Margery still, thank God, for she has had no part in this concealment. She has no suspicion that Christine Bodine and her mother are one and the same."

This mention of Margery helped Reinette, and the pain in her heart was not quite so heavy, or her resentment toward Mrs. La Rue so great. She was Margery's mother, and whatever happened, Reinette would stand by the girl whom she loved so much.

"Please, mademoiselle, have you heard the bell; it has rung three times, and dinner is growing cold," Pierre said, putting his head in at the door; and then Reinette roused herself to find that it was getting dark, for the November twilight was fast creeping into the room.

"Yes, Pierre, I know; I am not coming—I am not hungry. Tell them to clear the table," she said, abstractedly; and then, as Pierre looked inquiringly at her she continued: "Pierre, come here, and shut the door, and come close to me, so no one can hear. Pierre, I've found Christine Bodine!"

"You have found her? Where?" Pierre said, looking wonderingly at his young mistress, whose white face and excited manner puzzled and alarmed him.

"Here, Pierre, in Merrivale. While I was searching for her across the water she was here, not a mile away, and never told me. Pierre, Mrs. La Rue is or was Christine Bodine!"

"Mon Dieu," Pierre ejaculated, with a shrug of his shoulders and a rapid movement of his hands, "Madame La Rue Christine Bodine! I am very much, yes, I suppose I am very much astonished!"

But he was not. He had never shared Reinette's implicit faith in Christine, and he put things together rapidly, and to himself he thought:

"Yes, madame is Christine. I am not surprised;" but to Reinette he said, "Who told you? There must be some mistake, madame surely would never have kept silent so long."

"There is no mistake. I can trust you, Pierre, and I begin to feel as if you were the only one I can trust. Everything and everybody is slipping away from me. This is the letter from the agent in Mentone, who paid her the money for Messrs. Polignie in Paris. You know you were in their office once with father and saw him give his check for twelve hundred and fifty francs to be sent to her. Read the letter, Pierre, and you will know all I do."

She handed it to him, and striking a light he read it through, while Reinette watched him narrowly to see what effect it had upon him. But aside from frequent ejaculations of surprise he made no comment, and just then the dinner-bell rang again, this time long and loud as if the ringer were growing impatient.

"Oh, that dreadful bell," Reinette exclaimed, putting her hands to her ears to shut out the sound. "Will they never stop ringing it, or understand that I am not coming? Go, Pierre, and tell them to clear the table away; tell them I am sick and tired, and wish to be let alone; tell them anything to keep them away from me. No body must come to-night but you. Go quick, before they ring again, or Mrs. Jerry comes herself. She must not know what we do."

Thus entreated Pierre departed with the message to Mrs. Jerry, and then went back to Reinette who sat with her hands clasped tightly together and a look on her white face which puzzled him, for he did not know that she was bravely fighting down a suspicion to harbor which would be to dishonor her father in his grave.

"Pierre," she said, lifting her dry, heavy eyes appealingly to him, and speaking like a sick child which wants to be petted; "Pierre, I am strangely shaken by this news, because I do not understand why Christine should wish to hide her identity from me, when she knew how I wanted to find her. It looks as if there was something which she wished to keep from me—something wrong in her life after she left us—and was married to M. La Rue. I had so much faith in and love for her, and now—oh, Pierre, it makes me cold, and sick, and faint. Forget that I am a woman; try and fancy me a little girl again, as I was when you first came to Chateau des Fleurs, and take me up and carry me to the couch. I could not walk there to save my life, for the strength has all gone from my body."

Pierre had carried her in his arms many a time in the years gone by, and now he took her up gently, and laying her upon the couch, brought a pillow for her, and fixed it under her head, and covered her with her shawl, and put fresh coal on the grate, for the November night was cold and chill, and outside the first snow of the season was beginning to fall.

"Now sit down by me, Pierre," she continued "and rub my hands, they are so numb and lifeless, and let me talk to you of the olden time, when we lived in the country and were so very happy."

"Yes, mademoiselle," Pierre said sitting down beside her and rubbing and chafing the limp white fingers which seemed to have no vitality in them.

"Pierre," she began, "we were so happy when papa was alive; he was so good. He was always kind to you, was he not?"

"Yes, always."

"And he was good to everybody, Pierre?"

"Yes everybody."

"And—and—you were with him in places where he would be under less restraint than when with me, and you think he had as few faults as most men, I am sure?"

"He had not a single fault," Pierre said, emphatically, lying easily and unhesitatingly, thinking the end justified the means.

He knew now that Reinette was wishing to be reassured of her father's truth and honor, and though he had but little faith that his late master had possessed either of those virtues to an overwhelming degree, he could not say so to the daughter; he would sooner tell her a hundred lies, and take his chance of being forgiven by and by.

"Thank you, Pierre," she said. "You make me so happy. I like to think of father as a good, true, honest man; and I believe Christine was good."

"Did the servants at Chateau des Fleurs ever mention her as other than a nice woman?"

"They never mentioned her at all. I never heard her name except from you and monsieur, and from him only twice—once in the office of Messrs. Polignie, and once in Liverpool."

"Yes, Pierre," Reinette said, with a quick, gasping breath, "I am sure Christine is a good woman. My mother trusted her and bade father be kind to her always. I have it in a letter written before she died, and when Christine was with her. Mrs. La Rue is a good woman."

She kept asserting this as if she feared Pierre might doubt the fact, but if he did, he gave no sign, and merely replied:

"She must be good to be the mother of Miss Margery."

"Yes, Pierre," and Reinette roused herself up, and pushing her heavy hair back from her face, said, joyfully: "I see it now; I understand why she has not told me. She did not wish Margery or me to know that she once served in the capacity of my nurse, lest she should feel humiliated, and I, with my abominable pride, might think less of her; that is it, I am sure."

"Unquestionably," Pierre said, ready to assent to anything his young mistress might suggest, no matter how absurd.

"And, Pierre," she continued, "I shall, of course, tell Mrs. La Rue that I know who she is, but it is not necessary that all the world should know. We need tell no one else."

"No, mademoiselle; but what of Monsieur Beresford? He wrote to M. Albrech, too; he will get an answer; he will know."

"Of course," Queenie said, impatiently. "But I can trust him. I shall tell him to keep silent; and now leave me, and do not let Mrs. Jerry, or any one, come near me. I am tired, and shall soon retire."

So Pierre left her alone with her thoughts, which kept her awake the most of the night, and the next morning found her suffering with one of her head-aches, and unable to leave her bed. It was a stormy November day, and the wind blew in gusts over the hill, and drove before it clouds of snow, which was drifting down from the gray sky in great white feathery masses, but bad as was the day, it did not prevent Mr. Beresford from riding over to Hetherton Place, where he was met by Pierre with the message that Miss Hetherton had the headache, and could not see him. Mr. Beresford seemed disappointed, and was about turning away from the door, when he said, as if it had just occurred to him:

"By the way, do you know if Miss Hetherton received any letters from France yesterday?"

"She did receive one," Pierre said, looking straight at the lawyer, and feeling sure that he, too, had heard from Mentone, and knew the secret of Christine Bodine.

And he was right, for the same mail which brought the letter to Reinette had also in it one for Mr. Beresford from Mentone. It was a curious compound of English and French, which took Mr. Beresford nearly two hours to decipher. But he managed it at last with the help of grammar and dictionary, and had a tolerably accurate knowledge of its contents, which surprised and confounded him almost as much as Queenie's letter had confounded her. But in his letter were a few words, or rather insinuations, which were omitted in Queenie's and which affected him more than all the rest, and threw a flood of light upon Mrs. La Rue's reason for keeping her identity with Christine Bodine a secret from Reinette. Did Queenie know what he knew or suspected, Mr. Beresford wondered, and if so, how did she take it? What would she do? A burning, intense desire seized the usually calm, sober lawyer to have these questions answered. He must see Reinette and judge from her face how much she knew, and so he went to Hetherton

Place. But Queenie would not see him. She was sick, and she had received a letter from France. So much he learned, and he rode back to his office, where, for the remainder of the day, he seemed in a most abstracted frame of mind, paying but little attention to his clients, who had never seen him so absent-minded and grave before, and wondered of what he was thinking. Not of them and their business, but of Reinette and the change her coming to Merrivale had made in his hitherto quiet life. How she had turned everything upside down. It was like a romance whose pages he was reading, and now a fresh leaf had been turned which he wished to decipher, and since he could not see Reinette he must seek help in another quarter, and he, who had always been noted for minding his own business better than any man in Merrivale, waited impatiently for evening, when he meant to begin the new chapter.

CHAPTER XXX

TRYING TO READ THE PAGE

The night set in dark and stormy even for November and the wind howled dismally through the tall elms which grew upon the common, while both sleet and rain were falling pitilessly, when Mr. Beresford left his office, equipped for an evening call. He was going to see Margery La Rue, whom he found alone, as her mother had retired to her room with a toothache and swollen face. Margery let him in herself, and looked fully the surprise she felt when she saw who her visitor was. It was not so much that he should come that night as that he should come at all which astonished the young girl, who, with a woman's intuition, had read the proud man pretty accurately, and guessed that persons like her, whose bread was earned by their own hands, had not much attraction for him. But it was his early training, which was at fault, and not the real heart of the man himself. His mother had seldom done so much for herself as to arrange her own hair, and when her immense fortune slipped away from her, and left her comparatively poor, and compelled her sons, two as noble boys as ever called a woman mother, to choose professions and care for themselves, she could not bear the change, and with a feeling that she would rather die than live and work, she died, and very few mourned for her. With such a mother and a long line of ancestry on her side, as proud and exclusive as herself, it is not strange that Mr. Beresford should have imbibed some notions not altogether consistent with democratic institutions. He thought a great deal of family and blood, and though he was always polite and courteous to Margery when they met, he had unconsciously made her feel the gulf between them, and she had good cause to gaze on him wonderingly as she opened the door, and held it open a moment as if expecting him to give her some message from Queenie, as he had done when Phil went away. Laughing good-humoredly as he stepped past her into the hall, he said:

"I am coming in, you see, though I do not wonder that a call on such a wild night as this surprises you. But it is the weather which brings me here. I believe I have had the blues or something to-day, and need to talk to some one, and as Phil is gone, and Reinette is sick, I have come to call on you. I hope I am not unwelcome."

He was talking rather strangely, and not at all in a strain complimentary to Margery, who, nevertheless, passed it off pleasantly, and said, with her pretty accent, which struck Mr. Beresford with a degree of newness.

"Thank you, Mr. Beresford; I surely ought to feel honored to be No. 3. Let me see; you said that as Mr. Rossiter was gone, and Reinette sick, you were reduced to the alternative of coming here to be rid of the blues. Is that it? or have my French ears misinterpreted your English meaning?"

"That is the way it sounded, I will admit," Mr. Beresford replied, "but I am a bungler anyway, so please consider that I have made you number one, for really I have been intending to call for some time."

He took the seat she offered him, and moved it a little more in front of her, where he could look directly at her as she bent over her work, which, with his permission, she had resumed, and which, as it was a sacque for Miss Anna, must be finished as soon as possible.

How graceful every motion was, and how well her dress of black cashmere, with soft lace ruffles at her throat and sleeves, became her, and how very beautiful she was both in face and form, with her golden hair rippling over her finely shaped head, her dazzling complexion, her perfectly regular features, and, more than all, her large, clear, sunny blue eyes, veiled by long, fringed lashes, and shaded by eyebrows so heavy and black, that they seemed almost out of place with that hair of golden hue. But they gave her a novel and distingue look, and added to her beauty, which, now that he was studying her, struck Mr. Beresford as something remarkable, and made his eyes linger on the fair face with more admiration even than curiosity. But the likeness he sought for was not there, unless it were in the occasional toss of the head on one side—the significant shrug of the shoulders, or gestures of the hands—and something in the tone of the voice when it grew very earnest as she talked to him of Reinette, who was not like her in the least. In feature and complexion, Margery was the handsomer of the two. Mr. Beresford confessed that to himself with a kind of jealous pang, as if, in some way, a wrong were done the dark-faced, dark-eyed Queenie, who, put side by side with Margery La Rue, would, nevertheless, win every time, and make people see only herself, with her wonderful sparkle, and brightness, which threw everything else into the shade. Queenie was the diamond, and Margery the pearl, and they were not at all alike, and Mr. Beresford felt puzzled, and inclined to believe the agent in Mentone a slanderer, especially after he had talked with Margery awhile, of her friend.

"You have known Reinette a long time?" he said and she replied:

"Yes, a long time—ever since we were little girls—though it seems but yesterday since she climbed the narrow, winding stairs up to that low room, where I staid all day long with no company but the cat, and nothing besides my playthings to amuse me, except to look down into the narrow street below, the Rue St. Honore, and watch the carts, and carriages, and people as they passed, and wonder when mother would come home, and if she would bring me, as she sometimes did, a bon-bon, or a white, tender croissant, which I liked so much better for my supper than our dark, sour bread."

"Yes," Mr. Beresford said, leaning forward and listening eagerly to what Margery was telling him of her early life, and wondering a little that she should be so communicative.

"Most girls would try to conceal the fact that they had once known such poverty," he thought, but he did not know Margery La Rue, or guess that it was in part her pride which made her talk as she was talking.

She was naturally reserved and reticent with regard to herself, but to him, whose value of birth, and blood, and family connections she rightly guessed, she would speak openly, and show him that it was something more than a mere dressmaker—a sewing-woman—whom he was honoring with his society, and in whom he was interested in spite of himself. She divined that readily, by the kindling of his eyes when they met hers as she talked, and by some of those subtle influences by which a woman knows that the man she is talking with is entertained and pleased with herself as well as with what she is saying.

So, when he said to her, with a kind of pity in his tone, "And you were so desolate as that when Reinette found you?" she answered:

"Yes, more desolate than you can guess—you who have never known what poverty means in a large city like Paris. But I was not unhappy, either," she added, quickly. "I had too much love and petting from my mother for that. I was only lonely in her absence; for she worked at a hair-dresser's and was gone all day, and I kept the house and got the meals for father till he died."

"Your father—yes," Mr. Beresford repeated. "What was he, what did he do, and when did he die?"

He seemed very eager in his questionings, and mistaking his meaning altogether, Margery's cheeks flushed, but her voice was steady and clear as she replied:

"I do not know that he did anything. I think it is a fashion in France more than here for the women to work and the men to take their ease. At all events, father had no regular occupation that I know of. Sometimes he acted as guide to strangers, for he could speak a little English, and sometimes he was employed for a few days as waiter at some of the Duval restaurants, and once he took mother and me there to dine. That is the white day of my life, as connected with him. Reinette heard of me from old Lisette, the laundress, who lived on the floor below, and she came up to our humble room in her scarlet cloak and hood trimmed with ermine, and filled it with glory at once. You know what a halo of brightness seems to encircle her, and affect

148

everything around her. And how she did sparkle and glow, and light up the whole room, as she sat there in that hard wooden chair with me standing awkwardly by, in my coarse high-necked working apron, with broom in hand, and gazing at her as if she had been a being from another sphere."

How rapid and excitedly she talked, gesticulating with her hands, which were as small and white as those of any lady, and how large and bright her blue eyes grew, as she described that first interview with Reinette so vividly that Mr. Beresford could see the low room, far up the winding stairs, the humble furniture, the bare floor, the smoldering fire on the hearth, the wooden chair, the dark-eyed little girl in scarlet and ermine who sat there with the captured cat in her lap, talking to another child quite as beautiful as herself, though of another type of beauty, and clad in the coarse garments of the poor. He could see it all so plainly, and forgetting for a time why he was there, he listened still more intently, while Margery went on to tell him of the Champs d'Elysees, where she wore the scarlet cloak and played she was Mr. Hetherton's little girl, while Queenie sat demurely at her side, clad in homely garments, and making believe that she was Margery La Rue, whose home was up the winding stairs in the Rue St. Honore.

"I think that one act bound me to her forever," Margery said, "though it was the beginning of many make-believes and many deeds of kindness, for through Queenie's influence her father paid my expenses in part at the English school which she attended, and where I learned to speak your language and all I know besides, and after that she stood my fast friend in everything and treated me more like a sister than an inferior, as I am, by birth and social position. I think her love has never failed me since the day she first came to me and brought the glorious sunlight with her. So, do you wonder that I love her? I would lay down my life for her, if need be—would sacrifice everything for her, and I sometimes wish that I might have the chance to show how much I love her, and would endure for her sake."

Margery paused here, and with clasped hands, and eyes which had in them a rapt, far-away look, seemed almost to see looming on the horizon not far in the distance the something for which she longed, and which, when it came, would test her as few women have ever been tested in their love for another.

It was not possible that the dark shadow touched her now, although it was so near, and yet she shivered a little and drew a long breath as she at last came back to the present and turned her eyes upon Mr. Beresford, who said to her:

"Did you even see Queenie's father?—did you know him, I mean—you or your mother?"

"No, neither of us," Margery answered promptly. "I saw him once when Queenie and I were riding in the Bois, and she made him come and speak to me, but I did not like him much. He impressed me as one very proud and haughty, who only endured me for Queenie's sake. He was fine-looking, though, and his manners were very elegant. Did you know him, Mr. Beresford?"

"Scarcely at all, as I was a mere boy when he went away, but I have heard much of him from the villagers; he was not very popular, I imagine," Mr. Beresford replied, and then the conversation drifted into other channels, and they talked of Phil and Anna, and her engagement with the major, which was generally understood, but nothing more was said of Margery's early life.

Mr. Beresford had not succeeded in reading the page just as he had expected to read it, and was a good deal puzzled and perplexed when, at rather a late hour, he said good-night to Margery, and went back to his rooms at the hotel, with his mind full of what she had told him of her life as connected with Reinette Hetherton, and full too with thoughts of herself, and after he had retired to his bed, and a feeling of drowsiness began to steal over him, there came to him another face than Queenie's—a fairer face, with golden hair and eyes of blue—and in his troubled dreams the face hid Queenie's from him, and a voice with more of a foreign accent than Queenie's was sounding in his ears.

It was very late when he awoke, with a confused vision of black eyes and blue eyes dancing before him, and hastily dressing himself and swallowing his breakfast, he started for his office, where to his surprise he found Reinette Hetherton waiting for him.

CHAPTER XXXI

THE INTERVIEW

Reinette had thought and thought till her head seemed bursting with the effort to solve the mystery of her nurse's silence. Had she done anything that she was ashamed to tell, and if so what was it, and did it concern any one but herself?

"No, I will not believe it," she said more than once, with a striking out of her hand as if thrusting something aside. "I will not believe it. There is some good reason for her conduct which she can give me, and I am going to her to know the truth, but the world will not be as charitable as I and will say bad things of her, no doubt. So to the world she must remain Mrs. La Rue, and nobody will ever know that she is Christine, except Mr. Beresford, who, of course, knows it now, for Louis Arnaud has written to him, no doubt. But I can trust him, and I shall ask him to keep the knowledge to himself."

After this decision Reinette grew calmer; the violent throbbing in her temples ceased, and she slept comparatively well that night. But though the morning found her stronger and better, she felt nervous and unstrung, and shrunk with a great dread from confronting Mrs. La Rue and wringing her secret from her, if secret there were to wring.

"I am so hurt and disappointed," she thought, as she dressed herself for her calls. "I have loved Christine so much, and wanted so to find her, and now she is this woman whom, for some unaccountable reason, I never liked, though she is Margery's mother and greatly superior to her class. There surely is something wrong and I am going to find it out."

The waiting for Mr. Beresford seemed a long time to the excited girl, though in reality it was not more than ten minutes from the time she entered the office before she was closeted with the lawyer in his private room, where he received his clients who came to him on special business. And Reinette's was very special, or at least very private, and when the door was closed she plunged into it at once, by saying:

"Mr. Beresford, you have written to Monsieur Albrech, in Mentone, and asked about Christine Bodine."

She did not put it interrogatively, but as an assertion, and blushing guiltily, the lawyer replied:

"Yes, I did write to him, asking information of the woman's whereabouts. You were so anxious to find her, you know."

"Hush!" Queenie said, pouring the full scorn of her blazing eyes upon him. "Do not try to excuse yourself in that way. It was curiosity rather than a desire to serve me which prompted you to write, and you have had your reward. Louis Arnaud, Monsieur Albrech's clerk, has answered your letter."

"Yes, he has," Mr. Beresford replied, and Reinette continued:

"I know it. I have one from him, too. Here it is, and I will read it to you."

She drew the letter from her pocket, and read it through in a clear, steady voice, as if its contents were just what she had expected.

"You are not surprised, of course," she said, when she had finished. "He told you that Christine was Mrs. La Rue. Where is the letter, and how did you make it out?"

"It was written partly in English and partly in French, so I did pretty well," Mr. Beresford replied, and she continued:

"Did he write you anything more than he did me? I have a right to know if there is any reason why she should have kept herself from me in this manner. Show me the letter, Mr. Beresford."

Mr. Beresford knew she would persist in her demand until something was done to quiet her, and, going into the adjoining room where a fire was burning in the grate, he took Louis Arnaud's letter from his pocket and threw it into the fire; then, making a feint of hunting through pigeon-holes and on the table where piles of paper lay, he asked his clerk, so loud that Reinette could distinctly hear him, if he had seen a certain letter which he described. The clerk had not, but was finally driven to admitting that he might have torn it up that morning with other letters of no importance. He was reprimanded for his carelessness, and then Mr. Beresford returned to Reinette, feeling like a hypocrite, but thinking the end justified the means. But Queenie was not deceived, and with a smile which had much bitterness in it, she said to him before he could speak:

"Do not trouble yourself with more deception. Your clerk never destroyed that letter, for you are not the man to leave it lying round. It is safe somewhere, as you know, and you do not wish to show it to me. There was something in it which you will not tell me. But no matter; I am going to Christine, and she cannot keep from me why she has made no sign that she was my old nurse, when she knew how much I wished to find her."

"Possibly she feared you might not think as much of Margery, if you knew she was your nurse's daughter," Mr. Beresford said, and Reinette replied:

"I have thought of that, but she should have known me better than to think anything could change my love for Margery. Perhaps she displeased papa after mother died, and he dismissed her for it, but paid her money all the same, because mother wished it. That would explain why father never was willing to talk to me about her, and always said he did not know where she was."

"You used to question him of her, then?" Mr. Beresford said, and Reinette answered:

"Yes; and he would tell me nothing. Evidently he did not like her, but I knew how strong his prejudices were if once he took a dislike to one, and so I attached no importance to them."

"How long did she live with you as your nurse after your mother's death?" Mr. Beresford asked, and Reinette replied:

"I do not know; a year or so, I think, though all my knowledge of that part of my life seems to be a blank; and where was Margery then?"

She put this question more to herself than to Mr. Beresford, who, nevertheless, replied:

"Perhaps Christine was married unknown to your father, who, when he found it out, was angry, as it took a valuable nurse from his child."

"Yes, yes, thank you," Reinette, said, eagerly. "It was something of that nature, no doubt, and you lawyers are shrewd enough to see it, while I might have groped in the dark forever. I am glad you thought of that, and Mr. Beresford, you must tell no one what you heard from Louis Arnaud. There are many suspicious people in the world who would say hard things of Christine and—possibly—connect the trouble in some way with—with—father—and I will not have his name coupled with hers in any way. My father was a gentleman and a Hetherton."

Mr. Beresford bowed an acquiescence to the fact that her father was a gentleman and a Hetherton. And if there was any merit in being the latter, she certainly was a very fair representative of it as she stood up so proud and calm, and uttered her protest against her father's name being mixed with that of Christine Bodine.

"I am going there now," she said, adjusting her shawl and drawing on her gloves, "and when I see you again I shall know everything there is to know of Christine Bodine."

Mr. Beresford felt a little doubtful on that subject, but said nothing, and going with her to her carriage helped her in, and then in a very thoughtful mood returned to his office, wondering what would be the result of that call on Christine Bodine.

CHAPTER XXXII

CHRISTINE

It was more than a toothache and swollen face which had ailed Mrs. La Rue, and sent her to her room on that night when Mr. Beresford called upon Margery. She had a toothache, it is true, and was suffering from the effects of a severe cold, under cover of which she hid the terrible pain which was making her sick with nervous apprehension lest, at last, she was to be confronted by the girl whom she feared and shrank from more than from all the world beside, unless it was Margery, her dearly loved, beautiful child, who had brought her the letter which affected her so strangely. It had been forwarded from Oak Bluffs, and postmarked originally at Mentone, and it read as follows:

"Madame La Rue.—Inclosed find a note from Miss Hetherton, who has written asking your whereabouts and that this might be forwarded to you. In my absence, my clerk, Louis Arnaud, took charge of my business letters, and, it seems, answered the young lady, telling her your address. Had I been home this would not have occurred, but it cannot now be helped. Hoping no great harm will come of it, I am

"Your ob't servant,
"M. Albrech."

This letter Margery had taken from the office, and wondered in a vague kind of way what it contained, and why M. Albrech had written to her mother again, when she had supposed her business relations with him finished. Since the time when Margery first learned to write, it had been a distinctly understood thing that both she and her mother were to respect each other's correspondence, and Margery would as soon have broken the seal of a letter directed to a stranger as to her mother, consequently she had never known just what was in the letters which had passed between Mrs. La Rue and M. Albrech, of Mentone. She had always known since her father's death that her mother had at stated times received a certain amount of money from some source unknown to her; and she knew, too, that latterly the annuity had ceased, because, as her mother said, the person who paid it was dead. That the sum was very small she had been made to believe, and her mother had told her once, when she asked what became of it, that it was safely invested in stocks and bonds in Paris, and was to be kept for her as a dowry when she was married, or to be used before if absolutely necessary.

"But who gives it to you?" Margery had once inquired, and her mother had replied:

"A gentleman in Paris, whose wife was very fond of me. I was her maid first, and after she died took care of her child."

And Margery, wholly unsuspicious, accepted this explanation as all there was to tell, and received the impression somehow that the gentleman's name was Polignie, and never dreamed of the guilt, and sin, and terrible remorse which haunted her mother so continually, and had made her grow old so fast. Margery could remember her when she was bright and pretty, with a sparkle in her dark eyes and a bloom upon her cheeks, which now were sunken and pale, while her long, black hair was streaked with gray, and within the last few months had been rapidly growing white. She had brought the Mentone letter, and given it to her mother without so much as looking at her, and thus she failed to see how white she was as she took the letter and went to her room to read it alone.

"Probably it has something to do with my money," she thought, seeking to reassure herself as she broke the seal and opened the envelope from which Queenie's note dropped into her lap.

Picking it up she read the address: "Christine Bodine, care of M. Albrech," and recognizing the handwriting, which she had often seen on notes sent to her daughter by Reinette, she gave a low, gasping cry, while for a moment everything around her grew black, and she could neither see nor hear for the great fear overmastering her.

"Tracked at last," she whispered, as she tried to read what M. Albrech had written, and could not for the blur before her eyes.

For months Mrs. La Rue's remedy for nervousness had been morphine, which she took in constantly increasing doses, and she had resort to it now, and, swallowing half a grain, grew calm at last, and read her agent's letter; and then picking up the dainty note with Reinette's monogram upon the seal, kissed it passionately, and cried over it as if it had been some living creature instead of a bit of perfumed paper, on which these lines were written:

"Hetherton Place,

"Merrivale, Worcester Co., Mass., U. S. A.

"My Dear Christine:—Have you forgotten the little baby you used to bear in your arms years ago, in Paris and at Chateau des Fleurs? Little Queenie they called me, though my real name was Reinette, and I am the daughter of Mrs. Frederick Hetherton, who died in Rome, and to whom you were so kind. I have it in mother's letter written to father, in which she tells him how good and true you were to her and bade him always be kind to you for her sake. And I think he tried to be, for I have ascertained that he set apart a certain amount of money for you, which was all very well, though I should have shown my gratitude in an altogether different way. I might have given you money if you needed it, but I should also have made you come home to us, and should have loved and petted you because you knew my mother, and were so good to her. And that is what I wish to do now.

"Papa is dead, as you perhaps know. He died on the ship before we reached New York, and I am living alone at Hetherton Place, his old home, which is almost as lovely as Chateau des Fleurs, with a much finer view. Christine, did you know my mother was an American? She was, and her home was here in Merrivale, where my father found her and where I have a host of relatives on her side. But still I am very, very lonely, and I want you to come and live with me in America. I will try and make you so happy, and you will seem to bring me nearer to my mother, for you will tell me of her; what she did and what she said of me the few days she had me before she died. I am sure to love you because she did, and in her first letters to her mother and sister after she reached Paris she spoke of her good Christine, who was so much to her.

"You see I am writing on the assumption that you have no other ties. I always think of you as my dear old nurse, Christine, whom I sometimes fancy I can remember. Did you not come to me once in the Bois when another nurse had charge of me, and kiss, and cry over me, and give me a quantity of bon-bons? Some such scene comes up to me from the misty past, and you had such bright black eyes and so much color in your cheeks, and looked so pretty. Was that you, and why did you not stay with me always? Write immediately and answer all these questions, and tell me you will come to your loving

"Reinette."

Oh, how the wretched woman writhed as she read this letter, with thuds of pain beating in her heart, and her eyes dim with burning tears. It was so kind, so affectionate in its tone, and so familiar too; so unlike what Reinette's manner toward her had been.

"Queenie, my darling, would you write to me thus if you knew?" she moaned, as she rocked to and fro in her anguish, while at her work below Margery sat singing a little song she had learned in the Tabernacle at Oak Bluffs:

> "There is rest for the weary,
> There is rest for you."

"Rest for the weary," Mrs. La Rue repeated, as the clear, sweet tones floated up to her. "And I am weary, oh! so weary; but there is no rest for me, except in death, which some say is a long dreamless rest, and that I can have so soon, for my friend is always near me," and she glanced toward the shelf where stood a vial of laudanum to which she had resort when morphine did not avail to quiet her and bring forgetfulness. "But I must see Margery once more," she thought. "I must kiss her again, and hear her call me mother."

It was nearly time now for the evening meal, and summoning all her strength and calmness, Mrs. La Rue went down stairs, and under cover of the fast-increasing darkness, managed so well that Margery suspected nothing, and attributed her mother's pallor and weakness to the neuralgia from which she was suffering.

"I am going to bed early to-night," Mrs. La Rue said, when supper was over, and the table cleared away. "I am feeling quite ill."

Then Margery looked at her closely, and asked if it was anything more than neuralgia which ailed her. Was there bad news in the letter?

"No—yes; but nothing I can now explain," Mrs. La Rue replied; then going up to her daughter, she kissed her twice, and said: "Good-night, my darling. Do not speak to me when you come up to bed; I may be asleep."

Margery kissed her back, with no thought of what was in the mind of the miserable woman as she slowly climbed the stairs, and, going to her room, shut the door, and taking down her friend, poured out what was to give her forgetfulness and rest. Drop by drop the dark liquid fell into the glass, until there were forty drops in all, and she held it to the light, and looked at it, and smiled as she thought of the morrow, when she would be deaf to Margery's call, and deaf to Queenie's reproaches, if she should come, as she might do now at any time.

"But I shall be gone from it forever, and Margery will think it an overdose taken accidentally to ease the pain. Yes, this is better than the river; and yet I am so hot and feverish that the cold water would be grateful to me, and this is just the night for such a deed, only Margery then would know I meant it, and I must not lose her respect. I must carry that with me at least. No, to sleep and never waken is the best. So, Margery, darling, and Queenie, too, good-by!"

She raised the glass to her lips just as the door-bell rang a loud, clanging peal, which made her start so violently that the glass dropped from her trembling hand, and the poison was spilled on the floor.

It was Mr. Beresford who rang, and Christine heard him speaking to Margery in the hall. The sound of their voices quieted her and for the time turned her from her terrible resolve. "I will not die to-night; I will wait," she said as she cleared away all traces of the broken glass, and then, undressing herself, went to bed, but not to sleep, for her thoughts were busy with the past, when she was young and innocent, and first entered the service of Margaret Hetherton. She could not remember her father who died when she was two years old. Her mother had kept a cheap French pension in the suburbs of Paris, and Christine had often assisted in waiting upon the guests who frequented the house. As she was very pretty and bright and piquant she naturally attracted a good deal of attention, and sometimes words were said to her which she knew were insults, and which she repelled with scorn for she was then honest and pure as a child, and would have shrunk with horror from the future had it been shown to her. At the age of eighteen her mother died and she was left alone without money or employment. It was then that she saw an advertisement in the morning paper to the effect that a waiting-maid was wanted by a young American lady, who could be seen at the Hotel Meurice every day for a week between the hours of twelve and two. As the terms offered were unusually liberal she resolved to apply for the situation, notwithstanding that she had had no experience.

At the appointed hour she presented herself to Margaret, who was reclining upon a white satin couch, while partly behind her Mr. Hetherton stood with folded arms, and a critical look upon his face.

Accustomed as he was to the world, he saw at a glance that Christine Bodine knew nothing of the habits of a fine lady, such as he meant his wife to be, now that she was removed from the Fergusons, a thought of whom made him shudder. Indeed, the girl, when questioned for references, and the address of her last employer, acknowledged freely that she had no references, and had never served as maid.

"But I can learn," she said; "and I will serve madame so faithfully. I should so like you to try me," and she looked imploringly at Margaret, who saw something in the girl which pleased her.

She was so young, and very pretty and plain in her dress, and looked so good and trusty that her heart warmed toward her. References were nothing to her, and turning to her husband she said, in a low tone:

"Oh, Frederick, I like her so much. I am sure she will suit. Let us take her."

But Frederick demurred, urging that she had no style, no appearance of a maid.

"But she is good, I am sure, and I want her," the young wife pleaded, and Christine was retained, and entered upon her duties the next day.

How peaceful, and happy, and innocent those first few months spent in Mrs. Hetherton's service seemed to Christine now as she looked back upon them, and how sweet, and kind, and patient her mistress had always been with her, treating her more as an equal and a friend than as a servant, and thereby frequently calling down upon herself sharp reproofs from her husband, who did not approve of her familiarity with a maid. It showed at once a low-born taste, he said, and he wished his wife to conquer all such feelings, and, forgetting the past, remember that she was now Mrs. Frederick Hetherton, of Paris. But Margaret could not forget the past, or cease to pine for the dear ones at home, the plain, old-fashioned mother, whose ways she knew were homespun in the extreme, and not at all like the elegant manners of her proud husband, but who, nevertheless, was her mother, for whom she cried every day of her life. Laying her head on the lap of her faithful Christine she would sob out her homesickness, and talk by the hour of Merrivale and its people, until Christine knew every rock and crag, and winding brook in the pleasant New England town, and knew pretty well what the Fergusons were, and how they stood in Merrivale.

They were of mutual benefit to each other—this mistress and maid, for while Christine anticipated every wish of Margaret, waiting upon her as if she had been a duchess, and teaching her the French language as well as the German, of which she had some knowledge. Margaret in turn taught her a little English, and during the many weeks when she was alone and her husband away with his friends, she gave her lessons in history, and geography, and arithmetic, so that Christine, who was apt and bright, became a much better scholar than was common to persons of her class, and astonished her mistress with her rapid improvement. Even Mr. Hetherton began to notice her at last and marvel at the change in her, and when he was home he often found himself lingering longer in his wife's apartments when Christine was there, with her saucy smile, her bright eyes, and her pretty way of saying things. Without any motive except that she wished to please him because he was madame's husband she made herself necessary to him, and, carefully studying his wishes, ministered to him with the alacrity of a slave, and when he offered her money for extra services she refused to take it, and said that what she did was done for love of him and madame, who trusted and clung to the girl with a love which made the poor woman shiver with remorseful pain, as she remembered it now, when the sins of the past were confronting her so fearfully, and making her almost shriek aloud, as she recalled those days in Rome, when the husband was seeking his own pleasure, while the wife grew paler and thinner each day, and yet strove so hard to keep up, by talking of the great happiness in store for her, and surprise for him, if all went well with her, and she lived through the trial awaiting her.

"Frederick is so fond of children, and he will be so happy and surprised when he hears of it. I am glad I did not tell him," she said, when at last the waiting and suspense were over, and a little girl baby was pillowed on her arm.

Christine could see that baby now, and feel the touch of its soft hands, and see the white, worn face upon the pillow, and the great blue eyes which followed her so wistfully and questioningly, and at last had in them a look of terror and dread, as the days went by and no strength came to the feeble limbs, or vitality to the nerves. She was dying, and she knew it at last, and throwing herself into Christine's arms, she sobbed like a little child.

"It is hard to die," she said, "when I am so young and have so much to live for, now baby is born. And home is so far away, and mother, too, and Frederick—where is he, Christine? He ought to be here, and I so sick and lonely."

Christine knew that very well, and her tears fell like rain upon the golden head resting upon her bosom, while she tried to comfort the young mother, who was so surely passing away.

"Monsieur must come soon," she said; "and then madame will be better, and we shall go back to Chateau des Fleurs and be so happy there."

But Margaret knew better. She would never go to Chateau des Fleurs—never see her husband again, and that grieved her the most, for all his neglect and coldness had not killed her love, and she longed for him now so much when she lay dying in Rome, with only her baby and Christine with her—Christine, to whom she said "God bless you, and reward you according to your kindness and faithfulness to me!"

Margaret had meant it for a blessing, but it was really a curse, and it had followed Christine ever since, until now, when her sin was finding her out, and making her writhe with anguish and fear.

"And yet I was kind to her," she whispered; "and she died in my arms, with her head upon my breast, and she kissed me twice upon my lips; one was for me, she said, and one for the baby when she was old enough to know. Ah, me, those kisses! how they burn like fire! and I am burning, too—burning! Is there a hell, I wonder, and is it worse than the torment I am enduring?"

Her mind was disordered, and she raved incoherently of Rome, and Chateau des Fleurs; and Paris, and Margaret, and Reinette, until she was utterly exhausted, and growing quiet, at last fell into a sleep so deep that she did not hear Margery when she let Mr. Beresford out and came up to her room.

"Poor mother, she is resting sweetly, and I hope will be better to-morrow," Margery said, as she bent over the sleeping woman, whose face looked so white, and worn, and pinched.

The next morning, however, Mrs. La Rue did not attempt to get up. She was too weak and sick, she said, and should keep her bed all day. "And Margery," she added, with quivering lip and a pleading tone, "don't let any one in here, will you, if they come asking for me? Not any one; promise, Margery."

"No, mother, no one shall disturb you," Margery said, soothingly, "and fortunately I have not much work on hand to-day, and can stay with you a great deal. I must finish Miss Ferguson's sacque, and that is all. Now try to sleep again. I can't have such a woeful-looking, pale-faced little mother on my hands. I shall have to send her off and get another one."

She spoke playfully, but every word was a stab to the miserable woman, who said again:

"Remember, Margery, nobody is to come up here."

"No, mother, nobody. You are safer than the old bishop in his castle on the Rhine, for the rats did reach him there, and not so much as a mouse shall harm you here, so au revoir," and with a kiss—the last—the very last, she would ever give as she gave that, she ran down stairs just as a carriage stopped at the gate and Reinette came rapidly up the walk.

CHAPTER XXXIII

REINETTE'S INTERVIEW WITH MARGERY

Reinette did not ring, but entered unannounced, like one who had but one thought, one purpose, and was resolved to carry it out with as little ceremony as possible. It was fortunate for all parties that this was Margery's dull season, and there were no girls there with prying eyes and curious ears to listen, for Reinette was greatly excited now that the moment drew near when she could confront Christine, and she plunged at once into business by saying to Margery, "Where is your mother? I have come to see her."

"Mother is sick," Margery replied; "she is very nervous and cannot see any one. I am sorry, but you will have to wait. Maybe I can do as well," she continued, looking wonderingly at Queenie, who, utterly disregarding what she said, had started for the stairs.

"No, you will not do as well. I must see her; it is very important and I cannot wait," Queenie said, still advancing toward the stairs, while Margery put herself between them and her friend, whose strange conduct surprised her so much.

"But you cannot see her. I promised no one should disturb her," she said again, and now she laid her hand on Queenie's shoulder to detain her, for Queenie's foot was on the first stair and she looked resolute enough to storm a fortress as she persisted in her determination to go up.

But not less resolute than her own was the face which confronted her as Margery roused up and said in a voice Queenie had never heard from her before: "Miss Hetherton! You astonish me. I tell you mother is sick and cannot be disturbed. You must not go up."

"And I tell you I must. I have important news from Mentone, which concerns your mother and me, and I must see her."

"What news?" Margery asked, thinking suddenly of the letter her mother had received from Mentone the previous night, and experiencing a vague feeling of fear and dread of some impending evil. "What news have you heard which concerns my mother?" she repeated, looking steadily at Reinette.

Reinette hesitated a moment, kept silent by something in Margery's face, but when she said for the third time, "Tell me what news you have received from France," she replied: "Margery, it shall never make any difference between us, but your mother is Christine Bodine, whom I have been trying to find."

"My mother Christine Bodine! Impossible! She was Marie La Mille," Margery gasped, as she clutched Reinette's shoulder with a grip which was painful.

"I have it from her agent in Mentone, who has received money for her at different times from Messrs. Polignie in Paris—money my father deposited for her with them years ago. Now let me go! I must see her!" Queenie said, darting up the stairs, no longer restrained by Margery, who had let her pass without further protest.

Clasping her hand to her head as if smitten with a blow, Margery staggered back, and leaning against the wall for support, tried to think what it all meant, while her mind traveled rapidly back over the past, gathering up a thread here and there, until she had no doubt that what Queenie had told her was true. Her mother was Christine Bodine. But why this concealment? What was she hiding? What had she done?

Margery's first impulse was to hurry to her mother's room, where there was already the sound of excited voices, her mother's and Queenie's blended together, as each strove to be heard, and once she caught her own name, as if her mother were calling her to come.

Then she did start, and was half way up the stairs, when the door-bell rang violently—a sharp, imperious ring, which she recognized as Anna Ferguson's. She was expecting that young lady, and knowing that however fierce a storm might be blowing, she must keep it from the world, she calmed herself with a tremendous effort, and opening the door to Anna, listened patiently for several minutes, while the girl examined her sacque and said it would do very well, only the price was too high.

"Ma never asked anything like that for a common sacque."

"Very well. Pay me what you like," Margery said, anxious to be rid of her customer, who had asked, in her supercilious way:

"Isn't that Queenie up stairs? And isn't she talking pretty loud for a well-bred person?"

"Oh, will she never go?" Margery thought, just as the bell pealed a second time, and Grandma Ferguson came in, bringing a bundle almost as large as herself, and entering at once into full details of what she wished to have made, and how.

"I s'pose Anny is goin' to be married," she said, looking hard at her granddaughter, "though she hain't noticed me enough to tell me so, right out; but everybody's talkin' it, and I thought I might as well have a new silk gown. My moiry antique is pretty well whipped out, and a nice silk is allus handy. I got brown—a nice shade, I call it," and she unrolled a silk of excellent quality, but of a yellowish brown, which would be very unbecoming to her.

"Oh, grandma, why didn't you get black instead of that horrid snuff-color?" Anna said, contemptuously, as she glanced at the silk, and then went out, leaving the old lady a good deal crest-fallen, and a little doubtful with regard to the dress she had lately thought so pretty.

Margery soothed her as well as she could, and heard her suggestions, and took her measure, and showed her some new fashion-plates, and did it all with her ears turned to her mother's room where the talk was still going on, now low and earnest and almost pleading, and again so high and excited, that grandma asked if that was not Rennet's voice and what she was talking so loud for. Then Margery excused herself for a moment and ran up stairs to her mother's room, the door of which was ajar, and that accounted for the distinctness with which the sound of voices was borne to the parlor below.

Mrs. La Rue had risen from her bed and put on a dressing-gown which Reinette was buttoning for her while she was trying to bind her long, loose hair into a knot behind. Her face was white as ashes, and in her eyes there was a hunted look, as of one pursued to the last extremity. But when she saw Margery, their expression suddenly changed, and thrusting out both hands, she cried: "Oh, Margery, go away; this is no place for you."

Advancing into the room and closing the door, Margery said in a low, firm tone of voice: "Miss Hetherton, I don't know what all this is about, but mother is too weak and sick to be thus excited. Will you leave her until a fitter time?"

"Don't call me Miss Hetherton, as if you were angry at me," Reinette replied without looking up from buttoning Mrs. La Rue's dressing-gown. "I cannot go now. Your mother knew my mother and is going to tell me about her. She is Christine Bodine."

"Yes, I am Christine. God pity me," the miserable woman exclaimed, and over Margery's face there swept a look of unutterable pain and disappointment.

She had said to herself that this which Reinette had told her was true; that her mother was Christine, and still there had been a faint hope that there might be some mistake; but there was none; her mother had declared it herself, and with a low cry she turned away, saying as she did so: "There are people in the parlor, and your voices are sometimes louder than you suppose, and though they cannot understand you, they will know you are excited and that there is trouble of some kind. Speak lower; do. If this thing I hear be true we surely need not tell it to the world; we can keep it to ourselves."

"Yes, Margery, that is what I mean to do," Queenie said, while Mrs. La Rue exclaimed, with a ring of joy in her voice as if some unexpected relief had come to her: "Yes, yes, we need not tell; we will not tell; we will keep the secret forever."

"But you must tell me all you know about my mother," Queenie said, while Margery went down stairs, for the bell was ringing again and Grandma Ferguson was growing impatient of waiting to know if she should trim her brown silk with velvet or fringe.

This time it was Mrs. Rossiter and her daughters, and into Margery's mind there flashed the thought, "Are all the Fergusons coming here to-day, and what would they say if they knew who my mother was?" But they did not know or dream of the exciting interview in the room above, where Reinette questioned so rapidly and impatiently the woman who almost crouched at her feet in her abasement and answered amid tears and sobs. The Rossiters had merely come to ask when Miss La Rue could do some work for them, and they left very soon taking grandma with them, to the great relief of Margery, who locked the door upon them, determined that no one else should enter until Reinette was gone and she knew herself why the truth had been withheld from her.

Up stairs the talk was still going on, though the voices now were low and quiet as if the storm was over: but would the interview never end? would Reinette never leave her free to go to her mother herself and demand an explanation? Slowly, as it seemed, the hour hands crept on until it was twelve o'clock, and then at last a door opened and shut, and Queenie came down the stairs, her eyes red with weeping, but with a look of content upon her face which surprised Margery a little.

"She cannot be very angry with mother," she thought and her heart began to grow lighter as Queenie came up to her, and putting her arms around her neck, said to her:

"Margie, it makes you seem nearer to me, now that I know your mother was my nurse, and I love you more than ever. But how white you are, and your hands are like lumps of ice. Are you sick?" she continued, as she looked with alarm at Margery's face, which was as white as ashes.

"Not sick, but a good deal upset with what I have heard," Margery replied; "but tell me," she continued, "what does mother say? Why has she never told you who she was?"

"She says it was for your sake; that she feared lest I might think less of you if I knew you were the daughter of my former nurse," Queenie replied, and looking earnestly at her, Margery asked:

"And you believe this to be the only reason, don't you?"

"No, I do not," Queenie answered, promptly. "It is true in part, no doubt, but there is something she did not tell me, and which I am resolved to find out. But I did not tell her so, she seemed so scared—so like a frightened child. Margery, I believe your mother is more than half crazy."

"Yes, yes," and Margery caught eagerly at the suggestion. "You are right; she is crazy. I can see it now, and that will account for much which seems so strange. Oh, Queenie, be patient; be merciful. Remember, she is my mother."

"And my nurse," Queenie rejoined. "She was with my mother when I was born and when she died. I shall not wrong her; do not fear me," and Queenie's lips touched Margery's in token that through her no harm should come to the poor woman who, in the chamber above, sat in a low chair rocking to and fro, with a sickening dread of the moment when she must stand face to face with Margery and meet the glance of those clear, blue eyes which might read the story she had not told Reinette.

CHAPTER XXXIV

REINETTE's INTERVIEW WITH CHRISTINE

When Reinette went up the stairs to Mrs. La Rue's room, she had no definite plan of action; indeed, she had no plan at all, except to confront and confound the woman who had deceived her so long, and whom she found sitting up in bed with so terrified a look on her face, that she stood an instant on the threshold gazing at her ere she plunged impetuously into the business which had brought her there. Secure in Margery's promise that no one should disturb her, Mrs. La Rue had grown comparatively quiet, and was just falling off to sleep when she was roused by the sound of carriage wheels stopping at the gate, and a moment after she heard Reinette's voice speaking earnestly to Margery, and felt that the hour she had dreaded so long had come at last. Reinette had heard from Mentone and had come for an explanation.

"Fool, that I did not end it all last night, when I had the nerve to do it," she said, as, starting up in bed, she listened until footsteps came up the stairs, and Reinette Hetherton stood looking at her.

But not long; the girl was in too great haste to wait, and advancing to the bedside she began: "Christine, you see I know you; I have found you at last; traced you through Messrs. Polignie to your agent in Mentone, whose clerk put me on your track; so, there can be no mistake. You are Christine Bodine, my old nurse, whom I have so wished to find; and you knew I wished it all the time, and did not tell me who you were. Why did you treat me so, Christine? What is your excuse? You have one, of course."

She spoke so rapidly, pouring out question after question, that for a minute Mrs. La Rue was stunned and answered nothing, but sat staring blankly at her, like one in a dream. At last, however, her lips moved, and she said, faintly: "Yes, I am Christine, and I don't know why I didn't tell you."

"You don't know why you didn't tell me? That is very strange," Reinette replied. "If there is nothing to conceal, if all your dealings with my parents were honorable and upright, I see no reason for hiding from me the fact that you were once my nurse. Christine, I did not come to quarrel with you," and Reinette's voice softened a little. "I have loved you too much for that, but I have come to hear about my mother. You were with her when she died. You nursed me when I was a baby. You know what mother said to me and of me. She loved you, Christine, and trusted you. I have it in a letter written to my father before she died, when he was away in Russia or Austria. And that is why he paid you money, was it not, Christine?"

She was looking fixedly at the woman on whose white face blood-red spots were beginning to show, and who answered falteringly:

"Yes, that is why he gave me the money. Oh, Reinette, leave me; go away; don't try to unearth the past. There are things you should not know—things I cannot tell. God help me. I wish I had died before I ever saw your face."

She looked so pale and death-like that Reinette bent anxiously over her, and bringing the camphor bathed her forehead, and held it to her nostrils until she was better, and raising herself from the pillows upon which she had fallen, she said:

"I cannot lie here. I feel that I am smothering. I must get up, while I talk to you, but oh, you'll be so sorry. You'll wish you had never come. Bring me my wrapper there on the chair, and my woolen shawl, for I am shivering with cold."

Her teeth were chattering, and her lips were blue and pinched as Queenie brought the wrapper and helped her put it on, kneeling on the floor to button it herself, and occasionally speaking soothingly to her, though her own heart was beating rapidly with a dread of what she might hear. Then it was that Margery appeared on the scene, and by suggesting that no one but themselves need know what had so long been hidden, changed Mrs. La Rue's intentions altogether. For a few brief moments there had been in her mind a resolve to make a clean breast of it, and to tell the truth, and then when that was done, she would kill herself, and so escape the storm sure to follow her revelations.

"Better die," she thought, "than live to be questioned and suspected by the Rossiters, and Fergusons, and everybody, as I should be if they knew I was Christine."

But when the idea was suggested that only Margery and Reinette need know, she changed her mind, and in what she would now tell the latter, there was to be a deep, dark gulf bridged over in silence.

"Help me to my chair. I am very, very weak," she said to Reinette, when Margery had gone.

Reinette complied with her request, and leading her to a chair placed her gently in it, and drew the shawl closer around her. At this little act of attention Christine broke down entirely, and throwing her arms around Reinette, sobbed out:

"Oh, my darling, my baby whom I nursed. I have so longed to hold you in my arms as I held you years ago. Reinette, Reinette, kiss me—because—because—I am—Christine."

It was not in Reinette's nature to resist such an appeal, and she kissed the poor trembling woman twice, and then drawing a chair to her side spoke very softly to her, and said:

"Now tell me."

"Tell you what, child? What do you wish most to know?" Christine asked, and Reinette replied:

"About my mother. You are the first I have ever seen who knew her after she was Mrs. Hetherton. I have heard what she was when a girl—the sweetest, loveliest creature, they say, with eyes like the summer sky, and a face so fair and pure, and I wish to hear from beginning to end all you know about her, and when you saw her first, and where, and about her death in Rome, when I was born, and only you there to care for either of us."

"Would you mind holding my hand while I tell you of my first days with Mrs. Hetherton?" Christine said, and Reinette took the cold, clammy hand between both of hers and rubbed and chafed it as tenderly as Margery herself would have done.

She was beginning to feel very kindly toward this woman who had known her mother; the insinuations in Messrs. Polignie's letter were forgotten for the time, and she saw before her only one who had cared for her when an infant and had seen her mother die.

"Begin," she said, "I am impatient to hear."

And so Christine began, and told her of the advertisement for a waiting maid, which she had answered in person; told her of the handsome rooms at the Hotel Meurice, and of the beautiful young lady who was so kind to her, and made her more a companion than a maid, notwithstanding that her proud husband frequently protested against it and talked of bad taste, which sometimes made madame cry.

"And did she tell you of Merrivale and her old home? Did you know she was an American?" Queenie asked, and Mrs. La Rue replied:

"Yes, she told me all about her home and Merrivale, and I was familiar with every rock, and hill, and tree, I think, especially the elms upon the common, and the poplars near her home. She was so fond of Merrivale and her friends, and used often to cry for the mother so far away."

"Was she very homesick?" Reinette asked, and Mrs. La Rue answered her:

"At times, yes, when monsieur was away with his associates, or staid out so late nights, as he sometimes did."

Reinette's breath came quickly for a moment, and her voice shook as she asked, very low, as if afraid some one might hear:

"Was not father kind to her always?"

"If beautiful dresses and jewelry, and horses and carriages, and plenty of money means kindness, then he was kind, for she had all these in profusion, but what she wanted most she did not have, and that was her husband's society," Mrs. La Rue said, and then Reinette drew back a little haughtily and answered:

"Christine, you did not like my father. I see that in all you say, but he was very dear to me, and I loved him so much! You were prejudiced against him, but I insist upon your going on just the same and telling me everything. Why did she not have his society? Where and how did he pass his time, if not with her? He loved her, I am sure. You know he did. You know he loved my mother."

She kept asserting this, for there was an expression on Mrs. La Rue's face which she could not understand and which did not quite please her.

"He was very proud of her beauty, and in his way fond of her, but I do not think it was in Monsieur Hetherton's nature to love any one long. Her habits did not suit him; his did not suit her; she breakfasted at nine; he breakfasted at eleven in his room, and frequently dined out, returning generally to see her dressed for the opera or concert, and dictating about her toilet until we were both at our wits' end. Her tastes were too simple for him. He wished her to wear velvet and satin, and diamonds and pearls, while she would have liked plain muslin gowns and a quiet home in the country, with hens, and chickens, and pets. She was very happy at Chateau des Fleurs, and would have been happier if monsieur had staid more with her, but he was much in Paris, and Switzerland, and Nice, and so we were alone a great deal, and she taught me many things and was very kind to me."

"But why did not my father stay with her more?" Reinette asked, and Mrs. La Rue replied: "He was fond of travel, and hunting, and racing, and had many gentlemen friends there, whose influence was not good, and he complained that Chateau des Fleurs was lonely. If he only had a child—a son—he could bear it, he said; but as it was, the place was unendurable, and so he staid away weeks at a time, while your mother pined and drooped like some fair lily which had neither water nor sunshine."

"Oh, this is very dreadful," Queenie said, with a choking sob. "I am glad grandma will never know what you have told me. But go on and tell me the rest. I insist upon knowing the whole."

So Mrs. La Rue told of the weeks and weeks which her mistress passed alone at Chateau des Fleurs, while Mr. Hetherton was seeking his pleasure elsewhere; of his great desire for a son to bear his name; of Mrs. Hetherton's failing health and removal at last to Southern France, and then, as the season advanced, to Rome; of the great joy which came to her so unexpectedly and which she purposely kept from her husband, wishing to surprise him when he joined her in Rome, as he promised to do; of the weary weeks of waiting, hoping against hope, for he was always coming in a few days at the most and never came; and then of a girl baby's birth sooner than it was expected, and the scene which followed, when the young wife died, with her little girl clasped to her bosom and her own head pillowed on Christine's arm.

Here Christine stopped suddenly and covering her face with her hands sobbed hysterically as she recalled that scene, while Reinette, too, cried as she had never cried before for the dying mother in Rome, who had held her babe to the very last and prayed that God would bless it and have it in his keeping and make it a comfort and a joy to the husband and father, who was far away, joining in a midnight revel where wine, and cards, and women, such as Margaret Ferguson never knew, formed a conspicuous part.

"Her baby was a great comfort to her," Mrs. La Rue said, when she could speak, "and she would have it where she could feel its little hands upon her face, even after blindness came upon her, and she could no longer see. The English physician had been in, and told me she probably would not last the night through, and that I must have some one with me. But she said, 'No; Christine and baby are all I want,' and when he was gone she made me sit by her, while she talked, as she had done many a time, of her home over the sea, of her sister, and her mother, to whom she sent messages. I remember her very words. 'Tell them,' she said, 'that I have never ceased to love them, and to long for them with such longing as only homesick creatures know, and if I have seemed neglectful, and have not written as I ought it was because—I couldn't. I can't explain, only I love them so much; and now if I could lay my head on mother's lap, as I did when I was a little girl, and it ached as it is aching now, I should die more willingly. Dear old mother! poor old father! with his hard, brown hands, which have worked so hard for me—God bless them, and comfort them, when they hear I am dead!'"

"Oh, Christine!" Reinette sobbed, "grandma ought to know this—she and Aunt Mary, too. They have never heard one word of her last days, for father only wrote that she was dead, and did not even tell them of my birth. I ought to tell my grandmother; she will be so glad to know."

"No, no! oh, no! better not. You said you would not!" Christine exclaimed in terror. "It would lead to so much talk—so many questions about your father, and—Reinette, forgive me—but his record was not the fairest. Even you, his daughter, would not like to see its blackest pages."

Reinette's face was crimson with shame and resentment, and in her eye was that peculiar gleam which so bewildered and confounded those on whom it fell. The fair structure she had built about her father's memory was tottering to atoms, but she would struggle bravely to keep it together as long as possible, and she replied:

"If there were pages so black in father's life, do not show them to me, lest I should say you told me falsely. He was my father, and I loved him so dearly. He was kind to me always—and I will stand by him forever. But you have not finished. I want to know just how mother died."

So Christine went on and told of the long hours when the dying woman lay with her baby clasped to her bosom, and her head pillowed on the strong arm of her maid, who held her thus until the darkness was passed and the early dawn of the mild spring morning began to creep into the room, when Margaret roused a little, and said:

"It is almost over, Christine. I am going home to Jesus, whose arms are around me so that I am not afraid. Tell them at home I was so happy, and death had no terror for me. Tell them I seem to hear the children singing as they used to sing in the old church in Merrivale, and the summer wind blows in and out, and brings the perfume of the pond lilies with it, and the river flows on and on amid the green meadows—away—away—just as I am floating so quietly out upon the sea of eternity, where the lilies are fairer and sweeter than those which lift their white heads to the sunshine in the ponds of Merrivale. And now, Christine, place my baby so I can kiss her once more, for sight and strength have failed me."

The child's face was lifted to the pale lips which kissed it tenderly, and then, just as the warm Italian sunshine lighted up the distant dome of St. Peter's with a blaze of gold, and all over the great city, and far out upon the Campagna the morning was warm and bright, the young mother lay dead in the silent room, with only her servant and baby with her.

There was a fresh burst of tears and sobs from Reinette as she listened to the story, and when it was ended she threw her arms around her nurse's neck and nearly strangled her with kisses, as she said:

"I can forgive you everything now that I know how good and true you were to my mother."

With something like a moan Christine freed herself from the girl, and went rapidly on:

"I did not know just where your father was, for he was never long in the same place, and as we could not wait to hear from him, and I did not know what to do, strangers took the matter in hand and buried her in the Protestant grave-yard at Rome, where you father has never been since."

"And I?" Reinette said. "You took me to him?"

"Yes, I took you to Chateau des Fleurs," Christine replied, while her face grew scarlet and then turned ashen pale, and Queenie never dreamed of the chasm which she leaped in silence, or of the bitter remorse which brought those livid spots to the face of Christine, who did not look at her now, but shut her eyes and leaned wearily back in her chair.

"I am so weak, and talking all this tires me so," she said; but Reinette was not satisfied, and her next question was:

"What did father say when he first saw me?"

Christine did not reply to this, but sat with her hands locked together, and a look upon her face as if she was living over some painful scene.

"Tell me; how did he act? What did he say?" Reinette repeated, and then, with a smile full of irony and bitterness Christine answered:

"He swore because you were not a boy!"

"Oh-h! this is terrible," Reinette exclaimed, as her face grew very red.

But she was too proud to let her nurse see how she was pained, and she continued:

"Yes, I can understand how a man like him would be disappointed if he wanted a son very much; but he loved me afterward. I am sure of that. How long did you stay with me at Chateau des Fleurs, and why did you leave? Was it M. La Rue?"

"Yes, I was married to Monsieur La Rue and had to leave, but I saw you sometimes when you were a little child, playing in the grounds of the Chateau."

"I remember it—a woman came one day when I was with my nurse and kissed and cried over me, and gave me some bon-bons; and that was you," Reinette said and Mrs. La Rue assented, while Reinette continued:

"And you lived all the time in Paris, and never let me know or brought Margery to see me; and, oh, Christine when I found her up in that room that day and she told you of me, did you know then who I was?"

"Yes, I knew," was the reply, and Reinette went on:

"You knew, and never tried to see me? That is very strange. And did father know, when Margery was at school with me, and afterward at the chateau? Did he know she was your daughter?" "No, it would have made him very angry," Christine replied, "and lest he should find it out I took her to Southern France and tried to cut off all intercourse between you. Her letters to you I did not post and yours to her I withheld. You remember you did not hear from her for months." "Yes, I remember," Reinette replied. "We talked about it and wondered where the letters went, but we never suspected you, and I must say I think it was a very mean thing for you to do. Father would not have been angry. Why should he, Christine?" and Reinette grew more earnest in her manner. "You may as well tell me the truth, for I am resolved to wring it from you, and I will not tell Margery either. You had done something to displease my father; now, what was it? I insist upon knowing."

"Nothing, nothing," Christine gasped. "He was very proud, and I knew he would not like you to be too intimate with people like us; that is all—everything."

"And was that the reason why after he was dead and you met me here you kept silent? Were you afraid I, too, was proud, and would think less of Margery, if I knew."

"Yes, yes; you have guessed it," Mrs. La Rue said, quickly, as if relieved that Reinette had put so good a reason into her mind.

She was very tired, and had borne so much that it seemed to her she could bear no more, and clasping her hands to her head, she said, imploringly:

"Leave me now, please; there is nothing more to tell, and I am so tired and sick, and—and—there is Margery yet to see. Oh, Miss Hetherton, make it easy as you can to Margery. Don't let her think ill of me. I could not bear that. I would rather have the bad opinion of the whole world than hers. She is so good, so true, and hates deception so much. Go now, and leave me to myself. I believe—I think—yes, I am sure I am going mad."

Reinette looked at her in surprise.

"There is something else," she thought, "something behind, which she has not told, and I mean to know what it is; but I will leave her now," and taking Christine's hot hands in hers she said, very kindly, "Good-by, Christine; I am going, but another time you will tell me more of my mother."

Then pressing her hand to her lips she ran down the stairs to Margery, who was waiting anxiously for her, and who for the first time in her life was glad when Reinette said good-by and left her alone to seek her mother.

CHAPTER XXXV

MARGERY AND HER MOTHER

For a full quarter of an hour after Reinette's departure Margery sat motionless, with her head bent down, thinking of all the incidents of her past life as connected with her mother, and recalling here and there certain acts which, viewed in the new light shed upon them, seemed both plain and mysterious. Buzzing through Margery's brain, and almost driving her mad, was the same suspicion which had at times so disturbed Reinette, but, like Reinette, she fought it down. But not for the dead man whose costly monument was gleaming cold and white in the grave-yard of Merrivale. He was nothing to her, save as the father of her friend, who, for his daughter's sake, had been kind to her so far as money was concerned. But it was for the woman up stairs, her mother, that her heart was aching so, and the hot blood pouring so swiftly through her veins. To lose faith in her whom she had believed so good, and who had taught her always that truth and purity were more to be prized than all the wealth in the world, would be terrible. And yet that mother's life had for years been one of concealment, for which she could see no excuse. That given to Queenie was not the true reason. There was something else, "and I must know what it is," she thought, "even if it kills me."

Starting to her feet at last, and forgetting how weak and sick her mother was, she went half way up the stairs and called:

"Mother, will you come down, or shall I come up?"

The voice was not the same which Mrs. La Rue knew as Margery's. There was a hardness and sternness in it which boded no good to her, and a mortal terror took possession of her as she thought:

"My hour has come. She will wring it from me. Well, no matter. It will be better for her, perhaps."

"Say, mother, will you come down, or shall I come up?" came again from Margery, and this time Mrs. La Rue replied:

"Oh, Margery, Margery! not yet—not yet! Spare me a little longer. I have been so tried and worried. I am not quite right in my head; wait awhile before you come, dear Margery."

There was a world of pathos in those two words—"dear Margery"— pathos and pleading both, as if the mother were asking mercy from her child. And Margery recognized the meaning, but her heart did not soften or relent. Indeed, she could not understand herself, or define the strange feeling which had taken possession of her and was urging her on to know what it was her mother had hidden so long and so successfully.

But she did not then go up; she waited awhile, and going to the kitchen, prepared a tempting dinner, which she arranged upon a tray, and then took to the room, where Mrs. La Rue still sat just as Reinette had left her, her face as white as marble, her eyes blood-shot and dim, and her whole attitude that of a guilty culprit awaiting its punishment.

And she was awaiting hers, and when the first blow came in the person of Margery bringing her the nicely-prepared dinner, she seemed to shrivel up in her chair, and her head dropped upon her breast. But she did not speak, and when Margery drew a little table to her side, and placing the tray upon it, poured out her tea and held it to her lips, she swallowed it mechanically, as she did the food pressed upon her. At last, however, she could take no more, and putting up her hand, she made a gesture of dissent, and whispered faintly:

"Enough!"

How sick and old, and crushed she looked! But for this Margery would not spare her; and when, after taking the dinner away, she returned to her mother, and sat down where Queenie had sat, she said:

"Now, tell me."

"Tell you what?" Mrs. La Rue asked, and Margery replied.

"Tell me the whole truth, every word of it, as you did not tell it to Queenie."

"What did I tell her?" Mrs. La Rue said, in a bewildered kind of way, as if the events of the last few hours were really a blank to her.

"You told her you were Christine Bodine, her former nurse," Margery began, and her mother interrupted her with:

"And I am, Margery; that was the truth. I was Christine Marie La Mille Bodine; but I dropped the first name and the last, and for years was only Marie La Mille."

"Yes, I know," Margery returned. "You deceived me with regard to your name, and you kept your identity a secret from Reinette when you knew how much she wished to find you, and you gave her as a reason that you feared lest she would think less of me if she knew I was the child of one who had once served her mother."

"Yes, that's it—that's it, Margie!" Mrs. La Rue gasped, as she clutched the skirt of Margery's gown and rubbed it caressingly.

"Mother," Margery said, and her voice was low and stern, "that excuse might do for Queenie, but not for me, who knows all our past life. There is something you are keeping from me, and which I must know. What is it? Why were you afraid to let Queenie know who you were?"

"There is nothing—nothing—believe me, Margie, nothing," Mrs. La Rue said, still caressing the gown, as if she would thus appease her daughter, who continued:

"Yes, there is something; there has been a something always since I can remember. I see it now—your fits of abstraction, your moods of melancholy, amounting almost to insanity, and which have increased in frequency since we came to America and met Reinette. The money you received at stated times was from her father, was it not?"

"Ye-es," came in a whisper from Mrs. La Rue's white lips, and Margery went on:

"You must then have always known his whereabouts. When we lived in Paris, and father was alive you knew that Mr. Hetherton was there in the city, too; and did you ever see him?"

"Never—never! He would have spurned me like a dog," Mrs. La Rue answered, energetically, and Margery continued:

"But you knew he was there, and when Queenie came to me that day when I wore her scarlet cloak and she my faded plaid, you knew who she was, and did not speak?"

"Yes, I knew who she was, and did not speak," moaned Mrs. La Rue, and Margery went on:

"And when I was at school with her, and her father paid the bills, and when I visited her at the chateau, you knew, and did not tell me. But did you tell my father? Did he know who Queenie was?—know of Mr. Hetherton?"

"No, he did not," Mrs. La Rue replied, "nor was it necessary. I was a faithful wife to him, and there was no need for him to know."

"Mother," Margery began, after a moment's pause, "why did you wish to hide from Queenie who you were? I have a right to know. I am your daughter, and if there has been any wrong I can share it with you. I would rather know the exact truth than think the horrible things I may think, if you do not tell me. Why did you take another name than your own, and why did you not reveal your self to Queenie, but leave her to grope in the dark for what she so much wished to find? Tell me. I insist upon knowing."

Driven to the last extremity, and forgetting herself in her distress, Mrs. La Rue replied:

"I had sworn not to do it; had taken a solemn vow never to let Queenie know who I was."

"Had made a vow? Had sworn not to do it? Who made you swear? Who required that vow from you? Was it Mr. Hetherton?" Margery asked, and her mother replied:

"Yes, Mr. Hetherton; curse him in his grave! He has been my ruin. I was so happy and innocent until I knew him. He wrung the vow from me: he paid me money to keep it; he——"

She stopped here, appalled by the look on Margery's face—a look which made her cower and tremble as she had never trembled and cowered before.

Wrenching her dress away from the hands which still held it, and drawing herself back, Margery demanded:

"Tell me what you mean? You have said strange things to me, mother. You have talked of ruin, and innocence, and money paid for silence, and as your daughter I have a right to know what you mean. And you must tell me, too, before I look on Queenie's face again. What is it, mother? What was the secret between you and Mr. Hetherton? What have you done, which you would hide from me? Speak, and I will forgive you, even if it brings disgrace to me. If you do not tell, and suffer me to live on with these horrid suspicions torturing me to madness, I can never touch your hand again in love, or think of you as I have done."

She had risen from her chair, and stood with folded arms looking down upon the wretched woman, who moaned:

"Do not, Margie, do not drive me to tell, for the telling will involve so much—so much! Some will be disgraced and others benefited; do not make me tell, please do not."

She stretched her arms toward Margery, who stood immovable as a rock, and said, with a hard ring in her voice:

"Disgrace to me, I suppose. Well, I can bear that better than suspense and uncertainty."

"No, Margie, not disgrace to you, thank Heaven! not disgrace to you in the way you think," Mrs. La Rue cried.

And with this horrid fear lifted from her mind, Margery came nearer to her mother, and said:

"If there is no disgrace for me, then tell me at once what it is. I shall never leave this room till I know."

"Then listen."

And raising herself erect in her chair, while the blood came surging back to her face, and her eyes flashed with the fire of a maniac, Mrs. La Rue continued:

"Listen; but sit down first. The story is long, and you will need all your strength before it is through. Sit down," and she pointed to a chair, into which Margery sank mechanically, while a strange, prickling sensation ran through her frame, and she felt a sickening dread of what she was to hear.

"I am ready," she said; but her voice was the fainter now of the two, for her mother's was calm and steady as she commenced the story, which she told in all its details, beginning at the day when she first saw Mr. Hetherton's advertisement for a waiting-maid for his wife.

For a time the story was pleasant enough to listen to, for Mrs. La Rue dwelt at length upon the goodness and sweetness of her mistress, who trusted her so implicitly; but at last there came a change, and Margery's eyes grew dark with horror and pain, and her cheek paled, as she listened to a tale which curdled the blood in her veins and seemed turning her into stone.

Without the sleety rain was beating in gusts against the windows, and the wind, which had risen since noon, roared down the chimney and shook every loosened blind and casement, but was unheard by the young girl, who, with a face like the faces of the dead and hands locked so tightly together that the blood came through the flesh where the nails were pressing, sat immovable, listening to the story told her by the woman, whose eyes were closed as she talked, and whose words flowed on so rapidly as if to utter them were a relief and eased the terrible remorse which had gnawed at her heart so long.

Had she looked at the girl before her she might have paused, for there was something awful in the expression of Margery's face as she listened, until the story was ended, when, with a cry like one in mortal pain, she threw up both her hands and fell heavily to the floor, while purple spots came out upon her face, and the white froth, flecked with blood, oozed from her livid lips.

Margery knew the secret of Christine Bodine!

CHAPTER XXXVI

MARGERY'S ILLNESS

When Reinette left the cottage that morning she drove to the office of Mr. Beresford, to whom she communicated the result of her interview with Mrs. La Rue, telling him the reason given by the woman for her silence, and professing to believe it.

"It was very foolish in her, of course," she said, "for, if possible, I love Margery the better now that I know who her mother is, but there is no accounting for the fancies of some people. Christine seems very much broken, and does not wish to be questioned, as she would be by grandma and Aunt Mary if they knew what we do, so we must keep our own counsel. I can trust you, Mr. Beresford."

The lawyer bowed and looked searchingly at her to see if no other thought had been suggested to her by her interview with Christine. But if there had she gave no sign of it, and her face was very bright and cheerful as she said good-by and was driven home, where she sat down to write to Phil, who had left Rome and was journeying on toward India, where she was to direct her letter.

It was four o'clock by the time the long letter was finished, and as the rain by this time had ceased, and there was a prospect of fair weather, Reinette determined to take the letter to the office herself and then call upon her grandmother, and possibly upon Mrs. La Rue.

Christine's pale face had haunted her all the afternoon, and she longed to see her again and assure her of her faith in and love for her.

Depositing her letter in the office, and bowing to Mr. Beresford, who happened to be passing in the street, she drove next to her grandmother's, but was told by the girl that Mrs. Ferguson had gone to see Miss La Rue more than an hour ago, and had not yet returned.

"Very well, I will go there, too," Reinette said, and her carriage was soon drawing up before the cottage where the doctor's gig was standing.

"Dr. Nichols here? Mrs. La Rue must be worse. I am glad I came," Reinette thought, as she went rapidly up the walk and entered unannounced.

"How is Mrs. La Rue, and where is Margery?" she asked of a woman whom she met in the hall, and whom she recognized as a neighbor.

"Don't you know? Haven't you heard? Margery has had an apoplectic fit, and is dying," was the woman's reply, and with a shriek of terror and surprise Reinette fled past her up the stairs to Margery's room, where she paused a moment on the threshold to take in the scene which met her astonished view.

By the window, which was raised to admit the air, the doctor stood, with a grave, troubled look, while near him sat Mrs. La Rue, with a face which might have been cut from stone, so rigid and immovable was every feature, while her eyes, deep-set in her head, with dark circles around them, seemed like coals of fire as they turned upon Reinette, who shuddered with fear at their awful expression. At sight of her the woman's lips moved, but made no sound—only her fingers pointed to the bed where Margery lay breathing heavily, but with no other sign to show that she was living. She looked like one dying, and had looked thus since the moment she fell to the floor at the end of her mother's story.

For a few moments Mrs. La Rue had been as helpless and almost as insensible as her daughter; then, rousing herself with a great effort, she knelt beside the unconscious girl, and lifting her head covered the white face with kisses and tears, and called upon her by every tender epithet to open her eyes and speak, if only to curse the one who had wrought so much harm. But Margery's ears were deaf alike to words of love or pleading, and she lay so still, and looked so awful, with that bloody froth about her lips, that, at last, in wild affright, her mother called for help, and the woman who lived next door was startled by a succession of cries, each louder than the preceding, and which came apparently from Mrs. La Rue's cottage. Entering at a rear door, and following the direction of the sounds, she came to the chamber where Margery still lay upon the floor, with her mother bending over her and shrieking for aid. To lift Margery up and carry her to bed, and send for a physician, was the woman's first work, and then she tried what she could do to restore the insensible girl, who only moaned faintly in token that she knew what was passing around her. When questioned by the physician, who was greatly puzzled by the case, Mrs. La Rue said that Margery had not seemed well for some time—had overworked, she thought, and that she had fallen suddenly from her chair while talking to her after dinner. This was all the explanation she would give, and, more perplexed than he had ever been in his life, the physician bent his energies to help the young girl who, it seemed, even to him, was dying, for the most powerful restoratives and stimulants failed to produce any effect, or to move so much as an eyelid.

It was just then that Grandma Ferguson came in. She had remembered some directions with regard to the brown silk, which she had failed to give in the morning, and had come again to see about it. Finding no one below, and hearing the sound of voices above, she called at the foot of the stairs:

"Mrs. La Rue! Mrs. La Rue! Where be you all?"

"Hush! Margery is very sick," the neighbor, whose name was Mrs. Whiting, answered, going to the head of the stairs, and putting her finger to her lips.

At the sound of Mrs. Ferguson's voice a tremor seemed to creep all over Margery, whose head moved a little and whose eyes partly unclosed as the old lady entered the room, and, in great concern, asked what was the matter.

"I mistrusted something ailed her this mornin'," she said, "for she did not appear nateral at all, and her hands was just like ice. Have you tried a mustard paste the whole length of her backbone? My Margaret sometimes had such faintin' spells, and that always brought her to."

Grandma was standing at the foot of the bed as she talked, and when she mentioned her daughter Margaret, Margery's eyes unclosed again, and her lips moved as if she would speak. Then she was quiet, and did not stir again until Reinette came in, and at sight of her sprang forward exclaiming:

"Oh! what is it? what is it? Margery, Margery! What has happened to her?"

At the sound of her voice the same tremor which had run through Margery's frame when Grandma Ferguson came in, returned, and this time with greater intensity. There was a faint, moaning cry, which sounded like "Queenie, oh, Queenie!" and, stepping forward, the physician said:

"Speak to her again, Miss Hetherton. She seems to know you, and we must rouse her, or she will die."

Thus importuned, Reinette knelt beside her friend, covering her face and hand with kisses, and saying to her, softly:

"Dear Margery, do you know me? I am Queenie. Speak to me, if you can, and tell me what is the matter? What made you sick so suddenly?"

"No, no! oh, no! Go away! I cannot bear it! You hurt!" Margery said, as she tried to disengage her hand from Reinette. And those were the only words she spoke for several days, during which she lay perfectly still, never moving hand or foot, but apparently conscious most of the time of what was passing around her, and always seeming happier when Grandma Ferguson was with her, and agitated when Reinette came in with her caresses and words of sympathy and love.

It was a most singular case, and greatly puzzled the physician, who said once to Reinette:

"It seems like some mental shock more than a bodily ailment. Do you know if anything has happened to disturb her, which, added to over-fatigue, might produce this utter and sudden prostration?"

Queenie hesitated a moment, and then replied:

"She did hear something which surprised her greatly, but I should hardly think it sufficient to affect her so much."

"Temperaments differ," the doctor replied, while Queenie thought to herself:

"Can it be possible that Margery takes it so to heart, and does she fear that it will make any difference in my love for her? It shall not, and I will prove it to her."

After this Queenie took up her abode, for the time being, at the cottage, of which she was really the head, for Mrs. La Rue did nothing but sit by Margery and watch her with a pertinacity and earnestness which annoyed the sick girl, when she came to realize what was passing around her, and made her try to escape the steady gaze of those strange eyes always watching her.

"Do not look at me," she said at last one day. "Move back, please, where I cannot see you."

Without a word Mrs. La Rue moved back into the shadow, but did not leave the room, except at intervals to eat and sleep, and thus the whole charge of the cottage fell upon Reinette, who developed a wonderful talent for housekeeping, and saw to everything. Much of her time, however, was passed with Margery, on whom she lavished so much love that her caresses seemed at times to worry the sick girl, who would moan a little and shrink away from her.

"What is it, Margie, darling? Do I tire you?" Reinette asked her, one day, when they were alone for a few moments, and Margery had seemed uneasy and restless.

For a moment Margery did not answer, but lay with her eyes shut while the great tears rolled down her cheeks; then, suddenly raising herself in bed, she threw her arms around Reinette's neck and sobbed:

"Oh, Queenie, Queenie, you do not know, I cannot tell you how much I love you, more than I ever did before, and yet I am so sorry; but you will love me always, whatever happens, won't you?"

"Why, yes, Margery. What can happen, and why shouldn't I love you?" Queenie asked, as she held the beautiful golden head against her bosom, and kissed the quivering lips. "Margery," she continued, "do you feel so badly because of your mother's silence! She has explained it to me, and I am satisfied. Don't let that trouble you anymore. No others beside ourselves need know who she is, and thus all talk and comment will be spared."

"I know, I know," Margery replied, "but, Queenie, you told me you believed there was something else-some other reason, and you meant to write to France; do you mean it still? Will you try to find it out?"

"Yes, I think so," Queenie answered, "just for my own curiosity. I shall make no bad use of it. I shall not harm you."

"No, no; you must not seek to know," Margery exclaimed, with energy. "There was something, Queenie. I have wrung it from her. She did right to keep silent. She ought not to have spoken. And Queenie, if you love me, promise me you will never try to find it out—never write to anyone in France. Promise, or I shall certainly die."

She had disengaged herself from Queenie's embrace, but was sitting upright in bed, with a look upon her face like one who is really losing her senses. It startled Reinette, who answered unhesitatingly:

"I promise. I will not write to any one in France, but may be you will tell me some time. Will you, Margery?"

"Never—never, so help me Heaven!" was the emphatic reply, as Margery fell back among her pillows wholly exhausted.

For a moment Reinette stood looking curiously at her; then seating herself upon the side of the bed, and taking Margery's hand, she said:

"You make me half repent my promise made without stopping to consider, for my curiosity is very great. But I shall keep it, do not fear; only tell me this—was it anything very dreadful which your mother did?"

"Yes," Margery replied, "it was very dreadful—it would make you hate her and me, too, if you knew. Don't talk to me or any one about it. Don't mention it again."

"But tell me one thing more," Queenie persisted; "I have a right to know. Was my father involved in it?"

She held her breath for the answer, and looked earnestly at Margery, whose eyes grew larger and brighter, and whose face was scarlet as she answered at last:

"At first he was, but for the last, the thing for which I blame mother most, he was not to blame."

"Thank God for that," Queenie exclaimed joyfully, while her tears fell in torrents. "Oh, Margery, you don't know what a load you have taken from me—a load I did not mean any one should ever suspect, because—because—Margery, I don't mind telling you—I've had some dreadful thoughts about Christine. Forgive me, Margery, do," she continued, as she saw a strange look leap into her friend's eyes, a look which she construed into one of resentment toward her for having harbored a suspicion of her mother, but which arose from a widely different reason, and was born of bitter shame and a great pity for herself.

"I've nothing to forgive, at least in you," Margery said, as she covered Queenie's hands with kisses and tears, which fell so fast and so long that Queenie became alarmed, and tried to comfort and quiet her.

"Don't, Margie, don't," she said; "it distresses me to see you so disturbed. If father was not to blame I do not care for the rest, but I could not bear to lose faith in him whom I have loved and honored so much."

"You never shall, darling; never, never," Margery exclaimed, and Reinette little dreamed how much the girl was thrusting from her, or how terrible was the temptation which for one brief instant almost overcame her.

But she put it down, and in her heart registered a far more solemn vow than her lips had uttered that never, through any instrumentality of hers, should Queenie know what she knew and what had affected her so powerfully, taking away all her strength and seemingly all her vitality so that she did not rally or take the slightest interest in anything about her.

At last the physician said Margery must have a change and then Reinette insisted upon taking her to Hetherton Place.

"She will be so quiet there, with nothing to excite her, and I shall take care of her all alone. You, I suppose, will have to stay here and see to the cottage," she said to Mrs. La Rue, who assented in silence, for she knew that her presence was a constant source of pain and excitement to Margery, who undoubtedly would improve more rapidly away from her.

But she doubted if Hetherton Place was the spot to take her, and Margery doubted, too, but Queenie carried her point, and bore her off in triumph, leaving Mrs. La Rue alone in the cottage to combat her remorse and misery as best she could. Everything which love could devise or money do was done to make Margery happy at Hetherton Place. The sitting-room and sleeping-room across the hall from Reinette's, which were to have been Mr. Hetherton's, were given to her, and all the rarest flowers in the greenhouse were brought to beautify them. And there the two girls took their meals, and sat and talked, or rather Queenie talked, while Margery listened, with her hands folded listlessly together, and her eyes oftentimes shut, while around her mouth there was a firm, set expression, as if she were constantly fighting something back, rather than listening to Reinette, who chatted gayly on, telling how delightful it seemed to have Margery there, and how she wished she could keep her always.

"You ought to have just such a home as this. It suits you better than the cottage, where it is work, work all the time, for people who are some of them small enough to think you beneath them because you earn your own living," she said, one afternoon when they sat in the gathering darkness, with no light in the room, save that which came from the fire in the grate. "Yes," Reinette continued, "I do believe you would make a fitter mistress of Hetherton Place than I do. You are always so quiet, and dignified, and lady-like, while I am hot and impulsive, and do and say things which shock my high-bred cousins, Ethel and Grace."

Margery did not reply, but she was glad her companion could not see the pallor which by the faint, sick feeling at her heart, she knew was spreading over her face. Just then lights were brought in by Pierre, and in a moment the supper which the girls took together at that hour appeared, and was arranged upon a little round table, which was drawn near to Margery's easy-chair.

"This is so nice," Queenie said, "and carries me back to Chateau des Fleurs, when we were little girls, and used to play at make believe. Do you remember it, Margie?"

"Yes, yes; I remember; I have forgotten nothing connected with you," Margery replied, and Queenie went on:

"I made believe so much that you were I, and I was you, that I used at times to feel as if it were real, and that my rightful home was up in Number Forty, in the Rue St. Honore. And once I dreamed that I was actually there, alone with the cat, and had to sweep the floor and wash the dishes as you used to do."

"And how did you like it?" Margery asked.

"How did I like it?" Queenie repeated, "I did not like it at all. I rebelled against it with all my might. I thought I was wearing the apron which you wore the first time I ever saw you, and I dreamed I wrenched it off and tore it into shreds, and was going to throw myself out of the window, when my maid woke me and asked what was the matter that I cried out so in my sleep. I told her I was Margery La Rue, living in Rue St. Honore, and wearing coarse clothes, and she could not pacify me till she brought my prettiest dress, and showed it to me, with my turquoise ring, papa's last present. That made me Reinette Hetherton again, and I grew calm and quiet. It was very foolish in me, was it not?"

Margery did not answer at once, but sat looking at her friend, while the drops of perspiration stood thickly on her forehead and about her mouth, and at last attracted Queenie's notice.

"What is it, Margery?" she said. "Are you too warm? Let me put a screen between you and the fire."

The screen was brought, and, wiping the drops of sweat away, Margery rallied and tried to seem cheerful and natural, though all the time there was a terrible pain tugging at her heart as she kept whispering to herself, "God help me to keep my vow."

That evening Mr. Beresford called, and was admitted to Margery's sitting-room. He had not seen her before since her illness, though he had sent to inquire for her several times, and had heard various reports with regard to the cause of her sudden attack. He had heard that she had dropped to the floor in a fit, and had been taken up for dead, and that overwork and loss of sleep was the cause assigned. But, shrewd and far-seeing as he was, Mr. Beresford did not believe in the overwork and loss of sleep. As nearly as he could calculate, the fainting fit had come on about two hours after Reinette's interview with Mrs. La Rue.

There had been ample time for Margery to see her mother and demand an explanation, and that an explanation had been made different from the one given to Reinette he did not doubt; and he was curious to see the girl who was beginning to interest him so much.

The mother had confessed to her daughter he was sure; but how would the daughter bear it and what would be her attitude toward Reinette, and what would the latter say or do if she knew what he suspected, and what he fully believed, after he had been a few moments in the room and detected the new expression on Margery's face; the new light and ineffable tenderness in her eyes when they rested on Queenie. And yet there was something in those eyes and in Margery's manner which baffled the keen-witted lawyer, who was accustomed to study the human face and learn what he wished to know by its varying expressions.

There was nothing about Margery indicative of humiliation or shame. On the contrary, it seemed to him that there was in her manner a certain reassurance and dignity he had never noticed before, and he studied her curiously and wondered if after all he was mistaken and the insinuations of the clerk in Mentone false. How inexpressibly sweet and lovely Margery was, with just enough of the invalid about her to make her interesting and Mr. Beresford found it difficult to decide which of the two girls pleased and fascinated him more, Queenie or Margery. Both were very lovely, and he was so much interested and attracted that it was very late when he at last said good-night to the two young ladies, telling Reinette he was going to write the next day to Phil, who must be in India by this time.

For two weeks longer Margery remained at Hetherton Place; but though everything was done for her comfort that love could devise, she did not seem happy, neither did her strength come back to her, as Queenie had hoped it would. It was very rarely that she ever laughed, even at Queenie's liveliest sallies, and there was upon her white face a look of inexpressible sadness, as if there were a heavy pain in her heart, of which she could not speak. To Reinette she was all sweetness and love, and her eyes would follow the gay young girl as she flitted about the house, with an expression in them which it was hard to fathom or explain, it was so full of tenderness, and pity, too, if it were possible to connect that word with a creature as bright and merry-hearted as Queenie Hetherton was then. Toward Mrs. La Rue, who came occasionally to see her, her manner was constrained, though always kind and considerate. But something had come between the mother and her daughter—something which even Queenie noticed and commented on to Margery, with her usual frankness.

"Your mother acts as if she were afraid of you," she said to Margery one day, after Mrs. La Rue had been and gone. "She actually seemed to start every time you spoke to her, and she watched you as I have seen some naughty child watch its mother to see if it was forgiven and taken again into favor. I hope, Margery, you are not too hard upon her because of that concealment from me. I have forgiven it, and nearly forgotten it, and surely her own daughter ought to be more lenient than a stranger."

Reinette was pleading for Mrs. La Rue, and as she went on, Margery burst into a passionate fit of weeping.

"Thank you, Queenie," she said, when she could speak—"thank you so much. I must have been hard toward mother if even you noticed it; but it shall be so no longer. Poor mother! I think she is not altogether right in her mind."

The next time Mrs. La Rue came to Hetherton Place she had no cause to complain of her reception, for Margery's manner toward her was that of a dutiful and affectionate child, and when Mrs. La Rue asked:

"Are you never coming home to me again, Margery?" she answered her:

"Yes; to-morrow, or next day sure. I have left you too long already."

"And are you going to stay—always—just the same?" was Mrs. La Rue's next question, to which Margery replied:

"Yes; stay with you just the same, and try to make you happy."

They were alone in Margery's room when this conversation took place, and when Margery said what she did, Mrs. La Rue sank down on the floor at her feet, and clasping her knees, cried, piteously:

"Oh, Margie! my child, my child! God will bless you for what you are doing. Oh, if I could undo it all, I would suffer torture for years and years. My noble Margie, there are few in the world like you."

And she spoke truly; for there have been few like Margery La Rue, who, knowing what she knew, could, for the love of one little dark-eyed girl, keep silence, and, resolutely turning her back upon all the luxury and ease of Hetherton Place, return to her far less pretentious home and take up the burden of life again—take up the piles of work awaiting her, for her patrons knew her worth, and would go nowhere else as long as there was a prospect of her ultimate recovery. Even Anna Ferguson had kept her work for Margery, and had postponed her wedding that her bridal dress might be made by the skillful fingers of the French girl, who at last fixed the day for her return to her own home.

Reinette would fain have kept her longer, but Margery was firm in her determination. She had been at Hetherton Place nearly three weeks, and had grown so accustomed to the ease, and luxury, and elegance about her that the life seemed to belong to her, and was far more to her taste than the hard work at the cottage—the stitch, stitch, stitch, from morning till night for people, who looked down upon her even while they acknowledged her great superiority to the persons of her class. It was hard to leave it all, hard to leave Queenie and——this she confessed to herself secretly—hard to lose the opportunity of seeing Mr. Beresford, who had been at the house so often, and in whom she knew she was beginning to feel a deep interest.

He spent his last evening with them, and, at Queenie's earnest solicitation, Margery played and sang for him, while he listened amazed as the clear tones of her rich, musical voice floated through the rooms, and her white hands fingered the keys as deftly and skillfully as Queenie's could have done.

That Margery could sing and play was a revelation to Mr. Beresford, who stood by her side, and turned the leaves for her.

"You have given me a great pleasure," he said, when she at last left the piano and resumed her seat by the fire. "This is a surprise to me. I did not suppose——"

He did not finish the sentence, but stopped awkwardly, while Margery, who understood his meaning perfectly, finished it for him.

"You did not suppose," she said, laughingly, "that one of my class could have any accomplishments save those of the needle, and it is surprising. But I owe it all to Queenie. You remember I told you it was through her influence with her father that I was sent to one of the best schools in Paris. I think I have naturally a taste for music, and so made greater proficiency in that than in anything else. If I have pleased you with my playing I am glad, but you must thank Queenie for it."

"Yes," Mr. Beresford answered, thoughtfully, looking curiously at each of the young girls, and trying to decide which was the more attractive of the two.

Queenie always bewildered, and intoxicated, and bewitched him, and made him feel very small, and as if in some way he had made himself ridiculous, and she was laughing at him with her wonderful eyes, while Margery, on the contrary, soothed, and quieted, and rested him, and, by her gentle deference of manner, and evident respect for whatever he said, flattered his self-love, and put him in good humor with himself, and during his ride home that night he found himself thinking more of her sweet face, and of the blue eyes which had looked so shyly into his, than of Reinette's sparkling, brilliant beauty, which seemed to grow more brilliant and sparkling every day.

He had said to Margery that he was glad she was to return to town on the morrow, and that he hoped to hear her sing again very soon. And as he talked to her he kept in his the hand which he had taken when he arose to say good-night, and which was very cold, and trembled perceptibly as it lay in his broad, warm palm. Was it Margery's fancy, or was there a slight pressure of her fingers, as he released them—a touch different from that of a mere acquaintance, and which sent through her frame a thrill of joy which surprised and bewildered her.

It was not all fancy she was sure, and for hours she lay awake, feeling again the clasp of Mr. Beresford's hand and seeing the look in his eyes when they rested upon her.

"If he knew! Oh! if he knew!" was the smothered cry in her heart, as she bravely fought back the temptation assailing her so sorely, and vowed again that through her he should never know what might bring him nearer to her if there was that in his heart which she suspected.

Next morning Margery was later than usual, for she lingered long over her toilet, taking, as it were, a regretful leave of all the articles of luxury with which her room was filled. The white cashmere dressing-gown, with the pink satin lining, which Queenie had made her use, and the dainty slippers which matched them, were laid away for the last time. She should never more wear such garments as these, for probably she should not again be a guest at Hetherton Place. It would not be well for her to be there often, for after three weeks' experience of a life so different from her own, there came over her for a moment a sense of loathing for her work, a horrid feeling of loneliness and homesickness, as she remembered the cottage, which she knew was so much prettier and pleasanter than any home she had ever known. But it was not like Hetherton Place, and for a moment Margery's weaker nature held her in bondage, and her tears fell like rain as she went from one thing to another, softly whispering her farewell.

Queenie was going to the village with her immediately after breakfast, and the carriage was waiting for them now, she knew, for she heard it when it came to the door, and she had heard, too, the sound of horses feet coming rapidly into the yard, and looking from her window, had seen David, Mr. Rossiter's man dismounting from his steed which had evidently been ridden very hard.

Going down to the dining-room at last she saw Reinette standing near the conservatory with an open letter clutched in both hands, her head thrown back, disclosing a face which seemed frozen with horror, and her whole attitude that of one suddenly smitten with catalepsy. At the sound of footsteps, however, she moved a little, and when Margery went to her, asking what was the matter, she held the letter toward her, and whispered faintly:

"Read it."

CHAPTER XXXVII

THE LETTER

Phil's last letter had been addressed to his mother from Rome, and in it he had written that he was to start for India the next day with a young man whose acquaintance he had made on the voyage from New York to Havre, and who had persuaded him to go for a week or two to Madras, where his father was living. Since that time nothing had been heard from Phil, until the young man whose name was William Mather, wrote from Madras, as follows:

"Mr. and Mrs. Rossiter:—Respected Friends: I do not think I am an entire stranger to you, for I am very sure your son Philip wrote of me to you in some of his letters. We were together in the same ship, occupied the same state-room, and, as we were of the same age, and had many tastes and ideas in common, we soon became fast friends. I have never met a person whom I liked so much upon a short acquaintance as I did Philip Rossiter. He was so genial, so kind, so unselfish, and let me say, with no detriment to him as a man, so like a gentle, tender woman in his manner toward every one, that not to like him was impossible.

"My parents are American by birth, but I was born in Madras, where my father has lived for many years. Seeing in your son a true artist's love and appreciation for everything beautiful, both in nature and art, I was anxious for him to see my home, which I may say is one of the most beautiful places in Madras. So I begged him to accompany me thither before going on to Calcutta, and he at last consented. I was the more anxious for this as he did not seem quite well; indeed, he was far from being well, although his disease, if he had any, was more mental than physical. Frequently during the voyage he would go away by himself and sit for hours looking out upon the sea, with a look of deep sadness on his face, as if brooding over some hidden grief, and once in his sleep, when he was more than usually restless, he spoke the name Queenie—whom he said he had lost, but in his waking hours he never mentioned her. I think, however, that he wrote to her from my father's house at the same time he wrote to you. Probably you have received his letter ere this. He was delighted with my home, and during the few days he was with us improved both in health and spirits. He was very fond of the water, and as I have a pretty sailing-boat and a trusty man to manage it, we spent many hours upon the bay, going out one morning fifteen or twenty miles along the coast to a spot where my father has some gardens and a villa. Here we spent the day, and it was after sunset when we started to return, full of anticipated pleasure in the long sail upon the waters, which at first were so calm and quiet. Gradually, however, there came a change, and a dark cloud which, when we started, we had observed in the west, but thought nothing of, increased in size and blackness and spread itself over the whole heavens, while fearful gusts of wind, which seemed to blow from every quarter, tossed and rocked our boat as if it had been a feather. I think now that Jack, our man, must have drank a little too much at the villa, for he seemed very nervous and uncertain, and as the storm of wind increased, and in spite of all our efforts carried us out to sea instead of toward the coast, which we tried to gain, he lost his self-possession entirely and when there came a gust stronger than any previous one, he gave a loud cry and a sudden spring, and then we were struggling in the angry water with the boat bottom side up beside us.

"I seized your son's arm, and with my other hand managed to get a hold upon the boat, which Mr. Rossiter and Jack also grasped, and there in the darkness of that awful night we clung for hours, constantly drifting farther and farther away from the shore, for the gale was blowing from the land, and we had no power to stem it. Far in the distance we saw the lights of vessels struggling with the tempest, but we had no means of attracting the attention of the crew, and our condition seemed hopeless, unless we could hold on until morning, when we might be discovered and picked up. For myself, I felt that I could endure it, but I feared for my friend. He was breathing very heavily, and I knew his strength was failing him, besides his position was not so easy as mine, as he had a smoother surface to cling to."

"'If you can get nearer to me,' I said, 'I can support you with one hand. Suppose you try it.'

"He made a desperate effort to reach me, while I held my hand toward him, and then—oh, how can I tell you the rest—there came a great wave and washed him away.

"I heard a wild cry above the storm, and by the lightning's gleam I caught one glimpse of his white face as it went down forever. Of what followed, I am scarcely conscious, and wonder how I was enabled to keep my hold with Jack upon the boat until the storm subsided, and the early dawn broke over the still angry waves, when we were rescued from our perilous situation by a small craft going on to Madras. I cannot express to you my grief, or tell to you my great sorrow. May God pity you and help you to bear your loss. If there is a Queenie in whom your son was interested, and you know her, tell her I am certain that, whether waking or sleeping, she was always in the mind of my dear friend, and that a thought of her was undoubtedly with him when he sank to rise no more. Indeed, I am sure of it, for his last cry which I heard distinctly, was for her, and Queenie was the word he uttered just before death froze the name upon his lips. You can tell her this, or not, as you see fit.

"Again assuring you of my heartfelt sympathy,

"I am, yours, most respectfully,

"William J. Mather."

And this was the letter the Rossiters had received and read, and wept over—the mother going from one fainting fit into another, and refusing to be comforted, because her son Philip was not. And then they sent it to Queenie, who read it with such bitter anguish as few have ever known, for in her heart she felt that with her cruel words and taunts she had sent him to his death. She was his murderer, and she felt as if turning into stone as she finished the letter and stood clutching it tightly, with no power to move or even to cry out. It was like that dreadful phase of nightmare when the senses are alive to what is passing around one, but the strength to stir is gone. There was a choking sensation in her throat, as if her heart had leaped suddenly into her mouth, and if she could she would have torn the collar from her neck in order to breathe more freely.

When Margery came in she rallied sufficiently to pass the letter to her, and that broke the spell and set her free from the bands which had bound her so firmly. At first no words of comfort came to Margery's lips. She could only put her arms around her friend, and, leading her to her room, make her lie down, while she stood over her and rubbed her hands and bathed her face, which though white as marble, was hot to the touch, like faces burning with fever.

"You won't go? You will not leave me?" she said to Margery, who replied:

"Of course I shall not leave you. You staid with me, and I must stay with you."

Later in the day Mr. Beresford, who had heard the dreadful news, came to Hetherton Place, bringing the letter which poor Phil had written to

Queenie from Madras, and which, together with one for his mother, had come in the same mail which brought the news of his death.

When Queenie heard he was below asking for her she started from her pillow, where she had lain perfectly motionless for hours, and said to Margery:

"Yes, I will see him. I must vent these horrible feelings on some one, or I shall go crazy! Show him up at once."

Years ago Margery had seen Queenie in what she called her "moods," when her evil spirit had the ascendant, and she fought and struck at anything within her reach, but of late these fits had been of rare occurrence, and so she was astonished, on her return to the room with Mr. Beresford, to see the girl standing erect in the middle of the floor, her nostrils dilated and her eyes blazing, as they flashed upon Mr. Beresford, whose heart was full of sorrow for his loss, and who went toward her to offer his sympathy. But Queenie repelled him with a fierce gesture of both hands, striking into the air as if she would have struck him had he been within her reach.

"Don't speak to me, Arthur Beresford," she cried, and there was something awful in the tone of her voice. "Don't come near me, or I may do you harm. I am not myself to-day, I'm that other one you have never seen. I know what you are here for without your telling me. You have come to talk to me of Phil, to say you are sorry for me, sorry he is dead, but I will not hear it. You, of all men, shall not speak his name to me, guilty as you are of his death. I sent him away. I murdered him, but you were the first cause; you suggested to me the cruel words I said to him, and which no man could hear and not go away. You talked of Sardanapalus, and effeminacy, and weakness, and lack of occupation, and every word was a sneer, because, coward that you were, you thought to raise yourself by lowering him, and fool that I was, when he came to me and told me of a love such as you are incapable of feeling, I spurned him and cast your words into his teeth and made him loathe and despise himself and made him go away, to seek the occupation, to build up the manhood you said he lacked; and now he is dead, drowned in those far off eastern waters, my Phil, my love, my darling. I am not ashamed to say it now. There is nothing unmaidenly in the confession that I love him as few men have ever been loved, and I wish I had told him so that night upon the rocks; I wish I had trampled down that scruple of cousinship which looks to me now so small. But I did not, I broke his heart, and saw it breaking, too; I knew it by the awful look upon his face, not a look of disappointment only; he could have borne that; few men, if any, die of love alone; but there was on his face a look of unutterable shame and humiliation as if all the manliness of his nature had been insulted by my taunts of his womanish habits and ways. Oh, Phil, my love, my love; if he could know how my heart is aching for him and will ache on forever until I find him again somewhere in the other world! Don't speak to me" she continued, as Mr. Beresford tried to say something. "I tell you I am dangerous in these moods, and the sight of you who are the first cause of my anguish, makes me beside myself. You talked some nonsense once about waiting for my love. I told you then it could not be. I tell it to you now a thousand times more strongly. I would rather be Phil's wife for one second than to be yours through all eternity. Oh, Phil, my love, if I could die and join him; but life is strong within me and I am young and must live on and on for years and years with that death-cry always sounding in my ears as it sounded that awful night when he went down beneath the waters with my name upon his lips. Where was I that I did not hear it, and know that he was dying? If I had heard it I believe I, too, should have died and joined him on his journey through the shades of death. But there was no signal; I did not hear him call, and laughed on as I shall never laugh again, for how can I be happy with Phil dead in the sea?"

She was beginning to soften; the mood was passing off, and though her face was pale as ashes, the glitter was gone from her eyes, which turned at last toward Margery, who had looked on in utter astonishment.

"Oh, Margie, Margie, help me. I don't know what I have been saying. I think I must be crazy," she said, as she stretched her arms towards Margery, who went to her at once, and leading her to the couch made her lie down while she soothed and quieted her until a faint color came back to her face, and her heart-beats were not so rapid and loud.

Across the room by the window Mr. Beresford was still standing, with a troubled look upon his face, and seeing him Queenie called him to her, and putting her icy hand in his, said to him very gently:

"Forgive me if I have wounded you. I am not myself when these moods are upon me. I don't know what I said, for my heart is with Phil, and Phil is in the sea. Now go away, please, and leave me alone with Margie."

Mr. Beresford bowed, and pressing the hand he held, said, in a choking voice:

"God bless you, Queenie, and comfort you, and forgive me if anything I said was instrumental in sending Phil away. He was the dearest friend I ever had, the one I liked the best and enjoyed the most, and I never shall forget him or cease to mourn for him. Good-by, Queenie; good-afternoon, Miss La Rue."

He bowed himself from the room, and was soon riding slowly homeward, with sad thoughts in his heart of the friend he had lost and who seemed to be so near him that more than once he started and looked around as if expecting to meet Phil's pleasant face and hear his well-remembered laugh. Mr. Beresford belonged to that class of men, who, without exactly saying there is no God and no hereafter, still doubt it in their hearts, and by trying to explain everything on scientific principles, throw a vail over the religion they were taught to hold so sacred in their childhood. But death had never touched him very closely, or borne away that for which he mourned with a very keen or lasting sense of loss and pain. His father had died when he was a boy, and though his mother lived till he was a well-grown youth, she had not attached him very strongly to her. He had been very proud of her as an elegant, fashionable woman who sometimes came in her lovely party dress to look at him before going out to some place of amusement, but he had never known what it was to be petted and caressed, and when she died his sorrow was neither deep nor lasting, and in his maturer manhood, when the seeds of skepticism were taking root, he could think without a pang that possibly there was beyond this life no place where loved ones meet again and friendships are renewed; nothing but oblivion—a long, dreamless sleep.

But now that Phil was dead—Phil, who had been so much to him—Phil, whom he loved far better than the cold, unsympathetic elder brother who had died years ago, he felt a bitter sense of loss, and pain, and loneliness, and as he rode slowly home in the gathering twilight of that wintry afternoon, and thought of that bright young life and active mind so suddenly blotted out of existence, if his theory was true, he suddenly cried aloud:

"It cannot be; Phil is not gone from me forever. Somewhere we must meet again. Death could only stupefy, not quench, all that vitality. There is something beyond; there is a rallying point, a world where we shall meet those whom we have loved and lost. And Phil is there, and some day I shall find him. Thank God for that hope—thank God there is a hereafter."

CHAPTER XXXVIII

MOURNING FOR PHIL

It was very bitter and deep, and all the more so because the blow had fallen so suddenly, without a note of warning. At the Knoll there was a small and select dinner party the evening the letter came. Some friends from Boston were visiting in the house, and Mrs. Rossiter had invited a few of the villagers to meet them, and in her evening dress of claret velvet, with diamonds in her ears and at her throat, she looked as lovely and almost as young as in her early girlhood when she won the heart of the grave and silent Paul Rossiter. Dinner had been over some little time, and she was standing with her guests in the drawing-room when the fatal letter was brought to her. She saw it was from Madras, and that the handwriting was a stranger's; and though it was directed to her husband, who immediately after dinner had wandered off to his conservatories, where he spent most of his time, she opened it unhesitatingly, feeling sure that it contained tidings of her son, and feeling, too, with that subtle intuition which so often precedes dreadful news, that the tidings were not good. But she was not prepared to hear that Phil was dead; and when she read that he would never return to her again, she gave one long, agonizing shriek, and dropped upon the floor in a faint so nearly resembling death that for a little while they feared she was really dead. Fortunately the family physician was among the guests, and so relief was immediate, or she might never have returned to consciousness, so terrible was the shock to her nervous system. For hours she passed from one fainting fit into another, and when these were over lay in a kind of semi-stupor, moaning at intervals:

"Oh, my boy! my Phil, my darling—dead—gone from me forever—my boy, my boy!"

If Mrs. Rossiter had a weakness it was her love for her son. Phil had been her idol, and if her husband and both her daughters had lain dead at her feet and Phil had been spared to her, she would not have felt so badly as she did now when she still had husband and daughters, but Phil was not. Nothing availed to soothe or quiet her, and the house which had heretofore been so bright and cheerful, and full of gayety, became a house of sorrow and gloom. The servants trod softly through the silent halls, and spoke only in whispers to each other, while Ethel and Grace, with traces of bitter weeping upon their fair, sweet faces, sat from morning till night with folded hands looking hopelessly at each other as if paralyzed by the awful calamity which had fallen upon them. They were of no use to their mother, who lay in her darkened room, refusing to see any one except her husband, whom she kept constantly with her, and who gave no sign of what he thought or felt. Quiet, patient all enduring, he sat by his wife's bedside and listened to her moans, and did what she bade him do; left her when she said so; returned to her when she sent for him, and if he felt pain or grief himself uttered no word, and never mentioned Philip's name.

Of Mr. Rossiter we have said comparatively nothing, as he has but little to do with the story, except as the father of Phil. He was a very peculiar man— silent, unsocial, undemonstrative, and, save for his love and admiration for his wife, apparently indifferent to everything except his four conservatories, and what they contained. Had he been poor and obliged to earn his own living he would unquestionably have been a gardener, so fond was he of flowers and plants of every kind. He had walked miles through the tangled glades of Florida, hunting for some new specimens of ferns or pitcher-plants, and his greenhouses were full of exotics from every clime. Here, and in the room adjoining, where he kept his catalogues and books of pressed leaves and flowers, he spent most of his time, and if beguiled away from his favorites for a few moments he was always in a hurry to return to them. It was in one of his conservatories that the news of his son's death reached him. After dinner was over he had asked his gentlemen guests to go with him and see a new kind of fern, gathered the previous autumn in some of the neighboring swamps, and he was talking most eloquently of its nature and habits when his wife's shriek reached him, and the next moment a servant rushed in, exclaiming:

"Oh sir, come quick, Mrs. Rossiter has fainted, and Mr. Philip is drowned."

"Drowned! My son drowned! Did you say Philip was dead? It will go hard with his poor mother," he said very calmly, as he put the pot of ferns carefully back in its place.

But the hands which held the pot trembled, and the palms were wet with great drops of sweat, as he went slowly to the room where his wife lay in a swoon. He was a small man, and weak, too, it would seem, but it was he who lifted the fainting woman up and bore her to her chamber and loosened her dress, and took the diamonds from her throat and ears, and the flowers from her hair, as quickly and skillfully as her daughters could have done. There was a good deal of Phil in his nature, and he showed it in his womanly and quiet manner at the sick bed.

"Poor Mary, I am so sorry for you," he said, and pressed his lips to the forehead of his wife, who clung to him as a child in pain clings to its mother.

But there were no tears in his eyes, as the days passed by, no change in his manner, as he went about his usual vocations and watered his ferns and tended his orchids and picked off the dead leaves from the roses and carnations, and smoked the lilies and roses on which insects were gathering.

"Where have you been so long?" his wife asked him once, when he came to her after an absence of more than an hour.

"Been watering my ferns," was his reply, and with a half reproachful sob his wife continued:

"Oh, Paul, how can you care for such things with Philip dead?"

"I don't know, Mary" he answered, apologetically. "I am sorry if I have done anything out of character; the little things seem so glad for the water, and if I was to let every fern, and orchid, and pitcher-plant die, it would not bring Philip back."

Had he then no feeling, no sorrow for his son? Mrs. Rossiter almost thought so; but that night waking suddenly from a quiet sleep, she missed him from her side and raising herself in bed, saw him across the room by the window, where the moonlight was streaming in, kneeling upon the floor with his face buried in a pillow he had lain upon a chair, the better to smother the sobs which seemed almost to rend his soul from his body, they were so deep and pitiful.

"Phil, Phil, my boy, how can I live without him? I was so proud of him and loved him so much. Oh, Phil, they think me cold and callous, because I cannot talk and moan as others do, but God knows my bitter pain. God help me, and Mary, too. Poor Mary, who was his mother, and loved him, maybe, more than I did. God comfort her and help her to bear, no matter what I suffer."

This was what Mrs. Rossiter heard, and in a moment she was beside the prostrate man—her arms were around his neck, and his bowed head was laid against her bosom, while she kissed his quivering lips again and again, as she said to him:

"Forgive me, Paul, if I have been so selfish in my own grief as not to see how you, too, have suffered. Phil was our own boy, Paul; we loved him together, we will mourn for him together, and comfort each other, and love each other better because we have lost him."

Then Paul Rossiter broke down and cried as few men ever cry, and sobbed till it seemed as if his heart would break, while his wife, now the stronger and calmer of the two, supported him, and tried to comfort him. There was perfect accord and confidence between the husband and wife after that, and Mrs. Rossiter roused herself to something like cheerfulness and interest in the world about her for the sake of the man who, except to her, never mentioned Philip's name, but who grew old and gray and bent so fast and sometimes even forgot to water his ferns and let them dry and wither in their pots, where they might have died but for his wife, who took charge of them herself, and gave them the care they needed.

Like their father, Ethel and Grace were very quiet in their grief, which was not the less acute for that. A thought of Phil was always in their hearts, though they never spoke of him voluntarily, and always changed the conversation as soon as possible when his name was mentioned. But oh, how they missed him everywhere: missed his quick, springing step upon the walk as he came in, bright, and fresh, and gay, from doing nothing—his cheery whistle, or snatches of song, or his playful badinage, and all the thousand little acts by which a good, kind brother can make himself beloved. If they could have seen him dead—if his body could have been brought home and buried in quiet Merrivale, under the shadows of the pines, where they could have kept his grave bright with flowers and watered it with their tears—it would have been some solace for their pain. But alas! he had no grave, no resting-place, save those deep, dark Eastern waters, and who could tell what horrid monster of the deep might have torn and mangled his manly form ere it reached the bottom of the sea! It was too horrible to think of; and the faces of his mother and sisters grew whiter and thinner each day, for each day they missed more and more the young man who had been the sunlight of their home.

Poor Grandma Ferguson, too, was completely prostrated at first with the suddenness of the blow, and could only sit and cry like a little child for the boy whom she had loved so dearly, and who had always been kind and affectionate to her.

"No matter if I ain't nothin' but a homespun, uneddicated critter; he never acted an atom ashamed of me, and when he had some high young city bucks visitin' him he allus brought 'em to see me and get some of my strawberry short-cake or mince pies," she said to a neighbor who was trying to comfort her. "He never sassed me but once, and then he was a boy, and didn't know no better, and he was sorry, too," she said; and she went on to relate the circumstances of his coming to her the night before he went away to school, and asking her forgiveness for the rude words he had said to her, when she kissed him and called him her baby.

He was her only grandson, and her heart was very sore and full of pain; and, laying aside her brown silk dress, which she had thought to wear at Anna's wedding, she clothed herself in deepest black, and thought and talked of nothing but her boy, her Phil, "drownded in the Ingies."

As for Anna, she cried herself into a sick headache the first day, and declined to see the major, when he called. But she received him the next day, and was a good deal comforted by the beautiful necklace and pendant of onyx and pearls he brought to her with a view to assuage her grief, which was not very lasting. She liked Phil well enough, and his sudden death was a great shock to her, but she liked the major better, or, rather, she liked the costly presents he made her, and the position he would give her when she became his wife, as she expected to do in a few weeks. The grand wedding, however, which she was intending to have, must now be given up; and this, perhaps, added a little to her sorrow and regret for Phil's untimely end.

Outside of his family, too, there was deep mourning for the young man who had been so popular with every one, and of whom it was said that he had not a single enemy. But nowhere was there a heart so full of pain and remorse as at Hetherton Place where Queenie shut herself in her room and refused to see any one except Margery and Pierre.

She had read with a fresh burst of anguish Phil's letter written her from Madras—a letter full of tenderness and love, showing how he kept her still in his heart as the dearest, sweetest memory of his life, and at the close containing a few words of passionate entreaty that she would overcome her scruples, and bid him come back to her by and by.

"Not now," he wrote, "not while I am the shiftless, aimless block you were right to despise, but after I have shown that there is something in me besides a love of indolence and feminine occupations, will you reconsider, Queenie, and see if you cannot love me?"

"Yes, Phil, oh, Phil!" Queenie cried, as she finished reading this letter, which she covered with her kisses, and then kept under her pillow where she could find it readily when the fancy took her to read it.

Everything Phil had given her or helped to make, was brought to her chamber where she could see it, for she refused to go down stairs, but stayed constantly in her own room, sometimes pacing restlessly to and fro, but often lying down with her face to the wall and her eyes open day and night, for she could neither sleep nor cry, and her head seemed bursting with its pressure of blood and pain.

"If I could cry," she said once to Margery, as she pressed her hands to her throbbing temples, "it would loosen the tightness in my throat and about my heart, but I cannot, and I am so tired, and sick, and faint, I shall never cry again or sleep."

And it would almost seem as if she spoke the truth, for no tears came to cool her burning eyelids, and her eyes grew larger and brighter each day, while sleep such as she once had known had deserted her entirely. They gave her bromide, and morphine, and chloral in heavy doses, but these only procured for her snatches of troubled sleep which were quite as exhausting as wakefulness for she always saw before her that dark waste of waters, with the white face of her lover upturned to the pitiless sky, and heard always that wild cry for her who had been his evil star. Every morning the family at the Knoll sent to inquire for her, and every evening Mr. Beresford rode over to Hetherton Place to ask how she was. And sometimes he staid for half an hour or more, and talked with Margery, not always of the sick girl, or Phil, but of things for which each had a liking and sympathy—of pictures, and statuary, and books—and Mr. Beresford was surprised and delighted to find how intelligent Margery was, and how much she knew of the literature of other countries than France.

"I always had a fancy for everything English or American, particularly the latter," she said to Mr. Beresford, one evening when they had been discussing English and American authors, and he had expressed his surprise that a French girl should be so well posted.

"You like our country, then?" he said. "Did you ever wish you were part or whole American instead of French?" and he shot a curious glance at her to see what effect his question would have upon her.

For an instant her cheeks were scarlet, and then she turned very white about her lips, and her voice was not quite steady as she replied, "I pray God to make me content in that station to which he has called me, and if he has willed it that I should be French, then French I will remain forever."

It was a strange answer, and seemed made more to herself than to Mr. Beresford, who felt more certain than ever that Margery knew what he suspected, and was bravely keeping it to herself, for fear of wounding and humiliating Queenie. What a noble woman she seemed to him, and how fast the interest he felt in her ripened into a liking during the days when he went nightly to Hetherton Place, ostensibly to ask after Queenie, but really for the sake of a few minutes' talk with Margery La Rue, who was fast learning to watch for his coming, and to feel her pulses quicken when he came, and taking her hand in his, held it there while he put the usual round of questions with regard to Queenie and herself, appearing at last almost as much interested in her welfare as in Queenie's.

It was the dawning of a new life for Margery, this feeling, that Mr. Beresford, the proudest man in Merrivale, found delight in her society and loved to linger at her side. It made everything else so easy, and her life was not one of perfect rest, for Queenie did not improve as the days went on, and to soothe, and quiet, and minister to her was not an easy matter. She could not sleep, and the physician who attended her was beginning to fear for her reason, when she one day said to Margery, "Where is your mother? Why has she never been to see me? Doesn't she care for me any more?"

"She cares very much," Margery replied, "and she has been here several times to ask for you, but as you would not see your cousins or grandmother, she did not suppose you would see her. Will you see my mother?"

"Yes, send for her," was Queenie's answer, and Pierre was dispatched to Mrs. La Rue, with the message that Miss Hetherton was anxious to see her.

And so Mrs. La Rue went to Hetherton Place, and up to the room where Queenie sat in her easy-chair, with her face so pale and pinched, and her eyes so large and bright, that the impulsive Frenchwoman uttered a cry of alarm, and going to her, threw her arms around her, and cried, "Oh, Queenie, my child, that I should find you so changed."

"Yes, Christine," Queenie replied, freeing herself from the stifling embrace, "I suppose I am changed. I feel it myself, and believe I shall die if I do not sleep. I have not slept a good sleep since I heard Phil was dead, and I have sent for you to hold me in your arms, just as you must have done when I was a baby, after mother died. Sing me the old lullabies you used to sing me then, and maybe I shall sleep. I feel as if I should—there is such a heaviness about my lids and pressure on my brain. Take me, Christine. Play I am a baby again. I can't be very heavy now," and she smiled a faint, shadowy smile, as she put up her arms to the woman who took her up so gladly and covered the wan face with kisses and tears, while she murmured words of pity and endearment.

"There, that will do—it wearies me," Queenie said, and she laid her tired head upon Christine's shoulder and closed her heavy eyelids. "Rock me to sleep, Christine, as you did at Chateau des Fleurs," she whispered, faintly, and, sitting down in the chair, Christine rocked the poor little girl, and sang to her, in a low, sad voice, a lullaby of France, such as she used to sing when, as now, the dark curly head was pillowed on her breast.

Attracted by the sound, Margery stole softly to the door and looked in, but Christine motioned her away and went on with her song of "Mother Mary, guard my child," until nature, which had resisted every exertion and every drug, however powerful, gradually began to yield—the head pressed more heavily, the rigid nerves softened, a slight moisture showed itself under the hair upon the forehead, and the eyes, which had been so wild and bright, were closed in slumber.

Queenie was asleep at last, and when Margery came again to the door of the room and saw the closed eyes and the parted lips, from which the breath came easily and regularly, she exclaimed:

"Thank God, she sleeps at last. You have saved her life—or, at least, her reason; but let me help you lay her down. She is too heavy for you to hold, and you are not strong."

"No, no," Mrs. La Rue answered, almost fiercely. "No, no, I will not give her up, now that I have her in my arms. I am not tired. I do not feel her weight any more than I did when she was a baby, and if I did, think you I would not do it all the same—I who have so longed to hold her as I do now. Go away, Margie, and leave us alone again."

So Margery went away a second time, and busied herself below with some work she had been persuaded to take, and which was a part of Anna's bridal trousseau, for that young lady had insisted upon her making the traveling dress, which was all there was now to finish of the elaborate and expensive wardrobe for which, it was said, the major's money paid.

And while Margery worked in the sitting-room below, Mrs. La Rue sat in the chamber above, holding the sleeping girl, until her limbs were cramped, and numb—and ached with intolerable pain, while rings of fire danced before her eyes, and in her ears there was a humming sound, and a fullness in her head, as if all the blood of her body had centered there. And still she did not move, lest she should awaken the sleeper, but sat as motionless as a figure carved from stone, sometimes shutting her tired eyes, and again fixing them with a steady gaze upon the upturned face resting on her arm.

Two hours had gone by, and Mrs. La Rue was beginning to feel that her strength was failing her, when Queenie at last awoke, and said, very sweetly and kindly:

"I have been asleep, I am sure, and I feel so much better. How good in you, Christine, to hold me so long. It must have tired you very much. Thank you, dear old Christine!"

And taking the pallid face between both her hands, Queenie kissed it lovingly, thereby paying the tired woman for her two hours' endurance.

Queenie was much better after that long sleep. The spell which bound her so relentlessly was broken, and she improved steadily both in health and spirits, but would let neither Mrs. La Rue nor Margery leave her.

"I shall sink right back again into that dreadful nervousness if you go away," she said. "I need you both to keep me up—Margery to cheer me by day, and Christine to soothe me to sleep at night, when the world is the blackest, and Phil's dead face seems so close to mine that I can almost feel its icy touch, and can hear his bitter cry for me. Only Christine's song can drown that cry, which, I think, will haunt me forever."

So the two women stayed, Margery busying herself with the work which her former customers persisted in bringing to her as soon as they heard she was free to do anything of that sort, and Christine devoting herself to Queenie, to whom she talked of the days when she first entered the service of Mrs. Hetherton in Paris. Reinette was never tired of hearing of her mother, and the same story had to be told many times ere she was satisfied.

"It brings her so near to me to hear all this," she said to Christine, one evening when they sat together by the firelight in Queenie's room, and Christine had been describing a dress which her mistress wore to a grand ball at which dukes and duchesses were present. "I like to think of her in that lovely dress, and she was happy, too, I am sure, though you have sometimes talked as if she were not. I know my father loved her very much, though he might not have shown it before you. Men are different from women. Did he never pet her in your presence?"

"Oh, yes, sometimes, and called her his little Daisy—that was his pet name for her," Christine replied, and Reinette rejoined:

"Daisy is such a sweet name. I wish it were mine, though Queenie does very well. I like pet names so much. Did you ever have one? I hardly know what could be made of Christine."

Mrs. La Rue was gazing steadily into the fire, and did not at once reply, and when at last she did, she said, "I have been called Tina."

"Tina," Reinette exclaimed, starting suddenly, while like a flash of lightning there shot through her brain the memory of the long black tress she had burned and the letter whose writer had signed herself Tina. "Who used to call you Tina?" she demanded. "Was it your husband?"

Not a muscle of Christine's face moved, nor did her voice tremble in the least, as she replied:

"Yes; there was more sentiment in his nature than any one would suppose from seeing him. He was very fond of me at times."

Just then Pierre came in bringing candles and a tray with his mistress' supper upon it, and the conversation was brought to a close, nor was it resumed again, for after tea Margery came up and sat with Reinette and her mother until the latter asked to be excused, and retired to her room.

CHAPTER XXXIX

TINA

Reinette kept saying the name over to herself after Margery left her, and when at last she was in bed it repeated itself again and again in her brain, while a horrible suspicion, the exact nature of which she could not define, was forcing itself into her mind. To sleep was impossible, and with all her old wakefulness upon her, she tossed restlessly from side to side until she heard the clock strike one.

"I cannot lie here," she said, and putting on her dressing-gown she drew her chair to the grate where the fire which Pierre had replenished just before she retired was burning, and with her face buried in her hands, began to think such thoughts as made the drops of perspiration stand thickly upon her forehead and about her lips.

"Who was the Tina who wrote to my father?" she asked herself.

Not Christine; that would be too horrible. Christine had been her mother's maid, and it was not like a proud man like Frederick Hetherton to think of such as she. There were other Tinas in the world. The writer of the letter was some bright-eyed, bright-faced girl of humble origin, who had caught her father's fancy for a few days and been flattered by a kind word from him, and possibly, he was for the moment more interested in her than he ought to have been. That was all; and she was foolish to be so disquieted.

Thus Queenie reasoned, or tried to, but all the time a terrible fear was tugging at her heart, and she was living over again that dreadful death scene on the ship when her father made her swear to forgive him whatever might come to her knowledge. She had thought at first that he meant her American relations, of whom he had never told her, and she had forgiven that long ago. Then came the mystery concerning Christine and her concealment of her identity, but Reinette had recovered from that and still there was a nameless terror at her heart, as she sat alone in her room while the clock struck the hours two and three, and the fire in the grate grew lower, and the winter night seemed to grow thicker and colder around her.

At last, when she could keep still no longer, she arose, and pacing the room hurriedly, beat the air with her hands, as she was wont to do under great excitement.

"What is it I fear?" she asked herself. "What is it I suspect? Let me put it into words, and see if it sounds so very dreadful. I suspect that Christine Bodine, in her girlhood—when, I dare say, she was rather pretty and piquant, after mother died made herself very necessary to my father and attracted him more than she ought to have done. Such people are very ambitious, and susceptible, too; and if my father was at all familiar in his manner toward her, she probably was flattered at once, and maybe cheated herself, into the belief that he would marry her, when such an idea never existed in his brain. She probably wrote to him, and he answered and at last made her see how mistaken she was in supposing he could ever think of her after having known my mother. And then, by way of amends, he settled that money upon her. Yes, that is probably the fact of the case," she continued, and the tightness around her heart gave way. She could breathe more freely, and her hands ceased to beat the air, until like lightning there flashed into her mind:

"But where was Mr. La Rue, and where was Margery, when Christine wrote those letters to my father? Christine told me she was married soon after mother died, and that father was angry about it, as it took her from me. Oh, if I only knew the truth—and I can know it, in part, at least, by reading those letters which I hid away, swearing never to touch them, unless circumstances should seem to make it necessary; and it is necessary, I am sure. I must know the truth, or lose my mind. I am so unsettled since poor Phil died, and to brood over this will make me crazy in time. Yes, I must know who was the Tina who wrote those letters to father."

Reinette had reached a decision; and, lighting her candle, she opened the door of the closet where she had hidden the letters months before. There was the box on the upper shelf just where she had left it, and where she could not reach it without a chair. This she brought from her room, and stepping into it, stood a moment looking at the box, while a feeling of terror began to take possession of her, and she felt as if the dead hand of her father were clutching her arm and holding her back.

"I do not believe I will do it," she said, as she came down from the chair with a sense of that dead hand's touch still upon her arm. "It seems just as if father were speaking to me and bidding me let the letters alone. I wish I had burned them when I found them, and then I should not be tempted. And why not burn them now, and so put it out of my reach to read them?" she continued, as she stood shivering before the hearth and listening to the storm which was beginning to beat against the windows.

February was coming in with gusts of snow and the shrieks of the wild north wind, which swept furiously past the house, and seemed to Reinette to have in it a sound of human sobbing. She thought of her father in the quiet grave-yard in Merrivale, with the tall pine overhanging his grave—of her mother, far off in Rome, where the violets and daisies blossom all the year round—and of Phil, asleep beneath the Eastern waters, with nothing to mark his grave, and her heart ached with a keener pain than she had ever felt before as she stood in her slippers and dressing-gown and shivered in the cold, gray, winter night. And always above everything else the name of Tina was in her mind, with a burning desire to solve the mystery and know who Tina was, and what she had been to Mr. Hetherton.

"I may as well burn them first as last," she thought, and going again to the closet and mounting upon the chair she took the box from the shelf, and carrying it to the fire sat down upon the floor and began to open it.

There were four boxes in all, one within another, and Queenie opened each one till she came to the last and smallest, where lay the envelope containing the letters.

"There can be no harm in glancing at the handwriting, and then if I ever see Christine's, as I sometime may, I shall know if they are the same," she thought, and took out the yellow, time-worn package, which seemed to her so different from anything pertaining to herself or to her surroundings.

Looking at the outside begat an intense longing to know what was inside—to have her doubts confirmed or scattered to the winds, and at last she made a desperate resolve, and jerking her arm, which it seemed to her the dead hand still held firmly, she said, aloud:

"I shall read these letters now, though a thousand dead hands hold me."

Queenie felt herself growing very calm as she said this, and though outward the storm raged with greater fury, and the sobbing of the wind was wilder and louder than before, she neither heeded nor heard it, for she had opened the letters, and selecting that which bore date farthest back, began to read. And as she read, she forgot how cold she was—forgot that the fire was going out—forgot the fearful storm which shook the solid foundations of the great house, and screamed like so many demons past the windows—forget even that Phil was dead in the Indian sea, so horrible were the sensations crowding upon her and overmastering every thought and feeling save the one dreadful conviction that now she knew who Tina was, and that the knowledge paralyzed for the time every other sensation.

CHAPTER XL

THE LETTERS

They were written at different times, with an interval of some months between two of them—but all were dated at Marseilles, where the writer seemed to be living in lodgings, for in the first letter she said: "The rooms suit me exactly, and are very pleasant and a constant reminder of your kindness. I have found a trusty woman to stay with me, and if I could see you oftener I should be quite content, only I never can forget the sweet lady who died in my arms, believing in me as the best of servants. What would she say if she knew how soon I took her place in your affection? Sometimes I think she is here in the room watching me, and then I am afraid, and rush into the street until the terror is past."

"That was Christine, sure, for mother died in her arms," Reinette whispered, faintly, while a prickly sensation was in every nerve, and her lips quivered convulsively.

And still she read on, taking next the second letter, the one which had contained the lock of hair, and which was written two or three months after the first. Evidently Mr. Hetherton had been in Marseilles and seen the writer, for she spoke of his recent visit and the great pleasure it had given her. It was in this letter that she called herself his little Tina, and had written: "I have been sick most of the time since you were here, and that is why I did not answer your letter at once. You were so kind to me and treated me with so much tenderness that I cannot help believing you mean to make me your wife before the world just as you said you made me your wife before Heaven. But why put it off any longer? Can you not bring a clergyman here, and not wait till people call me a bad woman, which God knows I never meant to be. Oh, if you would take me to Chateau des Fleurs as your wife. I would be your very slave and make up to you in love and fidelity what I lack in culture. You say I am very pretty. You praised my eyes and hair when you were here, and so I send you a lock of the latter, and hope it will sometimes remind you of your little Tina."

"That's the tress I burned," Queenie whispered, feeling as if she, too, were burning and writhing on live coals just as the lock of blue-black hair had writhed and hissed in the flame.

But there was still another letter, and she read it, while every hair of her head seemed to stand on end, and instead of burning with heat she shook with cold, as she devoured the contents, which threw such a flood of light upon what had gone before, and which she had not suspected. She had read enough to make her hate Christine, and almost hate her father, who, she felt, was most to blame, but she had no suspicion of the real state of things until she began to read the third letter, which showed great physical weakness on the part of the writer.

"Dear Mr. Hetherton," it began, "I have been so sick that the old woman who attends me thought I should die, but I am better now, though still so weak as scarcely to be able to hold my pen. But I must tell you of my dear little girl who was born two weeks ago, and who now lies sleeping at my side."

"What!" Reinette exclaimed, aloud, clasping both hands to her forehead as if a heavy blow had fallen there. "What does she say? A little girl born in Marseilles—that was—Margery."

She could scarcely articulate the last word, for her tongue was thick and parched, and in her ears was a sound like the roar of the wind outside.

"Oh, oh!" she cried, throwing up her hands as if in quest of some support; then they dropped helplessly at her side, and she fell forward upon her face, with the blood gushing from her nose and staining her dressing-gown. How long she lay thus, she did not know, for since the clock struck three she had taken no note of time, but when she came to herself the cold gray of the early dawn was stealing into the room, and far away in the vicinity of the kitchen she heard the sound of some one stirring. The fire was out, and the candle was out, and she was cold, and stiff, and bewildered, and could not at first remember what had happened. But it came back to her with the rustling of the letter she still held in her hand—came with a terrible pain, which made her cry out faintly as she staggered to her feet, and lighted another candle, for she had not finished the letter yet. But she finished it at last and laid it with the others, while there swept over her a feeling of delight, mingled with the horror she had at first experienced.

Margery was that little girl born in Marseilles, and whom Christine was sure Mr. Hetherton would love, because he was so fond of children.

"Yes, that was Margery," she said, "and if so, she is my sister. Does she know, I wonder? Did Christine tell her the day she was so suddenly taken ill, and is that the reason she has seemed so different since? seemed to shun me at times as if afraid of me? Yes, she knows, and I shall tell her that I know, too, and that I love her better than ever. She is not to blame. No one can censure her, or cast a slight upon her, for she is my sister, and I shall proclaim her as such, and bring her to live with me, and share my fortune with her, and make her take her father's name. But Christine must not stay. I could not endure to see her every day, and be thus reminded of all I had lost in losing faith in my father. Christine must go. She was false to mother, false to me; and where was I when she was living in Marseilles? She could not have cared for me long after mother died. I do not believe she ever took me to Chateau des Fleurs, or ever was my nurse, as I have supposed. I have wasted too much love on her, but I know her now, and shall deal with her accordingly."

Such, in substance, were Reinette's thoughts as she sat shivering in the cold, cheerless room, while the morning light crept in at the windows, and she could see herself distinctly in the glass upon the mantel.

It was a very white, haggard face which looked at her from the mirror, and the eyes almost frightened her with their expression. About her mouth and on the front of her dress were spots of blood which had dropped from her nose while she was unconscious, and which added to her unnatural appearance. The stains upon her face she washed away; and exchanging her dressing-gown for a fresh one, crept into bed, for she was very cold and dizzy and faint, while, in spite of the wild excitement under which she was laboring, there was stealing over her a heavy stupor which she could not throw off, and when at the usual hour Pierre came to make her fire, he found her sleeping so soundly that he went softly out and left her alone. An hour later, Margery looked in, but Queenie was still asleep, nor did she waken when, as cautiously as possible, a fire was kindled in the grate to make the room more comfortable, for the morning was bitterly cold, and the frost lay thickly upon the windows. Margery could not see Queenie's face, as it was turned toward the wall, and so she had no suspicion of the frightful storm which had swept over the young girl during the night. The letters still lay upon the table, and Margery saw them there, but did not touch them or dream what they contained, and after putting the room a little to rights she went quietly out, leaving her friend to sleep until the clock struck ten. Then, with a start, Queenie awoke, and opening her eyes, looked about her with that vague sense of misery and pain we have all felt at some period of our lives, when the first thought on waking was, "Why is it I feel so badly?"

To Queenie it came very soon why she felt so badly, and with a moan she hid her face in her pillow, while something like a cry escaped her as she whispered:

"I thought him so good and true, and now I know him to have been so bad. He was false to mother, false to Christine, and doubly false to Margery, whom he repudiated and disowned. Why did he not bring her home like a man when I first told him of her? Why did he not say to me, 'Queenie, I have done a great wrong which many people in this country think of no consequence, but which, nevertheless, is a sin, for which I am sorry and would make amends. Little Margery La Rue is your sister, and I wish to bring her home to live with you and share equally with you as if no cloud hung over her birth. Will you let her come, Queenie?' Oh, if he had done this I should have taken her so gladly, and been spared all this pain. Oh, father, father, you have dealt most cruelly with both your children, Margery and me!"

Queenie had risen by this time and was making her toilet, for she meant to appear as natural as possible to Mrs. La Rue and Margery until the moment came for her to speak and know every particular of her sister's birth. While she was dressing Margery came to the door, but it was locked, and Queenie called to her:

"Excuse me, Margie, if I do not let you in. I am not quite dressed, but shall come down very soon."

She was very white when she did at last go down to the dining-room, and Margery noticed it and said: "Are you sick this morning? You are as pale as ashes, and there are dark circles around your eyes. Oh, Queenie, I am so sorry for you;" and thinking only of Phil as the cause of Queenie's pale face and hollow eyes, Margery drew her head down upon her arm and smoothed the shining hair caressingly.

Then Queenie came nearer crying that she had since she first heard Phil was dead. Grasping Margery's hand she sobbed hysterically for a moment, though no tears came to cool her aching eyeballs.

"I must not give way," she said, "for I have a great deal to do to-day. Where is your mother, Margie? I must see her. Find her, please, and bring her here; or no, we will go into the library. No one will disturb us there, and we must be alone. Call your mother, Margie, I cannot wait."

What did it mean, and why was Queenie so strange this morning, like one unsettled in her mind? Margie asked herself, as she went in quest of her mother, to whom she gave Queenie's message.

"What can she want with me, I wonder?" Mrs. La Rue thought, as she went to the library, where she found Reinette curled up in a large easy-chair, which she did no more than half fill.

Her head was leaning against the cushioned back, and her face looked very white and wan, while her eyes wore a peculiar expression as they fixed themselves on Mrs. La Rue. It was the same chair and the same position Queenie had occupied on the occasion of her first interview with Phil, who had stood leaning his elbow upon the mantel while he looked at her curiously. Something brought that day back to Queenie's mind, and a sob which was more for the dead Phil than for the secret she held escaped her as she bade good-morning to Mrs. La Rue, who said:

"What is it, Petite?"

This was the name Mrs. La Rue had often applied to her during the last few days, and Queenie had liked it heretofore, but now she shuddered and shrank away, and when Mrs. La Rue laid her hand upon her head and asked if it ached, she cried out:

"Don't touch me, or come near me. I don't know whether my head aches or not. But my heart is aching with a pang to which physical pain is nothing. Christine, I have lost all faith in you—faith in father—faith in everything. I know the whole now—you are Tina, the shame-faced, who wrote those letters to my father and sent him a lock of your hair!"

CHAPTER XLI

QUEENIE LEARNS THE TRUTH

This was not at all the way in which Queenie had intended to commence. She was going to come to it gradually, or, as she had expressed it to herself, "hunt Christine down." But when she saw her, her hot, passionate temper rose up at once, and she blurted out what she knew and then waited the result. It was different from what she anticipated. She had expected Christine to crouch at once at her feet and, cowering before her, confess her guilt and sue for pity and pardon.

But Christine did nothing of the sort. Quiet and gentle as she usually seemed, there was still in her a fierce fiery spirit, which, when roused, was something akin to the demon which ruled Queenie in her moods. When charged with being Christine Bodine she was worn in mind and body, and had shown only nervousness and agitation, for Queenie had not approached her then as she did now. There was no disgust, no hatred, in her manner when she said: "You are Christine, my old nurse." She had merely been excited and reproachful; but now she was angry, and attacked the woman with so much bitterness, and shrunk away from her with so much loathing that Christine was roused to defend herself, though at first she was stricken dumb when she heard of the letters which she remembered so well, and which would tell what she had kept so long.

Standing but a few feet from Queenie she gazed at her a moment, with a pallid face, on which all the worst emotions of her nature were visible. And when at last she spoke, it was not in the low, half-deprecating, apologetic voice habitual to her, but the tone was loud and clear, and defiant, in which she said:

"What letters have you seen, and where did you find them?"

Her manner, so different from what had been expected, made Queenie still more angry, and she replied with all the sternness and dignity it was possible for her to assume:

"It does not matter to you where I found them. It is sufficient that I have found them, and know your barefaced treachery, and how you must have deceived my mother who trusted you so implicitly, and who died, believing you to be good, and honest, and true to her, when all the time you were vile and low. You knew when you held her dying head upon your bosom what you were at heart, and yet you dared lay your hands on her dead form, dared care for her baby, and kiss it with lips which never shall meet mine again, and then you wrote to my father and called yourself his little Tina, as if you really supposed he could care for you! Men like him never love women like you, and my father was not an exception. He cast you off as we do a worn-out garment; he hated the thoughts of you, hated himself, and repented so bitterly.

"I see it all now, and understand his remorse on shipboard before he died. He was thinking of the past, and his thoughts were like a scorpion, stinging him to madness and making him long to confess to me the wrong he had done. But he could not, weak as he was then and worn; he could not tell me, when he knew how much I loved and honored him, but he made me promise solemnly to forgive him if I ever found it out, and I promised, and I'll keep the promise, too, though just now, I feel hard and bitter toward him, and were he living I should rebel against him so hotly and say I never could forgive him, as I never can you, whom I loved and respected, but whom I now know to be false in everything. You have made me believe a lie, from first to last, until I can credit nothing you have told me, and am ready to doubt if your name is really La Rue, or if that man were your husband."

"He was my husband. I never deceived you there," Christine exclaimed.

"But he was not Margery's father," Reinette continued, holding her breath for the answer, which did not come at once.

While she had been talking so rapidly, Christine had stood rigid and immovable, with a strange look upon her face and a gleam in her eyes such as mad people sometimes wear when they are becoming dangerous. Queenie's sudden and unexpected attack had so confounded and bewildered Christine that she felt her brain reeling, and was conscious of a feeling as if she were losing control of herself and should not long be responsible for what she said. When Queenie spoke of M. La Rue as one who possibly was not her husband, she roused in her own defense and answered; but at Queenie's next question she hesitated, while the blood came surging into her face, which was almost purple in spots, before she replied.

"No, he was not Margery's father," and the woman's voice was hard and pitiless, while the gleam in her eye was wilder and more like a maniac as she went on:

"Queenie Hetherton, if you drive me too far I may say what I shall be sorry for and what you will be sorry to hear. The worm will turn when trodden upon, and a miserable wretch like me will not be pressed too sorely without trying to defend herself. I am wicked and sinful, it is true; but in one sense I was not false to Mrs. Hetherton, and God knows what I have suffered—knows of the years of anguish and remorse when I would have so gladly undone the past if I could; but it was too late. You have found those letters, it seems. Your father was foolish to keep them; he ought to have burned them, as I did his; but—but—the fact that he did not tells me he cared more for me than I supposed—that in his proud heart there was something which bound him to me lowly born as I am," and over Christine's face as she said this there came a smile of pleasure and gratification in the thought that Frederick Hetherton had kept her letters, even though they had failed to produce any result.

The look made Queenie angrier than she had been before, for she interpreted it aright, and her pride rose up against it.

"My father never cared for you," she said. "It was only a fancy, which would never have existed at all if you had not tried to attract him."

"It is false!" Mrs. La Rue exclaimed, taking a step forward, with flashing eyes, before which even Queenie quailed. "It is false. I did not try to attract him at first, but he noticed and talked to and flattered me until my head he turned and I thought all things possible. The wrong was on his side. I was not bad nor had a thought of badness in my heart, and you, Queenie, of all others, should not speak to me as you have done. Margery did not, and hers is the greater wrong."

"Then you have told Margery!" Reinette exclaimed, and before Mrs. La Rue could answer, Margery herself came to the door asking:

"Did you call me, Queenie? I thought I heard my name."

"No, no," Mrs. La Rue almost screamed, as she turned like a tigress upon Margery. "Go away, I tell you, go away. I am losing my senses, and with you both standing here, and Queenie talking to me as she has talked, I shall tell what I have sworn not to tell. Go away, Margery—go!"

But Margery did not move except to advance a little farther into the room, where she stood, with a blanched cheek and wondering, frightened eyes, gazing first at her mother and then at Queenie, who stretched her arms toward her and, with quivering lips and a voice full of unutterable pathos and love, said:

"You are my sister. Come to me."

But Margery did not move, and her face grew whiter and more death-like, as she whispered to her mother:

"What does she mean? Have you told her? Does she know it all, and still call me sister?"

"Hush, Margie. No, she does not know it all," Mrs. La Rue replied; and, sinking into a chair and bowing her head upon her hands, Margery exclaimed:

"Thank God for that! Oh, Queenie, I don't know what you know or how you learned it; but if you love me, if you care for your own happiness, seek to know no more. Let the matter end here. If you believe I am your sister, love me as such; I shall be content with that."

She did not look up, but sat with her head bowed down as if with grief or shame. Queenie thought it the latter, and crossed the room to where Margery sat, and, kneeling beside her, wound both arms around her neck and said:

"Margie, I know you are my father's child, and I love you so dearly that this shall make no difference with me. You were not to blame, my darling. You had no part in the wrong; it was my father, may God forgive him, and this woman, who I am sorry to say is your mother, and whom I cannot forgive.”

“This woman!” and Christine’s voice rang out awfully clear and distinct, as she threw her arm toward the two girls. “Say no more of this woman, nor pity Margery because she is her mother; Margery’s parentage is as good as yours. Yes, better—better, Queenie Hetherton, for she is Frederick Hetherton’s own child, and you—”

She did not finish the sentence, for, with a wild cry, Margery put Queenie’s clinging arms from her neck, and rushing to Christine, laid her hand upon her lips.

“Mother, mother,” she cried, in a voice of intense entreaty, “are you mad? Have you forgotten your vow, your promise to me? Will you kill Queenie outright?”

“Kill her? No. She is not the kind which such things kill,” Christine answered, fiercely, as she pushed Margery from her. “You ask if I am crazy. Yes, and well I may be—I, who have kept this horrible secret for so many years. Twenty and more—twenty and more; kept it since you were born. How old are you, Margery? How long since you were born in Rome? There’s a buzzing in my brain, and I do not quite remember.”

She was softening a little, and taking advantage of this Margery took her hand to lead her from the room, saying very gently. “Poor mother, you are not right to-day. Come with me and rest; and you, Queenie, don’t mind anything she may have said. She is not responsible when she is this way.”

“But I do mind,” Queenie said, stepping before the door through which Margery would have passed. “I do mind, and I cannot forget. Christine has said strange things to and of me—things she must explain. If you are Frederick Hetherton’s own child, as she affirms, and were born at Rome, who am I?”

“I tell you she is not in her right mind, and you are not to believe what she says,” Margery replied, trying to put Queenie aside, so that she might lead her mother from the room.

But Queenie kept her place by the door, against which she leaned heavily, while her breath came in quick gasps, and her voice was unsteady as she said again, and this time to Christine, whose eyes were fastened upon her, holding her by a strange spell she could not resist.

“Tell me, Christine, as you hope for pardon hereafter when you stand with me face to face with God, is Margery my sister?”

“Yes, Margery is your sister,” Mrs. La Rue replied, still holding Queenie with her awful eyes. “Margery is your sister—your father’s child.”

“My father’s own lawful child?” was the next question, and then Margery cried out, “Oh, mother, have pity; remember all it involves!”

“Hush, Margery. Be still, and let me know the worst,” Reinette said, lifting her hand with the manner of one who would be obeyed at any cost. “Tell me, Christine,” she continued, “Is Margery the lawful child of Frederick Hetherton?”

“Yes, she is.”

“And was she born in Rome?”

"Yes, she was born in Rome, and her mother was Margaret Ferguson," Christine replied, without the slightest quaver in her voice or change of expression in her pitiless face.

Margery had released her hold of the woman's arm and sank upon the floor, where she sat with her knees drawn up, her arms encircling them, her head resting upon them, and her whole body trembling as with an ague chill. She had done all she could to avert the calamity. She had tried to save Queenie from the blow which she knew would fall so crushingly, and she had failed. Her mother was a maniac for the time being, and was doing what she had sworn never to do. She was telling Queenie, and Margery was powerless to prevent it.

"Margaret Ferguson's daughter!" Queenie repeated in a whisper, which, low as it was, sounded distinctly through the room, and told how the young girl's heart was wrung with a mortal fear as she continued: "then who am I, and who are you?"

For a moment there was a death-like silence in the room, for Christine, half crazed though she was, shrank from declaring what she knew would be the bitterest dreg in all the bitter cup. How could she tell the truth to that young girl who had been so proud of her blood and of her birth, and who even in her pain, when every limb was quivering with nervous dread and excitement, stood up so erect before her like one born to command. But she must do it now; she had gone too far to recede—had told too much not to tell the whole, and when Queenie asked again, "who am I, and who are you?" she answered, "I am your mother;" but she said it very softly and low, for her heart was full of a great pity for the girl, over whose face there came that pallid, grayish look which comes upon the face of the dying when the death pang is hard to bear, and who writhed a moment in agony as the insect writhes when put upon the coals.

She was still looking fixedly at Christine, though she did not see her, for there was a blackness before her wide-open, staring eyes, and in her ears there was a sound like the roar of many waters, when the skies overhead are angry and dark. For a second the scene around her had vanished away. She did not see Margery upon the floor, with her arms still encircling her knees and her head bowed upon them—did not see the woman standing so near to her, and who had spoken those terrible words, but strangely enough saw the far-off Indian sea and Phil's white face as it sank beneath the waves with a wild cry for her upon his lips. Mechanically she put up her hand to brush that vision away, and then the present came back to her with all its horror so much worse than the death of Phil had been, and she remembered the words Christine had spoken, "I am your mother!"

"My-my-my-m-mo-th-er," she tried to say when she could speak, but the words died away upon her white, quivering lips in a kind of babbling sound, which was succeeded by a hysterical laugh so nearly resembling imbecility that Margery looked up, and a cold shudder curdled her blood as she saw the face from which all resemblance to Queenie had vanished, and on which that ghastly, meaningless laugh was still visible.

Struggling to her feet she wound her arm around Queenie, saying to her mother, as she did so:

"You have destroyed her intellect. You have made her an imbecile."

But Margery was mistaken. Queenie's mind was not destroyed, though for many hours she remained in that condition, when her reason seemed to be tottering and her white lips had no power to frame the words she wished to say. They did not send for a physician, though it was Christine's wish to do so; but Margery said:

"No, we will not parade this secret before the world. I can bring her to herself if any one can, and when I do I shall, if possible, persuade her that it is all a delusion of her brain—that she did not hear aright. Oh, why did you tell her? Why did you break your promise?"

"Because I was angry, was crazy, and did not know what I said," Christine replied. "Her manner toward me provoked me more than her words, and roused in me a demon which would not be quieted, and so I told her all; and I am glad, for now I carry no dreadful secret to make my days so full of pain and my nights one long black horror. I have told the truth, and can call her my daughter now—my child—for she is my own flesh and blood—the little black-haired creature which lay in my arms and flashed her bright eyes on me—on me—her mother."

And as she said this, Mrs. La Rue's face glowed with excitement and her eyes shone with all the fire of her fresh girlhood when Frederick Hetherton had told her she was pretty. Margery had been dear to her as her own life, which she would at any time have given for the girl whom she had so wronged: but with her confession there had swept over her a great wave of motherly love and tenderness for the poor little girl who, in her own room, whither Margery had taken her, sat in the great easy-chair, motionless as a stone, with her hands lying helplessly upon her lap, and her eyes, from which all the sparkle and brightness were gone, looking always from the window across the snow-clad hills and meadows to the spot where the tall evergreens marked the burial-place of the dead. Sometimes Margery went and spoke to her. But Queenie did not answer until late in the afternoon, when Margery came and stood between her and the window. Then she said, entreatingly:

"Move away, please. I am looking over to where father lies, and thinking of all he said to me before he died. Oh, Margie," and the poor little white face quivered and the voice was very sad and piteous, "Is a lie to the dead worse than a lie to the living? I told him I would forgive him, whatever it was, and I cannot, I cannot, and my heart is so bitter and hard toward him and her, and all the world except you. Oh, Margie, Margie, you will not turn against me? You will love me just a little, I could not help it, and I love you so much. I would have stood by you in the face of the whole world; stand by me, Margie, will you?"

She was looking at Margery with her heavy, pleading eyes, and her hands were lifted in supplication as she spoke, while her voice told how abased and humiliated she felt. In a moment Margery knelt beside her and was covering the hands with tears and kisses as she said: "Queenie, Queenie, my love, my darling, will I stand by you? Will I love you? As well ask if the sun will rise again as to question my love for you, my sister. It is very sweet to call you thus, even though a shadow lies over us now; but that will pass away. There is brightness beyond and happiness, too—and, Queenie, you must not believe all mother said. She is not in her right senses.

"She knows it now, and wonders at herself. You may believe I am your sister, but not the rest—the part which touched you the closest—because—because——"

"Hush, Margery," Queenie said, withdrawing her hands from Margery and leaning back wearily in her chair. "You cannot deceive me. I am that child born in Marseilles. Margaret Ferguson was your mother; Christine Bodine is mine."

Here a shudder ran through Queenie's frame so long and deep that her teeth chattered as if she were seized with a chill, and both her hands and lips were purple with cold.

After a pause she continued:

"I think the hardest part of all is losing faith in father. I cannot forgive him, though I promised him I would. If he had left me in obscurity, where I belonged, it would have been better; but now the fall has crushed me utterly. And, Margery, what of you? How came you in that position—you, the lawful daughter of the house, while I, was raised to such a giddy height of prosperity that in my foolish pride I held myself better than the most of mankind? Why was it? Do you know?"

"Yes," Margery replied; "but it will be better for mother to tell you."

"Mother! Do you call her that still?" Queenie asked, and her voice expressed all the bitter scorn which she then felt for the woman who had so injured her.

"Yes, I call her mother still," Margery answered, softly. "She is all the mother I have ever known, she was more sinned against than sinning. She did not understand what she was doing. She is not a bad woman. Our father was the most in fault, for she was young and ignorant and foolish enough to believe that she was his wife. She is purer far than many a woman of to-day who stands high in society, and before whom the world bows down because of her position."

Margery was pleading for the woman who had done the greater wrong to her, and Queenie listened wonderingly, while there came back to her some words her father had said to her when dying: "If you find your mother, remember I was more to blame than she." She had found her, but she could not at once forgive her, but she said at last: "Where is she, Margie? Ask her to come up."

CHAPTER XLII

CHRISTINE'S STORY

Margery found her mother in the library standing by the window, with that gloomy abstracted look upon her face which she had so often seen there before she learned the cause and knew of the keen remorse always gnawing at her heart-strings and making her life so wretched. Christine had done the worst she could do to Queenie. She had told her the truth; and though a great burden was lifted from her, and in one sense she felt freer and happier than she had felt in years, she was weighed down with a sense of remorse and regret, and filled with a dread of the future. That Queenie could ever love, or even respect her, was impossible, reared as she had been in a very hot-bed of pride and aristocracy, and taught from her infancy that such as Christine Bodine were creatures of an entirely different grade from herself.

"She may compel herself to be civil to me," Christine thought, "though I ought not to hope for that; but if she only knew how much I love her and how the affection, smothered so long, has grown since I confessed myself her mother, she would forgive me, perhaps."

"Mother," Margery said just here, and with a start Christine turned toward her; "Mother, Queenie wishes to see you. Will you go to her now?"

"Yes," Mrs. La Rue replied, in a frightened voice, for there swept over her a great fear of the girl to whom she must tell her story, and grasping Margery's arm she whispered, "Does she hate me? Will she scorn me? Will she make me feel that I am but the dust beneath her feet? Oh, Margie, go with me. I cannot meet her alone. She is so hot, so imperious, so proud, so different from you, who have never reproached me, except for her sake. Come, Margie, you must go, too; and if she is too hard upon me, say a word for me, will you, Margie?"

She was like a child shrinking from the rod, and Margery's heart ached for the woman who clung to her nervously as they went up the stairs together to Queenie's room. Pierre had been there before them, full of concern for his young mistress, whose sudden and strange illness he did not understand.

As they entered, Queenie lifted her eyes to them, but made no sign of recognition to Christine, who, like some guilty culprit, sank into a chair, where she sat shaking in every limb.

After the first glance at her, Queenie shut her eyes and said languidly and slowly, as if speaking were wearisome, "I wish you to tell me of Margery and myself; tell me why she was deserted and left to live in the Rue St. Honore, while I was taken to Chateau des Fleurs and treated as the daughter of the house. That is all."

While Queenie talked she did not once look at Christine, but sat with her eyes closed and her whole attitude one of extreme weariness. But she heard Margery as she was stealing from the room and called her to come back.

"You must stay with me, Margery," she said, "I want to hold your hand so that I can feel there is something left when all else slips from me."

So Margery came back and sitting down by Queenie took one of the hot, feverish hands in hers, and caressed it occasionally as Christine told her story.

"I must commence at a period prior to Margery's birth," she said, "or I cannot make you understand how ignorant of the world I was when I entered Mrs. Hetherton's employ, and how innocent and unsuspecting too. And when Monsieur began to notice me, and speak to me pleasantly, and tell me what a good girl I was I thought nothing of it, but redoubled my efforts to please him. But when he flattered me and said I was more a lady than many a one who wore her diamonds and pearls, I was angry and told him he must never speak to me like that again; and he did not, though he was always very kind and polite, and I felt intuitively that he respected me as one superior to my class, and admired me, too, for I was pretty then, with ways something like Queenie's."

There was a slight sound like a moan from Queenie, and Christine continued:

"That he could ever think of me for a wife never entered my brain till I sat by my dying mistress and heard her say, 'I am so glad, for Frederick has wanted a child so much, and a daughter will make him very happy, and keep me in his mind. Christine, it may be very foolish in me, but I do not like to think that Frederick will marry again—that another woman will take my place, and possibly be loved more than I have been, and now that he has a little daughter to care for, there is not so much danger of it. He will be satisfied with little Margery, he will call her by that name. I have told him so in the letter which you will give to him. Stay with him, Christine, and be a comfort to him, you and Margery.' These were nearly the last words she said to me, for in less than an hour she was dead, and I was alone with her baby in my arms, and the horrible temptation to which I afterwards yielded kept suggesting itself to me, making me shudder and grow faint as I reflected what a monster I was to harbor such a thought for an instant. And still it recurred to me over and over again until it did not seem so very dreadful, and I began to consider it seriously, as something which might be done. I was not then the simple peasant girl I had been when I first entered my mistress' service. The familiarity with which she had treated me, the evident liking of my master whom I could influence at times more readily even than his wife, the notice I received from strangers, especially Americans who frequently mistook me for Mrs. Hetherton's companion, rather than her maid, had turned my head and made me discontented with my position. I wanted to be a lady, and as I sat with Margery in my arms, the devil whispered to me that now was my opportunity to try for something higher, and test the power I knew I held over my master. He had made one misalliance—he might make another. If he was very proud he was very susceptible too—he liked to be cared for and petted, and I, who understood him so well, would make myself so necessary to him that he could not live without me, and would perhaps make me his wife at last. Thus I reasoned when suddenly it occurred to me that the baby was an obstacle in my way. He was passionately fond of children, and a daughter in his house would change everything. My mistress had said so, and I believed it. With the baby at Chateau des Fleurs I could never hope to be more than nurse and maid, as I was now. And then Satan told me to hide the child for a time, till I saw what I could do with the father. If I succeeded I would tell him the truth, and brave his anger, for I should still be his wife. If I failed I would send his daughter to him with the letter my mistress entrusted to me, and in which she told him of its birth and the name she had given it. In any event I did not mean to hide Margie forever, but I did not know then how one sin leads to another or what a hard master is the evil one when you give yourself to him as I did, for I resolved at last to do the wicked thing which was comparatively easy. Of Margery's expected birth Monsieur knew nothing, for his wife had purposely kept it from him to make the surprise and pleasure greater. He had not seen her in some months, and would have no suspicion of the existence of the little girl. We had lived very quietly in Rome, and few knew or cared for the young mother who died alone with me. But when she was dead strangers kindly came forward and when they heard that Mr. Hetherton was away in Austria or Russia, I did not know which, they took the matter in hand and buried her in the Protestant burying ground, but left me to do what I pleased with the baby, which I took to Paris, to an old woman whom I had known for years, and to whom I entrusted it, telling her it was mine, and hiring her to care for it until I was in a position to claim it. She asked me no questions, for the gold I paid her was a conclusive argument in my favor and would, I knew, insure kind care for the child.

"My next step was to go to Chateau des Fleurs to await the coming of my master, for I had written him from Rome, telling him of his wife's death, and my intention to return to the Chateau with whatever effects she left in my care. The letter was some time in finding him; but on its receipt, he hastened home at once, and for a day or two seemed crushed with grief and remorse. Then for a short time he drank hard and deeply, and kept his room, where bottle after bottle of wine and brandy was sent, and in his drunkenness he was more like a brute than a man.

"This drunken revel was succeeded by an illness of several weeks' duration, during which I nursed him with the utmost care, playing my part so well that the result came sooner than I anticipated, but was not what I desired. I must be his wife or nothing, and at last weakened bodily and mentally by disease and the brandy he drank in so large quantities he promised to make me his wife on condition that I kept it a secret until he chose to tell of it himself. As there was no Protestant clergyman near Chateau des Fleurs he said we would marry ourselves, and he made me believe that by joining hands and promising to take each other for man and wife after the manner of the English Prayer Book, we should really become so. 'Such things were common in America,' he said, 'when a priest was not easy of access.' Of course, when it was convenient this private ceremony, though perfectly legal, must be repeated in public, and this he swore solemnly should be done, and I trusted him and went blind-folded to my ruin, but innocent—oh, Queenie, as innocent as you are to-day."

"Yes," Queenie rejoined, with a look of unutterable anguish upon her face, for now she had lost all faith in and respect for her father, but as yet had no relenting towards the poor deceived mother. "Yes, go on."

Christine flushed a little as she went on rapidly: "I believe I was his wife and wished to remain at the Chateau, but he would not hear to me. 'We must go to Marseilles,' he said, and thither he went, and he hired a suite of rooms for me, but did not remain there himself, though he came often to see me, and treated me with kindness and consideration, but did not bring the clergyman as he had promised to do. 'He had not met one of the right sort,' he said, and there was no haste as I was really his wife. And so matters went on until a great fear took possession of me that all was not right, and then you were born, and when you were three or four weeks old he came to me and seemed to love you so much, and was so kind to me that I begged him on my knees to acknowledge me to the world, and take me with him to Chateau des Fleurs. Then it was that he undeceived me and told me how I had been duped, and did it as coolly as if to ruin an innocent girl was nothing but pastime for gentlemen like him, and he laughed at me for taking it as I did, for at first I raved like a mad woman, but it did no good.

"'Christine,' he said, 'you must be very weak to suppose for a moment that I was in earnest, or that you could ever live at Chateau des Fleurs as other than a servant. Men of my stamp do not marry girls like you, or in fact marry at all in our sober senses. I will admit that I am far more to blame than you, but you can never be my wife, though I will care for the child. It is lonely at Chateau des Fleurs; a baby's voice and baby's prattle will make it more endurable. I have wanted a child so much, and if Margaret had left me one I should never have done what I have.'

"You will not believe me if I tell you that when I heard this my first impulse was to fall at his feet and tell him of the little girl in Paris, thoughts of whom had haunted me continually, making me sometimes cry out with pain and remorse. But I had gone too far to confess. He would never have forgiven me, and all my ambitious dreams for my own child would have come to naught. I had no hope for myself; his imperious manner and cold, disdainful words crushed all that; but there arose in me an intense desire to see you a lady, and I begged him to take you, whatever he might do with me, and he consented at last, but bade me stay where I was until I heard from him again. He wished to make some change in his household, he said, for if he took you home it would be as the child of his dead wife. I was only the nurse, who might or might not be retained; it would depend upon myself.

"Then he left me, and I knew I was no more to him than a cast-off garment, of which he was tired, and that in whatever arrangements he might make, no thought for me or my comfort would actuate him; and in my anguish I felt that my punishment was greater than I could bear, and I even thought to kill myself and you too. But a thought of little Margery prevented me. Somebody must care for her, and so I lived on and waited and hoped the time might come when I could restore her to her rights.

"On quitting Marseilles your father went to Chateau des Fleurs, and, on one pretext or another, dismissed all the servants in his employ, filling their places with strangers, who knew nothing of his past life, and who readily believed him when he told them of his wife who had died in Rome, and of his little daughter whom he was soon to bring home. A huge nursery, which communicated with his apartments, was fitted up with every possible luxury. And then he bade me come; and I took you to him as his lawful child, while I was only the head nurse—for he hired another woman to look after you, giving me the post of looking after her.

"I remember so well the day I took you to the Chateau and waited for his coming, but waited in vain, for though he knew I was in the house, he kept aloof from me and took his dinner, and read his paper, and smoked his cigar, and then at last he sauntered into the nursery with that air of elegant indifference and superiority so natural to him. I had not seen him since his visit to Marseilles, when you were a few weeks old; but he simply bade me good-evening, and asked if I had found everything in readiness. Then he walked up to the cradle, and when you raised your little hands toward him as if asking him to take you, he lifted you in his arms, kissed your lips, and laying your head upon his shoulder said: 'My daughter, my heiress, Reinette Hetherton.'

"I knew he had adopted you as his own. But I was only your hired nurse, who was entitled to consideration in the household because I had been the trusted maid of his wife. This raised me somewhat above my fellow-servants, who treated me with a great deal of respect, and asked me many questions concerning my late mistress and Mr. Hetherton, who puzzled them with his cold, quiet, haughty manner.

"With your advent at the Chateau all his former habits were changed, and he seldom left home except to go to Paris, where he never stayed more than a day or two. All his old associates were dropped, and few ever came to see him. And yet he did not seem to be lonely, so great was his love for you. From the moment he took you in his arms and kissed you, he was perfectly devoted to you, and had you brought to him in the library every night after his dinner was over. I generally took you to him myself, but he never noticed me by a word or look, and this so enraged me that I spoke out to him at last, and threatened to go away and take you with me, if he continued to treat me with so much contempt.

"'You can do so to-morrow, if you like, I shall be glad to have you,' was his reply, and I knew that he meant it.

"But my desire to see you a lady was stronger than my resentment, and so I stayed, content to be trodden down, if by that means you might rise. But those foolish words of mine sealed my fate, for from that time I think he began to plan how to be rid of me. The sight of me was distasteful to him, and when you were about a year and a half old, we had a bitter quarrel, which ended in a final separation; but I could not take you from all the luxury with which you were surrounded, and when he offered to settle upon me a certain sum of money if I would go away quietly, and promise solemnly, never to come near you, or let you know that I was your mother, I consented, and left you at Chateau des Fleurs the acknowledged and petted child of the house.

"How well I remember you, Queenie, as I saw you for the last time in your embroidered white dress, with coral clasps at your neck, and your hands full of flowers, which you offered to me when I bent over you, crying as if my heart would break. You were so beautiful and bright, and I loved you so much, that for a moment I was tempted to break my vow, and, defying my cruel master, publish to the whole world my wrongs, and, if possible, carry you off in triumph. But when I remembered the home to which I must take you, and how different all your future life would be, I abandoned the project, and left you there in the sunshine, with wealth and luxury all around you, and went out into the darkness, where only toil and poverty awaited me, with a constant sense of my wrong and the sin I had committed in hiding Margery."

Here Christine paused, and with closed eyes and clenched fists seemed to be living over again the scenes she had described, while Reinette raised herself from her reclining position in the chair, and winding her arms tightly around Margery's neck, rested her cheek upon the bowed head, and said:

"Well, Christine, you have let me see one side of the picture, have shown me myself, surrounded with riches and love, and sunshine and flowers, to which I had no right. Now show me the other side; take me to the garret where Margie, to whom belonged the sunshine and the flowers, was struggling with cold and hunger, and shrinking it may be, from harsh words and cruel blows."

"No, Queenie, never," Margery exclaimed. "Never hunger or cold or blows or harsh words. The woman who cared for me was always kind, and my childhood was a happy one, for I knew no other life, and the children of poverty are as much pleased with a toy which costs a penny as are the children of the rich with one which costs many francs; and after mother came and took me to live with her, I was very happy, for if she defrauded me of my birthright, she made it up in love and tender care."

Margery's generous defense of the woman who had wronged her so deeply, touched Queenie, and her voice was softer and her manner less imperious as she continued: "I know she loved you, Margie—know she has been kind to you, and I thank her for it; but I wish to hear about it all the same—wish to know where you lived, and how, after she left Chateau des Fleurs and went back to you. Tell me, please," and she turned to Christine: "tell me of Margie when she was a baby."

Christine was quick to detect the change in Queenie's voice and manner, and her face was brighter as she replied: "After I left you I went to Paris, to Florine's apartments, where I found a healthy, beautiful child, whom no one could see and not love. My heart was very sore and full of a great longing for my own baby girl left at Chateau des Fleurs, and when she toddled to my side and put up her sweet lips to be kissed, as was a habit of hers, I took her in my arms and into my heart and made a solemn vow to be true to her and never let her feel the want of a mother's love. I told her to call me mamma, and the name came prettily from her lips. I was younger and better looking than Florine, and she took to me readily, and slept in my arms and cried when I left her to look for lodgings and employment. I found both: the first with a hair-dresser in Rue de Richelieu, and the second on the upper floor of number —— Rue St. Honore, where you came to us one day and changed

Margery's whole life. Had I chosen to use the money your father paid me annually, we might have lived in much better style, but I shrank from touching more of it than it was absolutely necessary, and took pleasure in supporting her by my own hard labor. I would lay the money by for her until she married, if she ever did, or until she needed it more, I thought; and should she marry now she would not go empty-handed to her husband, for there are many thousand dollars invested for her in France.

"How I toiled and slaved for her, and how I loved her as time went on and she grew more and more into my heart; loved her so much, in fact, that your image gradually began to fade, and I could think of you without a pang. I saw you occasionally—once in the grounds at the Chateau, where I came upon you with your nurse, and several times in the streets of Paris, after your father brought you there. I used to take Margery out upon the Champs d'Elysees on fine afternoons when the streets were full of people driving out to the Bois, and hiring a chair I would hold her in my lap and watch for your father to pass. Though not the most showy—for his taste was too good for that—Mr. Hetherton's turn-out was the most elegant and probably the most expensive of all the private carriages in Paris, while his splendid thoroughbreds were the talk of the city. I always watched anxiously for him, and when he appeared, sitting up so proud and erect, with that look of haughty indifference and selfishness on his face, and with you beside him on the cushions, clad in dainty apparel, I used to hold little Margery tightly to my heart and bite my lips till the blood almost forced itself through the skin, so fearful was I lest I should shriek out the truth so loudly that he would hear it above the roll of the wheels and the tramp of the horses' hoofs. Something impelled me strongly to hold you high in my arms, and, making him see you, say to him: 'This is your lawful daughter, the child of your wife who died in Rome. Her place is there beside you, and not far up in the tenement house on the Rue St. Honore.'

"But it was too late now to confess, so I let you go by in all your splendor, and if at night I kissed Margery more tenderly than usual and held her closer to me as I undressed her for bed, it was by way of atonement for the great wrong I was doing her.

"It was about this time that I fell in with Gustave La Rue, who offered me marriage. He was a good-natured easy-going man, who would never trouble me much with questions concerning the past, provided I made his home comfortable and his life easy, and so I married him, and gave Margery his name, and said to strangers that she was his daughter. He was fond of children and always kind to her, and never pressed me hard with regard to her parentage but once, and then I swore to him that she was not my child; but he did not believe me, though he never suspected the truth."

"And when I went to your room in the Rue St. Honore, you knew I was Margery's sister?" Queenie said; and Christine replied:

"Yes, and kissed the chair you sat upon, and in my poor blind way thanked God for sending you there, and thanked him again when, through your influence, Margery was placed at the same school with you, and her education paid for by the man who never suspected the truth, or even knew that the little girl in whom his daughter was so interested was anything to me until her education was finished and she was a grown young lady, then he learned it accidentally and was very angry and bade me keep you apart, lest in some way you should learn who I was.

"It was then that the idea of emigrating to America was suggested to my mind by some ladies for whom Margery had worked, and who gave such glowing accounts of the country and the prospects for dressmaking that I began to consider the matter seriously, and finally made up my mind to go, without communicating with Mr. Hetherton upon the subject. I wrote him, however, from Oak Bluffs, and directed to the old address in Paris, but possibly he never received my letter."

"Yes, he did; I am sure he did," Queenie exclaimed. "There were letters forwarded to him at Liverpool, and one of them made him very angry, Pierre told me. He was present when papa read it, and after that he was very nervous and excited, and suggested to me that we give up America and go back to Paris. But I would not listen. I made him come, and he died on the voyage, and you were the cause of his death. He dreaded meeting you here, and the dread and the remorse killed him. Oh, papa—I can see him so plain as his eyes followed me, and he made me promise to forgive him if something ever came to my knowledge, and I promised; but it is so hard. Oh, Margie, if it were not for you, I could not keep my promise, and I don't know as I can at all, he was so bad—if all she says is true. It would have been better to have left me in Marseilles where I was born—left me to poverty and want—for then I should have known nothing better, and might have been as happy as the girls I have seen dancing on the street for the amusement of the crowd. But now, to fall so far—it makes me dizzy, and sick, and dazed, and there's a buzzing in my head, and a feeling as if I were crazed and could not understand it at all."

She was very white, with a drawn look about her lips, which alarmed Margery, who bent over her and said:

"You have heard enough. There can be nothing more to tell which will interest you. Mother must go out now, and leave you to rest."

"Yes, yes, Margie; tell her to go; I am so tired and sick," Queenie whispered, and without a word Christine left the room, and the two girls were alone.

CHAPTER XLIII

THE SISTERS

For a moment Queenie sat with her head dropped and her eyes closed; then, opening them suddenly and fixing them upon Margery, who knelt beside her, she said, "It is very dreadful, Margie, and I feel as if turned into stone. Oh, if I could cry; but I cannot, even though I know that everything is gone from me that I loved the most. Phil is dead—Phil, who would have stood by me even in this disgrace. He would have come to me and said, 'Dear little Queenie, I love you just the same, and want you for my wife,' and with him I might in time have been happy; but now there is nothing left to me, neither lover, friends, nor name, and that last hurts the worst and makes me so desolate; no name, no friends, not a single relative in the world except—except that woman, and she is my mother!"

Queenie said the last word with a choking sob, while Margery kissed and rubbed her hands which were cold as ice and lay helplessly upon her lap.

"You forget that you have me—forget that I am your sister—that whatever sorrow comes to you must be shared by me," Margery said, and Queenie replied, "No, I don't forget that. It is the only thing which keeps me from dying outright. Oh, Margie, you do not know how foolishly proud I was when I believed myself Queenie Hetherton—proud of my position, proud of my blood. And—I will confess it all to you who stand just where I thought I stood, I was so wicked and so proud that I rebelled against my mother's family—rebelled against the Fergusons, and though I tried to do my duty and tried to be kind and friendly, especially to grandma, I never came in contact with her, or with any of Uncle Tom's family, that I did not feel the little shivers run over me, and a shrinking away from them and their manner of speaking and acting. I could not help this feeling, though I hated myself cordially for it, and told myself many times that I was no better than they, and still in my heart I fancied I was infinitely their superior—I, who had no right to be born. Once I knelt in the room I supposed was my mother's, and prayed God to make me like the woman below stairs, whom I thought so coarse and vulgar—asked Him to humble me in any way, if that was what I needed to subdue my pride, but little did I dream the time would come when that prayer would be so terribly answered—when I would give my life to know the Fergusons were mine as I then believed them to be. Oh, if I could have the old days back again; if I could waken from this and find it a dream, but I never can. I am not Reinette Hetherton, I am nobody. I have neither name, nor friends, nor position, nor home; oh Margie, Margie, I had not thought of that before;" and Queenie bounded to her feet so suddenly that Margery was thrown backward upon the floor, where she sat staring blankly at the girl who it seemed to her had actually lost her mind.

She was walking rapidly across the floor, beating the air with her hands.

There were blood-red spots on her cheeks, and her eyes shone with a strange, unnatural light as they flashed first upon one object, and then upon another, and finally rested upon Margery, before whom she stopped and said in a whisper:

"Do not you know it? Do not you see that I am an outcast, a beggar, a trespasser where I have no claim? Frederick Hetherton's unlawful child has no right to a penny of his money. You are his heiress; you are his daughter, and I only an intruder, who have lived for years on what was not my own, and have, perhaps, sometimes felt that I was very good to give to you what was already yours, for you are Miss Hetherton, and I am Reinette—Bodine!"

Her lips quivered as she repeated the name, and her whole manner showed how hateful was the sound of it to her. But Margery scarcely noticed that, so intent was she on what had gone before. Springing to her feet, and winding her arm around Queenie, she held her fast, while she said:

"What folly is this! What injustice to me! I do not pretend not to understand you, for I do. You are excited now, and insane enough to think that you have no right to Frederick Hetherton's money because you are the child of Christine Bodine, whom you so despise. She is not a bad woman; the badness was on the other side. That ceremony which she thought true was true to her and in the sight of Heaven, so far as she was concerned, though it might not stand the test of the law. But in either case you are father's child as much as I am, and it was his wish that you should be his heir. He knew nothing of me, never dreamed of my existence, and, Queenie, the world need not know what we do. I would far rather remain Margaret La Rue forever than meet what we must meet should the truth be known. Stay as you are, here in your home, for it is yours, and, if you like, I will stay with you, and the secret of your birth shall be buried forever."

"No, Margie," Queenie said, disengaging herself from her sister's embrace. "I have no right here, and I cannot stay; not a penny of all my father's wealth is mine. You say truly that he did not dream of your existence; but if he had—if at the last moment of his life he had known that somewhere in the world there was a daughter lawfully his own, he would have repudiated me, and flown to you.

"I knew him, and you did not, and you cannot understand how proud he was. I knew he was more to blame than Christine if she tells the truth, and I can never forgive him, even if I did promise to do so, and I can never forgive her for hiding you, whom father would have loved so much, while I should never have been born.

"And yet he loved me, I am sure; but, had he known of you, all would have been changed, just as I shall change it now. He would have sent me away—not penniless, it was not his nature to do that; he provided for Christine, and would have made provision for me—but sent me from him just the same and taken his lawful daughter home, and after you are established here as Miss Hetherton, I shall go away—where, I do not know—but somewhere in the world there is a place for Pierre and me, and we shall go together. I cannot stay here with that mark upon me. I feel it now burning into my flesh, and know it is written all over me in letters of fire, which all the waters in the world cannot wash out. Truly, the sins of the parents are visited upon the children, and I am suffering so terribly—oh, Margie, it does ache so hard, so hard!" and with a gasping sob Queenie sank into her chair, where she sat writhing like one in agony.

For a moment Margery regarded her intently, then kneeling before her again and taking the hot, quivering hands in hers said to her: "Queenie, do you think I have forgotten the day when you came to me, a little, lonely girl, clad in garments so coarse that just to have worn them a moment would have roughened the delicate skin of one who, like you, had known only the scarlet, and ermine, and purple of life. And yet you did not shrink from me. You looked into my eyes with a look I have never forgotten. You touched my soiled hands with your soft, white, dimpled fingers, and the touch lingers there yet. You took the scarlet and ermine from your shoulders and put them upon me, and brought down heaven to me as nearly as it can be brought to us here upon earth. And now, when this great sorrow has come upon you, when it may be that I stand in the place you have held so long, when the scarlet and ermine are mine, will you not let me give it back to you as you once gave it to me, or at least share it with me—that is, supposing mother's statement is proved to be true?"

"Proved to be true!" Queenie said. "What do you mean by that?"

"I mean this," Margery replied, "The world will not accept the story as readily as you have done. There will have to be proof, I think, that I was born at Rome and that Margaret Ferguson was my mother."

"Do you doubt it, Margie?" Queenie asked, fixing her eyes searchingly upon her sister, who at last slowly answered, "No."

"Neither do I," was Queenie's quick rejoinder. "I know it is true—know I am Christine's daughter by the resemblance I bear to her, just as I know you are a Ferguson by the blue in your eyes and the golden hue of your hair, so like them all, so like to Phil. Oh, Phil! if I could go to him and tell him of my pain."

There was silence a few moments between the two girls, and it was Queenie who spoke first again.

"Go away now, Margie. My head is not quite straight. Go, and leave me awhile to myself."

Margery obeyed, thinking that Queenie wished to rest, but such was not her intention, and no sooner was she alone than she arose, and, bolting her door, went to her writing-desk, and taking out several sheets of paper began to write the story which Christine had told her. This done, she took the three letters which she had found among her father's papers, signed "Tina," and inclosing the whole in an envelope, directed it to Mr. Beresford. Then, ringing her bell, she asked that Pierre should be sent to her. The old man obeyed the summons at once, for he was very anxious about his young mistress and the sickness which had come so suddenly upon her. Stepping into the room, he made his bow, and then stood before her in his usual attitude of deference and respect, his head bent forward and his hands clasped, awaiting her orders.

"Sit down, Pierre," Queenie said. "You need not stand before me now. I have something to tell you, and the sooner I tell it, the better. A dreadful thing has come to light—a dreadful wrong been done to Margery. She is not Miss La Rue. She is that baby born at Rome. She is Margaret Ferguson's daughter, and I am—am—nobody! My father was Frederick Hetherton, and my mother is Christine Bodine, and they were never legally married. Do you understand me, Pierre?"

He did understand her, and the shock made him reel forward and grasp the back of a chair, to which he held, while he stood staring at his mistress as if to assure himself of her sanity.

"It is true," she continued, as she met his questioning look of wonder, and then, very rapidly, she told him how it had come to her knowledge, and what she meant to do.

"I will never believe it," was Pierre's emphatic reply, when he could speak at all. "It is a lie she told, the bad woman."

And yet in Pierre's heart there was a growing fear that what he had heard might be true, but even if it were, it should make no difference with him. He would stand by Queenie against the whole world. Where she went he would go, where she died, he would die, her faithful slave to the last. It did not matter to him whether she were a Hetherton or a Bodine, she was his sovereign, his queen, and he told her so, with many gestures and ejaculations, some of which were far from being complimentary to "La femme Bodine," as he called her.

"I knew I was sure of you," Queenie said to him, "and after a little we will go away from here and find a home somewhere, and I shall learn to work and take care of myself, and you, too, if necessary."

Pierre shrugged his shoulders significantly at the idea of being taken care of by this little girl who had been reared so tenderly. Queenie noticed the gesture, though she did not seem to, and went on:

"I have written to Mr. Beresford, who will know just what to do, and early to-morrow morning you must take it to him. Say nothing to Miss Margery or any one, but come to my door, quietly, as soon as you are up. I shall be waiting for you. And now go: it is getting late, and I am very tired."

Pierre obeyed and left her in a most bewildered state of mind, scarcely knowing what he had heard, and not at all able to realize its import. True to his promise, he was at Queenie's door the next morning before either Margery or her mother were astir, and received the package for Mr. Beresford, and a second and smaller one for Grandma Ferguson. This last Queenie had written after Peirre left her the previous night, and she bade him deliver it.

"There will be no answer to either; at least none for you," she said, and with a nod that he understood, Pierre hastened away to throw the bomb-shell at the feet of Mr. Beresford and Grandma Ferguson.

CHAPTER XLIV

THE EXPLOSION

Early as it was, Mr. Beresford was at his office. He had an important suit pending in the court which involved much thought and research, and he was hunting up certain points bearing upon it when Pierre came in, and with a simple "Bon jour, monsieur," laid the package upon the table and departed in the direction of Grandma Ferguson's. Mr. Beresford recognized Queenie's handwriting, and thinking she had probably sent him some business papers of her father's, which she had overlooked, he laid it aside for a time and went on with his own matters, so that it was an hour or more, and the one-horse sleigh which Grandma Ferguson had hired to carry her to Hetherton Place had driven rapidly past the door before he took the package in his hand and opened it. The three yellow, time-worn letters which Queenie had inclosed first met his eye, and he examined them curiously, noting that they were dated in Marseilles many years ago; but as they were written in French it would take him some time to decipher them, so he put them down and took up Queenie's letter, which he read through rapidly, feeling when it was finished so benumbed and bewildered that he walked several times across the floor of his office, and then went out into the open air to shake off the nightmare which oppressed his faculties and made his brain so dizzy. Then, returning to the letter, he read it again, weighing carefully every word, and jumping at conclusions, rejecting this statement as improbable, and that as impossible and saying to himself as Pierre had done, "I do not believe it." He had long ago suspected that Queenie and Margery might be sisters, but not in this way. Anon, however, a doubt stole into his mind that it might be true, and this doubt was succeeded by another, and another, until there were great drops of sweat upon the lawyer's face, and an intense pity in his heart as he thought of Queenie and all she would have to suffer.

"Poor little Queenie; so proud and so high-spirited; she cannot bear it, and I shall do all I can to prove the story false," he said; and then suddenly there swept over him another thought which made him reel in his chair, while the sweat-drops on his forehead and about his lips grew larger and thicker. "If the tale were true, then Margery was the daughter of the house; Margery was Miss Hetherton, of Hetherton Place, and——"

He did not allow himself to think any further, but, throwing out his hands, with a fierce gesture, he exclaimed, "Get thee gone, Satan! Is this a time to indulge in low, mean, selfish feelings? Were Margery a thousand times a Hetherton, she would be no sweeter or lovelier than she has seemed to me as Margery La Rue, nor will Queenie be one whit the worse for this stain upon her birth, if stain there be, which I doubt; at all events I will leave no stone unturned to prove the truth or falsity of this Bodine woman's statement. If I could only read her letters I might find something on which to base a conclusion."

Taking up the letter which bore date the furthest back, he began to decipher it slowly and carefully, succeeding better than he had anticipated, and when it was finished he possessed a pretty accurate knowledge of its contents. Then he took the second and the third, and went through with them both, while the conviction deepened in his mind that there was something in the story which would bear investigation.

"I must see Queenie at once," he said, "and Mrs. La Rue also, and hear from her if she has any other proof to offer, than her mere statement and these letters, which she may or may not have written."

Ordering his horse and giving some directions to his clerk in case clients called, he was soon riding rapidly toward Hetherton Place where Grandma Ferguson had been for more than an hour. Pierre had found the good woman seated at her breakfast-table, arrayed in her usual morning costume, a short, wine-colored stuff skirt, and a loose woolen sacque, with no collar on her neck or cap on her head. But her white hair was combed smoothly back and twisted into a little knot, and her face shone with content and satisfaction as she drank her coffee from her saucer or soaked her fried cake in it.

With his usual polite bow, Pierre handed the package to her, and then, departed without a word.

"Mrs. John Ferguson, Present," grandma read aloud. "What did Rennet want to put present on for, I wonder, and how finefied she writes. I don't believe I can make it out at all, the letters are so small and Frenchy," and tearing off the envelope she tried in vain to decipher the contents of the letter.

Queenie had written it under great excitement, and her handwriting, always puzzling to grandma, was more illegible than usual.

"Here, Axie, read it for me; 'tain't likely there's any secret," grandma said, and taking the paper in her hands, Axie began to read what Queenie had written.

It was as follows:

"Dear Grandma:

"You must let me call you that just this once, though you are not my grandmother. A dreadful thing has been done, and kept secret until yesterday, when I found it out, and it almost killed me. I am not the baby born at Rome; Margery is that baby; Margery is your grandchild, and I am nobody. I am the daughter of Frederick Hetherton and Mrs. La Rue, who was Christine Bodine, my old nurse. She has told me all the deception, and her hiding Margery from her father, who did not know of her existence. It is terrible—and I was so proud and hot tempered, and so bad to you sometimes, and now I'd give the world if you were really my grandmother.

"Come as soon as you can and see Margery and question Mrs. La Rue yourself.

"Queenie"

"Not her gra'ma! I not her gra'ma! Who then is her gra'ma, I'd like to

222

know?" Grandma Ferguson exclaimed, when Axie read the first lines of the letter.

But Axie did not answer. Her quick eye had gone rapidly on, and with an ejaculation of surprise, she read what Queenie had written, while her mistress turned white as ashes, and could only whisper her incredulity.

"Rennet not mine! not Margery's child! No, no, I cannot believe that," she said, and a sense of pain began to rise in her heart at the thought of losing in this way the little dark-eyed girl who had crept into her love in spite of her wilful, imperious ways. "Read it again, Axie," she continued; "You did not get it right before. Rennet never said no such thing, unless she's crazy. Yes, that's it," and grandma's face brightened, and her voice was more cheery. "Fretting for Phil has driven her out of her mind. She hain't slep', nor cried, nor et sence he died. I shall go over there at once, and do you run as fast as you can to the livery after a hoss and sleigh."

And so within an hour after Pierre delivered Queenie's letter to Grandma Ferguson she was alighting at the door of Hetherton Place. Margery, who knew nothing of Pierre's journey to the village, opened the door to the old lady, whose first exclamation was:

"How is she, and when did the spell come on her?"

"Do you mean Reinette, and how did you know anything ailed her?" Margery asked, and grandma replied:

"How do I know? Didn't that Frenchman fetch me a letter from her this mornin', in which she said she wasn't my granddarter, and that——"

Here grandma stopped, struck by the likeness to her daughter which had so impressed her the first time she saw Margery. She had paid no attention to the assertion in Reinette's letter that Margery was her granddaughter, but now, as she looked into the blue eyes confronting her so steadily, she saw there something which awoke within her a strange feeling of kinship and love, and she continued with a faltering voice: "She said that you was Margaret's girl. Be you Margery? Be you my granddarter?"

"I don't know, the story seems so incredible," Margery replied, but she took the hands extended toward her in her own, and covered them with kisses, as she continued: "If I am Margery Hetherton, it is very hard on Queenie, and you must love her just the same—love her better if possible."

"Yes, yes," grandma replied. "Nothing shall change my love for her. Where is she? Let me go to her at once."

Queenie, who was lying on the lounge, must have been almost asleep, for she heard nothing until a hand was laid gently upon her head, and a voice full of love and pity said to her:

"Rennet! poor little Rennet!"

Then she started up, with a low cry, caused partly by surprise and partly by the sharp pain which seemed to pass from her heart to her head and to force to the surface the tears which had been so long pent up, and which now fell like rain. She had never before heard her grandmother call her "Rennet" without a feeling of irritation, or, as she had expressed it to Phil, without a "jerking of her elbows," but now, as the familiar sound fell on her ears, there swept over her such a feeling of anguish, and regret, and intense longing for what she had lost, that the fountain of tears was broken up, and for some minutes she lay in the motherly arms held out to her, and cried so hard and piteously that Mrs. Ferguson became alarmed at last, and tried to soothe and quiet her. But Reinette could not be quieted.

"Let me cry," she said; "it does me good. You know I have not shed a tear before since poor Phil died, and I guess I am crying more for him than for my lost birthright—my——"

"Hush, Rennet;" grandma interrupted. "I don't know what you mean—don't want to know—and if there is anything, my advice is, keep it to yourself. I took you to my heart as my own that fust day I saw you at the train, a little scart thing among so many strangers. I loved you then; I've loved you ever sence, and allus will, no matter who you be."

"Don't you hurt me so!" Queenie cried with a keen pang of remorse, as she remembered how she had once rebelled against this woman, and refused to acknowledge her claim to relationship until it was proved beyond her power to gainsay it.

And now she would have given the world to have called her "grandmother," and known that it was true.

"I don't deserve your love," she said. "I have been so wicked, and have vexed you so many times, but, after Margery, you are dearer to me now than any living creature, though I am not your grandchild—Margery is that; Margery is the baby born at Rome and hidden away from her father. Mrs. La Rue has told us all about it. She is my mother."

Queenie spoke very low, and a flush stained her cheeks, where the tears were still falling though not so fast as at first. She was growing a little calmer and more composed, and was beginning to tell Mrs. Ferguson what she had heard, when Mr. Beresford was announced. To Margery, he had said, "Queenie has written me a strange story. Do you know anything about it?"

"Yes," Margery answered, with a quivering lip, "I heard mother tell her."

"And was that the first you knew of it?" he asked, scrutinizing her closely.

"No," she said, hesitatingly, as if the confession were a pain. "I knew it a few weeks ago——"

"When you were sick, and you kept it to yourself for her sake," Mr. Beresford interrupted her. "You are a brave girl, Margery. Few would have done what you have."

"If they loved Queenie as I do they would," she said. "Oh, Mr. Beresford, if it should be true, can we not keep it to ourselves? Need the world know it?"

"If it depended upon you and me, it might be done," he replied. "But I am afraid we could not manage Queenie. She seems determined to do you justice. Where is she, and can I see her?"

"Yes, let him come at once. I wish to have it over," Queenie said, when told that Mr. Beresford was in the house and had asked for her.

She heard him coming, and rising to her feet and brushing her tears away she stood erect, with the old, proud look flashing in her eyes, for she would not allow this man, who had once asked her to be his wife, to see how utterly crushed and humiliated she was. But when she caught sight of his face, so full of pity, and sympathy, and concern for her, she broke down utterly and cried harder even than she had done when grandma had called her Rennet. It was a perfect storm of sobs and tears, and Mr. Beresford, who had never witnessed anything like it, felt the moisture gathering in his own eyes as he looked at the little figure writhing in such pain.

"You must excuse me, for I cannot help it," she said, when she could speak. "It is not this alone which affects me so. It is everything. The death scene on the ship, when father's strange words foreshadowed this which has come upon me, and the loss of Phil, who would have stood by me in the face of everything."

"And do you not think I will do that, Queenie?" Mr. Beresford said, sitting down beside her and taking her hot hands in his as naturally as if he had been her brother or her lover.

And as he looked upon her, so broken, and crushed, and helpless, and yet so sweet and lovely withal, there swept over him again something of the same feeling which had prompted him to ask her to be his wife that night upon the rocks. True it was that recently he had learned to think of another face very different from the white, tear-stained one before him. But there was a great pity in his heart for the girl who had so dazzled, and bewildered, and bewitched him—a desire to comfort and reassure her, and he felt tempted to take her in his arms and soothe her as he would have soothed a little child. Grandma Ferguson had left the room as he came in, and the two were alone altogether, and Queenie's eyes, in which great tears were shining, were fixed upon him, and Queenie's lips he had once so longed to kiss were quivering in a grieved kind of way, and Queenie's hands were in his, and so it is not so very strange that for a moment he forgot the face he had thought fairer than the one which he finally took between his two hands and held, while he said:

"Queenie, you do wrong to talk as if anything for which you are not responsible can make a difference with your friends—with me, who once hoped to be more than your friend. Queenie, I asked you once to be my wife, when you stood upon a dizzy height of prosperity and now I ask you again when misfortune seems to be overtaking you. Will you be mine, Queenie, and let me shield you from the storm and prove to you that I have loved you for yourself rather than for your surroundings?"

Queenie's face was a study, as she drew it away from his encircling hands, and from sheer weakness and exhaustion lay wearily down upon the pillows of the lounge while she looked at him long and earnestly. Never before had Mr. Beresford seen so sweet, so soft and so womanly an expression in the dark eyes as he saw there now, and never had she seemed more desirable than she did when she answered him at last:

"I thank you so much, Mr. Beresford, for what you have said. It has done me a great deal of good, for if you can like me for myself alone there may be others who will do the same, and my life will not be quite so dreary. I will do you the justice to say that I believe you are in earnest now and mean what you say, but you are mistaken in the feeling which prompts you. It is pity for me, not love. But I thank you just the same, though I cannot accept your offer. When Phil went down beneath the waves my heart went with him, never to return. And you, Mr. Beresford, are destined for another. I know it; I have seen it, and am so glad. She is worthy of you, and was worthy before accident revealed that in everything she was your equal. And you will be so happy together sometime when it is all settled, as it must be at once. Send for Mrs. La Rue and hear her story; or rather, go to her. I could not listen to it again. She will convince you of the truth of what she says, and you must fix whatever there is to fix, so that Margery will have justice done her as Mr. Hetherton's daughter. Don't let a thought of me interfere with her rights. And now go to Mrs. La Rue."

She waved him from her with her old air of authority and he had no alternative but to obey, and wishing her good-morning he went below stairs to seek an interview with Mrs. La Rue.

As they had no suspicion of what had happened, it was a mere accident which sent the Rossiters to Hetherton Place that morning, and Mr. Beresford found them in the library with Grandma Ferguson, who had told them what she knew, and thrown them into a wild state of surprise and excitement.

"Oh, Mr. Beresford," Ethel said, going up to him as he entered the room, "is it true that Reinette is not our cousin?"

"I do not know," he replied; "I am going to question Mrs. La Rue. Shall I have her in here and let you hear what she has to say?"

"Yes, let her come," Mrs. Rossiter said; and in a few minutes Mrs. La Rue entered the room, calmer and more collected than she had been in months.

She had told the truth to Queenie. The worst was over. She could meet anything now; and at Mr. Beresford's request she began her story, which she repeated in a straightforward manner, never once crossing herself or hesitating in the least, except when some strong emotion overcame her as she spoke of Margery and the day Queenie came to her in the Rue St. Honore. No one could doubt that she was telling the truth, and Mr. Beresford did not doubt her, but he said to her when she had finished:

"Have you no other proof than your mere assertion of facts?"

"Yes," she replied; "I can give you the name of the pension in Rome where Mrs. Hetherton died, and of the physician who attended her, and the clergyman who buried her. These gentlemen, if living, will testify to the fact that she left an infant daughter, whom I took away with me. Then, old Florine is still alive in Paris, and will show that I brought Margery to her and took her away at such a date, while Jacques Berdotte and his wife Jeanne, in Marseilles, can tell you that they served me when Queenie was born; and I doubt not they will remember the American gentleman who came to see me, and to whom I went when I left their house. I think they are both alive. You can write and see. I have also Mr. Hetherton's last letter, written me from Paris when I was in the south of France, and he had heard that the girl Margery, in whom Queenie was so much interested, was my daughter. That will prove that Queenie is my child; and after that you surely will believe me without the letter which my mistress wrote to her husband not long before she died, and in which she speaks of her blue-eyed, golden-haired baby, whom she hopes he will love because it is so much like her. I did not destroy that letter, though tempted to do so many times."

She talked rapidly, and every word carried fresh conviction to Mrs. Rossiter, who was eager to see Margery and claim her as her sister's child. Of the meeting between Margery and her newly-found friends it is not my purpose to speak, except to say that at its close there was not in the minds of either a shadow of doubt as to the tie between them.

But amid their joy there was a keen pang of regret and pain for the little, desolate girl up stairs, who, when at last they went to her, received them at first with a calm, stony face and dry eyes, which seemed to flash defiance at any pity they might feel for her, but who finally broke down in a storm of sobs and tears, and, laying her head on Mrs. Rossiter's lap, begged her not to despise her for what she could not help.

"If I could die, I would," she said, "but I cannot. I am young, and life seems so lonely to me now, when once the days were too short for all I had to enjoy. Oh, why has God so dealt with me?"

It was hard to answer that question, or explain why to this young girl, whose life had been so full of sunshine, so much wretchedness should have come. Anna Ferguson said it was to punish her for her pride, and that it served her right for having felt above them all. Miss Anna heard the news with a wonderful degree of equanimity. She was not greatly surprised, she said, for she had always thought Reinette different from other young girls, and now she knew it was the bad blood there was in her. She pitied her, of course, and should go over and see her, but Reinette could not expect people to treat Christine Bodine's daughter just as they had treated Miss Hetherton.

This was the ground Anna took, but she met with no support from any one. On the contrary, the utmost sympathy was felt for Reinette when the story was known. Never before had Merrivale been so excited as it was now, for men, women, and children did nothing but talk of the affair from morning till night, and Margery, whom they all knew so well and had seen so many times, became as great an object of curiosity as the Queen of England would have been had she passed through the town.

To Margery this notoriety and scrutiny were exceedingly distasteful. She had fought the story of her birth as long as possible; had said that it could not be true, even after Mr. Beresford, in whose judgment she relied so much, had told her to believe it without other proof than he had gathered from Mrs. La Rue. Of course he was bound to obtain all the evidence possible, both from Rome and France, and this he had taken steps to do; and had suggested the possibility that the ceremony, which Christine had said took place at Chateau des Fleurs might be valid in France and thus legitimize Queenie. But there had been no witnesses, and Mr. Hetherton had never in any way acknowledged Christine as his wife. There could be no doubt on the subject, and Margery alone was the heiress of Hetherton Place. He called her Miss Hetherton, now, whenever he addressed her, as did the other people in town, and there always came an increase of color to Margery's cheek when she heard the name and thought of the little heart-broken girl who had shut herself up in her room and refused to see those of her former acquaintance, who, prompted partly by curiosity, and partly by genuine sympathy, came to assure her of their continued friendship and esteem.

"It is very kind in them, and I thank them so much; but I cannot see them yet," she would say, when Margery brought her the message.

And disappointed in their desire to see Reinette, the curious and meddlesome ones turned their attention to Mrs. La Rue, but she, too, avoided and baffled them; she had returned to the cottage in town, where she remained perfectly quiet, seeing no one and talking with no one except Margery and Mr. Beresford, to the latter of whom, as a lawyer, she was always communicative, giving him any information he wished for, and aiding him materially in procuring the proof, which, though he deemed it superfluous, he was desirous to obtain. To others she had said all she ever meant to say, and on the subject of her past life, her lips were sealed forever. Silent, cold, and impassive, she moved about her house, with no look of human interest on her white, stony face, except when Margery came, as she did every day, with news of Queenie. Then the pale cheek would flush for a moment and the heavy eyes light up with eager expectancy as she asked the same question. "Has she mentioned me yet?"

"No, not yet," was always Margery's answer, and then the color would fade away and the lips shut tightly together as if in pain, but no word of protest ever passed them, or complaint that she was not justly dealt with by the girl whose life she had blighted.

It was Grandma Ferguson who stayed constantly with Queenie during the first few days after the story was known, and it was wonderful to see the love and confidence between them. With Queenie the feeling was almost idolatrous which she felt for the woman whose coarse speech and common ways had once been so obnoxious to her, but to whom she now clung with more than a child's fondness for its mother. On her bended knees, with her head in grandma's lap, she had confessed all the past, even to her rebellious feelings on that day when she stood on the platform at the station and was claimed by relatives of whom she had never heard.

"I was so wicked and proud," she said, "for I thought myself equal to the greatest lady in Europe, and I hated the way you spoke to me—hated everything about you and went on hating it, especially the purple gloves and moire antique, which made my elbows jerk, they so offended my eye."

And grandma forgave the beautiful little sinner, and stroked the glossy, black hair, and told her not to mind, but get up and wipe her tears away, and be comforted.

"I ain't an atom like you," she said, "and never could be if I tried ever so hard. 'Taint the purple gloves, neither, nor the mory antique, which makes the difference: it is my whole make-up from the beginnin'. Some vessels is coarse, and some is fine. Some is jugs, and some is china, and I am a jug of the roughest kind, but I love you, Queenie, and will stick to you through thick and thin."

Then they talked together of Queenie's future, and where she would go when she left Merrivale, as she was resolved upon doing, for a time at least.

"I may come back to Margery after awhile," she said, "but now I must go where no one knows me, and pities me. I will not be pitied, and so I must go away."

"Then why not go to that place in Florida where your Gra'ma Hetherton used to live," Mrs. Ferguson suggested. "I've heard it was a fine place where they once kept a hundred niggers, though it must be awfully run down now."

"You mean Magnolia Park," Queenie rejoined. "It is near Tallahassee. I have heard my father speak of it. He used to go there when a boy, and he told me what a grand old house it was, standing in the midst of a grove of magnolias, with rooms enough to accommodate twenty or thirty guests. Yes, I should like to go there. I should like to see Florida. Pierre will go with me, and it will cost us but little to live."

"And let me give you that little," grandma said. "I've money in the bank, laid up for Anny; but now she's goin' to marry so rich, she does not need it. Let me give you a thousand dollars to start on, and when that's gone, you shall have more unless you are ready to come home, as you most likely will be."

The Florida plan struck Queenie very favorably. She had heard from her father of Magnolia Park, where Mrs. Hetherton had lived before her marriage, and knowing nothing of the dilapidated condition of the house, or the many difficulties to be met and overcome before she could be even comfortable there, she was anxious to go at once, and broached the subject to Margery, who naturally opposed it with all her powers. It was her wish that Queenie should remain at Hetherton Place, and share equally with her in their father's home and fortune.

But this Queenie would not do. After a time she might feel differently, she said, but now she must go away, and as Magnolia Park could not be of any great value to Margery she was willing to accept so much and go there to live. So Mr. Beresford was consulted and questioned with regard to the place, of which they knew very little. Originally it was a fine plantation, with at least a hundred negroes upon it, but these were scattered by the war, and since that time, or rather since he had done business for Mr. Hetherton, the farm had been let to different parties, who took the house furnished as it was when the last of Mrs. Hetherton's relations left it, and who were not supposed to have had any particular care for it. Now, however, it was untenanted, and only a few acres of the best land were rented to a man whose plantation adjoined it. It might be habitable, and it might not, but his advice was that Queenie stay in Merrivale, as it was getting near the last of February and not at all the time for going to Florida.

But Queenie argued differently. March was the month when many tourists flitted to the South, she said. She would have plenty of time to get acclimated before summer, and she seemed so anxious and excited, and determined that a consultation was held between Mr. Beresford, Grandma Ferguson, and Margery, which resulted in the decision that as soon as the necessary arrangements could be made, Queenie should leave Merrivale for

Magnolia Park, accompanied by Pierre and Axie, Mrs. Ferguson's colored girl, who was trusty and efficient, and delighted with the prospect of a change from the monotonous life in Merrivale. This giving up of Axie, who had lived with her so many years, was grandma's own proposition, which she strenuously insisted upon, saying, when Queenie remonstrated, that it would not be for long, as they'd soon get enough of that heathenish land of niggers and sand, and be back to the North again.

The last week in February was fixed upon for Queenie's departure, and the day before she left, the Hetherton carriage drove through the village to the cottage, where Mrs. La Rue was living alone. From it Queenie alighted, and entering unannounced remained there for half an hour or more. But of that interview nothing was ever known, except this: When, next day Margery called at the cottage and reported that Queenie had gone, Mrs. La Rue said, with a quivering lip and trembling voice:

"She kissed me and called me mother."

CHAPTER XLV

MAGNOLIA PARK

Thirty years before our story opens, Magnolia Park was one of the finest places in middle Florida. But after the death of Mrs. Hetherton, who had been born and married there, and who spent a part of every winter in her old home, there was no one left to care particularly for it, as Mr. Hetherton had lands enough of his own to look after. So the place began to go down, and when the war swept like a wave of fire over the South, it was left tenantless and unprotected save by an old negro, Uncle Sim, and his wife, Aunt Judy, who lived in the whitewashed cabin on the grounds, paying no heed to the rumors of freedom which reached them from time to time, as the terrible conflict between brother and brother went on. They were as free as they ever wished to be, they said, and all they asked was to be let alone and left to die on the old place. So they staid, and did their best to guard the house of which they were so proud, and which, at two different times, was made a kind of hotel for the soldiery, who were scouring the country. A night and a day the Boys in Blue halted there, carrying off whatever they conveniently could of the many valuable articles with which the house was furnished, and one of them, an officer, having a hand-to-hand fight with old Judy, who tried to wrench from him a pair of silver candlesticks he was stuffing in his pockets. He took away the candlesticks and also a black eye and a bloody nose which Aunt Judy had given him as a memento of his stay at Magnolia Park.

A week later, and a party of the Boys in Gray swooped down upon the place and spent the night in the house and fed on Judy's corn cakes and bacon, and killed Uncle Sim's big turkey, and turned the once handsome rooms into barracks, but were prevented from committing as extensive depredations as their predecessors had done simply because, aside from the six-legged piano on which they pounded Dixie vigorously, and the massive bedsteads and chairs and tables, there was little or nothing to steal. Warned by the lesson learned from their first visitors, Sim and Judy had dug a deep hole at the side of their cabin, and lining it with blankets had filled it with the remaining valuables of the house; then, covering them with another heavy blanket, they heaped dirt and sand upon them, and built over the spot a rude hen-house, where several motherly hens brooded over their young chickens. After this Sim and Judy lived in comparative ease until the war was over and peace and quiet reigned once more in Florida. Then the premises were let to a young Kentuckian, who soon grew tired of his bargain, and gave it up, and the house was empty again.

When Mr. Beresford first took charge of the Hetherton estate, he wrote to Frederick, asking why he did not sell the Florida lands, which yielded him nothing. But this Frederick would not do. Magnolia Park had been his mother's home, and a place where, as a boy, he had been very happy; and, as he could afford to keep it, he wrote to that effect to Mr. Beresford, telling him to let it if he could, and if not, to let it alone. So Mr. Beresford let it alone, except when some one wished to rent a few acres of the land, which was the case when Reinette decided to go there. Then he wrote to the man whose plantation adjoined Magnolia Park, telling him that a daughter of the late Mr. Hetherton was about to visit Florida, and asking him to see that a few of the rooms were made comfortable for her. Unfortunately this letter was miscarried or lost, so that Reinette's arrival was wholly unexpected, and produced the utmost consternation in the whitewashed cabin, where Uncle Sim and Judy were taking their evening meal, and feeding the four dogs hanging around them.

Queenie had traveled night and day until she reached the station at Tallahassee, where she took a carriage for Magnolia Park, a distance of two or three miles. The day was drawing to a close, and the sun was just setting when they turned off from the highway into the road, which wound through the fields for a quarter of a mile or more up to the house.

"Dat's 'em; dat's the place," said the driver, whose name was Boston, and he pointed to a huge wooden building standing upon a little rise of ground and surrounded by tall magnolias.

Once it must have been a little paradise, but now it was stripped of all its glory, and stood there desolate and dreary, with the paint all washed from its walls and the lights broken from the lower windows, while here and there a door was gone, and the shutters hung by one hinge, or swung loosely in the wind.

Involuntarily Queenie held out her hand to Axie, who took it in her strong palm, and said, encouragingly:

"It may be better inside. Anyway, I can soon fix it up, and the situation is lovely."

Attracted by the sound of wheels, the four dogs now came rushing down the road, barking so furiously that Queenie turned pale with fright, and clung closer to Axie. But when the noisy pack saw Boston, whom they knew, their barking changed into whines of recognition, which brought Uncle Sim and Aunt Judy round the corner of the house, where the latter stopped, and with her hands on her fat hips eyed the strangers curiously,

"Somebody gwine to visit Miss Strong, most likely; but why did Boston fetch 'em here?" she thought.

But when Queenie alighted, and going up to her told her that she was Miss Hetherton, granddaughter of Miss Lucy Marshall, who used to live at Magnolia Park, and that she had come to stay, her consternation knew no bounds, and while dropping a courtesy to Queenie, and saying to her, "An' sho' you're welcome, miss," she was thinking to herself, "For de dea' Lord's sake, whatever 'll I do wid sich quality as dis, and whar 'll I put her? There ain't a room in de whole house fit for a nigger or a cracker to sleep in. An' she's de real stuff dat ladies is made of. Can't cheat dis chile."

"Honey," she said at last to Queenie, who was looking ruefully around her. "I's no whar to ax you to sit down jes dis minute but in my cabin, whar I done scoured the flo' dis blessed day. If I had known you're comin' I'd done somethin'."

Queenie explained that a letter had been sent to some one announcing her expected visit, and added, with a little shiver, "Let me go to your cabin. I am very tired and chilly."

So Aunt Judy led the way to her quarters, which were as neat and clean as soap and water and her strong hands could make them. A pine knot was blazing on the hearth, diffusing a delightful degree of light and warmth through the room, and Queenie felt better and less desolate than when standing outside in the chill twilight, which had succeeded the warm spring day. Before entering the cabin, Axie, accompanied by Sim and Judy, made the tour of the house, deciding at once that to pass the night in that damp, cheerless place, was utterly impossible. Queenie might have gone to town and staid at a hotel until something like decency and cleanliness was restored to a few of the rooms, but Boston had left, and there was no alternative but to sleep in Judy's cabin. This, however, Queenie did not mind. Reared as she had been in France, she had none of the American prejudice against the African race, and ate her hot corncake which Aunt Judy baked for her, and drank her coffee from Judy's cups, with almost as keen a relish, as she had ever dined at the Meurice. Once, indeed, as she remembered Chateau des Fleurs, and Hetherton Place, and then glanced at her humble surrounding there came a great lump in her throat, and her hands involuntarily struck the air as if to thrust something from her. But she meant to be very brave, and when at last she was lifted by Aunt Judy into the clean, comfortable bed, which had been made for her upon the low kitchen table, she fell asleep almost immediately, and knew nothing more until the morning sun was shining in at the open door, and she heard Axie and Judy outside consulting together about the propriety of waking her.

Greatly refreshed with her night's rest Queenie felt better and decided that the place was not so bad, after all; but a close inspection of the premises after breakfast convinced her that, for the present at least, she must seek quarters elsewhere. Rooms there were in abundance, and furniture, but everything had gone to decay; everything was moldy and worm-eaten, and smelled of rats, and must and foul air. And still, as Axie said, there were great capabilities in the place, and with a little time and money, and a great deal of hard work, a portion of the house could be made not only habitable, but very comfortable and attractive. Meantime, Queenie must go away, for it was impossible for her to stay there while the renovating process was going on. But where to go was a question which troubled Queenie not a little, until Aunt Judy suggested an idea to her by saying, "Thar's Jacksonville on de river. Why not go thar a spell? Heaps of de gentry from de Noff is thar, and a sight of mighty fine dresses at dem grand hotels. Jacksonville is a mighty big city— bigger dan New York, I reckon."

Queenie had heard of Jacksonville, and she at once seized upon Judy's suggestion as something practicable. She would go to that winter Saratoga of the South and see what it was like. Possibly she might be amused with what she saw, and so the pain at her heart be lessened a little. She would go that very day, she said, for she was full of a burning restlessness and desire for change. But Judy, who knew something of the running of the trains, told her it was then too late; she must wait until the next day, and pass another night upon the kitchen table. From this, however Queenie was saved, for, while they were speaking, they caught the sound of wheels, and, shading her eyes with her hands, Aunt Judy saw entering the park a carriage with a lady in it. "Dar's Miss Strong from de Homestead," she exclaimed. "She's de ole Govenor's darter and de fustest lady in dese parts. Got a head full of brains, and writes for all de papers in de land. She be comen here, sho'-nuf." And Judy was right, for Boston had stopped at the Homestead the previous night, and had told of the young lady—Miss Hetherton—whom he had brought to Magnolia Park. Mrs. Strong remembered well the tall, handsome boy, Frederick Hetherton, who, when she was a child, had passed a winter at the Park, which was then one of the finest places in the State. She remembered, too, the stately lady, his mother, who had more than once dined at the Homestead, and she had no doubt that the young girl of whom Boston told her, was the granddaughter of that lady, and daughter of the boy Frederick. But why had she come to Magnolia Park so late in the season, and how was she to exist, even for a day, in that dilapidated, forsaken spot?

"I will go to see her at once and bring her home with me," was Mrs. Strong's first thought, upon which she acted immediately.

Introducing herself to Queenie, who advanced to meet her as she descended from her carriage, she said:

"If I mistake not, you are the daughter of Frederick Hetherton, whom I knew when I was a little girl. Though several years older than myself, he was

233

very kind to me, and I have spent hours with him under the shadow of these trees and those in the grounds of my own home."

The mention of her father by one who had seen and known him brought the hot tears at once to Queenie's eyes, but she dashed them aside, and explaining that Frederick Hetherton was her father, she led Mrs. Strong into the house, and sitting down beside her, answered as well as she could the questions which her visitor put to her concerning her home in Paris and her father's sad death on shipboard.

"I had heard something of this before," Mrs. Strong said to her, "for the lawyer who has charge of your father's affairs at the North wrote to a friend of mine who is supposed to look after the estate, that it now belonged to a young lady, the only direct heir of the Hethertons. It is rather a sorry place for a young girl to come to, but I suppose you do not intend remaining here long."

"Yes; always; I have no other home," Queenie replied, and her voice was choked with tears which she fought bravely back.

Mrs. Strong was a kind-hearted, far-seeing woman, and as she studied this girl, scarcely older than her own daughter Nina, whom she somewhat resembled, she felt strangely drawn toward her, and felt, too, that over her young life some terrible storm had swept.

"I will not ask her what it is," she thought, "but I'll be a friend to her, as I should wish some woman to befriend my Nina were she here alone with those strange attendants."

Then she said:

"I think I heard that Mr. Hetherton's wife died in Rome, years ago. It must have been at your birth."

For a moment Queenie sat as rigid as if turned into stone, her fists clinched, and her eyes staring at Mrs. Strong, who looked at her wonderingly. Then a tremor ran through her frame, and she shook from head to foot.

"Oh, I can't bear it! I can't bear it!" she cried, at last. "My head will burst if I keep it. I must tell you the truth; you seem so good and kind, and I want a friend so much. Mother did not die in Rome—that was Margery's mother; mine is still alive, and I had no right to be born."

Then, amid bursts of tears and broken sobs, Queenie told her story from beginning to end—from Chateau des Fleurs down to Magnolia Park, where she had come to hide from all who had ever known her. Had Queenie tried, she could not have found a more sympathizing listener to her recital, and when it was finished, Mrs. Strong's tears flowed almost as freely as her own, as she took the young girl in her arms, and kissing her lovingly, tried to comfort and reassure her, while at the same time she administered a little reproof.

"I think you should have staid with Margery," she said; "but since you are here, we will do the best we can for you. And now you must go home with me and stay until some of these rooms are made comfortable for you."

But to this Queenie objected. She had a great desire to see Jacksonville, she said, and was going there for two weeks or more.

"Jacksonville, and alone," Mrs Strong repeated, and Queenie replied that

Axie was going with her to see her settled, and then leave her with Pierre, while she returned to the Park to superintend the renovating process.

"There can be no harm in that, can there?" she asked, and Mrs. Strong replied:

"Oh, no, it is not an unheard-of thing for ladies to be at the hotel alone, but I think they usually have some acquaintances there, and you have none. If, however, you insist upon going, I shall write to the proprietor of the St. James to have a care over you, and also to some friends of mine, residents in town, whose attentions and friendship will be of great service to you, and shield you from the curious, gossiping ones who are to be found everywhere, and especially at large hotels. Cats, I call them, for they partake largely of the nature of that treacherous animal, smooth and purring if you stroke them the right way, but biting and scratching if you do not. There are plenty of them at the St. James, I dare say, but I think I can keep you from their claws, if you will go. Possibly the change may do you good. It will amuse you, at all events. But you must spend to-day and to-night with me; and to-morrow, if you still insist, you can take the train for Jacksonville."

To this plan Queenie assented, and spent the day and night at Mrs. Strong's, and the next morning started with Pierre and Axie for the St. James Hotel.

CHAPTER XLVI

AT THE ST. JAMES

It was too late in the season for guests to be coming from the North, but the increasing heat of the warm spring days was driving the people from points up the river, so that Jacksonville was full of visitors, and the St. James was crowded when Reinette arrived there in the train from Tallahassee.

"A small room will suit me; I do not care for a very expensive one," she said, timidly, as she stood before the clerk's desk, with Pierre and Axie on either side of her.

But the only vacant room in the house was one on the third floor front, and of this Queenie took possession, glad to escape for a time at least from the curious eyes which she felt were turned upon her. In all large hotels where the guests mingle freely together at table d'hote and in a common parlor, there is necessarily a good deal of gossip, and talk, and speculation with regard to strangers, especially if the latter chance to be at all out of the common order. And to this rule the St. James was not an exception. As Mrs. Strong had said, it had its cats, as what hotel has not? Idle, listless cats, who lead an aimless life, with nothing to do but scratch and tear each other, sometimes with claws unsheathed, but oftener with velvet paws and purring notes, and dark insinuations, which are far more dangerous, inasmuch as they cannot be met and combatted openly. Cliques, too, there were, the members of which, after criticising and talking each other up, turned their attention to any new-comers unfortunate enough to differ from the ordinary type of women, and Queenie was one of these. Everybody was interested in her. Everybody turned to look after her as she walked through the hall, or entered or left the dining-room, and many sought the books for information. But "Miss Hetherton, Merrivale, Mass.," told them nothing definite of the dark-faced little girl in black, who sat apart from them all, with a strange expression in the brilliant eyes, which swept the room so often and so rapidly, and which had in them a far-off look of weariness and pain rather than any particular interest in what was passing around her. Then one of the ladies tried Pierre. But at the first alarm the old man conveniently forgot every word of English he had ever known, and jabbered in his native tongue so rapidly that his interlocutor turned from him in dismay and opened her batteries upon Axie, whom she encountered in the hall. But Axie, too, was non-committal, or mostly so. Miss Hetherton was French and had always lived in Paris until quite recently, when she came to Merrivale, the old home of her father, who died upon the voyage, leaving her alone. Magnolia Park, near Tallahassee, belonged to the Hetherton estates, and thither the young lady had come for a change of air and scene, but finding that the place was a good deal run down and needed some repairs, she had decided to spend a little time at the St. James while they were being made.

This was Axie's explanation, which was wholly satisfactory, and as it was repeated with sundry additions, all in Queenie's favor, she was indorsed at once, and had she chosen, she might have been a belle and headed every clique in the house. But Queenie was far too sad and her heart was too full of pain to care for flattery, and yet in a way she was interested and amused with what she saw of life at the St. James, and liked to sit alone by herself in a quiet corner of the great parlor and watch the people around her—the devotees of whist, who night after night sat at the same table, with the same people, and usually with the same result; the dancers, who occasionally varied the monotony with a quadrille or a waltz; and the knots of lookers-on gathered here and there in groups, and whispering their confidences to each other. It was all very new and very strange to Queenie, who had never seen anything like it, and she was beginning to forget in part her great sorrow in the scenes around her, when an unexpected arrival brought the past back to her in all its bitterness, and made her shrink more than ever from intercourse with strangers. This arrival was none other than that of Mistress Anna Rossiter, nee Anna Ferguson, who had been three weeks a bride, and after doing Washington, as she expressed it, had resolved to see a little of Florida life before the season was fairly over and the Northerners gone home.

Miss Anna's wedding had been a very quiet one, owing to poor Phil's recent death, and only a few of the villagers had been honored with an invitation; but those so honored had been among the first in town—the Grangers, and Markhams, and Marshalls, against whom Anna had once rebelled so hotly because of fancied slights and indignities. It was now her turn to hold up her head, she thought: she was to be Mrs. Lord Seymour Rossiter, with a house in New York, and another on the Hudson if she liked. She was to have a maid, and diamonds, and her carriage, and servants in livery, for she liked those long coats and yellow boots, she said, and she meant to have her women servants wear caps, as she was told they did abroad.

Anna was very happy. The old days of dressmaking and drudgery were over. No more pricked red fingers for her, no more bundles to be carried home to those who bade her ring at the side instead of the front door.

All that was past and gone. The sign which had once so annoyed her was split and burned. It was hers now to snub instead of being snubbed, and so she began by slighting the very ones who had been kind to her, but whom she did not consider worthy of her notice in the days of her prosperity. She should begin her new life as she could hold out, and she would not have Tom, Dick, and Harry hanging to her skirts, she said, and she put aside the friends with whom she had been in the habit of associating intimately, and invited only those with whom it could scarcely be said she had ever been recognized as an equal. Margery was, of course, one of the guests, for she was now Miss Hetherton, of Hetherton Place, and it was an honor to claim her as a relation.

Mrs. La Rue was wholly ignored. A woman of her reputation, whose life had been a lie, had no right to expect civilities from the people she had deceived, Anna argued, and Mrs. La Rue's name was omitted from the list.

But the intended slight failed to touch the sad, remorseful woman, who now lived quite alone at the cottage, having resisted all Margery's entreaties that she should make her home at Hetherton Place. Since her confession, and especially since Queenie's departure for the South, she had fallen into a sad and silent mood, shrinking from every one, and preferring to live entirely alone, as solitude was best suited to such as she. And so she scarcely gave a thought to the wedding which took place one afternoon in the best room of Tom Ferguson's house, with only the elite of Merrivale looking on and commenting upon the airs of the bride and the childish delight of the bridegroom, who did not attempt to conceal his joy, but rubbed his hands in the exuberance of delight and kissed the bride many times the moment she was pronounced his wife.

There was a short trip to New York, and a long one to Washington, where Anna created a great sensation with her satins, and velvets, and diamonds, which she wore on all occasions. She had sold her youth and beauty for gold, and she meant to reap the full price of her charms. Every day she blossomed out in a new costume, with jewelry to match, and as she was really pretty, and could be very gracious when she tried, Mrs. Lord Seymour Rossiter, became the rage and was flattered, and admired, and complimented to her heart's content, and mentioned in the papers as the most distingue and lovely woman in Washington—notices which she read with great satisfaction at the breakfast-table every morning, and then passed to her husband, with the remark:

"How perfectly absurd! Did you ever read such nonsense?"

Anna was growing very fast, and talked of her relations, the Rossiters, and the Hethertons, and enjoyed herself immensely in her handsome suite of rooms at the Riggs House, where she would have spent a longer time, but for a letter received from Grandma Ferguson, which threw her into a wild state of alarm and apprehension. The good old lady had long wished to visit Washington and see the doin's, she wrote, and "she couldn't have a better time than when Anna was there to go round with her and show her the elephant. So, she'd about made up her mind to pick up and start, as her clothes were all nice and new, and Anna might expect her any day, and had better engage a room at once. A small one on the top floor would answer, as she did not mean to spend all her money on rooms, and she could just as well take some of her meals at a restaurant as not!"

"Oh-h!" and Anna fairly gasped as she read this letter, which she found lying by her plate one morning, when she came down to breakfast alone after a brilliant party, of which she had been the belle. "Oh-h!" and the cold sweat oozed from every pore as she thought of her grandmother swooping down upon her, and with her brown silk, and purple gloves, and pink ribbons, and dreadful grammar, demolishing the fair structure of blood, and family, and position, which she had secured for herself.

Knowing her grandmother as she did, she felt certain that she would come, if some decisive step were not taken to prevent it. And Anna took the decisive step, and turning her back upon the fresh fields of glory she had meant to win in Washington, she telegraphed immediately to her grandmother that she should leave the city that day, but said nothing of her destination.

"She would not mind following me to Europe, if she knew I was going there—the vulgar old thing!" she thought, with an indignant toss of fine-ladyism. "I will not have her spoiling everything. I am done with the old, hateful life. I am Mrs. Lord Seymour Rossiter and mistress of my own actions."

So she sent the telegram and then sought her husband, who had breakfasted before her and was reading his paper in his room.

"Dearest," she said, laying her hand caressingly upon his head, "I am so tired of Washington, where they say such silly things of me. Such a nonsensical article as there is in the paper this morning about the young and beautiful Mrs. Rossiter, whose sweet, fresh face and charming manners please every one, and whose dress is a marvel of taste and elegance. Why, they even estimated the value of my diamonds. I am sick of it all; it makes one so common; and then I know they would say the same of the next new-comer, if her dress was richer than mine. These reports are insufferable. Let's go away—to-night; go to Florida for a week or two: it is not too late, and I don't mind hot weather in the least. We shall be more quiet there, and I shall see more of you. Now, with the driving, and dressing, and calling, I scarcely have a bit of your company."

She was in his lap by this time and her fingers were lifting deftly his scant hair and fixing it over his bald spot. Whatever Anna might lack she knew how to manage her husband, who, throwing down his paper and encircling her slender waist, said to her:

"Sick of it, are you, Pussy? Why, I thought you liked it immensely: women generally do; but it shows your good sense not to want to be stared at and written up by a lot of snipper-snappers. But for heaven's sake don't go to Florida! You will roast alive."

The major had once been to St. Augustine in the days before the war, and it made him tired to think of the long, wearisome journey by land and the still worse trip by sea. But Anna's heart was set upon Florida, and she carried her point and left Washington that night with her three trunks and maid, who had been found in New York, and on whom Mrs. Anna called for the most trivial service, even to the picking up of her handkerchief, which it would seem she sometimes dropped on purpose, for the sake of showing her authority. Anna was very proud of her position and proud of her name, so out of the common order of names. Lord Seymour Rossiter had a sound of nobility in it, and she persuaded her husband to leave off the Mr. when he registered at hotels, "just to try the effect," she said. And so "Lord Seymour Rossiter, lady, and maid," was the record in the book at the St. James, which the bridal pair reached one evening about nine o'clock.

Of course such a registry attracted attention and comment, and before ten o'clock half the people in the parlor heard that a real live lord and lady had arrived, and great was the interest in and the curiosity to see them.

And Anna bore herself like a grand duchess, and had all the airs of twenty titled ladies, when next morning she stepped out of the elevator into the broad hall, the train of her blue morning dress sweeping far behind her, and a soft, fleecy white shawl wrapped gracefully and negligently around her. She knew she was creating a sensation, and her voice, never very low, was pitched a little higher as she asked the clerk if he had no private parlors—no sitting-rooms attached to the bedrooms. The clerk was very sorry, but there were no suites of rooms, he said; they were seldom called for, as the guests generally preferred sitting in the parlor, and hall, and upon the piazzas.

"Yes, but I do not," Anna replied, in her most supercilious tone; "and I think it very strange that a hotel like this should have no suites of rooms; but possibly you can obviate that difficulty by giving us an extra room. I should like the one adjoining mine. It will not be much trouble to take out the bed and convert it into a parlor."

She spoke as if the thing were settled, and was moving away, when the clerk stopped her by saying:

"But, madam, it is impossible to give you No. —, as it is already occupied by Miss Hetherton."

"Miss Hetherton! What Miss Hetherton, pray?" and Anna's voice lost the lady-like tone to which she had been trying to bring it since her accession of dignity.

Quietly turning the pages of the book back to a previous date, the clerk pointed to the entry, "Miss Hetherton, Merrivale, Mass.," while Anna repeated, scornfully:

"'Miss Hetherton, Merrivale Mass.!' Is she here, and alone?" while the elevating of her eyebrows, and the significant shrug of her shoulders expressed more than her words.

"You know the lady, then?" the clerk ventured to say; for, in spite of Anna's diamonds and airs, there was something about her which told him he could take more liberty with her than with many another guest of far less pretension.

"Know her? Yes; but I did not expect to find her here," Anna answered, and then swept on toward the dining-room door, where her husband was waiting for her.

Everybody looked up as she entered the room, and many whispers and many glances were exchanged as she passed on to her seat, which was quite at the end of the long hall; and so acute is the Yankee perception of the true and the false, the washed metal and the real, that even before she had been settled in her chair by her attentive husband, the verdict passed upon her by those for whose opinion she would care the most was, "Not a genuine lady, whatever her rank may be." There was too much show and arrogance about her, and the diamonds in her ears, and, more than all, the heavy cross and chain she wore, were sadly out of place at the breakfast-table.

Meanwhile another guest had entered the dining-room, a graceful little figure, clad in black, which was, however, relieved by plain linen collar and cuffs, and a cream-colored rose at the throat, which wonderfully heightened the effect and made Queenie an object to be looked after as she moved up the hall, the color deepening in her cheeks and her brilliant eyes lifted occasionally and flashing a look of recognition upon those she knew. Her seat was at the same table with Mistress Anna, who was never so startled in her life as she was when a hand was laid familiarly upon her shoulder and a voice she recognized said to her:

"Oh, Anna, are you here? I am so glad to see you!"

And Queenie was glad, for, though she had never liked Anna Ferguson much, the unexpected meeting with her in far-off Florida, where all were strangers, made her seem very near to the desolate, heart-sick girl, who could have fallen upon her neck and kissed her for the something in her face which brought the dead Phil to mind.

But Anna's manner was not provocative of any such demonstrations. She was not glad to see Queenie, for like all low, mean natures, she was ready to suspect others of what she knew she would do in similar circumstances, and when she learned that Queenie was in the hotel her first thought was that now her antecedents, of which she was so much ashamed, would be known, either from Queenie or Axie, neither of whom had much cause to love her, and thus the castle she had built for herself would be demolished.

And this was the reason why her manner toward Queenie was so cold and constrained, and even haughty, that the young girl felt repelled and wounded, and the hot blood mounted to her face and then left it deadly pale, as she took her seat at the table directly opposite Anna, who scarcely spoke to her again, except to ask some commonplace question or to remark upon the weather.

This little scene, however, was noticed by those sitting near, and the conclusion reached that the new-comer meant to slight Miss Hetherton; but it did not harm her one whit, for her sad, sweet face and quiet dignity of manner had won upon the guests, while, owing to Mrs. Strong's influence, some of the best and first people in town had called upon her, so that her standing was assured, and Anna's coldness could not matter, but it hurt her cruelly to be thus treated, when she was longing so much for sympathy, and she could scarcely restrain her tears until breakfast was over, and in the privacy of her room she could indulge her grief, with no one to see her but Axie, who learned at last the cause of her grief.

Axie was not a girl of many words, but there was a look in her black eyes which boded no good to Mrs. Anna, and, before the day was over, every one in the hotel at all interested in the matter knew exactly who Mrs. Lord Seymour Rossiter was and where she came from, and that at home, to use Axie's words, "she was of no kind o' count side of Miss Hetherton."

So Anna's star began to wane almost before it had risen, or would have done so but for her perseverance and push, which oftentimes compelled attention where it might not otherwise have been given. She was pretty, and fast, and rich, and this gained her favor with a certain class, and especially with the young men, with whom she was very popular. Night after night, while her husband played at whist or euchre in the gentlemen's room, she danced and flirted in the parlors, and wore her handsome dresses and diamonds, and furnished the cats with no end of gossip, and flattered herself that at last she was happy. With a woman's ready wit she soon discovered that she had made a mistake with regard to Queenie, and so she changed her tactics and tried to be very gracious to her, but Queenie did not need her patronage. She had scores of friends, and the days passed pleasantly and rapidly away. Axie had returned to the Park soon after Anna's arrival, and wrote her mistress at last that the house would be ready for her within a week, and at the end of that time Queenie left the Hotel with Pierre, and went to begin a new life in a home as unlike everything she had ever known as it well could be.

CHAPTER XLVII

THE YELLOW FEVER

It was very hot in Florida that summer, but it suited Queenie, who, like some tropical plant, seemed to thrive under the burning sun which affected even the negroes, accustomed to it as they were. Physically she had never been better than she was at Magnolia Park, or prettier either, for the bright color had crept back to her cheeks and her eyes had in them a look of softness and humility, while the expression of her face was ineffably sweet and gentle like the faces of some of the Madonnas. She had suffered terribly, and the fierce storm through which she had passed had left its marks upon her so that she would never again be quite the same dashing, impetuous girl she once had been. Margery wrote to her often,—long letters full of tenderness and affection, and entreaties for her to return to the home which was not the same without her.

From Grace and Ethel Rossiter she also heard frequently, and their letters touched her closely, as they always addressed her as their cousin, ignoring altogether the terrible thing which had separated her from them. Once in speaking of Margery Ethel said: "She is very lonely at Hetherton Place, though we go there often, and Mr. Beresford, we hear, is there every day."

This was underscored, and conveyed to Queenie's mind just the meaning Ethel meant it to convey. Mr. Beresford was daily growing more and more interested in Margery, and Queenie rejoiced that it was so. She was so glad for Margery to be happy in a good man's love, though her own sun had set in deepest gloom, and there was a ceaseless moan in her heart for poor Phil, while the load of humiliation which had come so suddenly upon her seemed sometimes greater than she could bear.

"If I only had something to do which would make me forget myself a little I should be happier," she thought, as morning after morning she awoke to the same monotonous round of duties, or, rather, occupation of trying to kill the time.

She had no real duties, for everything pertaining to the household arrangements was managed by Aunt Judy, who petted her young mistress as if she had been a queen, while both Pierre and Axie, watched vigilantly to anticipate every want before it was framed in words.

Mrs. Strong was absent on her plantation near Lake Jackson, and thus Queenie was left almost entirely alone and free to let her morbid fancies feed upon themselves. She did need something to do, and at last the something came, though in a very different form from what she would have chosen had it been hers to choose.

As the summer advanced it grew hotter and hotter until the nights were like the days, and there came no breath of air to relieve the dreadful heat.

There were rumors of sunstroke here and there, and talk of the sickness which must ensue if the state of things continued. And still in middle Florida it was comparatively healthy, and the air was free from malaria; but farther to the north, where a city spread itself over miles of territory, an ominous cloud was gathering. Once before the town had been scourged as with the plague, and the terror-stricken inhabitants had fled to the country for refuge from the pestilence, which oftentimes overtook them on the road and claimed them for its victims. And now it was coming again—was lurking in the corners of the lanes and alleys, where poverty and filth held high carnival—was breathed in the poisonous air which brooded over the doomed city like a pall, until at last it was there, and men spoke the awful word to each other in whispers, while their voices shook with fear and their hearts sank as they remembered the past and thought of the possible future. The yellow fever was in their midst, and though as yet confined to the poorer classes and the unfrequented parts of the city, the people knew too well that, like fire applied to cotton, it would spread until there was no house however grand, or spot however exclusive, which its shadow would not reach, its horrid presence threaten. The city was doomed, and as the days went by and the disease and danger grew, and the death roll increased, and men who walked the streets to-day were dead to-morrow, a panic seized upon the terror-stricken inhabitants, who fled before the horror as those who live on a frontier in time of war flee from the rapidly advancing enemy. Then it was, when the city was almost deserted, that the cry went up for help for the sick and the dying. And the North heard that cry as well as the South, and poured out her treasures with a most liberal hand, and "help for Memphis" was the watchword everywhere. Physicians were wanted, with nurses for the sick and deserted ones, and this demand it was which tried to the very quick the courage of those on whom it was made.

It was an easy matter to give of one's substance to the needy, to drop the money into the boxes placed everywhere for that purpose, but to take one's life in his hands and go into the very jaws of death, where the air was full of infection and the very flowers seemed to exhale a deadly poison, was a different thing. But there were hundreds of brave men and women who, from the New England hills, and the prairies of the West, and the pine glades of the South, went to the rescue, and by their noble heroism proved themselves more Christ-like than human. In her far-off Florida home Queenie heard the cry for help, and to herself she said:

"Here is something for me to do. Here is my chance, and I'll take it."

Had she known just what yellow fever was, she might have hesitated ere she made her decision, or having made it, might have drawn back from it at the frantic entreaties of Pierre, who, when she communicated her intention to him, fell upon his knees and with blanched face and chattering teeth begged her not to go where there was certain death for them both, for his place was with her: if she went, he must go also. Axie, too, tried to dissuade her from her purpose, but Queenie would not listen.

"I am not afraid," she said. "I shall not take the fever. I never catch things as some people do. I sat three hours once with a servant who had the smallpox, and who died two hours after, and I did not take it. Somebody must go, and I have nobody to care much if I should die. Nobody but Margery, and she would say I was doing right. So pack my trunk, like a good, brave girl, for I must be off to-morrow. Something which I cannot resist is calling me to Memphis. What it is I cannot tell, but I must go."

And so the next night the northern train for Savannah took in it Pierre and Queenie, bound for the fever-smitten city where the people were dying so fast and help was sorely needed. By some strange coincidence while Queenie was making up her mind to go to Memphis, Christine La Rue was already there. She, too, had heard the cry for help, and it roused her from the state bordering on insanity into which she was falling.

"I am going," she said, to Margery, "for I feel that I can do some good. I am not a bad nurse, and if I can save one life or ease one dying pillow, maybe it will atone to God for some of my misdeeds. I am not afraid of the fever, and if I should take it and die, better so than end my own life, as I am often tempted to do."

Her mind was made up, and Margery did not oppose her, but promised her plenty of money in case it should be needed. And so the mother and the daughter were bound for the same work—the one to have something to do, the other to atone. It was a fancy of Mrs. La Rue to assume the gray dress of a lay sister, as she felt freer and safer in this garb, and could go where she pleased. It was not her wish to be hampered by any restrictions; and when the physicians saw how efficient and fearless she was, they let her take her own course and do as she liked.

Sister Christine was the name by which she was known, and many a poor dying wretch blessed her with his last breath, and commended to her care some loved one struggling in the next room, perhaps, with the dread destroyer. Money Christine had in plenty, for Margery kept her supplied, and it was spent like water where it was of any avail, so that Sister Christine became a power in the desolated city, and was known in every street and alley of the town. Queenie had written to Margery of her intentions, and with a cry of horror on her lips Margery read the letter and then telegraphed to Christine:

"Queenie is or will be there. Find her at once and send her away. Queenie must not die."

There was a faint smile about Christine's lips as she read the dispatch, and then whispered to herself, "No, Queenie must not die," while her pulse quickened a little as she thought what happiness it would be to nurse the fever-tossed girl, should she be stricken down, and bring her back to life and health.

"I'll find her, if she is here, and keep a watch over her," she said; and two days after they met together high up in a tenement house, where, in a dark, close room, two negro children lay dead, and the mother was dying.

Queenie was doing her work bravely and well, seeking out the worst cases, and by her sweetness and tenderness almost bringing back the life after it had gone out. Always attended by Pierre, who carried with him every disinfectant of which he had ever heard, she went fearlessly from place to place where she was needed most, but found frequently that Sister Christine had been there before her. Naturally she felt some curiosity with regard to this mysterious person, whose praises were on every lip, and also a great desire to see her.

"If she could impart to me some of her skill, I might do more good and save more lives," she said to Pierre, and there was a thought of the woman in her heart as she bent over the dying negress, wiping the black vomit from her lips and the sweat-drops from her brow. "She might have saved her, perhaps," she said, just as the door opened and the gray sister came in.

Far gone as was the poor colored woman, she still had enough of sight and sense to recognize the new-comer, and something like a cry of joy escaped her as she managed to say:

"Sister Christine!"

In an instant Queenie sprang to her feet, and mother and daughter stood confronting each other for a moment, neither speaking, but each looking into the other's eyes with an eager questioning look. In Christine's there was love, and tenderness, and anxiety and fear, all blended together, while in Queenie's there was great surprise and something like gladness, too. She was the first to speak.

"Christine," she said, "Sister Christine they call you, though I never dreamed it was you, how came you here, and when?"

Christine told her how and when, and then repeated Margery's message—to find her and send her away.

"She says Queenie must not die, and I say so, too. Will you go before it is too late?" she asked, and Queenie answered her:

"No, my place is here, and I am glad you are here, too. It makes me feel safer and stronger."

"Oh, Queenie, Queenie, God bless you for saying even so much," and the woman who had stood undaunted by many a death-bed trembled like a leaf as she snatched Queenie's hand to her lips, and then went swiftly from the room, where her services were no longer needed, for while she was speaking the negress was dead.

That night a telegram went to Margery: "She will not go away, and she shall not die."

So there was nothing for Margery to do but pray earnestly and unceasingly for the young girl who seemed to bear a charmed life, so fearlessly did she meet every peril and overcome every difficulty. Almost as popular as Sister Christine, she was hailed with delight everywhere, and more than one owed his recovery to her timely aid. At last, however, she began to flag a little, and was not quite as strong to endure as she had been. There were about her no symptoms of the fever; she was only tired and worn, she said to Pierre, as she sat in her room one evening. The day had been damp and sultry, and the night had closed in with rain and fog, while the air was heavy as if laden with noxious vapors. Queenie had thrown off her street dress and put on a comfortable wrapper, when there came a quick, sharp ring, and Pierre brought her a note, or rather a bit of paper torn from a pocket tablet, and on which was written in French:

"Come immediately to No. 40, —— street. You are needed there.
"Christine."

The handwriting was very uneven, as if penned in great excitement, and as Queenie looked at it there swept over her an undefinable apprehension of something, she could not tell what—a feeling that this call from Christine on such a night was no ordinary call, and the need no ordinary one.

"I believe I am growing nervous myself, and that will never do," she thought, as she felt a faintness stealing over her and a kind of chill creeping through her veins communicated, she believed, by the message she had received.

Never before had Christine sent for her, but, on the contrary, had always tried to shield and spare her as much as possible from fatigue or exposure; but this "Come, you are needed," was imperative, and, with trembling hands and a strange sinking from what she was to do, she donned her usual every-day attire, and with Pierre started for No. . It was a private hotel, which had remained free from infection until within a day or two, when the fever had suddenly broken out in its most malignant form. Two of the inmates had already died, one the wife of the proprietor, who with his guests had fled in dismay, leaving behind a young man who had come to the city the previous day, and who was now lying senseless in an upper chamber, where Christine had found him, burning with fever and raving with delirium. It was a very bad case, aggravated by nervous excitement and fatigue; but she had done for him what she could, and then had sent for Queenie, whom she met on the landing outside the sick-room, and to whom she explained why she had sent for her.

"He is very sick," she said, "and needs the closest watching, and I know of no one who would be as faithful as you, for I must be elsewhere to-night. This weather has increased the danger tenfold, and there is no telling where it will end."

Then she gave some minute directions with regard to the treatment of the patient who, she said, was sleeping, and must be allowed to sleep as long as possible. She seemed greatly excited as she talked, and there was a glitter in her eyes, and occasionally an incoherency in her manner of expressing herself, especially with regard to the sick man, which made Queenie look curiously at her, wondering if she were altogether in her right mind. When all had been said which was necessary to say Christine still stood irresolute, as it were, looking fixedly at Queenie; then, with a sudden, upward movement of her arms, she wound them around the young girl's neck, and kissing her forehead, said:

"God bless you, my child, and keep you, and all those whom you love, from harm."

There were bright red spots upon her cheeks, but the lips which touched Queenie were cold as ice, as was the hand which accidentally brushed Queenie's cheek. Ordinarily Queenie would have resented this liberty, but she did not now. She was too much excited to resent any thing, and she was so glad afterward that it was so—glad that she had some thought and care for Christine, to whom she said, as she felt her lips and hand:

"How cold you are, and why do you tremble so? You surely must be ill.

Don't go out to-night; there must be plenty of vacant rooms here. Stay and rest yourself. We cannot let you die."

She had one of Christine's cold hands in her own, chafing and rubbing it as she spoke, but when she said, so kindly, "We cannot let you die," the woman drew it away suddenly, and bursting into a paroxysm of tears, exclaimed:

"Better so; better for me to die; but for you, oh! Queenie, you must live— you and——Oh, my child, summon all your strength and courage; you will need it. There is hard work ahead for you. Do you think you can meet it?"

Queenie did not know what the woman meant, but she was greatly moved and agitated, and shook from head to foot with a nameless terror.

"You, too, are cold are trembling, and that will never do. Drink this," Christine said, pouring from a flask which she always carried with her a quantity of brandy, and offering it to Queenie, who swallowed it in one draught.

The brandy steadied her nerves, and after standing a moment watching Christine as she went slowly down the stairs, holding to the banisters, like one suffering from great physical weakness, she turned toward the door of the sick-room, and opening it softly, went in.

CHAPTER XLVIII

THE OCCUPANT OF NO. 40

It was a large, handsome room, but it seemed gloomy and cheerless now, with only a night-lamp burning on the table, casting weird shadows here and there, and only partially revealing the form upon the bed of a tall young man, who lay with his face turned from the light and half buried in the pillow. Outside the counterpane one arm and hand were lying, and Queenie noticed that the latter was white and shapely as a woman's, and noticed, too, the mass of light brown, slightly curling hair, which clustered around the sick man's head and sent an indescribable thrill through her veins, as of something familiar. The man was young, she knew, though she had not seen his face, and dared not see it lest she should disturb him.

"Let him sleep; it will do him good and keep back the dreadful vomit," Christine had said, and not for worlds would Queenie disobey her. She held a human life in her keeping, and with her finger on her lip to Pierre, who crouched almost at her feet, she seated herself in an arm-chair just where she could see the outline of the figure upon the bed, and there for hours she sat and watched, and listened to the irregular breathing, while every kind of wild fancy danced through her brain, and her limbs began at last to feel prickly and numb, and a sense of cold and faintness to steal over her.

The air in the room was hot and oppressive though the windows were opened wide. Outside, the rain was falling heavily, and the sky as black as ink; there was no sound to break the awful stillness, except the occasional tread of some physician or nurse on duty, or the crash of distant wheels, whose meaning Queenie understood full well, shuddering as she thought of the rapid burials which the peril made necessary, and remembering what she had read of the great plague in London, where the death-cart rolled nightly through the street, while the dreadful cry was heard:

"Bring out your dead; bring out your dead."

The words kept repeating themselves over and over in Queenie's mind until her brain became confused; the present faded away into the far-off past, and she was one of those weary watchers in London, listening to the cry:

"Bring out your dead."

And she was bringing hers—was carrying the young man whose long limbs dragged upon the floor, and whose head drooped upon her shoulder, while his dead face, not yet cold, touched hers with a caressing motion which brought with it a thought of poor Phil, lying beneath the Indian waters.

It was a horrid nightmare, and Queenie struggled with it a moment, and then awoke with a cry of Phil upon her lips—a cry so loud that the sleeper upon the bed started a little, and moaned, and said something indistinctly, and moved uneasily, then settled again into slumber, and all was quiet as ever.

But Queenie stood erect upon her feet, rigid as a piece of marble, and almost as white, while her eyes, which seemed to Pierre to shoot out gleams of fire, were turned wildly toward the form lying so motionless across the room, with the white, shapely hand still outside the counterpane, and the light brown wavy hair upon the pillow. He had spoken—had called a name, which the excited girl had recognized as her own. She could not be mistaken. In answer to her cry for Phil the fever patient had aroused a little and responded:

"Queenie."

She was sure of it. He might not have meant her, it is true. There were other Queenies in the world, no doubt, but he had called her name—this man, who in her dream she was carrying to the death-cart, and who might perhaps, go there when the morning dawned.

There was a clock upon the mantel, and Queenie saw that it was half-past two. The early summer morning would soon break, and then she would see the face of this stranger who had called for Queenie, and whose head and hair were so like her lost Phil's that, as she looked, with straining, eager eyes, and whirling brain, it seemed to her at last that it was Phil himself—Phil, drowned and dead, perhaps, but still Phil, come back to her in some incomprehensible manner, just to mock her a moment, and then to be snatched away again forever. But she would see him first distinctly, would know if it were a phantom or a reality lying there upon the bed within her reach, for she had advanced a few steps forward, and could have touched the head upon the pillow.

"Pierre," she said, at last, when she could endure the suspense no longer—"Pierre," and her voice sounded to herself like the echo of something a thousand miles away, "am I going mad, or is that—is that—" and she pointed to the tall form on the bed.

Not comprehending her in the least, Pierre stared at her, with a great fear that her mind was really unsettled by all the terrible scenes through which she had passed.

"Is it what?" he asked, coming to her side, and she replied:

"Bring the light. I must see the face of this young man. I cannot wait till morning."

"But, mademoiselle," Pierre remonstrated, "think of the danger to him. Christine's orders were to let him sleep; he was not to be disturbed."

"Nor shall I disturb him; but I shall see him. Bring the light!" Queenie said, peremptorily, as she moved to the other side of the bed, toward which the sick man's face was turned.

Carefully pushing down the pillow, so as to bring the features more distinctly to view, Queenie stood for one brief instant gazing upon them; then, turning to Pierre, she whispered:

"Nearer, Pierre; hold the lamp a little nearer, please."

He obeyed her, and as the full rays of the light fell upon the white, pinched face of the sleeper, Queenie threw her arms high in the air, and, in a voice Pierre would never have recognized as hers, cried out:

"Oh, Pierre, Pierre! it is—it is—my Phil—come back to me again! Christine! Christine! come, and help!"

It was a loud, wailing cry, and the next moment Queenie lay across the foot of the bed, where she had fallen in a death-like swoon, while over her bent Christine. She had not left the house at all, but had sat below, waiting for some such denouement when the truth should become known to Queenie.

Christine had found the young man late the previous afternoon, and recognized him at once, experiencing such a shock as had set every nerve quivering, and made her feel that at last her own strength was giving way. To save him for Queenie was her great desire, and, with a prayer on her lips, and a prayer in her heart, she worked as she had never worked before to allay the burning fever and quiet his disordered mind.

Once, during a lucid interval, he looked into her face, and knew her.

"Christine," he said, faintly, "where is Queenie? I came to find her. Don't let me die till I have seen her."

"Queenie is here. I will send for her at once. Do not be afraid; I will not let you die. Your case is not very bad," Christine replied, speaking thus emphatically and against her own convictions, because she saw how frightened he was himself, and knew that this would only augment the disease and lessen his chances for recovery.

"Keep very quiet, and I'll soon have you well," she said, and Phil did whatever she bade him do, though his mind began to wander again, and he talked constantly of Queenie, whom he had come to find.

At last, however, he fell away to sleep, and then it was that Christine sent for Queenie, and establishing her in the room, went out into the adjoining chamber and waited, knowing that sooner or later she would be needed. All through the weary hours which preceded Queenie's cry for help she sat alone in the darkness, alternately shaking with cold and burning with fever, while in her heart was a feeling amounting to certainty that her work was done, that the deadly faintness stealing over her at intervals, and making her so sick and weak, was a precursor of the end. But she must live long enough to save Philip Rossiter, and give him back to Queenie, who might think more kindly of her when she was gone. So she fought back her symptoms bravely, and rubbed her cold, damp face when it was the coldest, and then leaned far out of the open window into the falling rain when it was the hottest.

And thus the time passed on until her quick ear caught the sound of voices and footsteps in the sick-room, and she heard Queenie's wild cry for her as if in that hour of peril she was the one person in all the world of whom there was need. Queenie had turned to her at last as the child turns to its mother in peril, and with swift feet Christine went to the rescue, and almost before Pierre knew she was there, she had the unconscious girl in her arms and was bearing her into the room, where for hours she had waited so patiently. Fixing her in a safe and upright position upon a cushion, she ran back to Phil, who, she knew, must be her first and principal care.

When Queenie's shriek echoed through the room so near to him, he had roused from his sleep, and was moaning and talking to himself, without, apparently, any real consciousness as to where he was. But Christine's soothing hands, and the medicine she administered quieted him, and leaving him in Pierre's care, she went back to Queenie, who was recovering from her swoon.

"Tell me," she gasped, when she was able to speak, "Was it a dream, or was it Phil? Tell me, Christine, is it Phil, and will he die?"

"It is Phil," Christine replied, "saved from the sea, I know not how, only that he is here, that he came seeking for you, and I found him with the fever, late yesterday afternoon, and did for him what I could. Then I sent for you, and the rest you know. Only be quiet now. I do not think he will die."

"Oh, save him, save him, and you shall have my love forever. I have been cold and proud, but I will be so no longer if you give me back my Phil," Queenie said, with choking sobs, as she knelt at Christine's feet and clasped the hem of her dress.

"I will do what I can," Christine replied, while again through every nerve throbbed the old, sick feeling which she could not put aside, even in her exquisite joy that Queenie might at last be won.

"Too late; it has come too late," she thought to herself, while to Queenie she said: "I must go to him now, for what I do must be done quickly. A few hours later and it will be too late."

So they went together to the sick-room, where Phil lay with his face turned more fully to the light and showing distinctly how pinched and pallid it was. Had Queenie's own life depended upon it, she could not have forborne going up to him and softly kissing his pale forehead; then she knelt down beside him, and so close to him that her dark hair touched the curls of light brown as she buried her face in her hands, and Christine knew that she was praying earnestly that he might be spared to her. At last, just as the dawn was breaking and the first gray of the morning was stealing into the room, he moved as if about to waken, and with a quick, imperative movement of her hand Christine put Queenie behind her, saying as she did so: "He must not see you yet. Keep out of his sight till I tell you to come."

Fearful lest she should attract his attention if she left the room, Queenie crouched upon the floor, close beside the bed, and waited with a throbbing heart for the moment when she might speak and claim her love. Phil was better; the long sleep had done him good, but there was a drowsiness over him still, and he only opened his eyes a moment, and, seeing Christine bending over him, smiled gratefully upon her, and said:

"You are so good to me."

Then he took the draught she gave him and slept again, this time quietly and sweetly as a child, while Queenie sat upon the floor, fearing to move or stir lest she should disturb him. Slowly the minutes dragged on until at last it was quite light in the room. The heavy rain had ceased; the dense fog had lifted, and the air which came in at the window was cool and pure, and seemed to have in it something of life and invigoration.

"The weather has changed, thank God," Christine murmured, while Queenie, too, whispered, "Thank God! thank God!"

Phil must have felt the change, for he breathed more naturally and there came a faint color to his lips, and at last, just as a ray of sunlight stole into the room and danced upon the wall above his head, he woke to perfect consciousness, and, stretching his hand toward Christine said:

"You have saved my life and I thank you; but for you I should have died when the dreadful sickness came. How long have I been here, and where is Queenie? I dreamed she was here."

As the tones of the voice she had never expected to hear again fell upon her ear Queenie could no longer restrain herself, but springing up, she bent over Phil and said:

"I am here—Phil, my love, my darling, and nothing shall part us again. I am not your cousin, and I can love you now."

She was kneeling beside him, with one arm under his neck, while with the other hand she caressed his face, and kissing him passionately continued:

"O, Phil, I thought you were dead, and it broke my heart, for I did love you all the time, and I found it out when it was too late and you were gone, and I mourned for you so much, and all the brightness went out from my life; but it will come back again with you, my darling! my darling!"

Her tears were falling like rain upon his face, and her voice was choked with sobs, as she made this avowal of her love, without a shadow of shame or feeling that she was doing anything unmaidenly. Phil was hers. Nothing could change that, or his love for her. She was as sure of him as she was that she breathed, and she had no hesitancy in pouring out the full measure of her affection for him. Both Christine and Pierre had stolen from the room, leaving the lovers alone in that first blissful moment of their reunion. For a time Phil lay perfectly still and took her caresses and kisses in silence. Then summoning all his strength, he wound his arms around the little girl, and hugging her close to him whispered:

"Heaven can scarcely be better than this. Oh, Queenie! my darling! my pet!"

He was very weak, and Queenie saw it, and drawing herself from him said:

"You must not talk any more now. You must get well, and then I can hear it all—where you have been and why you are not dead. Oh, Phil, it was so horrible—everything which has happened to me since you went away. I am nobody—nobody, Phil; no name, no right to be born, and I was once so proud. Did they tell you, Phil? Do you know who I am?"

"Yes, they told me; I know, poor little Queenie," Phil replied, with a tighter clasp of the hand which lay in his.

She did not ask him if it would make any difference with his love. She knew it would not. She had always felt sure of Phil; he was hers for ever, and the old joy began to come back, and the old light sparkled in her eyes, which shone like stars as she went on:

"It was so dreadful when I found it out, and I wanted to die, because you, too, were dead, or I thought you were, and I used to whisper to you in the dark nights, when I could not sleep, and I thought maybe you would come and let me know in some way that you were sorry for me. Where were you, Phil, when I was wanting you so much?"

"Very, very far away, but I cannot tell you now," said Phil, knowing himself that he must not talk longer then; but he would not let her leave him; he wanted her there beside him, where he could touch her hands, and look into her face and beaming eyes, which dazzled and bewildered him with their brightness.

So Queenie sat by him all that morning, seldom speaking to him, but often bending over him to kiss his forehead or hands, and occasionally murmuring;

"Dear Phil, and I am so glad—so happy. Nothing will ever trouble me again."

"Not even the Fergusons?" Phil answered her once, with his old, teasing smile, which made him so like the Phil of other days that Queenie laughed aloud, and, shaking her head gayly, said:

"No, not even grandma's purple gloves can ever worry me again. Oh, Phil, I have repented so bitterly of all my pride, and I shall never, never be so any more—shall never be angry with you, or any one, or indulge in one of my moods! I wish I could make you understand how changed I am, for I see you do not quite believe me."

Nor did he, though he smiled lovingly upon her, and lifting his hand feebly smoothed her fair round cheek, where her blushes were burning so brightly. He knew that Queenie could not change her nature any more than the leopard can change his spots—knew that at times she would be the same little willful, imperious girl she had always been, defying his authority and setting at naught his wishes. And he would not have her otherwise if he could; he should not know her if the claws were always sheathed and she was gentle and sweet as she was now. Loving and true she would always be, and so repentant when her moods were over that it would be well worth his while to bear with them occasionally, as he was sure to have to do. But he did not tell her so; he did not tell her anything, for he was too weak to talk, so he only looked his love and happiness through his eyes, which rested constantly upon her face, until at last even that became to him as something seen through a mist, not altogether real, and he again fell into a quiet sleep, with his hand resting in Queenie's.

CHAPTER XLIX

SISTER CHRISTINE

So absorbed had Queenie been with Phil that she had failed to notice anything which was passing around her, or to think of anything except her great happiness. She knew that some time during the morning Pierre had brought her coffee and rolls, which he had managed to find somewhere near, he said, and which he made her eat. He had also given her some orders with regard to Phil's medicines, saying that Madame La Rue bade him do so, and to say that Miss Hetherton must be very particular not to forget. And Queenie had not forgotten that, though all else was a blank to her until Phil went to sleep, and she sat watching him and wondering by what strange chance the sea had given up its dead and restored him to her. Then, as she heard a city clock strike eleven, she began to think how fast the hours had sped, and to wonder a little at Christine's prolonged absence from the room. And still that did not surprise her much, for she naturally supposed she had gone to some other sick bed, where she was needed more than there with Phil.

"There is a great deal of good in her, and I must always be kind to her because of what she has done for Phil," she thought, and she felt glad that all the old bitterness and resentment were gone, and that although she could not think of Christine as her mother, she could think of her quietly and calmly as of one who, if she had greatly sinned, had also greatly suffered for the sin and was trying to atone. "Phil and I will take care of her, though she cannot, of course, live with us. She will not expect that;" she thought, and her mind was busy with castles of the future, when Pierre looked in again just for an instant, and seeing Phil asleep, shut the door at once and went out again before she could ask him a question.

But in the glimpse she got of him, it seemed to her that there was an unusual look of concern upon his face, while through the open door she caught a faint sound of voices in the distance, and footsteps hurrying here and there. What was it? she asked herself, and felt tempted to go out and see, but Phil's hand was clasping hers and she would not free herself from it lest she should awaken him. So she still sat on till the clock struck twelve and the hum of voices was occasionally borne to her ears by the opening of some door further up the hall. There was somebody in the other part of the house besides Pierre—somebody sick, too; judging from the sounds, and she grew so nervous at last and curious upon the subject, that she gradually withdrew her hand from Phil's, and rising softly was about to leave the room, when Pierre looked in again, and this time she could not be mistaken with regard to the expression on his face, which was very pale and troubled as it looked wistfully at her.

"What is it, Pierre?" she asked in a whisper, going close to him and observing that he stood against the door as if to keep her from passing. "Whose voices do I hear, and is any one sick? I was just coming to ascertain. Let me pass, please."

"No, no, mademoiselle. Don't come. She said you were not to know. We are doing all we can for her." Pierre cried, in great alarm, thus letting out the secret he had been told to keep.

"Do all you can for her? For whom? Who is it that is sick, and said I must not know?" Queenie asked, as she put the old man aside, and opening the door, drew him with her into the hall. "Now tell me the truth," she continued. "Is some one sick whom I ought to see? Is it—Christine?"

"Yes," he answered, "it is Madame Christine, and she is very bad. She will die, the doctor fears, but she said you must not know. You must not leave Mr. Rossiter for her and she sent me many times to see how he was."

Pierre was right, for in a small room at the end of the hall Christine La Rue was dying. She who had braved so much and borne so much and passed through so many dangers unscathed, had at last succumbed to the terrible disease which she knew was creeping upon her, when she sent for Queenie to share her vigils by Phil's bedside.

"I must not give up yet; I must endure and bear until he is out of danger. I must save him for her sake," she thought, and fought down with a desperate courage and iron will the horrid sensations stealing over her so fast and making her sometimes almost beside herself with dizziness and languor.

But when the crisis was past and she felt sure Phil was safe, she could endure it no longer, and with one long, lingering look at Queenie, whom she felt she should never see again, she started for her own lodgings.

"I can die there alone and so trouble no one," she thought, as she made her way to the staircase.

But on the first landing her strength failed her and she fell upon the floor, where she lay, or rather sat in a half upright position, leaning against the wall with her face in her hands, until a voice roused her and she looked up to see a man standing before her and asking who she was and why she was there. It was the proprietor of the house, who, ashamed of his cowardice, had returned and going first through the rooms below where everything was as he had left it, started to ascend the stair to the chambers above, when he came upon Christine, whom he had often seen on her errands of mercy, but whom he did not recognize until she looked up and spoke to him. Then he knew her, and exclaimed:

"Sister Christine! What are you doing here, and what is the matter with you?"

"I am sick—I have the fever," she replied; "and if you are afraid, leave me at once."

He was mortally afraid, but he was not so unmanly as to leave a woman like Christine to die uncared for at the head of his own staircase, and helping her to the nearest room where there was a bed, he started for a physician. Meeting in the lower hall with Pierre, who had been out for Queenie's coffee, and who explained to him that his house held another patient, he told him of Christine and where she was, bidding him look after her until help came from some other quarter.

But Christine was past all human aid. The disease had attacked her in its worst form, and she knew she should not live to see another sun setting. She was very calm, however, and only anxious for Queenie and Phil.

"They must not be disturbed—they must not know," she said to Pierre, to whom she gave some orders concerning Phil's medicines, which Pierre took to his mistress.

"Don't tell her I am sick; don't let her know until I am dead. Then tell her I was so glad to die and leave her free, and that I loved her so much, and am so sorry for the past," she said to Pierre, who, half distracted with all he was passing through, wrung his hands nervously, and promised all she required.

But when Queenie began to suspect, and insisted upon knowing the truth, he told her, adding, as he saw her about to dart away from him toward Christine's room:

"You better not go there; she does not need you. One of the sisters is with her, and she said you must stay with monsieur. All her anxiety is for him and you—none for herself. She seems so glad to die!"

He might as well have talked to the wind for all the heed Queenie gave him. Bidding him sit by Phil until he awoke, and then come for her if she was needed, she went quickly to the room where Christine lay, with death stamped on every lineament of her face, but with a calm peaceful expression upon it, which told that she was glad for the end so fast approaching.

When Queenie entered, her eyes were closed, but they opened quickly, and a smile of joy and surprise broke over her face, when Queenie exclaimed:

"Oh, Christine, you are sick, and you did not let me know it, or I should have come before!"

For an instant Christine's lips quivered in a pitiful kind of way; then the great tears rolled down her cheeks as she whispered faintly:

"I am sick—I am dying; but I did not want you to know. I wished to spare you and him. How is he now?"

Queenie explained that he was sleeping quietly, and that she believed all danger had passed. Then, sitting down by the bedside, she took the hot, burning hands in hers, and rubbed and bathed them as carefully and gently as if they had been Phil's, instead of this woman's, toward whom she had felt so bitter and resentful. All that was gone now, and she was conscious of a strange feeling stirring within her as she sat and met the dying eyes fixed upon her with so much yearning tenderness and love. This woman was her mother. Nothing could change that; and whatever her faults had been, she was a good woman now, Queenie believed; and, as the dim eyes met hers so constantly and appealingly, she bent close to the pillow, and said:

"Mother, I am sorry I was so unforgiving and hard. It came so suddenly. Forgive me if you can."

A low, pitiful cry was Christine's only answer for a moment, and then she said:

"I have nothing to forgive; the wrong was all my own, and I deserved your scorn. But oh, Queenie, my child, you can never know how I was deceived, or how wholly I trusted your father whom I loved so much, and after I had kept Margery's birth a secret, I must go on concealing. There was no other way. He would have murdered me, or left me to starve with you. Oh, Margery. Margery, my other child! and, Queenie, you will not mind if I say my dearest child, for she has been all the world to me. Tell her so, Queenie; tell her I blessed her with my last breath, and loved her with all my strength, and soul, and might. She is so sweet, so good, so true! God bless her, and make her perfectly happy!"

During this conversation, which was carried on in French, the sister whom the physician had sent to attend Christine stood looking on wonderingly, and never dreaming of the relationship between the two. She was, however, anxious lest so much talking and excitement should be injurious to her patient, and she said so to Queenie, who replied:

"Yes, you are right. I should try to quiet her now. If you will be kind enough to look after the young man in No. 40, I will stay with Sister Christine. She wishes it to be so. She was my nurse in France. I knew her—her—"

Queenie hesitated a moment, and then added:

"Knew her daughter. She was talking of her to me."

This satisfied the woman, who, bowing assent, went from the room, leaving the two alone.

For a time Christine lay perfectly still, with her eyes closed, but her lips were constantly moving, and Queenie knew that she was praying, for she caught the words:

"Forgive for Christ's sake, who forgave the thief at the very last hour!"

And all the while Queenie held the hot hands in hers and occasionally smoothed the gray hair back from the pale brow where the sweat of death was gathering so fast. At last Christine opened her eyes and looked fixedly at Queenie, who said to her very gently:

"What is it? Do you wish to tell me something?"

"Yes," the dying woman answered, faintly. "I hope I am forgiven, and that I shall find rest beyond the grave. I used to pray so much in the cottage when I was alone—pray sometimes all night with my face on the cold floor. But the peace I asked for would not come. There was always a horror of blackness before me until I came here, when the darkness has been clearing, and now there is peace and joy, for I feel that God forgives me all my sin, and you, my child, have forgiven me too, and called me mother, and Phil is alive and safe. I've nothing more to live for, and I am so glad to die."

She talked but little after that, and when she did speak her mind was wandering in the past, now at Chateau des Fleurs, now in Rome, where she watched by her mistress' bedside, but mostly in Marseilles, where her baby was born, "her darling little girl baby," whom she bade Queenie be kind to when she was gone. Then she talked of Margery and Paris, and the apartments in the Rue St. Honore, until her voice was only a whisper, and Queenie could not distinguish a word. She was dying very fast, and just at the last, before her life went out forever, Queenie bent over her, and kissing her softly, whispered:

"Mother, do you know that I am here—Queenie—your little girl?"

"Yes, yes," she gasped, and a look of unutterable love and satisfaction shone in the eyes which looked up at Queenie. "I know you are Queenie—the baby born at Marseilles—my own—and you kiss me and call me mother. God bless you, my child, and make you very happy. I am glad for your sake that I am going away. Good-by, my darling, good-by!"

She never spoke again, though it was an hour or more before Queenie loosed her hold of the hand which clung so tightly to hers, and closing the eyes which looked at her to the last, smoothed the bed-clothes decently, and then going out to Pierre, who was waiting in the hall, told him that all was over.

Sister Christine was dead, and there was mourning for her in the city where she was so well known, and where her kindness and gentleness and courage had won her so many friends, some of whom followed her remains to their last resting-place, and wept for her as one long known and well beloved. Every respect which it was possible under the circumstances to pay her was paid to her. Many gathered about the grave where they buried her, just after the sun setting on the same day of her death. It was Queenie who prepared her for the coffin, suffering no other hands to touch her but her own.

"She nursed me when I was a baby, and I must care for her now," she said to Sister Agatha, when she remonstrated with her and offered to take the task from her hands.

And to Queenie it was a mournful pleasure thus to care for the woman who had been her mother, and who, she felt, was truly good and repentant at the last.

"I am glad I feel so kindly toward her—glad I called her mother," she thought, and was conscious of a keen pain in her heart as she looked upon the white dead face on which suffering and remorse had left their marks.

Notwithstanding the hour and her own fatigue, Queenie was among the number who stood by the open grave where all that was mortal of Christine was buried, and she would not leave until the grave was filled and all the work was done. Then, taking Pierre's arm, she went back to the hotel, and going to Phil's room laid her tired head upon the hands he stretched toward her and cried bitterly, while Phil soothed and caressed her until she grew quiet and could tell him all the particulars of Christine's death.

"There was much that was noble and good in her," she said, "and had she lived I would have tried to do right, and with you to help and encourage me I might have succeeded."

"Yes," Phil answered her, "I am sure you would; but it is better for her to be at rest."

And Phil was right; for had Christine lived she could only have been a source of unhappiness to Queenie, who, with the best of intentions, could never fully have received her as a mother. God knew best, and took to himself the weary woman, who had been more sinned against than sinning, and whose memory was held in the hearts of those whose lives she had been instrumental in saving as the memory of a saint.

CHAPTER L

PHIL'S STORY

He did not tell it until two days after Christine's burial, for Queenie would not listen to him until she felt that he was past all possible danger of a relapse. Then, with her head leaning upon his arm and his hand clasped in hers, she heard how he had escaped from death on that night when the boat was capsized and he found himself struggling for life in the angry waters.

"My friend wrote you," he said, "how the accident occurred and how for hours we clung to the boat, which was being drawn rapidly out to sea. For a time I kept up bravely, though for myself I cared but little to live, life was so dark and hopeless to me then. But I remembered my mother, who would mourn for me, and made every possible exertion to hold on. When we were capsized I struck my head just over the temple upon some iron surface of the boat, and I know now that the blow was of itself almost sufficient to cause my death. As it was, I felt stunned and bewildered and my strength was fast failing me when my friend bade me try and reach him, as he thought he could help me. I remember reaching out one hand toward him, while I tried to change my position, but my foot was caught in something which, when I lost my hold and floated away from the boat, was also detached and floated with me. It was the grating from the bottom of the boat, and it proved my salvation, for, as I came to the surface after sinking once beneath the waters, I caught at it and clung to it desperately, while the waves carried me far away from my companion, who, seeing me go down, naturally supposed I must be drowned. Indeed, I do not myself know how I was saved, or had the strength to endure the horrors of that night and hold to my frail support as I did.

"At last daylight broke over the waters, and a small vessel, bound for the southern coast of Africa, passed near me as I floated. I had then no power to signal them, my arms were so cramped and numb, but one of the sailors spied me, and a boat was at once lowered and sent to my rescue. How they got me on board I do not know, for all sense forsook me from the moment I felt a hand laid upon my shoulder, and when next I awoke to a consciousness of anything, I was lying in a close berth, and a dark face was bending over me, speaking in a language I could not comprehend. But the voice was kind, and the face a good-natured one, and I remember thinking that I should be cared for until I reached some point where I could make myself understood. My head was paining me dreadfully, and was probably the cause of the weeks and months of partial insanity which followed. I had taken a frightful cold, a burning fever set in, and for days I raved like a madman, they told me afterward and made several attempts to throw myself into the sea. It was useless for them to ask me anything, as their language was gibberish to me, as mine was to them. But one word they learned perfectly—it was on my lips so constantly—and that was your name. No matter what they said to me, I always answered Queenie, until every officer and common sailor in the boat knew the name, and could say it as well as I, though they little dreamed who the Queenie was I talked about so constantly."

"Oh, Phil!" Queenie cried, with streaming eyes; "and I was mourning for you, and thinking you were dead, and was so sorry for having sent you away. Can you ever forgive me, Phil, for all I have made you suffer?"

His answer, not given in words, was quite satisfactory, and then he went on:

"They thought at last it must be my own name, and called me Queenie whenever they addressed me or spoke of me. The voyage was rather long, owing to adverse winds and the bad condition of the ship, but they reached their destination at last, and gave me at once into the charge of some English who were living there. But these could get no satisfaction from me with regard to my home, or friends, or name. I had fallen into a weak, half-imbecile, frame of mind, and was very taciturn and reserved, refusing sometimes to talk at all, though always, when I did speak, begging them to carry me home. At intervals I suffered greatly in my head, and even now at times, if I touch the spot upon my temple where I received the blow, I experience a sensation like an electric shock, showing that the injury I received was a most serious one.

"And so the time wore on, and, as I was perfectly harmless, I was allowed to do as I pleased, and gradually, as I grew stronger in health, my mind regained its balance, and I was able to recall the past, or rather to remember up to the time when I was in the water holding to the grating of the boat. Everything else was a blank, and is so to me now. I have no recollection whatever of the voyage to Zanguibar, or of the months which followed my arrival there, and it was some little time before I could comprehend my position, or realize how long it was since I was at Madras and started with my friend on the excursion which ended so disastrously. My first act was to write at once to my father, who, I naturally supposed, must think me dead, but the letter was probably miscarried or lost, for it never reached him.

"At last a chance came for me to leave the coast, and I availed myself of it. An English sailing vessel, bound for Liverpool, took me on board, but, as if I were a second Jonah, we encountered heavy seas and violent storms, so that we were double the usual length of time in reaching Liverpool, where I took a steamer for New York, where I landed just a week before you found me here. Not wishing to shock my family, as I knew they would be shocked if they had never received my letter, I telegraphed to Mr. Beresford that I should be home on the next train from New York. The news took him as much by surprise as if one of the dead bodies in the grave-yard had walked in upon him, and I have been told that all Merrivale was wild with excitement, and that Uncle Tom, usually so quiet and undemonstrative, went himself and rang the fire-bell, to call the people out so as to tell them the news. I really believe the entire town was at the station to meet me when the train came in, and had I permitted it some of the men would have carried me in their arms up the hill to my very door, where Ethel and Grace and grandma were waiting to receive me. Mother was in bed, going from one fainting fit to another, and father was with her trying to quiet her. Poor old father, I used to think he cared more for his ferns and his flowers than for his children, but I have changed my mind, and never shall forget the expression of his face when he met me at the door, and, leading me to my mother, said to her, so tenderly:

"Here he is, Mary—here is our boy. Now please don't faint again. 'Praised be God.'

"To me he never spoke a word for full five minutes, but sat smoothing and patting my hands, and rubbing with his handkerchief a speck of dirt from my coat sleeve, while he looked at me so lovingly, with the great tears in his eyes and his lips quivering with his emotions. He has grown old so fast within the last few months. His hair is quite gray, and he stoops when he walks, though I do believe he was straighter when I came away, and younger, too, in looks. I did not know my friends were so fond of a good-for-nothing like me. It was almost worth my while to go and be drowned for the sake of all the petting I had at home the few days I remained there. But one thing was wanting. You did not come to meet me, and I wondered at it, for I think I had half expected to see your face among the very first to welcome me, and I felt disappointed and a little hurt at its absence. I did not know but you were Mr. Beresford's wife, and though the thought that it might be so hurt me cruelly, I had made up my mind to hide the hurt and make the best of the inevitable. It would be some comfort to see you, even if you belonged to another, and all the time I was receiving the welcome congratulations of my friends, I was thinking of and watching for you. But you did not appear, and no one mentioned your name until late in the evening, when Ethel asked me to go with her for a walk in the garden before retiring, and then she told me the strangest story I ever heard of you and Margery, who, it seems, is my cousin, while you——"

He paused a moment, while Queenie turned very white, and with a long, gasping breath, said, faintly:

"Yes, Phil, I know what I am. Don't remind me please."

"Queenie," and Phil drew the trembling girl closer to him, and stroking her bowed head continued: "Do you for a moment suppose that I have ever given the accident of your birth a thought, except to be glad, with a gladness I cannot express, that you are not my cousin? And when Ethel told me of your grief at my supposed death, and the love you were not then ashamed to confess for me, I felt that I must fly to you at once, and only my mother's weak condition and her entreaties for me to wait a little kept me from doing so. She and my sisters thought you were in Florida, for Margery had kept your secret, as you wished, and had not told them of your rash plan of coming here into this atmosphere of infection and death. But she told me when I went next day to see her, and told me, too, of all the remorse, and pain, and bitter humiliation you had endured; and, better than all the rest, of the perfect trust and faith you had in me—that were I living a hundred Christines could make no difference with me, and she was right. I would have called that woman mother for your sake had she lived, and treated her with as much respect as if she had been Margaret Ferguson instead of Christine Bodine. My cousin Margery I adopted at once. She is a noble woman, and so true to you. By the way, I fancy that Mr. Beresford visits Hetherton Place quite as often as he used to do in the days when I was so horridly jealous of him, and you played with us both as the cat plays with the mouse it has captured. And I am glad, for the match is every way suitable. Beresford is a noble fellow—a little too proud, perhaps, in some respects, and a trifle peculiar, too; but Margery will cure all that, and I would rather see him master of Hetherton Place than any one I know, if Margery must be its mistress. She wishes you to return and live with her; but of that by and by. When she told me where you were, my heart gave a great throb of terror for you, and I resolved to start at once and take you away if I should find you alive. I had a mortal fear of the fever, and this, I think, added to my mental excitement and the low state of my health, made me more liable to take it, as I did almost immediately, for I was sick and unable to leave my bed the very first morning after my arrival, and before I had time to inquire for you. You know how Christine found me and saved my life, for but for her I should most surely have died.

"And now, Queenie, I have been talking with the physician, who says I must leave the city at once if I would recover my strength, and he advises a stay of a few weeks in some quiet, cool spot among the mountains of Tennessee, where I shall grow strong and lazy again. You know that is my strong point—laziness."

He looked a little quizzically at her, but she paid no attention. She only said:

"I think that would be so nice. Have you decided upon the place?"

He told her of a little spot which the physician had recommended, where the air was pure and the water good, and then continued:

"But I cannot go alone; it would be so poky and forlorn, with nobody I know. I must have a nurse to look after me and keep me straight. Will you go with me, Queenie?" he said, looking earnestly into the eyes which met his so innocently, as, without a blush, Queenie answered:

"Of course I'll go with you, Phil. Did you think I would let you go alone?"

She was so guileless and unsuspecting of evil that it seemed almost a pity to open her eyes and show her that the world is not always charitable in its construction of acts, however innocent in themselves—that Mrs. Grundy is a great stickler for the proprieties, and that for a young girl to go alone to a hotel or boarding-house as nurse to a young man in no way related to her would make every hair of that venerable lady's head stand upright with horror. But Phil must do it, both for her sake and by way of accomplishing the end he had in view. So he said to her:

"I knew you would go with me; but, Queenie, do you know that for Queenie Hetherton to go to the mountains as a nurse to a great long-legged, rather fast-looking fellow like Phil Rossiter, would be to compromise herself sadly in the estimation of some people."

I doubt if Queenie quite comprehended him, for she looked at him wonderingly, and said:

"I don't know what you mean by my being compromised. I think it is an ugly word, and not at all one you should use with reference to myself, as if I should not always behave like a lady, whether I was taking care of you among the mountains, or here in Memphis, as I am doing now."

She was getting a little excited, and her eyes shone with the gleam Phil remembered so well and rather liked to provoke.

"Yes, I know," he said, "but don't you remember what you told me of the cats at the St. James, who used to spy upon the young people and make remarks about them? Well there are cats everywhere, and they would find us out in the mountains, and however quiet and modest you might be, they would set up a dreadful caterwauling because you were with me, and not at all related to me. They would tear you in pieces, till you had not a shred of reputation left. Do you understand now that as Queenie Hetherton you cannot go with me?"

"No, I don't understand," she answered wrathfully, "and I think it mean in you to ask me first if I will go, and then, when I say yes, to talk to me about cats, and compromise and reputation, as if I were bad, and immodest, and every sort of a thing. No, Phil, I didn't expect this from you; I must say I did not, and I don't like it, and I don't like you either—there! and I won't stay here any longer to hear such dreadful talk!"

For one who had pledged herself never to lose her temper again under any circumstances, Queenie was a good deal excited, as she wrenched her hand from Phil's and flounced from the room, leaving him to chuckle over her anger, which he had anticipated, and which he felt sure would result in her doing just as he wished her to do. And he was right in his calculations, for, after the lapse of an hour or two, during which Pierre had brought him his lunch, the little lady appeared in a most repentant frame of mind, and standing by him, with her hand on his shoulder, said:

"I am sorry, Phil, I was so angry with you. I did not think I ever should be again, but you did rouse me so with your cats, and compromising, and all that, after you had asked me to go. But I see you were right. It would not be proper at all, and people would be sure to talk. But you must take Pierre. I should feel safer about you, and can do very well without him. I know the way to Florida, and shall start to-morrow, for if it is improper for me to take care of you in the mountains, it is improper here, now you are so much better; so I am going back to Magnolia Park. But, Phil," and Queenie's voice began to tremble, "you'll come there next winter, won't you? You, and Ethel, and Grace, and Margery? That will make it quite proper and conventional, and it is so lonely there."

She was crying by this time, and Phil, who, as she was talking, had stolen his arm around her, drew her down upon his knee and, brushing away her tears, said:

"Yes, darling, if you are in Florida next winter, or next week, I shall be there, too; for in the words of Naomi, 'Where thou goest I shall go,' whether to the mountains or to the moon, and, as the mountains suit me best just now, what say you to going there at once?"

"But I thought you said I wasn't to go—that it would be very disreputable, or some other dreadful word like that? I don't understand you at all," Queenie said, hotly, and Phil replied:

"You are an innocent chick, that's a fact, and cannot see through a millstone. I said that as Queenie Hetherton you must not go scurriping round the world with a yellow-haired chap of the period like me; but as Queenie Rossiter, my wife, you will be a matron sans reproche."

"Your wife, Phil!" Queenie exclaimed, starting suddenly and trying to free herself from him. But he held her fast, and answered:

"Yes, my wife, and why not? You are bound to be that some time, and why wait any longer? We can be married here to-night or to-morrow, if you please, with Pierre and our landlord for witnesses, and we shall be as firmly tied as if all Merrivale were present at the ceremony. You do not care for bride-maids, and flowers, and flummery. I am sure Anna exhausted all that. And to me you are sweeter and fairer in this black dress, which was put on for me, than you would be in all the white satin robes and laces in the world. Shall it be so, love? Will you marry me to-morrow, and at once start for Tennessee?"

Queenie did not care for satins, or laces or bridal favors, but to be married so suddenly, and in such an informal manner, shocked her at first, and Phil had some little difficulty in getting her consent. But it was won at last. A desire to be with him, to go where he went, and have him to herself, prevailed over every other feeling, and early the next morning, with Pierre, and their landlord, and the sister who had cared for poor Christine as witnesses, Queenie and Phil were married, their wedding a great contrast to what Queenie had thought her wedding would be. But she was very, very happy, and Pierre thought he had never see his young mistress one-half so beautiful as she was in her simple black dress, with only bands of white linen at her throat and wrists, and the brightness of a great happiness in her face and in her brilliant eyes. She was Phil's at last. The joy she had thought never could be hers had come to her, greater far than she had ever dreamed, and in her happiness all the sad past was forgotten, and she could think of Christine without a pang.

"Next fall we will come here again, and place a tablet at mother's grave," she said to Phil, and by the name she gave the dead he knew that the old bitterness was gone, and that Queenie was content.

They took the first train for Brierstone, a quiet, lovely spot among the mountains of Tennessee, where, in the cool, bracing air, Phil felt himself growing stronger every hour, and where the bright color came back to Queenie's cheeks, and the old sparkle to the eyes which had shed so many bitter tears since the day when the news first came to her of the lover drowned in the Indian waters.

CHAPTER LI

CONCLUSION

As soon as they were located in their new quarters at the farm-house, which they had chosen in preference to the hotel, Phil sent the following telegram to his mother:

"Queenie and I were married two days ago, and are spending our honeymoon at Brierstone. Margery will explain.
"Phil."

Margery's little phaeton, which she had bought for her own use, was standing before the Knoll, where she was calling, and where Grandma Ferguson was spending the afternoon with her step-daughter, when the telegram was received, and thus the parties most interested had the news at the same time. And they were not greatly surprised, except at the place from which the telegram was sent. How came Phil in Tennessee, when they supposed him to be in Florida? It was Margery who explained to them, then, what she had purposely withheld for the sake of sparing them the anxiety they would have felt had they known that not only was Queenie in the midst of the yellow fever at Memphis, but that Phil was going there, too. Queenie had written her immediately after Christine's death, and had told her of Phil's illness, but added that he was past all danger, and there was no cause for alarm. Margery had wept in silence over the sad end of one whom she had loved as a mother, even after she knew the true story of her parentage. But, like Phil, she felt that it was better so, that by dying as she did Christine had atoned for the past even to Queenie, who must necessarily be happier with her dead than she could have been with her living. That Phil should have taken the fever so soon filled Margery with dismay lest he might have a relapse, or Queenie be smitten down, and her errand to the Knoll that afternoon was to tell her cousins, Ethel and Grace, the truth, and with them devise some means of getting the two away from the plague-smitten town. She had told them of Christine's death, but did not say how she received her information, and they were wondering why they did not hear from Phil, who must have been some days at Magnolia Park, when his telegram was brought in, and they heard for the first time that Queenie had been a nurse in Memphis, and of her falling in with Phil through Christine, but for whom he would have died. For a few moments they almost felt as if he were dead, and Mrs. Rossiter's face was very white as she listened to Queenie's letter, which Margery read, and in which were so many assurances of his safety that her fears gradually subsided and she could at last speak calmly of his marriage, of which she was very glad. It was sure to take place some time, she knew, and as Queenie ought to be with him during his convalescence, they could not have managed better than they did. But she was not willing to have them remain away from her any longer; they must come home at once, and she wrote to that effect to Phil, welcoming Queenie as a daughter whom she already loved, and insisting upon their immediate return to Merrivale. This letter Phil received in the heyday of his first married days, when he was perfectly happy with Queenie, who was as sweet, and loving, and gentle as a new bride well could be.

"Only think, I have not had a single tantrum yet, and we have been married two whole weeks," she said to Phil on the day when he received his mother's letter, to which she did not take kindly. "Do not let us go," she said, nestling close to him, and laying her head on his arm. "I am having such a nice time here with you all to myself, where I can act just as silly as I please. Do not go home just yet. I shall not be half as good there as I am here."

So Phil wrote his mother not to expect him for a few weeks, as the mountain air was doing him a great deal of good, and he was growing stronger every day. The same mail which took this letter to Mrs. Rossiter carried one to Margery from Queenie, who wrote in raptures of her happiness as Phil's wife, and begged Margery to come to Brierstone and see for herself.

"There is such a pleasant chamber right across the hall from mine, which you can have," she wrote, "and I want you here so much to see how happy we are, and how good I am getting to be."

And so one day early in September Margery came to Brierstone and took possession of the large, pleasant chamber opposite Queenie's, into whose happiness and plans she entered heart and soul; and ten days after her arrival Mr. Beresford came to escort her home. It was a settled thing now, the marriage between Mr. Beresford and Margery, and the four talked the matter over together and decided some things to which, without Mr. Beresford and Phil, Queenie would never have consented. It was Margery's wish that Queenie should share equally with her in their father's estate. And as this was also the wish of Mr. Beresford, while Phil himself said he saw no objection to it, and that it was probably what Mr. Hetherton would wish, could he speak to them, Queenie consented and found herself an heiress again, with money enough to support herself and Phil, even if he had no business or occupation. They talked that over, too, and Phil asked Queenie what she wished him to do.

"The only time I ever tried in earnest to do anything I came near losing my life," he said, "and so now I'll let you decide for me. Shall I turn lawyer, or preacher, or dressmaker? I really have more talent for the latter than for anything else. I might, with a little practice, be a second Worth; or I should make a pretty good salesman of laces and silks in some dry-goods store. So which shall it be—preacher, dressmaker, or clerk? I am bound to earn my own living in some way."

"You'll do nothing of the sort," Queenie answered, warmly. "A dressmaker or clerk! What nonsense! You are too indolent to be either; for, as a clerk, you would want to sit down most of the time, and dressmaking would give you a pain in your side. So you are going to be a farmer at Magnolia Park, which needs some one to bring it up. With money, and time, and care it can be made one of the finest places in Florida. Mr. Johnson, who lives on the adjoining plantation, told me so, and there are plenty of negroes to be hired; only they must have an overseer, to direct them."

"So I am to have no higher occupation than that of a negro overseer! Truly the mighty have fallen!" Phil said, laughingly, but well pleased on the whole with the prospect before him.

He liked nothing better than superintending outdoor work, and with Queenie believed that in a little time he could make Magnolia Park a second Chateau des Fleurs, if indeed he did not convert it into something like the famous Kew Gardens in England. It was to be their home proper, where all their winters were to be passed; but the summers were to be spent at the North, sometimes at Hetherton Place, sometimes at the Knoll, or wherever their fancy might lead them.

Thus they settled their future, and when Mr. Beresford and Margery went back to Merrivale the latter part of September, Phil and Queenie went with them, and were received with great rejoicings by the Rossiters and by the people generally, while even Mrs. Lord Seymour Rossiter, who was boarding for a few weeks at the hotel, drove down to the station to meet them in her elegant new carriage, which, with its thoroughbreds and its brass-buttoned driver, was making quite a sensation in Merrivale.

Anna was very happy in her prosperity, and very gracious to Queenie, who could afford to forget the slights put upon her at the St. James when she was lonely and sad, and was ready to accept all good the gods provided for her.

It was late in November when Phil and Queenie started at last for their

Florida home, where, during the holidays, they were joined by Margery, and where a little later Mr. Beresford came to claim the hand of his bride, for Margery was to be married at Magnolia Park, and the ceremony took place quietly one January evening, when the air was as soft and mild as the air of June at the North, and the young moon looked down upon the newly wedded pair. There was a short visit to the St. James, where Margery and Queenie reigned triumphant as belles for a few weeks, and then won fresh laurels at St. Augustine and Palatka. By this time Mr. Beresford's business necessitated his return to the North, but as Phil had no business except to oversee the negroes, and as these did not need overseeing then, he and Queenie tarried longer, and together explored the Ocklawaha and the upper St. John's, and fired at alligators, and camped out for two or three days on the Indian River, and hunted, and fished, and were almost as happy as were the first pair in Eden before the serpent entered there.

All this was good for Phil, whose constitution had received a great shock from his long illness in Africa, and who thus gained strength and vigor for the new life before him—that of improving and bringing up Magnolia Park, which had so long run to waste.

It is more than two years now since Queenie and Phil were married, and last winter they were at Hetherton Place, where a second Queenie Hetherton lay in its cradle and opened its big blue eyes wonderingly at the little lady who bent over it so rapturously, and called herself its "auntie." Queenie has no children, but she seems so much a child herself, and looks so small beside her tall husband, who can pick her up and sit her on his shoulder, or, as he says, "put her in his pocket," that a baby would look oddly in her arms. Bright, mirthful, and variable as the April sunshine, she goes on her way, happy in the love which has crowned her so completely, and not a shadow crosses her pathway, except when she remembers the past, which at one time held so much bitterness for her. Then for a moment her eyes grow darker, and with a sigh she says, "The worst of all was losing faith in father."

There is a tall monument to his memory in Merrivale, and a smaller, less pretentious one marks the grave of Christine in Memphis, erected "by her daughters." This was Margery's idea, "for," she said to Queenie, "she was to all intents and purposes my mother—the only one I ever knew."

Mrs. Lord Seymour Rossiter has been in Europe more than eighteen months, and has seen every thing worth seeing, and has gotten as far on her journey home as London, where she is stopping at the Grand Hotel, and has a suite of rooms, and a French maid, and a German nurse for the little Paul born a year ago in Florence, and who is never to speak a word of English until he has mastered both German and French. Major Rossiter is there, too, and plays whist, and smokes, and reads the papers, and goes to his banker's, and talks to his valet whom he employs, he scarcely knows why, except that Anna wishes him to do so.

Anna is very stylish, and grand, and foreign, and is high up in art, and castles, and ruins and knows all about Claude Lorraine and Murillo. She breakfasts in bed and lunches at two, and drives from five to six in Hyde Park, where her haughty face, and showy dress, and elegant turn-out attract almost as much attention as does the princess herself. Yesterday afternoon I paid my penny for a chair, and sitting down watched the gay pageant as it went by, and saw her in it, the gayest of them all, with her red parasol over her head and her white poodle dog in her lap. And when I thought of her past, and of Queenie and Margery, whose lives had been so full of romance, I said to myself: "Truly, there are events in real life stranger far than any recorded in fiction."

And so, with the summer rain falling softly upon the flowers and shrubs beneath my window, and the sun trying to break through the clouds which hang so darkly over England's great metropolis, I finish this story of Queenie.

London, July, 1880

THE END